W9-BSG-774

BLACK
HILLS

ALSO BY NORA ROBERTS

Honest Illusions	River's End	Key of Valor
Private Scandals	Jewels of the Sun	Northern Lights
Hidden Riches	Carolina Moon	Blue Dahlia
True Betrayals	Tears of the Moon	Black Rose
Montana Sky	Heart of the Sea	Blue Smoke
Born in Fire	The Villa	Red Lily
Born in Ice	From the Heart	Angels Fall
Born in Shame	Midnight Bayou	Morrigan's Cross
Daring to Dream	Dance Upon the Air	Dance of the Gods
Holding the Dream	Heaven and Earth	Valley of Silence
Finding the Dream	Face the Fire	High Noon
Sanctuary	Chesapeake Blue	Blood Brothers
Homeport	Birthright	The Hollow
Sea Swept	Remember When	The Pagan Stone
Rising Tides	(with J. D. Robb)	Tribute
Inner Harbor	Key of Light	Vision in White
The Reef	Key of Knowledge	

WRITING AS J. D. ROBB

Naked in Death	Judgment in Death	Origin in Death
Glory in Death	Betrayal in Death	Memory in Death
Immortal in Death	Seduction in Death	Born in Death
Rapture in Death	Reunion in Death	Innocent in Death
Ceremony in Death	Purity in Death	Creation in Death
Vengeance in Death	Portrait in Death	Strangers in Death
Holiday in Death	Imitation in Death	Salvation in Death
Conspiracy in Death	Divided in Death	Promises in Death
Loyalty in Death	Visions in Death	
Witness in Death	Survivor in Death	

BLACK HILLS

Nora Roberts

G. P. Putnam's Sons

New York

G. P. PUTNAM'S SONS
Publishers Since 1838
Published by the Penguin Group
Penguin Group (USA) Inc., 375 Hudson Street, New York, New York 10014, USA •
Penguin Group (Canada), 90 Eglinton Avenue East, Suite 700, Toronto, Ontario M4P 2Y3, Canada
(a division of Pearson Canada Inc.) • Penguin Books Ltd, 80 Strand, London WC2R 0RL, England •
Penguin Ireland, 25 St Stephen's Green, Dublin 2, Ireland (a division of Penguin Books Ltd) •
Penguin Group (Australia), 250 Camberwell Road, Camberwell, Victoria 3124, Australia (a division
of Pearson Australia Group Pty Ltd) • Penguin Books India Pvt Ltd, 11 Community Centre,
Panchsheel Park, New Delhi–110 017, India • Penguin Group (NZ), 67 Apollo Drive, Rosedale,
North Shore 0632, New Zealand (a division of Pearson New Zealand Ltd) • Penguin Books
(South Africa) (Pty) Ltd, 24 Sturdee Avenue, Rosebank, Johannesburg 2196, South Africa

Penguin Books Ltd, Registered Offices: 80 Strand, London WC2R 0RL, England

Copyright © 2009 by Nora Roberts
All rights reserved. No part of this book may be reproduced, scanned, or distributed in any printed
or electronic form without permission. Please do not participate in or encourage piracy of copyrighted
materials in violation of the author's rights. Purchase only authorized editions.
Published simultaneously in Canada

Library of Congress Cataloging-in-Publication Data

Roberts, Nora.
Black Hills / Nora Roberts.
p.   cm.
ISBN 978-0-399-15581-9
1. Black Hills (S.D. and Wyo.)—Fiction.   2. Animal sanctuaries—Fiction.   I. Title.
PS3568.O243B536   2009   2009002504
813'.54—dc22

Printed in the United States of America
1   3   5   7   9   10   8   6   4   2

BOOK DESIGN BY NICOLE LAROCHE

This is a work of fiction. Names, characters, places, and incidents either are the product of the author's imagination or are used fictitiously, and any resemblance to actual persons, living or dead, businesses, companies, events, or locales is entirely coincidental.

While the author has made every effort to provide accurate telephone numbers and Internet addresses at the time of publication, neither the publisher nor the author assumes any responsibility for errors, or for changes that occur after publication. Further, the publisher does not have any control over and does not assume any responsibility for author or third-party websites or their content.

To those who protect and defend the wild

PART ONE

HEART

Where your treasure is, there will your heart be also.

—MATTHEW 6:21

I

SOUTH DAKOTA

June 1989

Cooper Sullivan's life, as he'd known it, was over. Judge and jury—in the form of his parents—had not been swayed by pleas, reason, temper, threats, but instead had sentenced him and shipped him off, away from everything he knew and cared about to a world without video parlors or Big Macs.

The only thing that kept him from *completely* dying of boredom, or just going wacko, was his prized Game Boy.

As far as he could see, it would be him and Tetris for the duration of his prison term—two horrible, stupid months—in the Wild freaking West. He knew damn well the game, which his father had gotten pretty much right off the assembly line in Tokyo, was a kind of bribe.

Coop was eleven, and nobody's fool.

Practically nobody in the whole U.S. of A. had the game, and that was definitely cool. But what was the point in having something everybody else wanted if you couldn't show it off to your friends?

This way, you were just Clark Kent or Bruce Wayne, the lame alter egos of the cool guys.

All of his friends were back, a zillion miles back, in New York. They'd be hanging out for the summer, taking trips to the beaches of Long Island or down to the Jersey Shore. He'd been promised two weeks at baseball camp in July.

But that was before.

Now his parents were off to Italy and France and other stupid places on a second honeymoon. Which was code for last-ditch effort to save the marriage.

No, Coop was nobody's fool.

Having their eleven-year-old son around wasn't romantic or whatever, so they'd shipped him off to his grandparents and the boondockies of South holy crap Dakota.

Godforsaken South Dakota. He'd heard his mother call it that plenty of times—except when she'd smiled and smiled telling him he was going to have an *adventure,* get to know his *roots.* Godforsaken turned into pristine and pure and exciting. Like he didn't know she'd run off from her parents and their crappy little farm the minute she'd turned eighteen?

So he was stuck back where she'd run from, and he hadn't done anything to deserve it. It wasn't his fault his father couldn't keep his dick in his pants, or his mother compensated by buying up Madison Avenue. Information Coop had learned from expert and regular eavesdropping. They screwed things up and he was sentenced to a summer on a horseshit farm with grandparents he barely knew.

And they were really *old.*

He was supposed to help with the horses, who smelled and looked like they wanted to bite you. With the chickens who smelled and did bite.

They didn't have a housekeeper who cooked egg white omelets and picked up his action figures. And they drove trucks instead of cars. Even his ancient grandmother.

He hadn't seen a cab in days.

He had chores, and had to eat home-cooked meals with food he'd never seen in his *life.* And maybe the food was pretty good, but that wasn't the point.

The *one* TV in the whole house barely got anything, and there was no

McDonald's. No Chinese or pizza place that delivered. No friends. No park, no movie theaters, no video arcades.

He might as well be in Russia or someplace.

He glanced up from the Game Boy to look out the car window at what he considered a lot of nothing. Stupid mountains, stupid prairie, stupid trees. The same view, as far as he could tell, that had been outside the window since they'd left the farm. At least his grandparents had stopped interrupting his game to tell him stuff about what was outside the window.

Like he cared about a lot of stupid settlers and Indians and soldiers who hung around out here before he was even born. Hell, before his prehistoric grandparents had been born.

Who gave a shit about Crazy Horse and Sitting Bullshit. He cared about the X-Men and the box scores.

The way Coop looked at it, the fact that the closest town to the farm was called Deadwood said it all.

He didn't care about cowboys and horses and buffalo. He cared about baseball and video games. He wasn't going to see a *single* game in Yankee Stadium all summer.

He might as well be dead, too.

He spotted a bunch of what looked like mutant deer clomping across the high grass, and a lot of trees and stupid hills that were really green. Why did they call them black when they were green? Because he was in South crappy Dakota where they didn't know dick about squat.

What he didn't see were buildings, people, streets, sidewalk vendors. What he didn't see was home.

His grandmother shifted in her seat to look back at him. "Do you see the elk, Cooper?"

"I guess."

"We'll be getting to the Chance spread soon," she told him. "It was nice of them to have us all over for supper. You're going to like Lil. She's nearly your age."

He knew the rules. "Yes, ma'am." As if he'd pal around with some *girl*. Some dumb farm girl who probably smelled like horse. And looked like one.

He bent his head and went back to Tetris so his grandmother would leave him alone. She looked sort of like his mother. If his mother was old and didn't get her hair done blond and wavy, and didn't wear makeup. But he could see his mother in this strange old woman with the lines around her blue eyes.

It was a little spooky.

Her name was Lucy, and he was supposed to call her Grandma.

She cooked and baked. A lot. And hung sheets and stuff out on a line in back of the farmhouse. She sewed and scrubbed, and sang when she did. Her voice was pretty, if you liked that sort of thing.

She helped with the horses, and Coop could admit, he'd been surprised and impressed when he'd seen her jump right on one without a saddle or anything.

She *was* old—probably at least fifty, for God's sake. But she wasn't creaky.

Mostly she wore boots and jeans and plaid shirts. Except for today she'd put a dress on and left the brown hair she usually braided loose.

He didn't notice when they turned off the endless stretch of road, not until the ride turned bumpier. When he glanced out he saw more trees, less flat land, and the mountains roughed up behind them. Mostly, it looked like a lot of bumpy green hills topped over with bare rock.

He knew his grandparents raised horses and rented them at trailheads to tourists who wanted to ride them. He didn't get it. He just didn't get why anybody would want to sit on a horse and ride around rocks and trees.

His grandfather drove along the more-dirt-than-gravel road, and Coop saw cattle grazing on either side. He hoped it meant the drive was nearly over. He didn't care about having dinner at the Chance farm or meeting dumb Lil.

But he had to pee.

His grandfather had to stop so his grandmother could hop out to open a cattle gate, then close it again when they'd gone through. As they bumped along his bladder began to protest.

He saw sheds and barns and stables, whatever they were didn't matter. It was, as far as it went out here, a sign of civilization.

Something was growing in some fields, and horses were running around in others like they didn't have anything better to do.

The house, when it came into view, didn't look that different from the one his grandparents lived in. Two floors, windows, a big porch. Except the house was blue and his grandparents' was white.

There were a lot of flowers around the house, which somebody who hadn't had to learn to weed the ones around his grandparents' house might think were okay to look at.

A woman came out on the porch and waved. She wore a dress, too. A long one that made him think of the pictures of hippies he'd seen. Her hair was really dark and pulled back in a ponytail. Outside the house sat two trucks and an old car.

His grandfather, who hardly said anything, stepped out of the car. "'Lo, Jenna."

"It's good to see you, Sam." The woman gave his grandfather a kiss on the cheek, then turned to give his grandmother a big hug. "Lucy! Didn't I say don't bring a thing but yourselves?" she added when Lucy turned and took a basket from the car.

"I couldn't help it. It's cherry pie."

"We sure won't turn that down. And this is Cooper." Jenna held out a hand as she would to an adult. "Welcome."

"Thank you."

She dropped a hand on his shoulder. "Let's go on in. Lil's been looking forward to meeting you, Cooper. She's finishing up some chores with her dad, but they'll be right along. How about some lemonade? I bet you're thirsty after the drive."

"Um. I guess. May I use the bathroom?"

"Sure. We have one right in the house." She laughed when she said it, with a teasing look in her dark eyes that made the back of his neck hot.

It was like she knew he'd been thinking how old and dumpy everything looked.

She led him through, past a big living room, then a smaller one, and into a kitchen that smelled a lot like his grandmother's.

Home cooking.

"There's a washroom right through there." She gave his shoulder a careless pat, which added to the heat on the back of his neck. "Why don't we have that lemonade out on the back porch and visit awhile?" she said to his grandparents.

His mother would have called it a powder room. He relieved himself with some gratitude, then washed his hands at the tiny sink fixed in the corner. Beside it pale blue towels with a little pink rose hung on a rod.

At home, he mused, the powder room was twice as big, and fancy soaps sat in a crystal dish from Tiffany. The towels were a lot softer, too, and monogrammed.

Stalling, he poked a finger at the petals of some white daisies standing in a skinny wood pot thing on the sink. At home there would've been roses probably. He hadn't really noticed that kind of thing until now.

He was thirsty. He wished he could take a gallon of lemonade, maybe a bag of Cheetos, and stretch out in the back of the car with his Game Boy. Anything would be better than being forced to sit with a bunch of strange people on the porch of some old farmhouse for probably *hours*.

He could still hear them talking and fooling around in the kitchen, and wondered how long he could stall before going back out.

He peeked out the little window, decided it was the same shit. Paddocks and corrals, barns and silos, dumb farm animals, weird-looking equipment.

It wasn't as if he'd wanted to go to Italy and walk around looking at old stuff, but at least if his parents had taken him, there might be pizza.

The girl came out of the barn. She had dark hair like the hippie woman, so he figured it had to be Lil. She wore jeans rolled up at the cuffs, and high-top sneakers, and a red baseball cap over the hair done in two long braids.

She looked scruffy and stupid, and he immediately disliked her.

A moment later a man came out behind her. His hair was yellow, and worn in a long tail that enforced the hippie conclusion. He, too, wore a ball cap. He said something to the girl that made her laugh and shake her head. Whatever it was had her starting to run, but the man caught her.

Coop heard her squeal with laughter as the man tossed her in the air.

Had his father ever chased him? Coop wondered. Ever tossed him in the air, then swung him in giddy circles?

Not that he could remember. He and his father had *discussions*—when there was time. And time, Cooper knew, was always in short supply.

Country bumpkins had nothing but time, Cooper thought. They weren't under the demands of business like a corporate lawyer of his father's repute. They weren't third-generation Sullivans like his father, with the responsibilities that came with the name.

So they could toss their kids around all day.

Because it made something hurt in his stomach to watch, he turned away from the window. With no other choice, he went out to be tortured for the rest of the day.

LIL GIGGLED as her father gave her another dizzying swing. When she could breathe again, she tried to give him a stern look. "He is *not* going to be my boyfriend."

"That's what you say now." Josiah Chance gave his girl a quick tickle along the ribs. "But I'm going to keep my eye on that city slicker."

"I don't want any boyfriend." Lil gave a lofty wave of her hand with her expertise as an almost-ten-year-old. "They're too much trouble."

Joe pulled her close, rubbed cheeks. "I'm going to remind you of that in a few years. Looks like they're here. We'd better go say hello, and get cleaned up."

She didn't have anything *against* boys, Lil mused. And she knew how to mind her manners with company. But still . . . "If I don't like him, do I have to play with him?"

"He's a guest. And he's a stranger in a strange land. Wouldn't you want somebody your own age to be nice to you and show you around if you dropped down in New York City?"

She wrinkled her narrow nose. "I don't want to go to New York City."

"I bet he didn't want to come here."

She couldn't understand why. Everything was there. Horses, dogs, cats, the mountains, the trees. But her parents had taught her that people were as different as they were the same.

"I'll be nice to him." At first, anyway.

"But you won't run off and marry him."

"Dad!"

She rolled her eyes just as the boy came out on the porch. Lil studied him as she might any new specimen.

He was taller than she'd expected, and his hair was the color of pine bark. He looked . . . mad or sad, she couldn't decide which. But neither was promising. His clothes said city to her, dark jeans that hadn't been worn or washed enough and a stiff white shirt. He took the glass of lemonade her mother offered and watched Lil as warily as she watched him.

He jolted at the cry of a hawk, and Lil caught herself before she sneered. Her mother wouldn't like it if she sneered at company.

"Sam." Grinning broadly, Joe stuck out a hand. "How are things?"

"Can't complain."

"And Lucy, don't you look pretty?"

"We do what we can with what we've got. This is our grandson, Cooper."

"Glad to meet you, Cooper. Welcome to the Black Hills. This is my Lil."

"Hello." She cocked her head. He had blue eyes—ice-on-the-mountain blue. He didn't smile, nor did his eyes.

"Joe, you and Lil go clean up. We're going to eat outside," Jenna added. "We've got a fine day for it. Cooper, sit down here by me, and tell me what you like to do in New York. I've never been there."

In Lil's experience, her mother could get anybody to talk, make anybody smile. But Cooper Sullivan from New York City seemed to be the exception. He spoke when spoken to, minded his manners, but little more. They sat out at the picnic table, one of Lil's favorite things, and feasted on fried chicken and biscuits, on potato salad and snap beans her mother had put up last harvest.

Conversation ranged from horses and cattle and crops, to weather and books and the status of other neighbors. All the things, in Lil's world, that mattered.

Though Cooper struck Lil as stiff as his shirt, he managed to eat two helpings of everything, though he barely opened his mouth otherwise.

Until her father brought up baseball.

"Boston's going to break the curse this year."

Cooper snorted, then immediately hunched his shoulders.

In his easy way, Joe picked up the basket of biscuits, offered it to the boy. "Oh, yeah, Mr. New York. Yankees or Mets?"

"Yankees."

"Not a prayer." As if in sympathy, Joe shook his head. "Not this year, kid."

"We've got a strong infield, good bats. Sir," he added as if he'd just remembered to.

"Baltimore's already killing you."

"It's a fluke. They died last year, and they'll fade this year."

"When they do, the Red Sox will pounce."

"Crawl maybe."

"Oh, a smart-ass."

Cooper paled a little, but Joe continued as if he hadn't noticed the reaction. "Let me just say, Wade Boggs, and toss in Nick Esasky. Then—"

"Don Mattingly, Steve Sax."

"George Steinbrenner."

For the first time, Coop grinned. "Well, you can't have everything."

"Let me consult my expert. Sox or Yankees, Lil?"

"Neither. It's Baltimore. They've got the youth, the momentum. They've got Frank Robinson. Boston's got a play, but they won't pull it off. The Yankees? Not a chance, not this year."

"My only child, and she wounds me." Joe put a hand on his heart. "Do you play back home, Cooper?"

"Yes, sir. Second base."

"Lil, take Cooper on around back of the barn. You can work off the meal with a little batting practice."

"Okay."

Coop slid off the bench. "Thank you for dinner, Mrs. Chance. It was very good."

"You're welcome."

As the children walked away, Jenna looked over at Lucy. "Poor little boy," she murmured.

The dogs raced ahead, and across the field. "I play third base," Lil told Coop.

"Where? There's nothing around here."

"Right outside Deadwood. We have a field, and a league. I'm going to be the first woman to play major-league ball."

Coop snorted again. "Women can't play the bigs. That's just the way it is."

"The way it is isn't the way it has to be. That's what my mother says. And when I'm finished playing, I'm going to manage."

He sneered, and though it brought her hackles up, she liked him better for it. At least he didn't seem as stiff as his shirt anymore. "You don't know dick."

"Dick who?"

He laughed, and even though she knew he was laughing at her, she decided to give him one more chance before she clobbered him.

He was company. A stranger in a strange land.

"How do you play in New York? I thought there were buildings everywhere."

"We play in Central Park, and sometimes in Queens."

"What's Queens?"

"It's one of the boroughs."

"It's a mule?"

"No. Jesus. It's a city, a place. Not a donkey."

She stopped, set her fists on her hips, and fired at him out of dark, dark eyes. "When you try to make somebody feel stupid when they ask a question, you're the stupid one."

He shrugged, and rounded the side of the big red barn with her.

It smelled like animal, dusty and poopy at the same time. Coop couldn't figure out why anybody would want to live with that smell, or the sounds of clucking, snuffling, and mooing all the damn time. He started to make a sneering remark about just that—she was only a kid, after all, and a girl at that—but then he saw the batting cage.

It wasn't what he was used to, but it looked pretty sweet to him. Somebody, he supposed Lil's father, had built the three-sided cage out of fencing. It stood with its back to a jumbled line of brush and bramble that gave way to a field where cattle stood around doing nothing. Beside the barn, under the shelter of one of the eaves, sat a weatherworn box. Lil opened it, pulled out gloves, bats, balls.

"My dad and I practice most nights after dinner. Mom pitches to me sometimes, but she's got a rag arm. You can bat first if you want, 'cause you're company, but you have to wear a batting helmet. It's the rule."

Coop put on the helmet she offered, then checked the weight of a couple of bats. Holding one was almost as good as the Game Boy. "Your dad practices with you?"

"Sure. He played minor-league for a couple seasons back east, so he's pretty good."

"Really?" All derision fled. "He played professional ball?"

"For a couple seasons. He did something to his rotator cuff, and that was that. He decided to see the country, and he ended up out here. He worked for my grandparents—this used to be their farm—and met my mother. That was that, too. You wanna bat?"

"Yeah." Coop walked back to the cage, took a couple of practice swings. Set. She pitched one straight and slow, so he got the meat on it and slapped it into the field.

"Nice one. We've got six balls. So we'll field them after you hit." She gripped the next ball, took her position, pitched another easy one.

Coop felt the little lift inside as the ball sailed into the field. He smacked a third, then wiggled his hips and waited for the pitch.

She winged it, and blew it by him. "Nice cut," was all she said as he narrowed his eyes at her.

He choked up on the bat a bit, scuffed his heels. She fooled him with one that curved low and inside. He caught a piece of the next pitch, fouling it off so it rang as it hit the cage.

"You can toss those three back if you want," she told him. "I'll pitch you some more."

"That's okay. You take a turn." And he'd show her.

They switched places. Rather than soften her up, he burned one in. She caught enough of it to have it shooting foul. She caught the next, popped it up. But she got the fat of the bat on the third pitch. If there'd been a park, Coop was forced to admit, she'd have hit it out.

"You're pretty good."

"I like them high and inside." After cocking the bat against the cage, Lil started toward the field. "We've got a game next Saturday. You could come."

Some dumbass boondockie ball game. Would be, he thought, a lot better than nothing. "Maybe."

"Do you get to go to real games? Like at Yankee Stadium?"

"Sure. My father's got season tickets, box seats, right behind the third-base line."

"No way!"

It felt good—a little—to impress her. And it didn't suck to have some-body, even a farm girl, to talk ball with. Plus she could handle the ball and the bat, and that was a serious plus.

Still, Coop only shrugged, then watched Lil slip through the lines of barbed wire without mishap. He didn't complain when she turned and held the lines wider for him.

"We watch on TV, or listen on the radio. And once we went all the way down to Omaha to watch a game. But I've never been to a major-league ballpark."

And that reminded him just where he was. "You're a million miles from one. From anything."

"Dad says one day we'll take a vacation and go back east. Maybe to Fenway Park because he's a Red Sox fan." She found a ball, stuck it in her back pocket. "He likes to root for the underdog."

"My father says it's smarter to root for a winner."

"Everybody else does, mostly, so somebody has to root for the underdog." She beamed a smile at him, fluttered long lashes over dark brown eyes. "That's going to be New York this year."

He grinned before he realized it. "So you say."

He picked up a ball, tossed it hand to hand as they worked their way toward the trees. "What do you do with all these cows, anyway?"

"Beef cattle. We raise them, then sell them. People eat them. I bet even people in New York like steak."

He thought that was gross, just the idea that the cow staring at him now would be on somebody's plate—maybe even his—one day.

"Do you have any pets?" she asked him.

"No."

She couldn't imagine not having animals around, everywhere, all the time. And the idea of not having any brought a lump of genuine sympathy to her throat.

"I guess it's harder in the city. Our dogs . . ." She paused to look around, then spotted them. "They've been out running, see, and now they're back at the table, hoping for scraps. They're good dogs. You can come over and play with them sometimes if you want, and use the batting cage."

"Maybe." He sneaked another glance at her. "Thanks."

"Not many of the girls I know like baseball all that much. Or hiking and fishing. I do. Dad's teaching me to track. My grandfather, my mom's father, taught him. He's really good."

"Track?"

"Animals and people. For fun. There's lots of trails, and lots to do."

"If you say so."

She cocked her head at the dismissive tone. "Have you ever been camping?"

"Why would I want to?"

She only smiled. "It's going to be dark pretty soon. We'd better get the last ball and head back. If you come over again, maybe Dad will play or we can go riding. You like to ride?"

"You mean horses? I don't know how. It looks stupid."

She fired up at that, the way she'd fired up to hit the ball high and long. "It's not stupid, and it's stupid to say it is just because you don't know how. Besides, it's fun. When we—"

She stopped dead in her tracks. As she sucked in her breath, she grabbed Coop's arm. "Don't move."

"What?" Because the hand on his arm shook, his heart slammed into his throat. "Is it a snake?"

Panicked, he scanned the grass.

"Cougar." She barely breathed the word. She stood like a statue with that one trembling hand on his arm, and stared into the tangled brush.

"What? Where?" Suspicious, sure she was just screwing around and trying to scare him, he tried to pry her hand away. At first he saw nothing but that brush, the trees, the rise of rock and hill.

Then he saw the shadow. "Holy shit. Holy freaking shit!"

"Don't run." She stared as if mesmerized. "If you run, he'll chase you, and he's faster. No!" She yanked on his arm as Coop edged up, getting a firmer grip on the ball. "Don't throw anything, not yet. Mom says . . ." She couldn't remember everything her mother had told her. She'd never seen a cat before, not in real life, not near the farm. "You have to make noise, and, and make yourself look big."

Quivering, Lil rose to her toes, lifted her arms over her head, and began to shout. "Get away! Get away from here.

"Yell!" she shouted to Cooper. "Look big and mean!"

Her eyes, keen and dark, measured the cougar from tip to tail. Even as her heart pounded with fear, something else moved through her.

Awe.

She could see his eyes glint in the oncoming dusk, glint as they seemed to look right into hers. Though her throat went dry, she thought: He's beautiful. He's so beautiful.

He paced, powerful grace, watching them as if deciding whether to attack or retreat.

Beside her Coop shouted, his voice raw with fear. She watched the big cat slink toward deeper shadow. And then it leaped away, a blur of dull gold that dazzled her eyes.

"It ran away. It ran away."

"It didn't," Lil murmured. "It flew."

Through the roaring in her ears, she heard her father shouting for her, and turned. He charged across the field, scattering surprised cattle. Yards behind him Coop's grandfather ran, carrying a rifle she realized he'd gotten from the house. The dogs raced with them, as did her mother, with a shotgun, and Coop's grandmother.

"Cougar." She managed to get the word out just before Joe swept her off her feet and into his arms. "There. Over there. It's gone now."

"Get in the house. Coop." With his free arm, Joe pulled Coop against him. "Both of you, get inside. Now."

"It's gone, Dad. We scared it away."

"Go! Cougar," he said as Jenna sprinted past Sam and reached them.

"Oh, God. You're all right." She took Lil, giving Joe the shotgun. "You're all right." She kissed Lil's face, her hair, then bent down to do the same to Coop.

"Get them in the house, Jenna. Take the kids and Lucy, and get inside."

"Come on. Come on." Jenna draped her arms around both children, looked up at Sam's grim face as he reached them. "Be careful."

"Don't kill it, Dad!" Lil called out as her mother pulled her away. "It was so beautiful." She searched the brush, the trees, hoping for just one more glimpse. "Don't kill it."

2

Coop had a couple of bad dreams. In one the mountain lion with its glinting yellow eyes jumped through his bedroom window and ate him in big greedy bites before he could even scream. In another, he was lost in the hills, in the green and the rock, in the miles of it. No one came to find him. No one, he thought, even noticed he was gone.

Lil's father hadn't killed the cougar. At least Coop hadn't heard gunshots. When his grandfather and Mr. Chance had come back, they'd had cherry pie and homemade ice cream, and had talked of other things.

Deliberately. Coop knew all about that adult ploy. Nobody would talk about what had happened until after he and Lil were in bed, and couldn't hear.

Resigned to and resentful of his prison, he did his chores, ate his meals, played his Game Boy. He hoped, if he did what he was told, he'd get a parole day and be able to go back to the Chance farm and use the batting cage.

Maybe Mr. Chance would play, too, then he could ask him about what it was like to play professional ball. Coop knew his father expected him to go to law school, to work in the family firm. To be a big-shot law-yer one day. But maybe, maybe, he could be a ballplayer instead.

If he was good enough.

With his thoughts on ball, on escape, on the misery of his summer sentence, the big yellow-eyed cat might've been just another dream.

He ate his breakfast of flapjacks, as his grandmother called them, in silence at the old kitchen table while she fiddled around at the stove. His grandfather was already outside doing some farm thing. Cooper ate slowly, even though the Game Boy was forbidden at the table, because when he finished he'd have to go outside for chores.

Lucy poured coffee into a thick white mug, then brought it with her to sit across from him. "Well, Cooper, you've been with us two weeks now."

"I guess."

"That's about all the brooding time you're going to get. You're a good, bright boy. You do what you're told and you don't sass. At least not out loud."

There was a look in her eyes—a smart look, not a mean one—that told him she knew he sassed in his head. A lot.

"Those are good qualities. You also tend to sulk and don't say boo to a goat and drag around here like you're in prison. Those aren't such good qualities."

He said nothing, but wished he'd eaten his breakfast faster and es-caped. He hunched his shoulders, figuring they were going to have a *discussion*. Which meant, from his experience, she'd tell him all the things he did wrong, and how she expected more, and he was a dis-appointment.

"I know you're mad, and you've got a right to be. That's why you got these past two weeks."

He blinked at his plate, and a line of confusion formed between his eyebrows.

"The fact is, Cooper, I'm mad *for* you. Your parents did a selfish thing, and didn't take you into account when they did it."

He brought his head up about an inch, but his eyes lifted and met hers. Maybe it was a trick, he thought, and she was saying that so he'd say something bad. So he could be grounded or punished. "They can do what they want."

"Yes, they can." She nodded briskly as she drank her coffee. "Doesn't mean they should. I want you here, and so does your grandpa. I know he doesn't say much, but I'm telling you the truth. But that's a selfish thing, too, for us. We want you here, we want to get to know our only grandchild, have time with him we never got much of before. But you don't want to be here, and I'm sorry for that."

She was looking right at him, right at his face. And it didn't *feel* like a trick. "I know you want to be home," she continued, "with your friends. I know you wanted to go to baseball camp like they promised. Yeah, I know about that."

She nodded again, and sipping coffee stared off hard out the window. It seemed she *was* mad, as she'd said. But not at him. She really was sort of mad *for* him.

And that was something he didn't understand. That was something that had his chest getting all tight and achy.

"I know about that," she repeated. "A boy your age doesn't get a lot of say, a lot of choices. They'll come, but at this stage you just don't have them. You can make the best out of what you've got, or be miserable."

"I just want to go home." He hadn't meant to say it, only to think it. But the words came right out, pushing out of that tight, achy chest.

She shifted her gaze back to his. "Honey, I know. I know you do. I wish I could do that for you. You may not believe me, you don't know me very well so you may not, but I really want to give you what you want."

It wasn't a matter of belief, it was that she talked to him. Actually talked as if he mattered. So the words, and the misery with them, just bubbled out of him.

"They just sent me away, and I didn't do anything wrong." Tears rose into his voice. "They didn't want me to go with them. They didn't want me."

"We do. I know that's not much comfort to you right now. But you know that, you believe that. Maybe sometime later in your life, you'll need a place. You know you'll always have one here."

He spoke the worst. The worst that hid inside him. "They're going to get a divorce."

"Yes, I expect you're right about that."

He blinked and stared, because he'd expected her to say that wasn't true, he'd expected her to pretend everything would be fine. "Then what'll happen to me?"

"You'll get through it."

"They don't love me."

"We do. We do," she said, firmly, when he lowered his head again and shook it. "First because you're blood. You're kin. And second, just because."

When two tears plopped on his plate, Lucy kept talking. "I can't speak for what they feel, what they think. But I can say something about what they do. I'm so mad at them. I'm so mad at them for hurting you. People will say it's just one summer, it's not the end of the world. But people who say that don't remember what it's like to be eleven. I can't make you happy to be here, Cooper, but I'm going to ask you for something. For just one thing, and maybe it's a hard thing for you. I'm going to ask you to try."

"Everything's different here."

"It sure is. But you might find something in the different you like. And the backside of August won't seem so far away if you do. You do that, Cooper, you give it a real good try, and I'll talk your grandpa into getting us a new television set. One that doesn't need those rabbit ears."

He sniffled. "What if I try and I still don't like anything?"

"Trying's enough, if you mean it."

"How long do I have to try before the new TV?"

She laughed, full and hard, and for some reason the sound of it made his lips curve and his chest loosen up. "That's a boy. Good for you. Two weeks, we'll say. Two weeks of brooding, now two weeks of trying. You make a real effort, and you'll have that new TV set in the parlor, you betcha. Is that a deal?"

"Yes, ma'am."

"All right. Why don't you go out now, find your grandpa. He's got some project going out there, and he might need a hand."

"Okay." He got to his feet. Later, he wouldn't know why it spewed out. "They yell a lot, and they don't even know I'm there when they do. He's having sex with somebody else. I think he does that a lot."

Lucy blew out a long breath. "Are you listening at keyholes, boy?"

"Sometimes. But sometimes they're yelling about it, and I don't have to try to hear. They never listen to me when I talk. They pretend to sometimes, and sometimes they don't even pretend. They don't care if I like anything, as long as I'm quiet and out of their way."

"That's different here, too."

"I guess. Maybe."

He didn't know what to think as he walked outside. No adult had ever talked to him that way, or listened to him that way. He'd never heard anybody criticize his parents—well, except each other.

She'd said they wanted him. No one had ever said that to him before. She said it even when she knew he didn't want them, and it didn't feel like she'd said it to make him feel bad. It felt like she'd said it because it was true.

He stopped, looked around. He could try, sure, but what could he find to like around here? A bunch of horses and pigs and chickens. A bunch of fields and hills and nothing.

He liked her flapjacks, but he didn't think that's what she meant.

He stuffed his hands in his pockets and headed around to the far side of the house where he heard banging. Now he was going to have to hang around with his strange, mostly silent grandfather. How was he supposed to like *that*?

He cut around, and saw Sam over by the big barn with the white silo. And what Sam was hammering into the ground with some kind of metal stakes had Coop speechless.

A batting cage.

He wanted to run, just fly across the dirt yard. But made himself walk.

Maybe it just looked like a batting cage. It could be something for the animals.

Sam glanced up, took another whack at the stake. "Late on your chores."

"Yes, sir."

"Fed the stock, but you're going to need to get the eggs right soon."

"Grandma said you needed help with a project."

"Nope. 'Bout done." With the little sledgehammer in hand, Sam straightened up, stepped back. He studied the fence cage in silence.

"Eggs aren't going to jump in the pail on their own," he said at length.

"No, sir."

"Might be," he drawled as Coop turned to go, "I could pitch you a few after chores are done." Sam walked over, picked up a bat he'd leaned against the side of the barn. "You can use this. Just finished it last night."

Baffled, Cooper took the bat, ran his hands along the smooth wood. "You made it?"

"Don't see no reason for store-bought."

"It . . . it has my name on it." Reverently, Coop traced his fingers over the name etched in the wood.

"That's how you know it's yours. You plan on getting those eggs sometime today?"

"Yes, sir." He handed the bat back to Sam. "Thank you."

"You ever get tired of being so damn polite, boy?"

"Yes, sir."

Sam's lips twitched. "Go on."

Coop started to run toward the chicken house, stopped, turned back. "Grandpa? Will you teach me how to ride a horse?"

"Get your chores done. We'll see."

THERE WERE some things he liked, at least a little. He liked hitting the ball after supper, and the way his grandpa would surprise him every few pitches with crazy, exaggerated windups. He liked riding Dottie, the little mare, around the corral—at least once he'd gotten over being worried about being kicked or bitten.

Horses didn't really smell after you got to like them a little, or ride them without being scared shitless.

He liked watching the lightning storm that came one night like an ambush and slashed and burned the sky. He even liked, sometimes, a little, sitting at his bedroom window and looking out. He still missed New York, and his friends, his life, but it was interesting to see so many stars, and to hear the house hum in the quiet.

He didn't like the chickens, the way they smelled or sounded, or the evil glint in their eyes when he went in to gather eggs. But he liked the eggs just fine, whether they were cooked up for breakfast or stirred into batter and dough for cakes and cookies.

There were always cookies in his grandmother's big glass jar.

He didn't like when people came to visit, or he rode into town with his grandparents, the way they'd size him up and say things like, *So, this is Missy's boy!* (his mother, christened Michelle, went by Chelle in New York). And they'd say how he was the spitting image of his grandfather. Who was *old*.

He liked seeing the Chance truck ramble toward the farmhouse, even if Lil was a girl.

She played ball, and didn't spend all her time giggling like a lot of the girls he knew. She didn't listen to New Kids on the Block all the time and make girly eyes over them. That was a plus.

She did better on a horse than he did, but she didn't rag on him about it. Much. After a while, it wasn't like hanging out with a girl. It was just hanging out with Lil.

And one week—not two—after the talk at the kitchen table, a brand-new TV showed up in the parlor.

"No point in waiting," his grandmother said. "You held up your end just fine. I'm proud of you."

In all of his life, he couldn't remember anyone being proud of him, or saying so, just because he'd tried.

Once he'd been judged good enough, he and Lil were allowed to ride, as long as they stayed in the fields, within sight of the house.

"Well?" Lil asked as they walked the horses through the grass.

"What?"

"Is it stupid?"

"Maybe it's not. She's pretty cool." He patted Dottie's neck. "She likes apples."

"I wish they'd let us ride up into the hills, really see stuff. I can only go with one of my parents. Except . . ." She looked around, as if to check for cocked ears. "I snuck out one morning, before sunrise. I tried to track the cougar."

He actually felt his eyes bug out. "Are you crazy?"

"I read all about them. I got books from the library." She wore a cowboy hat today, a brown one, and flipped a long braid over her shoulder. "They don't bother people, hardly at all. And they don't much come around a farm like ours unless they're like migrating or something."

Excitement poured off her as she shifted to turn more fully toward the speechless Coop. "It was so cool! It was just so cool! I found scat and tracks and everything. But then I lost the trail. I didn't mean to stay out so long, and they were up when I got back. I had to pretend I was just coming out of the house."

She pressed her lips together, gave him her fierce look. "You can't tell."

"I'm not a tattletale." What an insult. "But you can't go off by yourself like that. Holy shit, Lil."

"I know how to track. Not as good as Dad, but I'm pretty good at it. And I know the trails. We hike a lot, and we camp out and everything. I had my compass, and my kit."

"What if the cougar had been out there?"

"I'd have seen it again. It looked right at me that day, right at me. Like it knew me, and it felt like . . . It sort of felt like it did."

"Come on."

"Seriously. My mother's grandfather was Sioux."

"Like an Indian?"

"Yeah. Native American," she corrected. "Lakota Sioux. His name was John Swiftwater, and his tribe—his, like, people—lived here for generations and stuff. They had animal spirits. Maybe the cougar was mine."

"It wasn't anybody's spirit."

She just continued to train her gaze on the hills. "I heard it that night. Late the night we saw it. I heard it scream."

"Scream?"

"That's the sound they make because they can't roar. Only the big cats—like lions—can roar. Something in their throat. I forget. I'll have to look it up again. Anyway, I just wanted to try to find it."

He couldn't help but admire what she'd done, even if it was crazy. No girl he knew would sneak out to track down a mountain lion. Except Lil. "If it'd found you, maybe you'd be breakfast."

"You can't tell."

"I said I wouldn't, but you can't sneak out and go looking for it again either."

"I think it would've come back by now if it was going to. I wonder where it went." She looked off again, into the hills. "We could go camping. Dad really likes to. We take like a nature hike and camp overnight. Your grandparents would let you."

"Like in a tent? In the mountains?" The idea was both terrifying and compelling.

"Yeah. We'd catch fish for supper and see the falls, and buffalo and all kinds of wildlife. Maybe even the cougar. When you get all the way to the peak, you can see clear to Montana." She shifted to look back as the dinner bell rang. "Time to eat. We'll go camping. I'll ask my dad. It'll be fun."

HE WENT CAMPING and learned how to bait a hook. He knew the rush-up-the-spine thrill of sitting by a campfire and listening to the echoing howl of a wolf, and the shock of watching a fish he'd caught more through luck than design flash silver in the sunlight at the end of his rod.

His body toughened; his hands hardened. He knew an elk from a mule deer and how to care for tack.

He could ride at a gallop, and that was the biggest thrill of his life.

He earned a guest spot on Lil's baseball team, and brought in a run with a strong double.

Years later, he'd look back and realize his life had turned that summer, and would never be the same again. But all Coop knew at the age of eleven was he was happy.

His grandfather taught him to carve and whittle, and to Coop's utter joy, presented him with a pocketknife—to keep. His grandmother showed him how to groom a horse, top to bottom, how to check for injury or illness.

But his grandfather taught him how to talk to them.

"It's in the eyes," Sam told him. "In the body, the ears, the tail, but first it's in the eyes. What he sees in yours, what you see in his." He held a lead line on a fractious yearling colt who reared and pawed the air. "Doesn't matter what you say so much, because they'll see what you're thinking in your eyes. This one wants to show he's tough, but what he is is a little spooked. What do we want from him, what're we going to do? Is he going to like it? Will it hurt?"

Even as he spoke to Coop, Sam looked into the colt's eyes, kept his voice soft and soothing. "What we're going to do is shorten up on the line here. A firm hand doesn't have to be a hard one."

Sam eased in, got that firm hand on the bridle. The colt quivered and danced. "Needs a name." Sam stroked a hand over the colt's neck. "Give him one."

Coop took his eyes off the yearling to gawk at Sam. "Me?"

"What kind of a name's Me for a horse?"

"I meant . . . Um. Jones? Can it be Jones, like Indiana Jones?"

"Ask him."

"I think you're Jones. Jones is smart and brave." With a little help from Sam's hand on the bridle, the colt gave a decisive nod. "He said yes! Did you see that?"

"Yeah, you betcha. Hold his head now, firm, not hard. I'm going to get the saddle blanket on him. He's used to that. Remind him."

"I . . . It's just the blanket. You don't mind the blanket, Jones. It doesn't hurt. We're not going to hurt you. You've had the blanket before. Grandpa says we're just going to get you used to the saddle today. It doesn't hurt either."

Jones stared into Coop's eyes, ears forward, and barely acknowledged the saddle pad.

"Maybe I can ride you some, after you're used to the saddle. Because I don't weigh enough to hurt you. Right, Grandpa?"

"We'll see. Hold firm now, Cooper."

Sam hefted the training saddle, eased it onto the horse. Jones jerked his head, gave a quick buck.

"It's okay. It's okay." He wasn't mad, wasn't mean, Coop thought. He was a little scared. He could *feel* it, he could see it in Jones's eyes. "It's just a saddle. I guess it feels funny at first." Under the afternoon sun, with sweat he barely noticed dampening his T-shirt, Coop talked and talked while his grandfather cinched the saddle.

"Take him out on the lounge, like I showed you. Just like you did with him before the saddle. He'll buck some."

Sam stepped back to let the boy and the colt learn. He leaned on the fence, ready to intervene if need be. From behind him, Lucy laid a hand on his shoulder.

"That's a sight, isn't it?"

"He's got the touch," Sam acknowledged. "Got the heart and the head, too. The boy's a natural with horses."

"I don't want to let him go. I know," she said before Sam could respond. "Not ours to keep. But it's going to break my heart a little. I know a true thing, and that's they don't love him like we do. So it breaks my heart knowing we have to send him back."

"Might be next summer he'll want to come."

"Might be. But oh, it's going to be quiet between times." She heaved a sigh, then turned at the sound of a truck. "Farrier's coming. I'll go get a pitcher of lemonade."

IT WAS the farrier's son, a gangly towheaded boy of fourteen called Gull who, in the late-afternoon shadows of the barn, gave Coop his first—and last—chaw of tobacco.

Even after he'd finished puking up his breakfast, his lunch, and everything else still in his system, Coop remained what Gull assessed as green as a grasshopper. Alerted by the sounds of retching, Lucy left her work on her kitchen garden to hustle to the back of the barn. There Coop, on his hands and knees, continued to heave while Gull stood, scratching his head under his hat.

"Jesus, Coop, ain't you done as yet?"

"What happened?" Lucy demanded. "What did you do?"

"He just wanted to try a chaw. I didn't see the harm, Miss Lucy, ma'am."

"Oh, for— Don't you know better than to give a boy his age tobacco?"

"Sure can puke."

Since he seemed to be done, Lucy reached down. "Come on, boy, let's get you inside and cleaned up."

Brisk and pragmatic, Lucy hauled him inside. Too weak to protest, Coop only groaned as she stripped him down to his jockeys. She bathed his face, gave him cool water to drink. After she'd lowered the shades against the sun, she sat on the side of the bed to lay a hand on his brow. He opened bleary eyes.

"It was awful."

"There's a lesson learned." She bent over, brushed her lips on his forehead. "You'll be all right. You'll get through." Not just today, she thought. And sat with him a little, while he slept off the lesson learned.

ON THE BIG flat rock by the stream, Coop stretched out with Lil.

"She didn't yell or anything."

"What did it taste like? Does it taste like it smells, because that's gross. It looks gross, too."

"It tastes . . . like shit," he decided.

She snickered. "Did you ever taste shit?"

"I've smelled it enough this summer. Horse shit, pig shit, cow shit, chicken shit."

She howled with laughter. "New York has shit, too."

"Mostly from people. I don't have to shovel it up."

She rolled to her side, pillowing her head on her hands, and studied him with her big, brown eyes. "I wish you didn't have to go back. This is the best summer of my whole life."

"Me too." He felt weird saying it, knowing it was true. Knowing the best friend of the best summer of his life was a girl.

"Maybe you can stay. If you asked, maybe your parents would let you live here."

"They won't." He shifted to his back, watched a circling hawk. "They called last night, and said how they'd be home next week, and meet me at the airport and . . . Well, they won't."

"If they did, would you want to?"

"I don't know."

"You *want* to go back?"

"I don't know." It was awful not to know. "I wish I could visit there and live here. I wish I could train Jones and ride Dottie and play baseball and catch more fish. But I want to see my room and go to the arcade and go to a Yankee game." He rolled toward her again. "Maybe you could visit. We could go to the ballpark."

"I don't think they'd let me." Her eyes turned sad, and her bottom lip quivered. "You probably won't ever come back."

"Yes, I will."

"Do you swear?"

"I swear." He offered his hand for a solemn pinky swear.

"If I write you, will you write me back?"

"Okay."

"Every time?"

He smiled. "Every time."

"Then you'll come back. So will the cougar. We saw him the very first day, so he's like our spirit guide. He's like . . . I can't remember the word, but it's like good luck."

HE THOUGHT about it, how she'd talked of the cougar all summer, had shown him pictures in the library books, and the books she'd bought herself with her allowance. She'd drawn pictures of her own and hung them in her room, among her baseball pennants.

In his last week on the farm, Coop worked with his penknife, and the carving tool his grandfather let him borrow. He said his goodbyes to Dottie and Jones and the other horses, bade a not very fond farewell to the chickens. He packed his clothes, along with the boots and work gloves his grandparents had bought him. And his beloved baseball bat.

As he had on the long-ago drive in, he sat in the backseat and stared out the window. He saw things differently now, the big sky, the dark hills that rose up in rocky needles and jagged towers and hid the forests and streams and canyons.

Maybe Lil's cougar prowled in them.

They turned in the far road to the Chance land to say another goodbye.

Lil sat on the porch steps, so he knew she'd been watching for them. She wore red shorts and a blue shirt, with her hair looped through the back of her favorite ball cap. Her mother came out of the house as they pulled up, and the dogs raced from the back, barking and bumping their bodies together.

Lil stood, and her mother came down, laid a hand on her shoulder. Joe rounded the house, stuffing work gloves in his back pocket, and flanked Lil on the other side.

It etched an image in Cooper's mind—mother, father, daughter—like an island in front of the old house, in the foreground of hills and valleys and sky, with a pair of dusty yellow dogs racing in madly happy circles.

Coop cleared his throat as he got out of the car. "I came to say goodbye."

Joe moved first, stepping forward and offering a hand. He shook Coop's and still holding it crouched to bring them eye-to-eye. "You come back and see us, Mr. New York."

"I will. And I'll send you a picture from Yankee Stadium when we clinch the pennant."

Joe laughed. "Dream on, son."

"You be safe." Jenna turned his cap around to lean down, kiss his forehead. "And you be happy. Don't forget us."

"I won't." He turned, suddenly feeling a little shy, to Lil. "I made you something."

"You did? What is it?"

He held out the box, shifting his feet when she pulled the lid off. "It's kind of stupid. It's not very good," he said, as she stared at the small cougar he'd carved out of hickory. "I couldn't get the face right or—"

He broke off, stunned, embarrassed, when she threw her arms around him. "It's beautiful! I'll always keep it. Wait!" Spinning around, she dashed into the house.

"That's a good gift, Cooper." Jenna studied him. "The cougar's hers now, she won't have it any other way. So you've put part of yourself into her symbol."

Lil bolted out of the house, skidded to a stop in front of Coop. "This is my best thing—before the cougar. You take it. It's an old coin," she said, as she offered it. "We found it last spring when we were digging a new garden. It's old, and somebody must've dropped it out of their pocket a long time ago. It's all worn so you can hardly see."

Cooper took the silver disk, so worn the outline of the woman stamped on it could hardly be seen. "It's cool."

"It's for good luck. It's a . . . what's the word, Mom?"

"A talisman," Jenna supplied.

"A talisman," Lil repeated. "For good luck."

"We've got to get on." Sam gave Cooper's shoulder a pat. "It's a long drive to Rapid City."

"Safe trip, Mr. New York."

"I'll write," Lil called out. "But you have to write back."

"I will." Clutching the coin, Coop got into the car. He watched out the back, as long as he could, watched the island in front of the old house shrink and fade.

He didn't cry. He was nearly twelve years old, after all. But he held the old silver coin all the way to Rapid City.

3

Lil walked her horse through the morning mists along the trail. They moved through high grass, crossed the sparkling waters of a narrow stream where tangled vines of poison ivy lurked before starting the upward climb. The air smelled of the pine and the water and the grass while the light shimmered with the delicacy of dawn.

Birds called and chattered. She heard the burry song of the mountain bluebird, the hoarse *chee* of a pine siskin in flight, the irritable warning of the pinyon jay.

It seemed the forest came to life around her, stirred by the streams and slants of misty light sliding through the canopy of trees.

There was nowhere in the world she'd rather be.

She spotted tracks, usually deer or elk, and noted them on the tape recorder in her jacket pocket. Earlier she'd found buffalo tracks, and of course, numerous signs of her father's herd.

But so far in this three-day jaunt she'd given herself, she'd yet to track the cat.

She'd heard its call the night before. Its scream had ripped through the darkness, through the stars and the moonlight.

I'm here.

She studied the brush as the sturdy mare climbed, listened to the birdcalls that danced through the sheltering pine. A red squirrel burst out of a thicket of chokecherry, darted across the ground and up the trunk of a pine, and looking up, up, she spotted a hawk circle on his morning rounds.

This, as much as the majestic views from the clifftops, as much as the towering falls tumbling down canyons, was why, she believed, the Black Hills were sacred ground.

If you felt no magic here, to her mind, you would find it nowhere.

It was enough to be here, to have this time, to scout, to study. She'd be in the classroom soon, a college freshman (God!), away from everything she knew. And though she was hungry to learn, nothing could replace the sights, the sounds, the smells of home.

She'd seen cougar from time to time over the years. Not the same one, she thought. Very unlikely the same cougar she and Coop had spotted that summer eight years ago. She'd seen him camouflaged in the branches of a tree, leaping up a rock face, and once, while riding herd with her father, she'd spotted one through her field glasses as he took down a young elk.

In all of her life she'd never seen anything more powerful, more real.

She made note of the vegetation as well. The starry forget-me-nots, the delicate Rocky Mountain iris, the sunlight of yellow sweet clover. It was, after all, part of the environment, a link of the food chain. The rabbit, deer, elk ate the grasses, leaves, berries, and buds—and the gray wolf and her cats ate the rabbits, deer, and elk.

The red squirrel might end up lunch for the circling hawk.

The trail leveled off, and opened into grassland, already lush and green and spearing with wildflowers. A small herd of buffalo grazed there, so she added the bull, the four cows, and the two calves to her tally.

One of the calves dipped and shoved, and came up again with his head draped with flowers and grass. Grinning, she paused to pull out her camera, take a few pictures to add to her files.

She could title the calf *Party Animal.*

Maybe she'd send it, and copies of some of the shots she'd taken on the trail, to Coop. He'd said he might be coming out this summer, but he hadn't answered the letter she'd sent three weeks before.

Then again, he wasn't as reliable about letters and e-mails as she was. Especially since he was dating that coed he'd met at college.

CeeCee, Lil thought with a roll of her eye. Stupid name. She *knew* Coop was sleeping with her. He hadn't said so, in fact had been pretty damn careful not to. But Lil wasn't stupid. Just like she was sure—or nearly sure—he'd slept with that girl he'd talked about in high school.

Zoe.

Jeez, what happened to regular names?

It seemed to her that guys thought about sex all the time. Then again, she admitted, shifting in the saddle, she'd been thinking about it a lot lately.

Probably because she'd never had it.

She just wasn't interested in boys—not the ones she knew, anyway. Maybe in college next fall . . .

It wasn't as if she *wanted* to be a virgin, but she didn't see the point in getting sweaty if she didn't really like the guy—and if he didn't heat her up on top of the like, then it was just a kind of exercise, wasn't it?

Just something to be crossed off the life-experience list.

She wanted, she thought she wanted, more than that.

She shrugged it off, put her camera away, took out her canteen to drink. She'd probably be too busy studying and working in college for sex. Besides, her priority now was the summer, documenting her trails, the habitats, working on her models, her papers. And talking her father into culling out a few acres for the wildlife refuge she hoped to build one day.

The Chance Wildlife Refuge. She liked the name, not only because it was hers, but because the animals would have a chance there. And people would have a chance to see them, study them, care about them.

One day, she thought. But she had so much to learn first—and to learn, she had to leave what she loved best.

She hoped Coop came, even for a few weeks, before she had to leave for college. He'd come back, like her cougar. Not every summer, but often enough. Two weeks the year after his first visit, then the whole wonderful summer the year after, when his parents divorced.

A couple of weeks here, a month or so there, and they'd always just picked up where they left off. Even if he did spend time talking about the girls back home. But now it had been two whole years.

He just had to come this summer.

With a little sigh, she capped her canteen.

It happened fast.

Lil felt the mare quiver, start to shy. Even as she tightened her grip on the reins, the cat leaped out of the high grass. Like a blur—speed, muscle, silent death—he took down the calf with the flower headdress. The small herd scattered, the mother bugling. Lil fought to control the mare as the bull charged the cat.

It screamed in challenge, rising up to defend its kill. Lil locked her legs, gripping the reins with one hand as she dragged out her camera again.

Claws flashed. Across the meadow Lil scented blood. The mare scented it as well and wheeled in panic.

"Stop, easy! It's not interested in us. It's got what it wants."

Gashes dripped from the bull's side. Hooves thundered, and the calls sounded like grief. Then it all echoed away, and there was only the cat and her kill in the high meadow.

The sound it made was like a purr, a loud rumble, like triumph. Across the grass, its eyes met Lil's, and held. Her hand trembled, but she couldn't risk taking her other off the reins to steady the camera. She took two wobbly shots of the cat, the trampled, bloody grass, the kill.

With a warning hiss, the cat dragged the carcass into the brush, into the shadows of the pine and birch trees.

"She has kittens to feed," Lil murmured, and her voice sounded thin and raw in the morning air. "Holy shit." She pulled out her recorder, nearly fumbled it. "Calm down. Just calm down. Okay, document. Okay.

Sighted female cougar, approximately two meters long, nose to tail. Jeez, weight about forty kilograms. Typical tawny color. Stalk-and-ambush kill. It took down a bison calf from a herd of seven grazing in high grass. Defended kill from bull. It dragged kill into the forest, potentially due to my presence, though if the female has a litter, they would be too young, probably, to visit kill sites with the mother. She's taking her kids, who wouldn't be fully weaned as yet, breakfast. Incident recorded . . . seven twenty-five A.M., June 12. Wow."

As much as she wanted to, she knew better than to follow the track of the cat. If she had young, she might very well attack horse and rider to defend them, and her territory.

"We're not going to top that," she decided. "I guess it's time to go home."

She took the most direct route, anxious to get back and write up her notes. Still it was mid-afternoon before she saw her father and his part-time hand Jay mending a fence in a pasture.

Cattle scattered as she rode through them and whoaed the horse by the battered old Jeep.

"There's my girl." Joe walked over to give her leg, then the mare's neck, a pat. "Home from the wilderness?"

"Safe and sound, as promised. Hi, Jay."

Jay, who didn't believe in using two words if one would do, tapped the brim of his hat in response.

"You need some help here?" Lil asked her father.

"No, we've got it. Elk came through."

"I saw a couple herds myself, and some bison. I watched a cougar take down a calf in one of the high meadows."

"Cat?"

She glanced at Jay. She knew the look on his face. Cougar equaled pest and predator.

"Half a day's ride from here. With enough game to keep her and the litter I imagine she's got fed. She doesn't need to come down and go after our stock."

"You're all right?"

"She wasn't interested in me," she assured her father. "Remember, prey recognition is learned behavior in cougars. Humans aren't prey."

"Cat'll eat anything, it's hungry enough," Jay muttered. "Sneaky bastards."

"I'd say the bull leading that herd agrees with you. But I didn't see any signs of her on the route back here. No sign she's extended her territory down this far."

When Jay just jerked a shoulder and turned back to the fence, Lil grinned at her father. "Anyway, if you don't need me I'm going to head in. I'm ready for a shower and a cold drink."

"Tell your mother we'll be a couple hours out here yet."

After she'd groomed and fed her horse and downed two glasses of sun tea, Lil joined her mother in the vegetable garden. She took the hoe from Jenna's hands and set to work.

"I know I'm repeating myself, but it was the most amazing thing. The way it moved. And I know they're secretive, skulky, but God knows how long it was back there, stalking that herd, choosing its prey, its moment, and I never saw a sign. I was looking, and I never saw a sign. I have to get better."

"It didn't bother you, to see it kill?"

"It was so fierce and fast. Clean, really. Just doing her job, you know? I think if I'd been expecting it, if I'd had time to think about it, I might've reacted differently."

She sighed a little, tipped up the brim of her hat. "The calf was so damn cute, with those flowers dripping around its head. But it was life and death, in seconds. It , . . this is going to sound weird, but it was sort of religious."

She paused to swipe at her sweaty forehead. "Being there, witnessing the moment, it just made me more sure of what I want to do, and what I need to learn so I can do it. I took pictures. Before, during, after."

"Honey, it may be squeamish, especially coming from a beef farmer, but I don't think I'd want to see that cougar chowing down on a buffalo calf."

Grinning, Lil went back to hoeing. "Did you know what you wanted, what you wanted to do, to be, when you were my age?"

"I didn't have a clue." Squatting, Jenna plucked weeds from around the ferny green of carrots. Her hands were quick and capable, her body long and lithe like her daughter's. "But a year or so after, your father came along. He gave me one cocky look, and I knew I wanted him, and he wasn't going to have much choice in the matter."

"What if he'd wanted to go back east?"

"I'd've gone back east. It wasn't the land I loved, not back then. It was him, and I guess we fell in love with this place together." Jenna pushed back her hat, looked over the rows of carrots and beans, the young tomatoes, and on to the fields of grain and soybeans, to the pastures. "I think you loved it with your first breath."

"I don't know where I'll go. There's so much I want to learn, and to see. But I'll always come back."

"I'm counting on it." Jenna pushed to her feet. "Give me that hoe now, go in and clean up. I'll be in in a bit, and you can help me start supper."

Lil cut across toward the house, taking off her hat to slap it against her pants to dislodge some of the trail dust before going in. A long, hot shower sounded better than good. After she'd helped her mother in the kitchen, she could take some time to start writing up her notes and observations. And tomorrow, she had to get her film into town, get it developed.

On her list of things to save for was one of the new digital cameras. And a laptop computer, she thought. She'd earned a scholarship, and that would help with college expenses, but she knew it wouldn't cover everything.

Tuition, housing, lab fees, books, transportation. It all added up.

She was nearly to the house when she heard the roar of an engine. Close, she determined, on their land. She walked around the house rather than inside to see who was coming and making such a racket out of it.

She set her hands on her hips when she saw the motorcycle roaring down the farm road. Bikers traveled the area regularly, and especially in the summer. Now and then one or more rode in looking for directions, or a couple days' work. Most approached a little more cautiously, she thought, while this one barreled straight in as if he . . .

The helmet and visor hid his hair and most of his face. But the grin flashed, and she knew it. Letting out a whooping laugh, she raced forward. He stopped the bike behind her father's truck, swung his leg over as he unhooked the helmet. He set the helmet on the seat, and turned in time to catch her in mid–flying leap.

"Coop!" She held on, tight, as he swung her in a circle. "You came."

"I said I would."

"Might." Even as she gave him a squeeze, something trickled inside her, a little like heat. He felt different. Harder, tougher, in a way that made her think of man instead of boy.

"Might turned into did." He dropped her on her feet, and still grinning, looked at her. "You got taller."

"Some. I think I'm done now. So did you."

Taller, and harder—and the scruff he hadn't shaven off in a day or two, she judged, added sexy. His hair, longer than the last time she'd seen him, curled and waved around his face so his chilled blue eyes seemed even clearer, sharper.

The trickle inside her went warm.

He took her hand as he turned to study the house. "It looks the same. New paint on the shutters, but it looks the same."

He didn't, she thought. Not exactly. "How long have you been back? Nobody said you were here."

"I've been back about ten seconds. I called my grandparents when I hit Sioux Falls, but I told them not to say." He released her hand, but only to wrap his arm around her shoulders. "I wanted to surprise you."

"You did. You really did."

"I stopped by here before I went there."

And now, she realized, everything she wanted and loved most was here for the summer. "Come inside. There's sun tea. When did you get that thing?"

He glanced back at the motorcycle. "Nearly a year ago. I figured if I could make it back this summer, it'd be fun to bike cross-country."

He stopped at the base of the stairs, cocking his head as he scanned her face.

"What?"

"You look . . . good."

"I do not." She shoved at her hair, gone to tangles under her flat-brimmed hat. "I just got back from the trail. I smell. If you'd gotten here a half hour later, I'd be cleaned up."

He just kept staring at her face. "You look good. I missed you, Lil."

"I knew you'd come back." Giving in, she went into his arms again, closed her eyes. "I should've known it would be today, when I saw the cougar."

"What?"

"I'll tell you all about it. Come inside, Coop. Welcome home."

Once her parents had come in, greeted Coop, settled down with him, Lil dashed upstairs. The long hot shower of her dreams became the fastest shower in history. Moving at light speed, she pulled out her small supply of makeup. Nothing too obvious, she ordered herself, and used a light hand with blush, added mascara and just a hint of lip gloss. Since it would take forever to dry her hair, she pulled it all back, still damp, into a tail.

She thought about earrings, told herself it was too obvious. Clean jeans, she decided, a fresh shirt. Natural, casual.

Her heart was beating like a marching band.

It was weird, it was strange, it was unexpected. But she had the hots for her best friend.

He looked so different—the same, but different. The hollows in his cheeks were new and fascinating. His hair was shaggy and sexy with the dark brown just starting to go streaky from the sun. He'd already started to tan a little—she remembered how he'd go brown in the sun. And his eyes, that glacier ice blue, just *pierced* some unexplored land inside her.

She wished she'd kissed him. Just a friendly hi-Coop sort of thing. Then she'd know what it was like, know what it felt like to have his mouth meet hers.

Calm down, she ordered herself. He'd probably laugh his head off if he knew what she was thinking. She took several deep breaths, then walked slowly downstairs.

She could hear them in the kitchen: her mother's laugh, her father's joking tones—and Coop's voice. Deeper, wasn't it deeper than it had been?

She had to stop and breathe again. Then fixing an easy smile on her face, she strolled back into the kitchen.

He stopped, in the middle of a sentence, and stared. Blinked. Just that instant, that surprise that flickered in his eyes, had her skin humming.

"So are you staying for supper?" Lil asked him.

"We were just trying to talk him into it. But Lucy and Sam are expecting him. Sunday," Jenna said with a finger wag. "Everybody here for a picnic on Sunday."

"Absolutely. I remember the first one. We can fit in some batting practice."

"Bet I can still outhit you." She leaned back against the counter and smiled in a way that had him blinking again.

"We'll see about that."

"I was hoping for a ride on that toy you've got out there."

"A Harley," he said in sober tones, "is nobody's toy."

"Why don't you show me what it can do?"

"Sure. Sunday, I'll—"

"I was thinking now. It's all right, isn't it?" She turned to her mother. "Just a half hour?"

"Ah . . . Do you have helmets, Cooper?"

"Yeah, ah, I bought a second one figuring . . . Yeah."

"How many tickets have you racked up riding that?" Joe asked him.

"None in the last four months," Cooper said with a grin.

"Bring my girl back like you took her."

"I will. Thanks for the tea," he said as he rose. "I'll see you on Sunday."

Jenna watched them go out, then looked at her husband. "Oh," she said.

He gave her a weak smile. "I was heading more toward: oh, shit."

Outside, Lil studied the helmet he offered. "So are you going to teach me to drive this thing?"

"Maybe."

She put the helmet on, watching him while she strapped it. "I can handle it."

"Yeah, I bet you could." He got on. "I thought about picking up a sissy seat, but—"

"I'm no sissy," she said, and swung on behind him. She snuggled her body behind his, wrapped her arms around his waist. Could he feel her heart thudding? she wondered. "Let her rip, Coop!"

When he did, zipping down the farm road, she let out a scream of delight. "It's nearly as good as riding a horse," she shouted.

"Better on the highway. Lean into the turns," he told her, "and keep a good grip on me."

Behind him, she smiled. She intended to.

COOP MEASURED OUT grain while the sun streamed through the loft windows. He could hear his grandmother singing as she fed the chickens, and their clucking accompaniment. In the stalls, horses chuffed and chewed.

It was funny how it all came back—the smells, the sounds, the quality of light and shadow. It had been two years since he'd fed a horse or groomed one, since he'd sat down at a big kitchen table at dawn to a plate of flapjacks.

It might have been yesterday.

The constant was a comfort, he supposed, when so much of his life was in flux. He remembered lying on a flat rock by the stream with Lil, years before, and how she'd known what she wanted. She still did.

He still didn't.

The house, the fields, the hills, just the same as he'd left them. His grandparents, too, he thought. Had he really thought them old all those years before? They seemed so sturdy and steady to him now, as if the eight years since hadn't touched them.

They'd sure as hell touched Lil.

When had she gotten so . . . well, prime?

Even two years before she'd just been Lil. Pretty, sure—she'd always been pretty. But he'd barely thought of her as a girl, much less a *girl*.

A girl with curves and lips, and eyes that put his blood on charge when she looked at him.

It wasn't right to think of her that way. Probably. They were friends, best friends. He wasn't supposed to notice she *had* breasts, much less obsess on what they'd felt like pressed into his back while they'd roared down the road on his bike.

Firm and soft and fascinating.

He sure as hell wasn't supposed to have a sex dream about getting his hands on those breasts—and the rest of her.

But he had. Twice.

He bridled a yearling, as his grandfather had asked, and let the filly out to the corral to work her on the line.

With the stock fed and watered, the eggs gathered, Lucy walked over to sit on the fence and watch.

"She's got some sass to her," she said when the filly kicked up her hind legs.

"Energy to spare." Coop switched leads, worked her in a circle.

"Picked her name yet?"

Coop smiled. Since Jones it had been tradition for him to name a yearling every season whether he made it out to the farm or not. "She's got that pretty, dappled coat. I'm thinking Freckles."

"Suits her. You've got a way, Cooper, with the naming, and the horses. You always did."

"I miss them when I'm back east."

"And when you're here, you miss back east. It's natural enough," she continued when he didn't speak. "You're young. You haven't settled yet."

"I'm almost twenty, Grandma. It feels like I should know what I'm after. Hell, by my age you were married to Grandpa."

"Different times, different place. Twenty's younger in some ways than it once was, older in others. You've got time to do that settling."

He looked back at her—sturdy, her hair shorter, with a bit of curl, the lines around her eyes deeper—but the same. Just as it was the same that he could say what was on his mind, or in his heart, and know she'd listen.

"Do you wish you'd taken more? More time?"

"Me? No, because I ended up right here, sitting on this fence watching my grandson train that pretty filly. But my way's not yours. I married at eighteen, had my first baby before I was twenty, and barely been east of the Mississippi my whole life. That's not you, Cooper."

"I don't know what me is. First?" He looked back at her. "You said first baby."

"We lost two after your ma. That was hard. Still is. I think it's why me and Jenna got close so quick. She had a stillbirth and then a miscarriage after Lil."

"I didn't know."

"Things happen, and you go on. That's all there is. If you're lucky you get something out of it. I got you, didn't I? And Jenna and Josiah, they got Lil."

"Lil sure seems to know what she wants."

"The girl does have her eyes forward."

"So . . ." He aimed for casual. "Is she seeing anyone? A guy, I mean."

"I took your meaning," Lucy said drily. "Nobody in particular I've heard about. The Nodock boy did a lot of sniffing around in that direction, but it didn't seem Lil was interested overmuch."

"Nodock? Gull? But, Jesus, he's twenty-two or -three. He's too old to be hanging around Lil."

"Not Gull, Jesse. His brother. Younger. He'd be about your age. Would you be sniffing in that direction, Cooper?"

"Me? Lil? No." Crap, he thought. Just crap. "We're friends, that's all. She's practically like a sister."

Her face bland, Lucy tapped her boot heel on the fence. "Your grandfather and I were friendly when we were coming up. Though I don't recall him ever thinking of me as a sister. Still, that Lil, she's got her eyes forward, like I said. Girl's got plans."

"She always did."

When work was done for the day, Coop thought about saddling one of the horses for a long, hard ride. He wished it could be Jones, but the yearling he'd once helped train had become one of the stars of his grandparents' tourist trade.

He considered his options, had just about settled on the big roan gelding named Tick, when he saw Lil walking toward the corral.

It was lowering to admit, but his mouth went dry.

She wore jeans and a bright red shirt, scuffed boots, and a worn-in gray hat with a wide, flat brim, and her long black hair loose under it.

When she got to the fence, she tapped the saddlebag slung over her shoulder. "I've got a picnic in here I'm looking to share. Anybody interested?"

"Might be."

"The thing is, I need to borrow a horse. I'll barter this cold fried chicken for a ride."

"Take your pick."

Angling her head, she gestured with her chin. "I like the look of that piebald mare."

"I'll get you a saddle, and let my grandparents know."

"I stopped in the house first. They're fine with it. We've got a lot of day left. Might as well take advantage." She draped the saddlebag over the fence. "I know where the tack is. Go ahead, get your own horse saddled."

Friends or not, he didn't see the harm in watching her walk away, or noticing how her jeans fit as she did.

They set to work, with a rhythm both of them knew well. When Coop lifted her saddlebag, he winced. "That's a lot of chicken."

"I've got my recorder and camera, and . . . stuff. You know I like to make a record when I'm out on a trail. I was thinking we could head for the creek, then take one of the spur trails through the forest. Get a good gallop on the way there, then it's pretty scenery."

He shot her a knowing look. "Cougar territory?"

"The couple I've tracked this year cover that area. But that's not why." She smiled as she swung into the saddle. "It's just a pretty ride, and there's a stream where the forest opens up. It's a nice spot for a picnic. It's a good hour from here though, if you'd rather something closer."

"I can work up a good appetite in an hour." He vaulted onto his horse, settled his hat more securely on his head. "Which way?"

"Southwest."

"Race ya."

He gave the gelding a light kick. They galloped across the farmyard and through the fields.

There'd been a time, Lil thought, when she'd been the better rider, and by a long shot. Now she had to admit they were on level ground. The mare was her advantage, being light and quick, so with the wind in her hair, Lil reached the thin line of trees less than a length in the lead.

Laughing, eyes bright, she leaned forward to give the mare a congratulatory pat on the neck. "Where do you ride in New York?"

"I don't."

She straightened in the saddle. "You're saying you haven't sat a horse in two years?"

He shrugged. "It's like riding a bike."

"No, it's like riding a horse. How do you . . ." She trailed off, shook her head, and began to walk the horse into the pines.

"How do I what?"

"Well, how do you stand not doing something you love?"

"I do other stuff."

"Such as?"

"Ride a motorcycle, hang out, listen to music."

"Chase girls."

He gave her a grin. "They don't run very fast."

She let out a hoot. "I bet they don't. How does CeeCee feel about you being out here all summer."

He shrugged again as they crossed a flat bordered by trees and boulders. "We're not serious. She's got her thing, I've got mine."

"I thought you two were tight."

"Not especially. I heard you were hooking up with Jesse Nodock."

"God, no!" Tossing back her head, she laughed. "He's nice enough, but kind of dopey. Plus all he really wants to do is wrestle."

"Wrestle? Why . . ." Something dark crept into his eyes. "You mean with you? You've been doing it with Nodock?"

"I have not. I went out with him a couple times. I don't much like the way he kisses. A little on the sloppy side of things, to my taste. He needs to practice his technique."

"You know a lot about technique?"

She slanted him a look, a slow smile. "I'm doing an informal study. Look." As they were riding abreast, she reached out to touch his arm, then pointed. In the far edges of the trees, a herd of deer stopped to stare back at them. Lil dug out her recorder.

"Six white-tail, four doe, two fawns. Aren't they sweet? A buck's been through here, too, not long ago."

"How do you know that, Tonto?"

"Look at the bark. Scrape marks from a buck rubbing his antlers. Some of that's fresh, Mr. New York."

This, too, was familiar, he thought. Riding with her, listening to her point out the tracks, the wildlife, the signs. He'd missed that.

"What else do you see?"

"Marmot tracks, and mule deer. There's a red squirrel up in that tree. You've got eyes."

"Not like yours."

"Cat's been through here, but not recently."

He watched her, only her. He couldn't seem to do otherwise, not when the sunlight dappled on her face, and those dark eyes were so alive, so intent. "Okay, how do you know?"

"Those scrape marks? That's cougar, but they're old, probably from a male marking his territory last mating season. He's moved on, at least for now. They don't stay with the female or the family. Screw and hit the road. That's a guy for you."

"About this informal poll."

She laughed, and clucked to the mare.

4

It was easy to fall into a routine, into the comfortable zone of it. Hot days, hard work, and sudden storms. Lil spent nearly every free moment with Coop, on horseback or hiking, batting balls, or on fast rides on his bike. She lay in the grass with him and counted stars, sat on the banks of a stream and shared picnics.

And he never made a move.

She didn't understand it. She'd barely looked cross-eyed at Jesse and he'd been all over her. Dirk Pleasant, too, when all she'd done was take a couple of spins on the Ferris wheel with him at the carnival last summer.

She *knew* the look a boy got in his eye now when he thought about a girl that way. She'd swear she'd seen that look in Coop's aimed in her direction.

So why wasn't he all over her?

Obviously it was time to take the bull by the horns.

She drove the bike, carefully, nearly to the end of the farm road. Concentrated, muttering instructions to herself on the turn, then drove it back to where Coop stood, watching her.

She kept the speed dignified, only because the couple of times she'd burned it, he'd gotten really mad.

"Okay, I've driven back and forth six times today." Though her hand twitched, she resisted gunning the engine. "You've got to let me take it out on the road, Coop. Get on, let's take a ride."

"You almost ditched it on the turn."

"Almost doesn't count."

"It does on my bike. I'm still paying for it. You want a ride, I'll drive."

"Come on." She got off, took off her helmet. Deliberately shook back her hair before taking the Coke bottle from him to drink. She tried on the sultry look she'd practiced in the mirror. "One mile up, one mile back." Smiling, she traced a finger down his throat, moved in a little closer. "It's a straight shot, and . . . I'll make it worth your while."

His eyes narrowed. "What're you doing?"

She cocked her head. "If you have to ask, I must not be doing it right."

He didn't step back; she didn't move the hand that rested lightly on his chest. His heartbeat speeded up a little. Surely that was a good sign.

"You need to be careful how you come on to guys, Lil. They're not all me."

"You're the only one I'm coming on to."

Temper—hardly the reaction she'd been after—lit in his eyes. "I'm not your practice dummy."

"I wasn't practicing. But I guess you're not interested." With a shrug, she set the Coke on the seat of the bike. "Thanks for the lesson." Insulted, embarrassed, she started for the first cattle gate.

She supposed he just went for city girls, with their city ways. Mr. New York City. Well, that was fine, that was just fine, she didn't need him to—

His hand gripped her arm, and he spun her around so fast her body plowed into his. Temper sparked off him just as it did her.

"What the hell's wrong with you?" he demanded.

"What the hell's wrong with *you*? You don't trust me to drive your stupid bike for a couple of miles, you don't want to kiss me. You act like I'm still nine years old. If you're not interested that way, then you should just say so instead of—"

He yanked her up to her toes, and his mouth was on hers. So hard, so fast. Nothing like the others, she thought, dizzy. Nothing like the other boys.

His lips were hot, his tongue quick. Something inside her went loose, as if a knot gave way, and every inch of her—inside and out—flashed with light, with heat.

It felt as if her heart would beat its way right out of her chest.

She shoved him back, trying to catch her breath. "Wait a minute, wait a minute."

Everything went bright and sharp. Dazzling. Who needed to breathe, she thought, and leaped back into his arms with a force that knocked them both to the ground.

She stopped his heart. He'd have sworn it stopped beating when he'd gone crazy and kissed her. For that instant, it had been like death—and then everything blasted back to life.

Now, somehow, he was rolling with her on the dirt road, over the prickly grass on its edge. He was hard, brutally hard, so when she pressed her hips up, pressed against him, he groaned in pleasure and torment.

"Does it hurt? What does it feel like?" Her words tore on ragged breaths. "Let me feel—"

"Jesus. Don't." He gripped her hand and pulled it back from its sudden and fierce exploration. Another minute of that and he knew he'd go off, and embarrass them both.

He pushed back to sit on the old road with his heart knocking between his ears. "What are we doing?"

"You wanted to kiss me." She sat up with him. Her eyes were huge, deep and dark. "You want more."

"Look, Lil—"

"So do I. You're going to be my first." She smiled as he stared at her. "It'll be right with you. I've been waiting until I knew it'd be right."

Something, she thought it might be panic, streaked across his face. "That's not something you can take back once it's done."

"You want me. I want you back. We'll figure it out." She leaned forward, laid her lips gently, experimentally on his. "I liked the way you kissed me, so we'll figure it out."

He shook his head, and the panic turned into a kind of baffled amusement. "I'm supposed to be the one talking you into having sex."

"You couldn't talk me into anything if I didn't want it."

"That's for damn sure."

She smiled again, started to lean her head on his shoulder. And was on her feet in a flash. "Oh, God, look at the sky. Look north."

It boiled. Coop pushed to his feet to grab her hand. "Let's get inside."

"It's miles off. Miles. It's going to spawn though. It's— There!"

The funnel whirled out of the churning mass, twisting its way to the ground like a deadly black finger. "My grandparents."

"No, it's miles off, and it's heading west, heading to Wyoming. We've barely even got wind here."

"They can turn." As he spoke he saw it simply *eat* through a line of trees.

"Yeah, but it's not. It won't. Look, look, Coop, can you see the rain wall? There's a rainbow."

She saw the rainbow, he thought, and he saw the black funnel storming its way across the plains.

He supposed that said something about both of them.

OUTSIDE LIL'S BEDROOM, Jenna took several bracing breaths. The light under the door told her Lil was still up. She'd half hoped that by the time she'd finished stalling, the light would be off.

She knocked, opened the door when Lil called out to come in.

Her daughter sat up in bed, her hair spilling around her shoulders, her face scrubbed for the night, and a thick book in her hands.

"Studying already?"

"It's on wildlife ecology and management. I want to be ready when I start classes. No, I want to be ahead," Lil admitted. "A freshman has to be really good to have a chance at any serious fieldwork. So I'm going to be really good. I'm already feeling competitive."

"Your grandfather was the same. Horseshoes or horse trading, politics or pinochle, he wanted to come in first." Jenna sat on the side of the bed. So young, she thought, looking at her daughter. Still a baby in so many ways. And yet . . .

"Did you have a good time tonight?"

"Sure. I know a lot of people my age think barn dances are hokey, but they're fun. It's nice to see everybody. And I like watching you and Dad dance."

"The music was good. Gets the feet moving." She glanced at the open book, saw what looked like some sort of strange algebra. "What in the world is that?"

"Oh, it's explaining equations for measuring population density of species. See, this is a formula for finding the merged estimate, that's the mean of the individual estates. And its variance is the mean of . . ." She stopped, grinned at her mother's face. "Do you really want to know?"

"Do you remember me helping you with math after you got through long division."

"No."

"That would be your answer. Anyway, you didn't dance much tonight."

"We liked listening to the music, and it was so nice out."

And whenever you came back in, Jenna thought, you had that dazed and smug look of a girl who'd done some serious kissing.

Please, God, let that be all.

"You and Cooper aren't just friends anymore."

Lil sat up a little straighter. "Not just. Mom—"

"You know we love him. He's a good young man, and I know you care about each other. I also know that you're not children anymore, and when you feel more than friendship, things happen. Sex happens," Jenna corrected, ordering herself to stop being a coward.

"It hasn't. Yet."

"Good. That's good, because if it does, I want both of you to be prepared, to be safe." She reached in her pocket and took out a box of condoms. "To be protected."

"Oh." Lil just stared at them, as dumbfounded as her mother had been by the equations. "Oh. Um."

"Some girls consider this the boy's responsibility. My girl is smart and self-aware, and will always look after herself, rely on herself. I wish you'd wait, I can't help wishing you'd wait. But if you don't, I want you to promise me you'll use protection."

"I will. I promise. I want to be with him, Mom. When I am—I mean just with him, I feel all this . . . this," she said lamely. "In my heart, and in my stomach, in my head. Everything's fluttering around so I can barely breathe. And when he kisses me, it's like, Oh, that's what's it supposed to be. I want to be with him," she repeated. "He pulls back because he's not sure I'm really ready. But I am."

"You've just made me feel a lot better about him. A lot better knowing he's not pressuring you."

"I think it might be, sort of, the other way around."

Jenna managed a weak laugh. "Lil, we've talked before, about sex, safety, responsibility, those feelings. And you've grown up on a farm. But if there's anything you're not sure of, or want to talk about, you know you can talk to me."

"Okay. Mom, does Dad know you're giving me condoms?"

"Yes. We talked about it. You know you can talk to him, too, but—"

"Oh, yeah, big but. It'd feel really weird."

"On both sides." Jenna patted Lil's thigh as she rose. "Don't stay up too late."

"I won't. Mom? Thanks for loving me."

"Never a problem."

———

Rely on yourself, Lil thought. Her mother was right, as usual, she decided as she packed provisions. A woman had to have a plan, that was the key. What to do, when and how to do it. She'd made the arrangements. Maybe Coop didn't know all of them, but the element of surprise was also key.

She put the packs in the truck, grateful that her parents had gone to town, so there didn't have to be any awkward be carefuls, even if they were unspoken.

She wondered if Coop's grandparents knew what was going on. Really going on. She'd opted not to ask her mother that one. Talk about awkward.

Didn't matter, don't care, she thought as she drove with the wind shooting through the open windows. She had three days free. Probably her last in a row for the summer. In another few weeks she'd be on her way north, on her way to college. And another phase of her life would begin.

She wasn't leaving until she'd finished this phase.

She'd thought she'd be nervous, but she wasn't. Excited, happy, but not nervous. She knew what she was doing—in theory—and was ready to put it into practice.

She turned the radio up and sang along as she drove through the hills, passed tidy farms and pastures. She saw men mending fences, and clothes flapping on lines. She stopped—she couldn't help herself—to take pictures and some quick notes when she spotted a good-sized herd of buffalo.

She arrived at the farm in time to see Coop saddling up. She hitched on her pack, grabbed the second, then gave a whistle.

"What's all that?"

"Some surprises," she called out as he walked over to help her.

"Jesus, Lil, it looks like enough for a week. We're only going to be a few hours."

"You'll thank me later. Where is everybody?"

"My grandparents had to run into town. They should be on their way back, but they said not to wait if we were ready before."

"Believe me, I'm ready." She hugged that exciting secret inside. "Oh, I talked to my college roommate today." Lil checked the cinches on the mare's saddle. "We got our dorm assignments, and she called, just to touch base. She's from Chicago, and she'll be studying animal husbandry and zoology. I think we're going to get along. I hope. I've never shared a room before."

"Not much longer now."

"No." She mounted. "Not much longer. Do you like your roommate?"

"He stayed stoned pretty much through two years. He didn't bother me."

"I'm hoping to make friends. Some people make friends in college that stay friends all the rest of their lives." They moved at an easy pace, all the time in the world, under the wide blue plate of sky. "Did you get stoned?"

"A couple of times and that was enough. It seemed like the thing to do, and the grass was right there. He's all, *Dude,* fire one up," Coop said in an exaggerated stoner's tone that made her laugh. "So why not? Everything seemed pretty funny—and mellow—for a while. Then I was starving and had a headache. It didn't seem worth it."

"Is he going to be your roommate again this term?"

"He flunked out, big surprise."

"You'll have to break in a new one."

"I'm not going back."

"What?" She jerked her mount to a halt to gape, but Coop kept going. She nudged the mare into a trot to catch up. "What do you mean, you're not going back? Back east?"

"No, back to college. I'm done."

"But you've only—you've barely . . . What happened?"

"Nothing. That's pretty much the point. I'm not getting anywhere, and it's not where I want to get, anyway. The whole prelaw shit was my father's deal. He'll pay as long as I do it his way. I'm not doing it his way anymore."

She knew the signs—the tightening of his jaw, the flare in his eyes. She knew the temper, and the bracing for a fight.

"I don't want to be a lawyer, especially not the kind of corporate stooge in an Italian suit he's pushing on me. Goddamn it, Lil, I spent the first half of my life trying to please him, trying to get him to notice me, to fucking care. What did it get me? The only reason he's paid the freight on college is because he has to, but it had to be his way. And he was pissed I didn't get into Harvard. Jesus, as if."

"You could've gotten into Harvard if you wanted."

"No, Lil." Exasperated he scowled at her. "*You* could. You're the genius, the straight-A student."

"You're smart."

"Not like that. Not with school, or not that way. I do okay, I do fine. And I fucking hate it, Lil."

Sad and mad, she realized. The sad and mad was back in his eyes. "You never said—"

"What was the point? I felt stuck. He can make you feel like you don't have a choice, like he's right, you're wrong. And Christ, he knows how to make you toe the line. That's why he's good at what he does. But I don't want to do what he does. Be what he is. I started thinking of all the years I'd have to put into becoming what I didn't want to become. I'm done with it."

"I wish you'd told me before. I just wish you'd told me you were so unhappy with all this. We could've talked about it."

"Maybe. I don't know. But I do know this whole deal's about him, not me. Him and my mother, and their endless war, and endless pursuit of the right appearances. I'm finished with it, too."

Her heart broke a little for him. "Did you have a fight with your parents before you left?"

"I wouldn't call it a fight. I said some things I wanted to say, and I got an ultimatum. I could stay and work in the family firm this summer or he'd cut me off. Financially, as he's cut me off in every other way since I was a kid."

They forded a stream in silence, just the splash of hooves through water. She couldn't imagine her parents stepping away from her, not in any way. "So you came here."

"It's what I'd planned to do, what I wanted to do. I've got enough money to get my own place. I don't need much. I was never going back to live with my mother anyway. Just never going there again."

A little bubble of hope swelled inside her. "You could stay here, with your grandparents. You know you could. Help out at the farm. You could go to school out here, and—"

He turned his head toward her, and she felt that little bubble pop and dissolve. "I'm not going back to college, Lil. It's not for me. It's different for you. You've been planning what you were going to study, what you were going to do, ever since you saw that cougar. And decided to chase cats instead of pop flies."

"I didn't know you were so unhappy. I get law wasn't your choice, and it was unfair of your father to push you there, but—"

"Fair's not the point." He shrugged, a gesture of a young man too used to unfair to be bothered by it. "It's not about that, and from now on it's not about him. It's about me. The whole college scene? That's not about me."

"Neither is staying here, is it?"

"It doesn't feel like it, not yet or not now anyway. I don't know what I want, for sure. Staying would be easy. I've got a place to stay, three squares, work I'm pretty good at. I've got family, and you."

"But."

"It feels like settling, before I know. Before I *do* something. Out here, I'm Sam and Lucy's grandson. I want to be me. I enrolled in the police academy."

"Police?" If he'd leaned over and shoved her off her horse she'd have been less stunned. "Where did that come from? You've never said any-thing about wanting to be a cop."

"I took a couple of courses in law enforcement, and one in criminol-ogy. They were the only things I liked about the whole pile of crap these last two years. The only things I was any good in. I've already applied. I've got enough course credits to get in, and I'll be twenty when I start. It's six months' training, and it just feels like I'd be good at it. So I'm going to try it. I need something that's mine. I don't know how to explain it."

She thought, I'm yours, but kept the words to herself. "Have you told your grandparents?"

"Not yet."

"You'll be working in New York."

"I'd've been going to school back east," he reminded her. "And if ev-eryone but me had their way, working in legal in my father's company back there. Wearing a suit every fricking day. Now I'll be doing something for me, or at least trying to. I figured you'd understand that."

"I do." She wished she didn't. She wanted him there, with her. "It's just . . . so far away."

"I'll come out when I can. As soon as I can. Maybe Christmas."

"I could come to New York, maybe on semester break, or . . . next summer."

Some of that sad lifted from his face. "I'll show you around. There's a lot to do, to see. I'll have my own place. It's not going to be much, but—"

"It won't matter." They'd make it work, somehow, she told herself. She couldn't feel this way about him, about them, and not make it work. "They have cops in South Dakota, too." She tried out a bright smile. "You could be sheriff of Deadwood one day."

He laughed at the idea. "First I have to get through the academy. A lot of people wash out."

"You won't. You'll be great. You'll help people and solve crimes, and I'll study and get my degree and save wildlife."

And they'd find a way, she thought.

———

SHE LED the way to the spot she'd chosen. She'd wanted it perfect—the day, the place, the moment. She couldn't let the future, the uncertainty of it interfere.

They had the sun, and it filtered through the trees to sparkle on the waters of the fast-running stream where purple dame's rockets danced in the light breeze. More wildflowers bloomed in the light, and in the shadows, and the birdcall was music enough.

They dismounted, tethered the horses. Lil unstrapped her pack. "We should set up the tent first."

"Tent?"

"I wanted it to be a surprise. We've got two days. It's okay with your grandparents, with my parents." She set the pack down, laid her hands on his chest. "Is it okay with you?"

"It's been a while since we camped. Last time your father and I shared a tent." Searching her face, he rubbed her arms. "Things have changed, Lil."

"I know. That's why we're here, with one tent and one sleeping bag." She leaned in, keeping her eyes open as she brushed her lips over his. "Do you want me, Cooper?"

"You know I do." He pulled her closer, took her mouth with a sudden and fierce possession that arrowed heat straight to her belly. "Jesus, Lil, you know I do. No point in asking if you're sure, if you're ready. You're always sure. But . . . We're not prepared. A tent's not enough for what we're talking about. At least, the kind of tent you've got in that pack."

It made her laugh, and hug him tight. "I have a box of tents."

"Sorry?"

"Condoms. I have a box of condoms. I never go camping unprepared."

"A box. That makes the one I'm carrying in my wallet kind of unnecessary—and okay, thank you, God—but where the hell did you get condoms?"

"My mother gave them to me."

"Your . . ." He closed his eyes, then gave up and sat on a rock. "Your mother gave you a box of condoms, then let you come out here with me?"

"Actually, she gave them to me a week ago, and asked me to promise to be sure and to be careful. I did, I am. I will."

A little pale, Coop rubbed his hands on the knees of his jeans. "Your father knows?"

"Sure. He's not home loading up the shotgun, Coop."

"It's weird. It's just weird. And now I'm nervous, damn it."

"I'm not. Help me set up the tent."

He rose. They worked quickly, efficiently, securing the small, light-weight tent.

"You've done this before, right?"

He glanced over at her. "You don't mean camping. Yeah. But I've never done this before with someone who hasn't—done it before. It's proba-bly going to hurt you, and I don't know if it's even any good for a girl the first time."

"I'll let you know." She reached out, laid a hand over his heart. All she could think was it was beating for her now. It had to be. "We could start now."

"Now?"

"Well, I'm hoping you'll get me warmed up first. I brought an extra blanket to spread out." She pulled it out of the pack. "And since you've got that condom in your wallet, we could start with that. Otherwise, it's all we're going to think about." Steady and sure, she took his hand. "Maybe you could lie down here with me, and kiss me awhile."

"There's nobody else like you in the world."

"Show me, will you? You're the only one I want to show me."

He kissed her first, as they stood in the sunlight beside the blanket, and put everything he had that was soft and gentle into it.

He knew she was right. It should be here, in the world that belonged to the two of them, the world that had brought them together, and linked them together forever.

They lowered to kneel, face-to-face, and she sighed against his lips.

He stroked her, her hair, her back, her face, and finally her breasts. He'd felt them before, felt her heart kick against his palm when he touched her. But this was different. This was prelude.

He drew off her shirt, and saw the smile in her eyes as she drew off his. Her breath caught when he unhooked her bra. Then her eyes fluttered closed as for the time he touched her there skin to skin.

"Oh. Well. That's definitely warming me up."

"You're like . . ." He searched for the right words as he cupped her breasts, used his thumbs to tease her nipples. "Gold dust, all over."

"You haven't seen all over yet." She opened her eyes, looked into his. "Things are coming to life inside me I didn't even know were there. Everything's all jumpy and hot." She reached out, rubbed her palms over his chest. "Is it like that for you?"

"Except I knew they were there. Lil." He bent his head and took her breast into his mouth. The flavor of her flooded him, the sound of her shock and delight raced wild through his blood.

Her arms came around him, urging him, and stayed around him when they collapsed on the blanket.

She hadn't known there would be so much. Storms and waves and shudders. Nothing she'd read—not the texts, not the novels—had prepared her for what happened to her own body.

Her mind seemed to lift out of it, release it, so there was nothing but *feeling*.

She raced her lips over his shoulder, his throat, his face, giving in to the urge to feed on him. When his hand stroked down her torso, fought open the button of her jeans, she quivered. And thought: Yes. Please, yes.

When she tried to do the same for him, he drew back.

"I need to . . ." His breath came ragged as he dragged his wallet out. "I might forget, just stop thinking."

"Okay." She lay back, touched her own breasts. "Everything feels different already. I think . . . Oh." Her eyes widened as he yanked off his jeans. "Wow."

Elemental male pride at her reaction had him slanting a glance at her as he ripped open the condom. "It'll fit."

"I know how it works, but . . . let me." Before he could sheath himself she sat up to touch him.

"Holy shit, Lil."

"It's smooth," she murmured as another wave of heat rolled through her. "Hard and smooth. Will it feel like that inside me?"

"Keep that up, you're not going to know for a while." His breathing fast and shallow, he caught her wrist, pulled her hand away.

He struggled to focus, concentrated on the protection. "Let me," he said as he lowered to her. "Just let me this first time."

He kissed her, long, slow, deep, and hoped his instincts ran true. She seemed to soften under him, and then as he stroked his hand down, quivered.

She was already wet, and that nearly undid him. Praying for control, he slipped a finger into her. Her hips arched up as her fingers dug into his back.

"Oh, God, oh, God."

"It's good." Hot, soft, wet. Lil. "Is it good?"

"Yes. Yes. It's . . ."

She felt something rise up, fly off, and take her breath with it. He was kissing her, kissing her, anchoring her, letting her go. She arched again, to find more. Then again, again.

This, she thought, this.

Swimming in the heat, she felt him shift, felt him press at the core of her. She opened her eyes, struggled to focus, watched his face, the intensity of those crystal blue eyes.

It hurt. For a moment the pain was so shocking through the pleasure she went stiff with denial.

"I'm sorry. I'm sorry."

She didn't know if he intended to stop or go on, but knew she was on the brink of something unimagined. She gripped his hips, and reared up to find it, to know it.

The pain struck again, another shock and burn—and he was inside her. With her.

"It fit," she managed.

He dropped his head on her shoulder with a breathless and choked laugh. "Oh, God, Lil. Oh, God. I don't think I can stop now."

"Who asked you to?" She dug her fingers in, lifted her hips again, then felt him move in her.

He trembled above her, and it seemed to her the ground trembled beneath. Inside her, everything opened, everything filled, and she knew.

She cried out with pleasure as she hadn't with the pain, and rode the crest of it with him.

5

They played in the stream, washing in the cool water, teasing and tormenting each other's bodies until they were breathless.

Wet and half naked, they fell on the food Lil had brought like a pair of starving wolves. With the horses tethered and dozing, they donned light packs to hike a short way along the trail.

Everything seemed brighter to her, clearer and stronger.

She paused among the shelter of the pines, pointed at tracks. "Wolf pack. The cats compete with them for prey. Mostly they leave each other alone. There's a lot of game, so . . ."

He gave her a poke in the belly. "I should've known there was a reason you picked this way."

"I wondered if the female I spotted covered this ground. She's probably more west of here, but it's good territory, as the wolves would tell you. We're going to build a refuge."

"For what?"

"All of them. For endangered and injured and abused. For the ones people buy or capture as exotic pets then realize they can't possibly keep. I'm still talking my father into it, but I will."

"Here? In the hills?"

She gave a decisive nod. "Paha Sapa—Lakota for Hills of Black, a sacred place. It seems right. Especially right for what I want to do."

"It's your place," he agreed. "So yeah, it seems right. But it seems like a lot."

"I know. I've been studying how other refuges are built, set up, how they run, what it takes. I have a lot more to learn. We've got some overlap with the National Park, and that could work in our favor. We'll need some funding, a plan, some help. Probably a lot of help," she admitted.

They stood on the trail of a world they both knew, but it felt to him as if they stood at some kind of crossroads. "You've been doing a lot of thinking, too."

"Yeah. I have. I'm going to work on it in school. Build a model, I hope. Learn enough to make it happen. It's what I want to do. I want to be a part of protecting all this, learning and educating. Dad knows I'm never going to be a beef farmer. I guess he's always known."

"That's where you're lucky."

"I know it." She ran her hand down his arm until their fingers linked. "If you decide being one of New York's Finest doesn't suit you, you could come back and give us a hand with it."

He shook his head. "Or sheriff of Deadwood."

"I don't want to lose you, Cooper." She turned into his arms.

So she felt it, too, he realized, and he only held her tighter. "You couldn't."

"I don't want to be with anyone but you. I don't want anyone but you."

He turned his head to rest his cheek on top of her head. Looked at the tracks they'd left behind. "I'll come back. I always come back."

She had him now, and tried to hold on to that as tightly as she held on to him. She would will him back if need be. Back to her, back to where he was happy.

One day they'd walk through this forest again, years from now. Together.

As they walked back to camp, she put everything between now and then out of her mind.

That night, while the stars seared the sky overhead, she lay in his arms, and heard the cry of the cat.

Her talisman, she thought. Her good-luck charm.

Because she couldn't understand why she felt so weepy, she turned her face into his shoulder and lay quiet until she could sleep.

JENNA WATCHED OUT the window. The hard, hot day threatened storms with a mottled bruising in the eastern sky. There would be other storms, and more bruising, she thought as she watched her girl and the boy she loved ride back from checking fences with Joe and Sam.

Even at that distance she could see what they were. Lovers now, so young, so fresh. All they could see were the summer blue skies, and not the storms blowing in.

"He'll break her heart."

"I wish I could say otherwise." Behind her, Lucy put a hand on Jenna's shoulder and watched as she watched.

"She thinks it'll all fall into place, the way she wants, the way she plans. That it'll be what it is now forever. I can't tell her different. She wouldn't believe me."

"He loves her."

"Oh, I know. I know. But he'll go, just as she will. They have to. And she'll never be quite the same again. There's no stopping that either."

"We hoped he'd stay. When he told us he wasn't going back to college, I thought, Well, that's all right. You'll stay here, and take over the farm one day. I had just enough time to think it—and to think how he might've given his education a better try if his father hadn't pushed so hard. Then he told us what he aimed to do."

"The police force." She turned from the window to study her friend. "How do you feel about that, Lucy?"

"Scared some, that's a fact. Hopeful he'll find his feet, and some real pride in himself. I can't tell him any more than you can tell Lil."

"My biggest fear is he'll ask her to go back with him, and she will. She's young and in love and, well, fearless. The way you are at that age." Jenna walked over to get out the pitcher of lemonade to give her hands something to do. "She'd just let her heart pull her along. It's so far away. Not just the miles."

"I know. I know what it was like when my Missy lit out, like there was a fire under her feet." At home in Jenna's kitchen as she was in her own, Lucy went to the cupboard for glasses. "He's not like his mother, not a bit. Neither's your girl. Missy, she never had a thought for anybody but herself. Just seemed to be born that way. Not mean, not even hard, just careless. She wanted anything but here."

She took her drink back to the window, sipping as she looked out. "Those two might want different things, but here's a part of it. Your girl has plans, Jenna. My boy there? He's trying to make some."

"I don't know if you ever get over your first love. Joe was mine, so I never had to get over him. I just hate knowing she's going to hurt. Both of them are going to hurt."

"They'll never let loose of each other, not all the way. Too much there. But, well, nothing we can do about it in the meantime but be here. Storm's coming in."

"I know."

THE WIND KICKED high and hard, ahead of the rain. Lightning slashed over the hills in whips of eerie blue, blinding white. It struck a cotton-wood in the near pasture, cleaving it like an ax. Ozone burned the air like a sorcerer's potion.

"It's a mean one." Lil stood on the back porch scenting the air. Inside the kitchen, the dogs whined, and were, she imagined, huddled under the table.

It could pass, she knew, as quickly as it came. Or it could beat and strike and wreak destruction. Hail to batter the crops and the stock, twisting winds to shred them. In the hills, in the canyons, animals would take shelter in lairs and dens, in caves and thickets and high grass. Just as people took it in houses, in cars.

The feeding chain meant nothing to nature.

The cannon blast of thunder boomed, rolled, echoed, and shook the valley.

"You won't get this in New York."

"We have thunderstorms back east."

Lil just shook her head as she watched the show. "Not like this. City storms are inconveniences. This is drama, and adventure."

"Try hailing a cab in Midtown during a storm. Baby, *that's* an adventure." Still, he laughed and took her hand. "But you've got a point. This is E Ticket."

"Here comes the rain."

It swept in, fast-moving curtains. She watched the wall rush through, and the world went a little mad. Pounding, roaring, slashing in one titanic roar.

She turned to him, clamped around him, and took his mouth with as much fury and power as the storm. Rain dashed them, hard pebbled drops the wind shoved under the porch roof. Thunder crashed, an ear-ringing explosion. The wind chimes and dinner bells clanged and rang insanely.

She drew back, but not before she'd added a quick, teasing bite. "Every time you hear thunder, you're going to remember that."

"I need to be alone with you. Somewhere. Anywhere."

She glanced toward the kitchen window. Her parents and the Wilkses stood watch on the front porch as she and Coop had chosen the back.

"Quick. Run!" Laughing, she pulled him off the porch, into the wild rain and wind. Instantly soaked, they raced for the barn.

Lightning forked the sky, electric sizzle. Together they dragged the door open to stumble inside, breathless and drenched. In the stalls, horses shifted restlessly as the rain pounded, as thunder rolled.

In the hayloft, they stripped off wet clothes, and took each other eagerly.

IT WOULD BE their last day together. When it was over he would say his goodbyes to Joe and Jenna, and then somehow to Lil.

He'd said goodbye before, but he knew it would be harder this time. This time, more than ever before, they were each taking different directions at that crossroads.

They walked their horses as they had so many times before, to the place that had become theirs. The fast-running stream at the verge of the pines where the wildflowers danced.

"Let's keep going. We'll come back," she said, "but when we stop, it'll be the last time. So let's keep going for a while."

"I might be able to come out for Thanksgiving. It's not that far away."

"No, it's not that far away."

"Christmas for sure."

"Christmas for sure. I'm leaving in eight more days." She hadn't started to pack, not yet. She'd wait until Coop had gone. It was a kind of symbol. As long as he was here, everything stayed. Everything was solid and familiar.

"Nervous yet? About college."

"No, not nervous. Curious, I guess. Part of me wants to go, get started, find out. The other part wants everything to stop. I don't want to think about it today. Let's just be."

She reached out, took his hand for a moment. They walked in a silence full of questions neither knew how to answer.

They passed a little falls engorged from summer storms, crossed a grassland green with summer. Determined not to drop into a brood, she took out her camera. "Hey!" He grinned when she aimed it at him. Then, with their horses close abreast, she leaned over, held the camera out.

"You probably cut off our heads."

"Bet I didn't. I'll send you a print. Coop and Lil in the backcountry. See what your new cop friends think about that."

"They'll take one look at you and think I'm a lucky guy."

They took a spur trail through tall trees and hefty boulders, with views that swept to forever. Lil pulled up. "Cougar's been through here. The rains washed most of the tracks away, but there're markings on the trees."

"Your female?"

"Maybe. We're not far from where I spotted her that day." Two months before, she thought. The kittens would be weaned by now, and big enough for their ma to take them with her when she hunted.

"You want to try to track her."

"Just a little ways. I'm not sure I can anyway. We've had a lot of rain in the last few days. But if she's territorial, she could be in the area where I first saw her. It'd be good luck," she decided on the spot. "For us both to see her on your last day, the way I did on your first."

He had the rifle if he needed it, though he didn't mention it. Lil wouldn't approve. "Let's go."

She led the way, searching for signs as the horses picked and plodded. "I wish I was better at tracking."

"You're as good as your father now. Maybe even better."

"I don't know about that. I was going to practice a lot more this summer." She sent him a smile. "But I've been distracted. The brush, the boulders. That's what she'd stick to if she was hunting. And I'm not sure . . ." She stopped, and eased her horse to the right. "Scat. It's cougar."

"I think it's good tracking to be able to tell one pile of shit from another."

"Tracking 101. It's not real fresh. Yesterday, the day before. But this is part of her territory. Or if not hers, probably another female. Their territories can overlap."

"Why not a male?"

"Mostly they steer clear of females, until mating season. Then it's all, Hey, baby, you know you want it. Of course, I love you. Sure, I'll respect you in the morning. Get it, then get gone."

He narrowed his eyes as she grinned. "You have no respect for our species."

"Oh, I don't know, some of you are okay. Besides, you love me." The minute the words were out, she straightened in the saddle. Couldn't take them back, she realized, and shifted to look him in the eye. "Don't you?"

"I've never felt about anyone the way I do about you." He gave her an easy smile. "And I always respect you in the morning."

There was a nagging thought at the back of her brain that it wasn't enough. She wanted the words, just the power of those words. But she'd be damned if she'd ask for them.

She continued on, aiming for the high grass shelf where she'd seen the cat take down the calf. She found other signs, more scrapings. Cougar and buck. Brush trampled down by a herd of mule deer.

But when they reached the grass, nothing roamed or grazed.

"Nice spot," Coop observed. "Is this still your land?"

"Yeah, just," she replied as she gazed across the vista.

She started across the grass toward the trees where she'd once watched the cougar drag her kill. "My mother said there used to be bear, but they got hunted out, driven out. The cougar and the wolf stay, but you have to look to find them. The Hills are a mixing bowl, biologically speaking. We get species here that are common to areas in every direction."

"Like a singles bar."

She laughed at him. "I'll take your word. Still, we lost the bear. If we could . . . There's blood."

"Where?"

"On that tree. On the ground, too. It looks dry."

She swung her leg across the saddle.

"Wait. If this is a kill site, she could be close. If she's got a litter she won't be happy to see you."

"Why is it on the tree? So high on the tree." Drawing out her camera, Lil walked closer. "She could've taken out an elk or deer, I guess, and it fought, or it hit the tree. But it just doesn't look like that."

"And you know how that would look?"

"In my head I do." She glanced back, saw he had the rifle. "I don't want you to shoot her."

"Neither do I." He'd shot nothing but targets, and didn't want to shoot the living, especially her cat.

Frowning, Lil turned back to the tree, studied it, the ground. "It looks like she dragged the kill off that way. See how the brush looks? And there's more blood." She crouched, poked at the ground. "There's blood on the ground, on the brush. I thought she took the buffalo calf that way. More east. Maybe she had to move her den, or it's another cat altogether. Keep talking and stay alert. As long as we don't surprise her or threaten her or her young, she won't be interested in us."

She inched her way, trying to follow the signs. As she'd said, the trail was rough here, steep, rocky. It didn't surprise her to see some signs of hikers, and she wondered if the cat had moved to avoid them.

"There's more scat. Fresher." She looked over and just beamed. "We're tracking her."

"Whoopee."

"If I could get a shot of her and her young . . ." She stopped, sniffed. "Do you smell that?"

"Now I do. Something's dead." When she started forward, he took her arm. "I can follow it from here. You stay behind me."

"But—"

"Behind me and the rifle, or we turn back. I'm stronger than you are, Lil, so believe me when I say we'll turn back."

"Well, if you're going to get all macho."

"I guess I am." He walked forward, following the stench.

"West," she directed, "a little more west. It's off the trail." She scanned brush, trees, rocks as they moved. "God, you wonder how she can stomach anything that smells like that. Maybe they abandoned the kill. Chowed down, moved on. Nothing picked clean is going to smell like that. It looks like a lot of blood around here, and then into the brush."

She stepped over. She didn't move in front of him, but beside him. It wasn't her fault the signs were on her side. "I see something in there.

Definitely something there." She strained to see. "If she still considers it hers, and she's around, she'll let us know quick. I can't see what it is, can you?"

"Dead is what it is."

"Yes, but what was the prey? I like to know what . . . Oh, my God. Cooper. Oh, my God."

He saw it as she did. The prey had been human.

LIL WASN'T PROUD of the way she'd handled herself, the way her legs had buckled, the way her head had gone light. She'd damn near fainted, and certainly would've gone down if Coop hadn't gotten hold of her.

She managed to help him mark the spot, but only because he'd ordered her to keep back. She made herself look, forced herself to see and remember what had been done before she'd gone back to her mount for her canteen to drink deeply.

She'd been steadier, and able to think clearly enough to mark the trail for those who would have to come for the remains. Coop kept the rifle out as they rode back home.

There'd be no final tryst by the stream.

"You can put the rifle away. It wasn't a cat that killed him."

"Her, I think," Coop said. "The size and the style of the boots, and what was left of the hair. I think it was a woman. You think wolves, then?"

"No, I didn't see any signs of wolves near there. It's the cougar's habitat, and they'd leave her alone. It wasn't an animal who killed her."

"Lil, you saw what I saw."

"Yeah." It was etched in her mind. "That was after. They fed after. But the blood on the tree, it was high, and there weren't any cat tracks there. No tracks until a good ten yards off. I think someone killed her, Coop. Killed her and left her there. Then the animals got at her."

"Either way, she's dead. We have to get back."

When the trail opened enough, they spurred to a gallop.

———

HER FATHER GAVE them whiskey, just a swallow each. It burned straight down to the sickness in her belly. By the time the police arrived, the idea of being sick had passed.

"I marked the trail." She sat with Coop and her parents and a county deputy named Bates. She used the map he'd brought, highlighting the route.

"Is that the way you went?"

"No, we took scenic." She showed him. "We weren't in a hurry. We came back this way. I saw the blood on the tree here." She made a mark on the map. "Drag marks, more blood. A lot probably washed away in the rain, but there was enough cover so you can see there's blood. Whoever killed her did it there, at the tree, because the blood's a good five feet up—close to five and a half, I'd say. Then he dragged her off the trail to about here. That's where the cougar found her. She must've dragged her from there, to better cover."

He made notes, nodded. He had a weathered and quiet look about him, almost soothing.

"Any reason you think she was murdered, Miss Chance? What you're describing sounds like a cougar attack."

"When's the last time we had a cougar attack a person around here?" Lil demanded.

"It happens."

"Cats go for the throat." Bates shifted his gaze to Coop. "Isn't that right, Lil?"

"Yeah, their typical kill method is the neck bite. It takes the prey down, often breaking the neck. Quick and clean."

"You rip out somebody's throat, there's going to be all kinds of blood. It'd gush, wouldn't it? This was more like a smear. It wasn't . . . spatter."

Bates lifted his eyebrows. "So, we've got a cougar expert and a forensic specialist." He smiled when he said it, kept the remark friendly. "I appreciate the input. We'll be going up, and we'll look into all that."

"You'll have to do an autopsy, determine cause of death."

"That's right," Bates said to Coop. "If it was a cougar attack, we'll handle it. If it wasn't, we'll handle that. Don't worry."

"Lil said it wasn't a cougar that killed her. So it wasn't."

"Has a woman gone missing? In the last few days?" Lil asked.

"Might be." Bates rose. "We'll head on up now. I'm going to want to talk to you again."

Lil sat silent until Bates went out to mount up with his two-man team. "He thinks we're wrong. That we saw what was left of a mule deer or something and got spooked."

"He'll find out different soon."

"You didn't tell him you were leaving in the morning."

"I can take another day. They should know who she is and what happened to her in another day. Maybe two."

"Can you eat?" Jenna asked.

When Lil shook her head, Jenna wrapped an arm around her, stroking when Lil turned her face to her mother's breast. "It was awful. So awful. To be left like that. To be nothing but meat."

"Let's go up for a while. I'm going to draw you a hot bath. Come on with me."

Joe waited, then got up and poured two mugs of coffee. He sat, looked Coop in the eye. "You took care of my girl today. She can take care of herself, I know that's true, most ways, most times. But I know you saw to her today. You got her back here. I won't forget it."

"I didn't want her to see it. I've never seen anything like it, and hope I never do again. But I couldn't stop her from seeing it."

Joe nodded. "You did what you could, and that's enough. I'm going to ask you for something, Cooper. I have to ask that you don't make her any promises you're not sure you can keep. She can take care of herself, my girl, but I don't want her holding on to a promise that has to be broken."

Coop stared into the coffee. "I don't know what I could promise her. I've got enough to rent an apartment, as long as it's cheap, for a few months. I've got to try to make the grade at the academy. Even if I do, a cop doesn't make a lot. I come into some money when I'm twenty-one. A trust fund thing. I get more when I'm twenty-five, then thirty, and like that. My father can tie it up some, and he threatened to, until I'm forty."

Joe smiled a little. "And that's worlds away."

"Well, I'll be living pretty thin for a while, but I'm okay with that." He looked up again, met Joe's eyes. "I can't ask her to come to New York. I thought about it, a lot. I can't give her anything there, and I'd be taking away what she wants. I've got no promises to give her. It's not because she doesn't matter."

"No, I'd say it's because she does. That's enough for me. You've had a hell of a day, haven't you?"

"I feel like pieces of me are coming apart. I don't know how they're going to go together again. She wanted to see the cougar—for us to see it together. For luck. It doesn't feel like we have any right now. And who-ever that is up there, she had it a lot worse."

HER NAME WAS Melinda Barrett. She'd been twenty when she'd set out to hike the Black Hills, a treat for herself for the summer. She was from Oregon. A student, a daughter, a sister. She'd wanted to be a ranger.

Her parents had reported her missing the same day she'd been found, because she'd been two days late checking in.

Before the cougar had gotten to her, someone had fractured her skull, then stabbed her violently enough to nick her ribs with the blade. Her pack, her watch, the compass her father had given her, the one his father had given him, weren't found.

Because she'd asked, Coop drove his bike to the start of the Chance farm road at dawn. Melinda Barrett's murder had delayed his start by two days, and he couldn't delay it longer.

He saw her standing in the early light, the dogs milling around her, the hills at her back. He'd remember that, he thought. Remember Lil just like that until he saw her again.

When he stopped and got off the bike, the dogs raced and leaped. Lil simply went into his arms.

"Would you call, when you get to New York?"

"Yes. Are you all right?"

"It's so much. I thought we'd have more time alone. Just alone to be. Then we found her. They don't have any idea who did that to her, or if they do, they're not saying. She just walked that trail, and someone killed her. For her pack? Her watch? For no reason? I can't get it out of my mind, and we haven't had our time." She tipped her face up, met his lips with hers. "It's just for a while."

"For a while."

"I know you have to go, but . . . did you eat? Do you need anything?" She tried to smile as tears drenched her throat. "Watch how I stall."

"I had flapjacks. Grandma knows my weakness. They gave me five thousand dollars, Lil. They wouldn't let me say no."

"Good." She kissed him again. "Good. Then I won't worry about you starving to death in some gutter. I'll miss you. God, I miss you already. Go. You need to go."

"I'll call. I'll miss you."

"Kick ass at the academy, Coop."

He got on the bike, took one last long look. "I'll come back."

"To me," she murmured when he gunned the engine. "Come back to me."

She watched until he was out of sight, until she was sure he was gone. In the soft, early light, she sat on the ground, and gathering the dogs to her, wept her heart out.

6

The little Cessna shuddered, then gave a couple of quick, annoyed bucks as it buzzed over the hills, the plains and valleys. Lil shifted in her seat. Not from nerves—she'd been through worse air than this and come out fine. She shifted for a better view. Her Black Hills were white with February, a snow globe of rises, ridges, and flats, ribboned by frozen streams, laced by shivering pines.

She imagined the wind on the ground was nearly as raw and mean as it could be up here, so a good, strong inhale would be like gulping down broken glass.

She couldn't have been happier.

She was nearly home.

The last six months had been incredible, an experience she'd never forget. She'd been drenched, had sweltered, been frozen, been bitten and stung—all while studying pumas in the Andes.

She'd earned every penny of the research grant, and hoped to earn more with the papers and articles she'd written, and would write.

Money aside—though in her position that was a luxury she couldn't afford—every mile she'd hiked, every bruise, every sore muscle had been worth the sight of a golden puma stalking prey in the rain forest, or perched like an idol on a cliffside.

But now she was ready for home. Back to her own habitat.

Work waited, and plenty of it. Six months equaled her longest field trip, and even keeping in touch when she could, she'd face mountains of work.

The Chance Wildlife Refuge was her baby, after all.

But before she dived in, she wanted a day, even a day to wallow in home.

She stretched out her legs as best she could in the confines of the cabin, crossed her hiking boots at the ankles. She'd been traveling, one way or the other, for a day and a half, but this last leg washed away any travel fatigue.

"Gonna get bumpy."

She glanced over at Dave, the pilot. "And it's been smooth as a lake so far."

He grinned, winked. "Gonna seem like it."

She gave her seat belt an extra tug, but wasn't worried. Dave had gotten her home before. "I appreciate you making the detour."

"No problem."

"I'll buy you a meal before you head up to Twin Forks."

"I'll rain-check that." He turned his Minnesota Twins fielder's cap bill-back as he always did for luck before a landing. "I figure I'll take off as soon as I refuel. You've been gone awhile this time. Must be anxious to get home."

"I am."

The wind slapped and yanked at the little plane on the descent. It rocked and kicked like a bad-tempered child in mid-tantrum. Lil grinned when she saw the runway of the municipal airport.

"You call me when you're back this way, Dave. My mother will fix you the prince of home-cooked meals."

"I'm on that."

She shoved her thick braid off her shoulder, peering down, her dark eyes searching. She spotted the blop of red. Her mother's car, she thought. Had to be. She braced against the turbulence, keeping that spot of red as her focal point.

The landing gear rumbled down, the red became a Yukon, and the plane dipped toward the runway. When the wheels touched, her heart lifted.

The minute Dave gave her the nod, she unbuckled to grab her duffel, her pack, her laptop case. Loaded, she turned to her pilot, managed to get a hand on his beard-grizzled face, and kissed him hard on the lips.

"Almost as good as a home-cooked meal," he said.

As she clanged her way down the short steps to the tarmac, Jenna rushed out of the tiny terminal. Lil dumped her gear, and met her mother on the run.

"There you are. There you are," Jenna murmured as they gripped each other in rib-crushers. "Welcome back, welcome home. Oh, I *missed* you! Let me look at you!"

"In a minute." Lil held on, breathed in the scents of lemon and vanilla that said *Mom*. "Okay."

She eased back, and the two women studied each other. "You look so beautiful." Lil reached out, flicked her fingers over her mother's hair. "I still can't get used to it short. Sassy."

"You look . . . amazing. How can you look amazing after six months of tramping around the Andes? After spending nearly two days on planes, trains, and God knows what else to get home? But you look amazing, and ready for anything. Let's get your stuff, get you out of the cold. Dave!"

Jenna hurried toward the pilot, caught his face, as Lil had, kissed him, as Lil had. "Thanks for bringing my girl home."

"Best detour I ever took."

Lil hefted her pack, her duffel, let her mother take the laptop. "Safe skies, Dave."

"I'm so happy to see you." Jenna wrapped an arm around Lil's waist as they walked against the wind. "Your dad wanted to come, but one of the horses is sick."

"Bad?"

"I don't think so. Hope not. But he wanted to stay close, keep an eye on her. So I get you all to myself for a while."

Once the gear was loaded, they settled into the car. The hybrid her green-minded parents used was neat as a parlor, and roomier than the Cessna's cabin. Lil stretched out her legs, let out a long sigh. "I'm dreaming of an endless bubble bath, with a bottomless glass of wine. Then the biggest damn steak this side of the Missouri."

"We happen to have all those in stock."

To cut the glare from the snowpack, Lil dug out her sunglasses. "I want to stay at the house tonight, catch up with you guys before I go to the cabin, get back to work."

"I'd kick your butt if you planned to do anything else."

"Yay. Tell me everything," Lil insisted as they drove out of the lot. "How is everybody, what's been going on, who's ahead in the Joe v. Farley Never-Ending Chess Tournament? Who's fighting, who's having sex? Note I'm trying not to ask specifically about the refuge, because once I get started I won't be able to stop."

"Then I'll just say everything's fine in the area you're not asking about. I want to hear all about your adventures. The journal entries you e-mailed were so rich, so interesting. You need to write that book, honey."

"One of these days. I have enough already put together for a couple more solid articles. Got some great photos, more than I sent you guys. I looked out of my tent one morning, not fully awake, really, just glanced out, and I saw a puma up in a tree, maybe twenty yards away. Just sitting up there, studying the camp, like she was thinking, What the hell do they think they're doing here?

"There were mists rising, and the birds had just started to chatter. Everyone else was asleep. It was just the two of us. She took my breath, Mom. I didn't get a picture. I had to force myself to ease back and get my camera. It only took seconds, but when I looked back out, she was gone. Like smoke. But I'll never forget how she looked."

Lil laughed and shook her head. "See, you got me started. I want to hear about here. About home." She flipped open her old sheepskin jacket as the car's heater pumped out blissful warmth. "Oh, look at the snow. You've all been hammered. Two days ago I was sweltering in Peru. Tell me something new."

"I didn't tell you when you were gone. Didn't want to worry you. Sam fell and broke his leg."

"Oh, God." Instantly the pleasure on her face, in her heart, dissolved. "When? How bad?"

"About four months ago. His horse shied, reared—we're not quite sure—but he fell, and the horse tromped on his leg. Broke it in two places. He was alone, Lil. The horse headed back without him, and that's what alerted Lucy."

"Is he all right? Mom—"

"He's doing better. We were all scared for a while there. He's fit, but he's seventy-six, and they were bad breaks. They put pins in, and he was in the hospital for over a week, then in a cast, and then therapy. He's just starting to get around again, with a cane. If he wasn't so tough . . . The doctors say he's remarkable, and he'll do fine. But it's slowed him down, no question."

"What about Lucy? Is she doing all right? The farm, the business? If Sam's been laid up all this time, have they got enough help?"

"Yes. It was a little rough at first, but yes, they're doing okay." Jenna took a quick breath, which told Lil more tough news was coming. "Lil, Cooper's back."

It was a sucker punch to the heart. Just reflex, she told herself. Just old memories taking a cheap shot. "Good, that's good. He'd be a lot of help. How long is he staying?"

"He's back, Lil." Jenna reached over to rub her hand on her daughter's thigh. Both the tone and the touch were gentle. "He's living at the farm now."

"Well, sure." Something inside her jittered, but she ignored it. "Where else would he stay while he's helping them out?"

"He came out as soon as Lucy called him, stayed a few days, stayed until we were all sure Sam wasn't going to need more surgery. Then he went back east, settled whatever he had to settle, and came back. He's staying."

"But . . . He has his business in New York." That something inside squeezed her sternum now, making it hard to breathe. "I mean, after he quit the police force and went private, he . . . I thought he was doing okay there."

"I think he was. But . . . Lucy told me he sold the agency, packed up, and told her he'd be staying. And he has. I'm not sure what they'd have done without him, truth be told. Everyone would've pitched in to help, you know how it is. But there's nothing like family. I didn't want to tell you about it on the phone, or by e-mail. Baby, I know it might be hard for you."

"No. Of course not." Once her heart stopped aching, once she could take a deep breath without pain, she'd be fine. "That was a long time ago. We're still friendly. I saw him, what, three or four years ago, when he came out to visit Sam and Lucy."

"You saw him for less than an hour, before you suddenly had to go to Florida, for the full two weeks he was here."

"I did have to go, or the opportunity came up. Florida panthers are endangered." She stared out the window, grateful for the sunglasses. Even with them everything seemed too bright, too *much*. "I'm fine about Coop. I'm glad he's here for Sam and Lucy."

"You loved him."

"Yes, I did. Past tense. Don't worry."

It wasn't as if she'd run into him every five minutes, see him every-where. She had her work, her place. He, apparently, had his. Plus, no hard feelings, she reminded herself. They'd been children; they'd grown up.

She ordered herself to put it away, all away, when her mother turned onto the farm road. She could see smoke puffing out of the chimney—a homey welcome—and a pair of dogs racing from the back to see what was up.

She had a quick and poignant memory of weeping into the comfort of another pair of dogs on a hot summer morning. Twelve years ago this summer for that first miserable goodbye, she reminded herself. And really, if she was honest, that had been the end. Twelve years was long enough, plenty long enough, to get over it.

She saw her father coming from the barn to greet them, and pushed all thoughts of Cooper Sullivan away.

SHE WAS HUGGED, kissed, plied with hot chocolate and cookies, slobbered on by the pair of hounds her parents had named Lois and Clark. Out the kitchen window the familiar view spread. The fields, the hills, the pines, the bright wink of the stream. Jenna insisted on washing the clothes stuffed in the duffel.

"I'd like to. Makes me feel like Mommy for the day."

"Far be it from me to deprive you, Mommy."

"I'm not a fussy woman," Jenna observed as she took the load Lil gave her. "But I don't know how you can get by with so little for so long."

"Planning, and the willingness to wear dirty socks when choices are limited. That's actually still clean," Lil began when her mother pulled another shirt out of the duffel. Jenna only lifted her eyebrows. "Okay, not so much clean as not filthy."

"I'll bring you a sweater, some jeans. That'll hold you until these are clean and dry. Take your bath, drink your wine. Relax."

She sank into the tub her mother had drawn. It was, Lil thought with a long, nearly orgasmic groan, nice to have someone fuss over her a little. Working in the field usually meant living rough, and in some cases close to primitive. She didn't mind it. But she sure as hell didn't mind having her mom draw her the Jenna Chance special bubble bath, and knowing she could indulge in it until the water went cold.

Now that she was alone, now that there was plenty of time, she let Coop back into her head.

He'd come back when his grandparents needed him—she had to give him credit for that. The fact was, no one could question his love or loyalty in that direction.

How could she hate the man, one who had, apparently, changed his life to see that his grandparents' home and their business were protected?

Besides, she had nothing to hate him for.

Just because he'd broken her heart, then squeezed the still dripping juices of it onto the ground so they had clung to his boot heels when he'd walked away from her—really, was that a reason to hate anyone?

She sank in a little more, sipped her wine.

But he hadn't lied, she had to give him that one, too.

He'd come back. Not at Thanksgiving, but at Christmas. Only for two days, but he'd come. And when he hadn't been able to come that summer, she'd accepted an offer to work in a refuge in California. She'd learned a lot over those weeks, and she and Coop had kept in touch as much as possible.

But things had already started to change. Hadn't she felt it even then? she asked herself. Hadn't some part of her known?

He hadn't been able to come out the next Christmas, and she'd cut her own winter break short for a field study.

When they'd met at a halfway-between point the following spring, it had been the end. He'd changed, she could see it. He'd been harder, tougher—and yes, colder. Still, she couldn't claim he'd been cruel. Just clear.

She had her life west, he had his east. Time to toss it in and admit they'd never make it work.

Your friendship matters to me. You matter. But, Lil, we've got to get on with what we are. We've got to accept who we are.

No, he hadn't been cruel, but he'd shattered her. All she'd had left was pride. The cold pride that had allowed her to say he was right, and to look him in the eye when she'd said it.

"Thank God I did," she muttered. Otherwise his coming back would be both mortification and misery.

The best way to deal with it, to get everything off on the right foot, was to face it head-on. As soon as she could manage it, she'd go over to see Sam and Lucy, and Coop. Hell, she'd buy him a beer and play catch-up there, too.

She wasn't a teenager with a fluttering heart and raging hormones anymore. As of the previous summer she was Dr. Lillian Chance, thank you very much. She was cofounder of the Chance Wildlife Refuge right here in her own corner of the world.

She'd traveled to, studied and worked in other corners of the world. She'd had a long-term, monogamous, *serious* relationship with a man. A couple of others not so long-term, not so serious, but she'd basically lived with Jean-Paul for nearly two years. Not counting the times she'd been traveling—or he'd been traveling—in different directions.

So she could handle sharing her corner of the world with a childhood sweetheart. Really, that's what they'd been, *all* they'd been. It was simple, even sweet, she decided.

And they'd keep it that way.

She dressed in the borrowed sweater and jeans, and lulled by the bath, the wine, her old room, opted to take a power nap. Twenty minutes, she told herself as she stretched out.

She slept like the dead for three hours.

THE NEXT MORNING, she woke in the hour before dawn, rested and ready. Because she hit the kitchen before her parents, she made breakfast—her specialty. When her father walked in for coffee, she had bacon and home fries in the skillet, and eggs already whisked in a bowl.

Handsome, his hair still full and thick, Joe sniffed the air like one of his hounds. He pointed a finger at her. "I knew there was a reason I was glad you're back. I figured I'd be eating instant oatmeal for breakfast."

"Not when I'm around. And since when have you had to eat instant anything in this house?"

"Since your mother and I compromised a couple months ago and I agreed to eat oatmeal twice a week." He gave her a mournful look. "It's healthy."

"Ah, and this was oatmeal day."

He grinned and gave her long ponytail a tug. "Not when you're around."

"Okay, full cholesterol plate for you, then I'll help you with the stock before I ride over to the refuge. I made enough for Farley, assuming he'd be here. Does oatmeal put him off?"

"Nothing puts Farley off, but he'll be grateful to get the bacon and eggs. I'll ride over with you this morning."

"Great. Depending on how things go, I'm going to try to drive over and see Sam and Lucy. If you need anything from town I can head in, take care of it."

"I'll put a list together."

Lil forked out bacon to drain as her mother came in. "Just in time."

Jenna eyed the bacon, eyed her husband.

"She made it." Joe pointed at Lil. "I can't hurt her feelings."

"Oatmeal tomorrow." Jenna gave Joe a finger-drill in the belly.

Lil heard the stomp of boots out on the back porch, and thought: Farley.

She'd been in college when her parents had taken him on—taken him in was more accurate, she thought. He'd been sixteen, and on his own since his mother took off and left him, owing two months' back rent in Abilene. His father, neither he nor his mother had known. He'd only known the series of men his mother had slept with.

With some vague idea of going to Canada, young Farley Pucket ducked out on the rent, hit the road, and stuck out his thumb. By the time Josiah Chance pulled over and picked him up on a road outside of Rapid City, the boy had thirty-eight cents in his pocket and was wearing only a Houston Rockets windbreaker against the wicked March winds.

They'd given him a meal, some chores to work it off, and a place to sleep for the night. They'd listened, they'd discussed, they'd checked his story as best they could. In the end, they'd given him a job, and a room in the old bunkhouse until he could make his way.

Nearly ten years later, he was still there.

Gangly, straw-colored hair poking out from under his hat, his pale blue eyes still sleepy, Farley came in with a blast of winter cold.

"Whoo! Cold enough to freeze the balls off—" He broke off when he saw Jenna, and his cheeks pinked from cold flushed deeper. "Didn't see you there." He sniffed. "Bacon? It's oatmeal day."

"Special dispensation," Joe told him.

Farley spotted Lil and broke out in a mile-wide grin. "Hey, Lil. Didn't figure you'd be up yet, all jet-lagged and stuff."

"'Morning, Farley. Coffee's hot."

"It sure smells good. Gonna be clear today, Joe. That storm front tracked east."

So as it often did, morning talk turned to weather, stock, chores. Lil settled down with her breakfast, and thought in some ways it was as if she'd never been away.

Within the hour, she was mounted beside her father and riding the trail to the refuge.

"Tansy tells me Farley's been putting in a lot of volunteer hours at the refuge."

"We all try to lend a hand, especially when you're away."

"Dad, he's got a crush on her," Lil said, speaking of her college roommate and the zoologist on staff.

"On Tansy? No." He laughed it off. Then sobered. "Really?"

"I got the vibe when he started volunteering regularly last year. I didn't think much of it. She's my age."

"Old lady."

"Well, she's got some years on him. I can see it from his end. She's beautiful and smart and funny. What I didn't expect was to get the vibe—which I did reading between the lines of her e-mails—that she may have one on him."

"Tansy's interested in Farley? Our Farley?"

"Maybe I'm wrong, but I got the vibe. Our Farley," she repeated, taking a deep breath of the snow-tinged air. "You know, in my world-weary phase of twenty, I thought the two of you were insane to take him in. I figured he'd rob you blind—at the least—steal your truck and that would be that."

"He wouldn't steal a nickel. It's not in him. You could see it, right from the start."

"You could. Mom could. And you were right. I think I'm right about my college pal, the dedicated zoologist, having eyes for our own goofy, sweet-natured Farley."

They followed the track at an easy trot, the horses kicking up snow, their breath steaming out like smoke.

As they approached the gate that separated the farm from the refuge, Lil let out a laugh. Her coworkers had hung a huge banner across the gate.

WELCOME HOME, LIL!

She saw the tracks as well—from snowmobiles and horses, animals and men. Through January and February, the refuge saw little in the way of tourists and visitors. But the staff was always busy.

She dismounted to open the gate. When they could afford it, she thought, they'd replace the old thing with electric. But for now, she waded through the snow to work the latch. It squealed as she dragged it clear so her father could lead her horse through.

"Nobody's been bothering you, have they?" she asked as she remounted. "I mean the public."

"Oh, we get somebody comes by every now and then, who can't find the public entrance. We just send them around."

"I hear we had good turnout, and good feedback, from the school field trips in the fall."

"Kids love the place, Lil. It's a good thing you've done here."

"We've done."

She scented animal before she saw them, that touch of wild in the air. Inside the first stretch of habitat a Canadian lynx sat on a boulder. Tansy had brought him in from Canada, where he'd been captured and wounded. In the wild, his maimed leg was a death sentence. Here, he had sanctuary. They called him Rocco, and he flicked his tufted ears as they passed.

The refuge gave homes to bobcat and cougar, to an old, circus tiger they called Boris, to a lioness who had once, inexplicably, been kept as a pet. There were bear and wolf, fox and leopard.

A smaller area held a petting zoo, what she thought of as hands-on education for kids. Rabbits, lambs, a pygmy goat, a donkey.

And the humans, bundled in cold-weather gear, who worked to feed them, shelter them, treat them.

Tansy spotted her first, and gave a whoop before racing over from the big-cat area. A pink flush from cold and pleasure bloomed on the cheeks of her pretty, caramel-colored face.

"You're back." She gave Lil's knee a squeeze. "Get on down here and give me a hug! Hey, Joe, I bet you're happy to have your girl back."

"And then some."

Lil slid off the horse and embraced her friend, who swayed side-to-side making a happy *mmmm* sound. "It's so good, so good, so *good* to see you!"

"Likewise." Lil pressed her cheek to the soft spring of Tansy's dark hair.

"We heard you'd caught Dave and managed to get back a day early, so we've been scrambling." Tansy leaned back and grinned. "To hide the evidence of all the drunken parties and fat-assing we've had going on since you left."

"Aha. I knew it. And that's why you're the only member of the senior staff out and about?"

"Naturally. Everyone else is nursing hangovers." She laughed and gave Lil another squeeze. "Okay, truth. Matt is in Medical. Bill tried to eat a towel."

Bill, a young bobcat, was renowned for his eclectic appetite.

Lil glanced back at the pair of cabins, one housing her quarters, the other offices and Medical. "Did he get much?"

"No, but Matt wants to check him out. Lucius is chained to his computer, and Mary's at the dentist. Or going to. Hey, Eric, come take the horses, will you? Eric's one of our winter-term interns. We'll make the introductions later. Let's—" She broke off at the harsh, bright call of a cougar. "Somebody smells Mama," Tansy said. "Go ahead. We'll meet you in Medical when you're done."

Lil wound her way, following the trail formed by feet trampling through the snow.

He was waiting for her, pacing, watching, calling. At her approach, the cat rubbed its body against the fencing, then stood, bracing his forepaws against it. And purred.

Six months since he'd seen her—scented her, Lil thought. But he hadn't forgotten her. "Hello, Baby."

She reached through to stroke the tawny fur, and he bumped his head affectionately to hers.

"I missed you, too."

He was four now, full-grown, lithe and magnificent. He hadn't been fully weaned when she'd found him, and his two littermates, orphaned and half starved. She'd hand-fed them, tended them, guarded them. And when they'd been old enough, strong enough, had reintroduced them to the wild.

But he'd kept coming back.

She'd named him Ramses, for power and dignity, but he was Baby.

And her one true love.

"Have you been good? Of course, you have. You're the best. Keeping everybody in line? I knew I could count on you."

As she spoke and stroked, Baby purred, hummed in his throat, and looked at her with golden eyes full of love.

She heard movement behind her, glanced back. The one Tansy had called Eric stood staring. "They said he was like that with you, but . . . I didn't believe it."

"You're new?"

"Um, yeah. I'm interning. Eric. I'm Eric Silverstone, Dr. Chance."

"Lil. What are you looking to do?"

"Wildlife management."

"Learning anything here?"

"A lot."

"Let me give you another quick lesson. This adult male cougar, *Felis concolor,* is approximately eight feet long from nose to tail and weighs about one-fifty. He can outjump a lion, a tiger, a leopard, both vertically and horizontally. Despite that, he's not considered a 'big cat.'"

"He lacks the specialized larynx and hyoid apparatus. He can't roar."

"Correct. He'll purr like your aunt Edith's tabby. But he's not tame. You can't tame the wild, can you, Baby?" He chirped at her as if in agreement. "He loves me. He imprinted on me as a kitten—about four months of age—and he's been in the refuge, among people, since. Learned behavior, not tame. We're not prey. But if you made some move he sensed as attack, he'd respond. They're beautiful, and they're fascinating, but they're not pets. Not even this one."

Still, to please herself and Baby, she pressed her lips in one of the small openings of the fence, and he butted his mouth to hers. "See you later."

She turned and walked with Eric toward the cabin. "Tansy said you found him and two other orphans."

"Their mother got into it with a lone wolf—at least that's how it looked to me. She killed it, must have or it would have taken the litter. But she didn't survive. I found the corpses, and the litter. They were the first cougar kittens we had here."

And she had a scar near her right elbow from the other male in that litter. "We fed them, sheltered them for about six weeks, until they were old enough to hunt on their own. Limited human contact as much as possible. We tagged them and released them and we've been tracking them ever since. But Baby? He wanted to stay."

She glanced back to where he'd joined his companions in his habitat.

"His littermates reacclimated, but he kept coming back here." To me, she thought. "They're solitary and secretive and cover a vast range, but he chose to come back. That's the thing. You can study and learn the patterns, the biology, the taxonomy, the behavior. But you'll never know everything."

She looked back as Baby leaped on one of his boulders and let out a long, triumphant scream.

Inside, she shed her outer gear. She could hear her father talking to Matt through the open door of Medical. In the offices, a man with Coke-bottle glasses and an infectious grin hammered away at a keyboard.

Lucius Gamble looked up, said, "Yeah!" and tossed his hands in the air. "Back from the trenches." He jumped up to give her a hug, and she smelled the red licorice he was addicted to on his breath.

"How's it going, Lucius?"

"Good. Just updating the Web page. We've got some new pictures. We had an injured wolf brought in a couple weeks ago. Clipped by a car. Matt saved it. We've gotten a lot of hits on the pictures there, and the column Tansy wrote for it."

"Were we able to release it?"

"It's still gimpy. Matt doesn't think it'll make it out there in the world. She's an old girl. We're calling her Xena, because she looks like a warrior."

"I'll take a look at her. I haven't done the tour yet."

"I put your shots from the trip on here." Lucius tapped his computer monitor. He wore ancient high-tops rather than the boots most of the staff favored, and jeans that bagged over his flat ass. "Dr. Lillian's Excellent Adventure. We've been getting *beaucoup* hits."

As he spoke, Lil glanced around the familiar space. The exposed log walls, the posters of wildlife, the cheap, plastic visitors' chairs, the stacks of colorful brochures. The second desk—Mary's—stood like a trim, organized island in the chaos Lucius generated.

"Any of the hits come with . . ." She lifted her hand, rubbed her thumb and fingers together.

"We've been going pretty steady there. We added a new webcam, like you wanted, and Mary's been working on an updated brochure. She had a dentist deal this morning, but she's going to try to make it in this afternoon."

"Let's see if we can get together for a meeting this afternoon. Full staff, including interns, and any of the volunteers who can attend."

She walked back and peeked into Medical. "Where's Bill?"

Matt turned. "I cleared him. Tansy's taking him back. Good to see you, Lil."

They didn't hug—it wasn't Matt's style—but shook hands, and warmly. He was about her father's age, with thinning hair streaked with gray, and wire-rimmed glasses over brown eyes.

He was no idealist, as she suspected Eric was, but he was a damn fine vet, and one willing to work for pitiful pay.

"I'd better get back. I'll try to cut Farley loose some tomorrow, so he can give you a couple hours." Joe tapped a finger on Lil's nose. "You need anything, you call."

"I will. I'll pick up the stuff on your list later, drop it off."

He went out the back.

"Meeting later," she told Matt, and leaned on a counter that held trays and bins of medical supplies. The air smelled, familiarly, of antiseptic and animal. "I'd like you to brief me, and the rest, on the health and medical needs of the animals. Lunchtime would be best. Then I can do a supply run."

"Can do."

"Tell me about our newest resident. Xena?"

Matt smiled, and the amusement lightened his often serious face. "Lucius named her that. It seems to have stuck. She's an old girl. A good eight years old."

"Top of the scale for the wild," Lil commented.

"Tough girl. Scars to prove it. She took a pretty hard hit. The driver did more than most people do. She called us, and stayed in the car until we got there, even followed us back here. Xena was too injured to move.

We immobilized and transported, got her in here, into surgery." He shook his head, removing his glasses to polish the lenses on his lab coat. "It was touch and go, given her age."

Lil thought of Sam. "But she's recovering."

"Like I said, tough girl. At her age, and given the leg's never going to be a hundred percent, I wouldn't recommend releasing her. I don't think she'd last a month."

"Well, she can consider this her retirement home."

"Listen, Lil, you know at least one of us has been staying at night while you were in the field. I was on a couple nights ago. Just as well, as I'd had to extract a tooth that morning from the queen mum."

Lil thought of their ancient lion. "Poor grandma. She's not going to have a tooth left at this rate. How'd she do?"

"She's the Energizer Bunny of lions. But the thing is, there was something out there."

"Sorry?"

"Something or someone was out there, around the habitats. I checked the webcam, and didn't see anything. But hell, it's pretty damn dark at two in the morning, even with the security lights. But something had the animals stirred up. A lot of screaming and roaring and howling."

"Not the usual nocturnal business?"

"No. I went out, but I couldn't find anything."

"Any tracks?"

"I don't have your eye, but we looked the next morning. No animal tracks, no new ones. We thought—we think—there were human ones. Not ours. No way to be sure, but there were tracks around some of the cages, and we'd had some snow after the last feeding of the day, so I don't know how else there'd have been fresh tracks."

"None of the animals were hurt? Any locks tampered with?" she added when he shook his head.

"We couldn't find anything, nothing touched, taken. I know how it sounds, Lil, but when I went out, it felt like someone was there. Watching me. I just want you to keep an eye out, make sure you lock your doors."

"Okay. Thanks, Matt. Let's all be careful."

There were strange people out there, she thought as she put her coat back on. From the No Animal Should Be in Prison—as some thought of a refuge—to Animals Are Meant to Be Hunted and Killed. And everything in between.

They got calls, letters, e-mails from both ends of the spectrum. Some with threats. And they'd had the occasional trespasser. But so far, there'd been no trouble.

She wanted to keep it that way.

She'd go have a look around herself. Odds were, after a couple of days there would be nothing for her to find. But she had to look.

She shot a wave to Lucius, opened the door.

And nearly walked straight into Cooper.

7

It was a toss-up who was more surprised, and disconcerted. But it was Lil who jolted back, even if she recovered quickly. She plastered on a smile and put a friendly laugh in her voice.

"Well, hi, Coop."

"Lil. I didn't know you were back."

"Yesterday." She couldn't read his face, his eyes. Both, so familiar, simply didn't speak to her. "Coming in?"

"Ah, no. You got a package—your place got a package," he corrected, and handed it to her. He wasn't wearing gloves, she noted, and his heavy jacket was carelessly open to the cold.

"I was sending something off for my grandmother, and since I was heading back to the farm, they asked if I'd mind dropping it off."

"Thanks." She set it aside, then stepped out and closed the door rather than let the heat pump out. She fixed her hat on her head, the same flat-brimmed style she'd always favored. Standing on the porch, she pulled on one of her gloves. It gave her something to do as he watched her in silence. "How's Sam? I just heard yesterday that he'd gotten hurt."

"Good, physically. It's hard on him, not being able to do everything he wants, get around the way he did."

"I'm going by later."

"He'll like that. They both will." He slid his hands into his pockets, kept those cool blue eyes on her face. "How was South America?"

"Busy, and fascinating." She pulled on her other glove as they walked down the steps. "Mom said you'd sold your detective agency."

"I was done with it."

"You did a lot, left a lot, to help two people who needed you." The finality in his voice, the flatness in it had her stopping. "It counts, Cooper."

He only shrugged. "I was ready for a change anyway. This is one." He glanced around. "You've added more since I was here."

She sent him a puzzled look. "When were you here?"

"I came by when I was out last year. You were . . . somewhere." He stood at ease in the cold, while the brisk wind kicked through the al-ready disordered waves of his dense brown hair. "Your friend gave me the tour."

"She didn't mention it."

"He. French guy. I heard you were engaged."

Guilt balled in her belly. "Not exactly."

"Well. You look good, Lil."

She forced her lips to curve, forced the same casualness he projected into her voice. "You too."

"I'd better get going. I'll tell my grandparents you're going to try to come by."

"I'll see you later." And with an easy smile, she turned to walk to the small-cat area. She circled around until she heard his truck start, until she heard it drive away. Then she stopped.

There, she thought, not so bad. The first time would be the hardest, and it wasn't so bad.

A few aches, a few bumps. Nothing fatal.

He did look good, she thought. Older, tougher. Sharper in the face, harder around the eyes. Sexier.

She could live through that. They might be friends again. Not the way they'd been, even before they'd become lovers. But they might be friendly. His grandparents and her parents were good friends, close friends. She and Coop would never be able to avoid each other gracefully, so they'd just have to get along as best they could. Be friendly.

She could do it if he could.

Satisfied, she began to scout around the habitats for signs of trespass—animal or human.

Coop looked into the rearview mirror as he drove away, but she didn't glance back. Just kept going.

That's the way it was. He wasn't looking to change it.

He'd caught her off-guard. They'd caught each other off-guard, he corrected, but her surprise had shown on her face, just for a beat or two, but clearly. Surprise, and a shadow of annoyance.

Both gone in a blink.

She'd gotten beautiful.

She'd always been so, to him, but objectively he could look back now and see that she'd been poised for beauty at seventeen. Touched by beauty at the cusp of twenty. But she hadn't crossed the finish line then, not like now.

For a second there, those big, dark, sultry eyes had taken his breath away.

For a second.

Then she'd smiled, and maybe his heart had twisted, just for another second, over what had been. What was gone.

Everything easy, everything casual between them. That's the way it should be. He didn't want anything from her, and had nothing to give back. It was good to know that, since he was back for good.

Oddly enough, he'd been considering coming back for several months. He'd even looked into what steps he'd need to take to sell his private investigator's business, close his office, sell his apartment. He hadn't moved on it, had simply continued his work, his life—because not moving was easier.

Then his grandmother had called.

With all the research done and filed in Maybe Someday, it had been a simple matter to make the move. And maybe, if he'd made the damn move earlier, his grandfather wouldn't have been alone, and in pain after his fall.

And that kind of thinking was useless, he knew it.

Things just happened because they did. He knew that, too.

The point was he was back now. He liked the work—he always had— and God knew he could use a little serenity. Long days, plenty of physical labor, the horses, the routine. And the only real home he'd ever known.

The Maybe Someday might have come before but for Lil. The obstacle, the regret, the uncertainty of Lil. But that was done now, and they could both get back to their lives.

She'd created something so solid and real, so Lil, with her refuge. He hadn't known how to tell her that, how to tell her that it was a source of pride for him, too. He didn't know how to tell her he remembered when she'd told him she would build this place, he remembered the look on her face, the light on it, the sound of her voice.

He remembered everything.

Years ago, he thought. A lifetime ago. She'd studied and worked and planned, and made it happen. She'd done exactly what she'd set out to do.

He'd known she would. She wouldn't have settled for less.

He'd made something. It had taken a lot of time, a lot of mistakes, but he'd made something of himself, and for himself. And he could walk away from that because the point had been to make it.

Now the point was here. He turned onto the farm road. Right here, he thought, right now.

When he went inside, Lucy was in the kitchen, baking.

"Smells good."

"Thought I'd do a couple of pies." She offered a smile, strained around the edges. "Everybody get off all right?"

"Group of four. Gull's got them." The blacksmith's son hadn't followed in his father's footsteps, but served as trail guide and man-of-work for Wilks's Stables. "Weather's clear, and he's keeping them to a couple of easy rides." Since it was there, he poured himself some coffee. "I'm going to go out and check on the new foals and their mas."

She nodded, looked in on her pies, though they both knew she could time them by instinct to the minute. "Maybe, if you don't mind, you could ask Sam to go out with you. He's having a mood today."

"Sure. He upstairs?"

"Last I checked." She flicked her fingers at the hair she now wore short as a boy's and had let go a stunning and shining silver. "Checking's one of the things, I expect, put him in the mood."

Rather than speak, he just put an arm around her shoulders and kissed the top of her head.

She would've checked, Coop thought, several times. Just as he had no doubt she'd been out to the barn to check on the foals. She'd have seen to the chickens and the pigs, getting all the chores done she could manage before Sam could try to do them.

And she'd have fixed his breakfast, just as she'd fixed Coop's. Seen to the house, the laundry.

She was wearing herself out, even with him there.

He went upstairs.

For the first couple of months after his grandfather had been released from the hospital, he'd stayed in the parlor they'd outfitted as a bedroom. He'd needed a wheelchair and help with the most personal functions.

And he'd hated it.

The minute he'd been able to manage the stairs, however long it took, however hard it had been, he'd insisted on moving back to the room he shared with his wife.

The door was open. Inside Coop saw his grandfather sitting in a chair, scowling at the television and rubbing his leg.

There were lines in his face that hadn't been there two years before, grooves dug by pain and frustration more than age. And maybe, Coop thought, some fear along with it.

"Hey, Grandpa."

Sam turned the scowl toward Coop. "Not a damn thing worth looking at on the television. If she sent you up here to check on me, to see if I need something to drink, something to eat, something to read, somebody to burp me like a baby, I don't."

"Actually, I'm heading out to check on the horses and thought you could give me a hand. But if you'd rather watch TV . . ."

"Don't think that kind of psychology holds water with me. I wasn't born yesterday. Just get me my damn boots."

"Yes, sir."

He got the boots, one of the pairs set neatly on the closet floor. He didn't offer to help, something his practical and insightful grandmother couldn't seem to stop herself from doing. But Coop judged that came from fear, too.

Instead he talked about the business, the current trail ride, then his stop at the refuge.

"Lil said she'd stop by and see you today."

"Be pleased to see her, long as it's not a sick call." Sam levered himself up, bracing a hand on the back of the chair as he got his cane. "What did she have to say about running around in those foreign mountains?"

"I didn't ask. I was only there a couple minutes."

Sam shook his head. He moved well, Coop thought, for a man who'd busted himself up four short months before. But the stiffness was there, the awkwardness, enough to remind Coop just how easy and economic Sam's gait had once been.

"Gotta wonder about your brain, boy."

"Sorry?"

"Pretty girl like that, and one everybody knows you had a hankering for once upon a time, and you can't spare more than a couple minutes?"

"She was busy," Coop said as they started toward the stairs. "I was busy. Plus, that was once upon a time. Another plus, she's involved with someone."

Sam snorted as he clumped downstairs, with Coop positioned to catch him if he lost balance. "Some foreigner."

"Have you developed a prejudice against things foreign just recently?"

Though his mouth was tight from the effort to negotiate the stairs, humor twinkled into Sam's eyes. "I'm an old man. I'm allowed, even expected, to be crotchety. 'Sides, involved ain't nothing. You young people today don't have the gumption to go after a woman because she's *involved*."

" 'You young people'? That would be part of the new and expected crotchety?"

"Sass." But he didn't complain when Coop helped him into his outdoor gear. "We're going out the front. She's back in the kitchen, and I don't want her raining all her worries and don't-do's down on my head."

"Okay."

Sam let out a little sigh, and put on his old, rolled-brimmed hat. "You're a good boy, Cooper, even if you are stupid about women."

"I'm stupid about women?" Coop led Sam outside. He'd shoveled the porch, the steps, a path to the trucks, others to outbuildings. "You're the one who has his wife nagging at him. Maybe if you did more in that bed at night than snore, she'd leave you alone in the daytime."

"Sass," Sam repeated, but he wheezed out a laugh. "I oughta give you a good whack with this cane."

"Then I'd just have to help you up when you fell on your ass."

"I can stand long enough to get the job done. That's what *she* won't get through her head."

"She loves you. You scared her. And now neither one of you will give the other one a break. You're pissed off because you can't do everything you want, the way you want to do it. You've got to walk with a stick, and might have to for the rest of it. So what?" he said without letting a drop of sympathy escape. "You're walking, aren't you?"

"Won't let me step out of my own house, on my own land. I don't need a nursemaid."

"I'm not your nursemaid," Coop said flatly. "She fusses around you, and at you, because she's scared. And you snap and slap back at her. You never used to."

"She never used to dog me like I was a toddler," Sam said with some heat.

"You shattered your goddamn leg, Grandpa. The fact is you're not steady enough to walk around in the damn snow by yourself. You will be, because you're too stubborn not to get where you want to go. It's going to take more time. You just have to deal with it."

"Easier to say when you're still eyeball-to-eyeball with thirty than when you're getting a glimpse of eighty."

"Then you should appreciate time more, and stop wasting it complaining about the woman who loves every crotchety inch of you."

"You've got a lot to say all of a sudden."

"I've been saving it up."

Sam lifted his weathered face to the air. "A man needs his pride."

"Yeah, I know."

They made their slow, laborious way to the barn. Inside, Coop ignored the fact Sam was out of breath. He could catch it while they looked at the horses.

They'd had three foalings that winter. Two had gone smooth and one had been breech. Coop and his grandmother had helped bring that one into the world, and Coop had slept in the barn that night and the next.

He stopped at the stall where the mare and the filly stayed, and slid over the door to go inside. Under Sam's watchful eye, Coop murmured to the mare, ran his hands over her to check for heat, for strain. Carefully, he examined her udder, her teats. She stood placidly under the familiar touch while the filly butted her head to Coop's ass to get his attention.

He turned, rubbed her pretty buckskin coat.

"That one's yours as much as hers," Sam told him. "You named her yet?"

"Could be Lucky, because God knows. But it doesn't suit her." Coop checked the filly's mouth, her teeth. He studied the big doe eyes. "It's clichéd, but this one's a princess. She sure thinks of herself that way."

"We'll put it down that way. Cooper's Princess. The rest is yours, too. You know that."

"Grandpa."

"I'll have my say here. Your grandmother and I talked about it over the years. We couldn't be sure you wanted it or not, but in the end, we made that legal. It's yours when we're gone. I want you to tell me if you want it or you don't."

Cooper rose, and immediately the filly deserted him to nurse. "Yes, I want it."

"Good." Sam gave a quick nod. "Now, are you going to play with those horses all day or see to the others?"

Coop stepped out, secured the gate, then moved on to the next.

"I got something else." Sam's cane rang on the concrete as he followed. "Man your age needs a place of his own. He's got no business living with a couple of old people."

"You sure are into 'old' these days."

"That's just right. I know you moved in to help out. That's what kin does. I'm grateful nonetheless. But you can't stay in the house this way."

"You kicking me out?"

"I guess I am. Now, we can build something. Pick out a spot that suits you."

"I don't see using the land to plant a house when we could be using it to plant crops or graze horses."

"You think like a farmer," Sam said, with pride. "But still in all, a man needs his place. You can pick out some land and go that way. Or if that's not what suits you, at least not right yet, you can fix the bunkhouse up.

It's a good size. Few walls in it, better floor. Might use a new roof. We can do that for you."

Coop checked the next mare, the next foal. "The bunkhouse would work for me. I'll get it fixed up. I won't take your money for it, Grandpa. That's the line. A man has to have his pride," he said. "I've got money. More than I need now."

Which was something he wanted to talk to his grandparents about. But not quite yet.

"So I'll look into it."

"That's settled then." Sam leaned on his cane and reached out to stroke the mare's cheek. "There's Lolly, there's a girl. Given us three fine foals over the years. Sweet as a lollipop, aren't you? Born to be a ma, and to take a rider up and give him a good, gentle ride."

Lolly blew at him, affectionately.

"I need to sit a horse again, Cooper. Not being able to makes it feel like I lost this leg steada busting it."

"Okay. I'll saddle a couple up."

Sam's head snapped up, and in his eyes shone both shock and hope. "Your grandma'll skin us."

"She'll have to catch us first. A walk, Grandpa. Not even a trot. Deal?"

"Yeah." Sam's voice quavered before he strengthened it. "Yeah, that suits me."

Coop saddled two of the oldest and quietest mounts. He'd thought he'd known, thought he'd understood how hard this enforced convalescence was on his grandfather. The look on Sam's face when he'd said they'd ride told him he hadn't. Not nearly.

If he was making a mistake, he was making it for the right reasons. It wouldn't be the first time.

He helped Sam mount, and knew the motion and effort caused some pain. But what he saw in his grandfather's eyes was pleasure, and relief.

He swung into the saddle himself.

A plod, Coop supposed. A couple of old horses wading through snow, and going nowhere in particular. But by God, Sam Wilks looked *right* on horseback. Years fell away—he could watch them slide off his grandfather's face. In the saddle his movements were smooth and easy. Economic, Coop thought again.

In the saddle, Sam was home.

White stretched out and gleamed under the sun. It trimmed the forests that climbed the hills, tucked outcroppings of rocks under its icy blanket.

But for the whisper of wind, the jingle of bridle, the world was as still as a painting in a frame.

"Pretty land we got here, Cooper."

"Yes, sir, it is."

"I've lived in this valley my whole life, working the land, working with horses. It's all I ever wanted in this world except for your grandma. It's what I know. I feel I've done something, knowing I can pass it to you."

They rode nearly an hour, going nowhere in particular, and mostly in silence. Under the strong blue sky, the hills, the plains, the valley were white and cold. The melt would come, Coop knew, and the mud. The spring rains and the hail. But the green would come with it, and the young foals would dance in the pastures.

And that, Coop thought, was what he wanted now. To see the green come again, and watch the dance of horses. To live his life.

As they approached the house, Sam whistled under his breath.

"There's your grandma, standing on the back porch, hands on her hips. We're in for it now."

Coop sent Sam a mild glance. "We, hell. You're on your own."

Deliberately, Sam led his horse into the yard.

"Well, don't the pair of you look smug and stupid, riding around on horseback in the cold like a couple of idiots. I reckon now you want coffee and pie, like a reward."

"I could do with pie. Nobody bakes a pie like my Lucille."

She huffed, sniffed, then turned her back. "He breaks his leg getting off that horse, you'll be tending to him, Cooper Sullivan."

"Yes, ma'am."

Coop waited until she stalked into the kitchen, then dismounted to help Sam down. "I'll deal with the horses. You deal with her. You've got the dirty end of the stick on this one."

He helped Sam to the door, then deserted the field.

He tended to the horses and the tack. Because there was no real need for him to go back to town, he dealt with a few minor repairs that had piled up. He wasn't as good with his hands as his grandfather, but he was competent enough. At least he rarely smashed his thumb with a hammer.

When he finished, he walked over to take a look at the bunkhouse. It was no more than a long, low—and rough—cabin, in sight of the farmhouse and the paddocks.

But with enough distance, Cooper judged, for everyone to have their privacy. And he could admit, he missed his privacy.

Its use was primarily storage now, though it got put to use seasonally, or when there was a need, or enough money, to warrant a hand or two living on the premises.

The way he saw it there was more money now—his—and more need—his grandparents'. After he fixed up the bunkhouse, it might be time to consider refiguring the tack room in the barn and making it into quarters for a permanent farmhand.

He'd have to take that kind of change slowly, Coop knew. One step at a time.

He went inside the old bunkhouse. Nearly as cold in as out, he thought, and wondered when the potbellied stove had last been fired up. There were a couple of bunks, an old table, a few chairs. The kitchen would serve for frying up a meal and little else.

The floors were scarred, the walls rough. There was a lingering scent of grease and possibly sweat in the air.

A far cry from his apartment in New York, he thought. But then, he was done with that. He'd have to see what could be done to make this habitable.

It could work, and with enough room for a small office. He'd need one here, as well as the one in town. He didn't want to have to go over to the house and share his grandparents' office every time he had something to do.

Bedroom, bathroom—and that needed serious updating—galley kitchen, office. That would do. It wasn't as if he'd be doing any entertaining.

By the time he'd finished poking around, outlining basic plans, he began to think about the pie. He hoped his grandmother had cooled off by now.

He walked over, stomped his boots, and went in.

And there was Lil, Goddamn it, eating pie at the kitchen table. His grandmother gave him the beady eye but rose to get a plate. "Go on and sit. Might as well spoil your supper. Your grandfather's up taking a nap, seeing as he's worn out from riding the range. Lil had to make do with me, and she came all the way out to see Sam."

"Well," was all Coop said. He took off his coat and hat.

"You keep Lil company. I need to go up and check on him." She slapped the pie and a mug of coffee down, then flounced out.

"Shit."

"She's not as mad as she's acting." Lil forked up some pie. "She told me the ride did Sam a world of good, but she's pissed the two of you went off without telling her. Anyway, it's good pie."

He sat, took the first bite. "Yeah."

"She looks tired."

"She won't stop; she won't even slow down. If she's got ten minutes to sit down, she finds something else to do. They bicker day and night like a couple of ten-year-olds. Then . . ." He caught himself, caught himself talking to her as he might have done years before.

Before it ended.

He jerked a shoulder, forked up more pie. "Sorry."

"It's all right. I care about them, too. So you're going to fix up the bunkhouse."

"Word travels fast, since I only decided on that a couple hours ago."

"I've been here nearly a half hour. Long enough to catch up on current events. You really mean to stay, then?"

"That's right. Is that a problem?"

She lifted her brows. "Why would it be?"

He shrugged, went back to his pie.

"Not looking to be sheriff of Deadwood, are you?"

He glanced up, met her eyes. "No."

"We were surprised when you quit the police force." She waited a moment, but he didn't respond. "I guess being a private investigator's more exciting, and pays better than police work."

"Pays better. Most of the time."

She nudged the pie plate away to pick up her coffee. Settling in, he knew, to talk. Her lips curved, just a little. He knew the taste of them— exactly—the feel of them on his.

And the knowing was next to unbearable.

"It must've been interesting. The work."

"It had moments."

"So is it like it is on TV?"

"No."

"You know, Cooper, you used to be able to actually hold a conversation."

"I moved here," he said shortly. "I'm helping run the farm and the horse business. That's it."

"If you want me to mind my own business, just say so."

"Mind your own business."

"Fine." She slapped her coffee down and rose. "We used to be friends. I figured we could get back there. Apparently not."

"I'm not looking to get back to anything."

"Clear enough. Tell Lucy I said thanks for the pie, and I'll be around to see Sam when I can. I'll try to make sure I stay out of your way when I do."

When she stomped out, he scooped up another bite of pie, glad to be alone again.

8

It took little time for Lil to swing back into routine. She had everything she wanted—her place, her work, like-minded people to work with, the animals. She caught up with the mail and phone calls best dealt with personally, spent time working on proposals for grants.

There was never enough money.

She needed time to get to know the new crop of interns who'd come on while she'd been in the Andes, and to look over the reports of animals they'd treated and released—the injured wild brought to them.

She fed animals, cleaned them and their enclosures, assisted Matt in treating them. Days filled to bursting with the sheer physical demands. Evenings she reserved for writing—articles, papers, grant proposals, the bits of behind-the-scenes color that could influence a browser on the website to click on Donations.

Every night, alone, she checked the scope for Baby's siblings, and other cats and wildlife they'd tagged over the years.

They'd lost some, to hunting season, to other animals, or just to age or accident. But she currently had six cougars who had originated in the Black Hills, tagged by her or one of the staff. One, a young male when tagged, had traveled to Iowa, another had ranged into Minnesota. The female from Baby's litter had localized in the southwest of the Black Hills, occasionally roaming over into Wyoming during mating season.

She plotted locations, calculated dispersal distances, and speculated on behavior and choice of territory.

She thought it was time to buy a new horse, and go tracking. She had time before the spring season to capture and evaluate, tag and release.

In any case, she wanted some time in her own territory.

"You should take one of the interns with you," Tansy insisted.

She should, she should. Education and training were essential arms of the refuge. But . . .

"I'll be quicker in and out on my own." Lil checked a radio transmitter, then packed it. "I've waited until late in the season for this. I don't want to dawdle. Everything's under control here," she added. "Plus someone's got to check on the camera up there. It's a good time for me to take a few days, deal with that and maybe get a capture and release."

"And if weather comes in?"

"I'm not going that far, Tansy. We're losing data with that camera out, so it has to be checked. If weather comes in, I'll head back, or wait it out."

She added a second transmitter. She could get lucky.

"I'll have the radio phone." She swung the tranquilizer gun over her shoulder by the strap, hefted her pack.

"You're leaving *now*?"

"Plenty of day left. With luck, I might have a capture tonight or tomorrow, tag it, and be on my way back."

"But—"

"Stop worrying. Now I'm going to go buy a good horse from a former friend. That works out, I'll leave from there. I'll stay in touch."

She hoped the former friend was in town or at the trailhead, dealing with his rental stock, customers, whatever he did with his days. She could horse-trade with Sam or Lucy, and avoid the annoyance of doing business with Coop.

Especially since he'd made it clear he wanted her to mind her own.

And to think she'd made a sincere effort to be friendly, to let bygones be. Well, screw that. If he wanted to be pissy, she'd be pissy right back.

But she wanted a good horse. Annoyance didn't mean taking chances on the trail, and her usual mount was getting too old for this kind of trip.

Odds were, Lil thought as she drove to the neighboring farm, she'd be able to do no more than verify territory and activity on this little trip. She might get a sighting, but an actual capture and tag was a long shot. Worth it though, to add to her proposed ten-year study.

And it would give her the chance to see what, if any, human activity there might be.

When she arrived, she noted the ring and buzz—hammer and saw— from the bunkhouse. She recognized one of the trucks parked by the building as belonging to a local carpenter. Curiosity had her heading in that direction.

A mistake, she realized when Coop stepped out.

Business, she told herself. Just do the business.

"I need to buy a horse."

"Something happen to yours?"

"No. I'm looking for one experienced on the trail. Mine's getting on. I'd be looking for one between five and eight, say. Steady, mature, sound."

"We don't sell horses that aren't sound. Going somewhere?"

She angled her head, spoke coolly. "Do you want to sell me a horse, Cooper?"

"Sure. I figure we both want me to sell you the right horse. Makes a difference if you want one for some pleasure riding on the trail, or one for working."

"I work, so I need a horse who'll work with me. And I want it today."

"You're planning on heading up today?"

"That's right. Look, I'm going to try for a quick trap-and-tag. I need a reliable mount who can handle rough ground and has some nerve."

"Have you spotted any cats near your place?"

"For somebody who wants me to mind my business, you sure are hell-bent on minding mine."

"My horse," he said.

"I haven't seen anything within the sanctuary. We've got a camera out, and I want to check on it. Since I'm doing that, I'm going to set up a live trap and see if I get lucky. I'm planning on two days, three at most. Satisfied?"

"I thought you took a team for tagging."

"If that's the primary goal. I've handled it myself before. I'd like to buy that horse, Cooper, before spring. If it's all the same to you."

"I've got a six-year-old gelding that might suit you. I'll bring him out so you can take a look."

She started to say she'd just go with him, then changed her mind. She'd stay put. Less need for conversation. Less chance she'd give in and ask if she could see what was going on inside the old bunkhouse.

She liked the look of the gelding right off. He was a handsome brown-and-white piebald with a long slash down to his nose. His ears and eyes stayed alert as Coop led him over to the paddock fence.

The sturdy build told her he'd carry her and her gear without trouble.

He didn't shy or sidestep when she checked his legs, his hooves. He jerked his head some when she checked his mouth, his teeth, but didn't try any nip.

"He handles well. Got some spunk so we don't use him unless the rider's experienced. He likes to move." Coop gave the gelding a rub. "He's steady, he just gets bored if he's doing nothing but plodding along in a line of others. Tends to stir up trouble. Likes to be in the lead."

"What are you asking?"

"Since you're buying a horse, you've got your saddle with you. Saddle him up, ride him around some. Take your time. I've got a couple things to see to."

She did just that. The gelding gave her one curious look, as if to say, This isn't usual. Then stood patiently while she saddled him, switched the tack for her own. When she mounted, he did a little shift and quiver in place.

Are we going? Are we?

She clucked her tongue and sent him into a quick, happy trot. She used sounds, her knees and heels, her hands to test him on commands. Well-trained, she concluded, but she'd expected no less from Wilks's stock.

She figured her high end, and the price she'd like to pay, while she worked the gelding through paces and turns.

He'd do, she thought. He'd do just fine.

She slowed to a walk when Coop came back, leading a bay mare already saddled. "Has this one got a name?"

"We call him Rocky. Because he just keeps going."

That got a laugh out of her. "He fits the bill. What are you asking?"

He named a price, right at her high end, then walked toward the house to retrieve a pack he'd set on the porch.

"That's a little steeper than I'm looking for."

"We can dicker on the trail."

"I'll give you . . . what?"

"I'm going with you."

Flustered, she nearly stuttered. "No you're not."

"My horse."

"Listen, Cooper." She cut herself off, took a breath. "Why do you think, mistakenly, you're going with me?"

"My grandparents could use some time without me underfoot. I'm tired of hearing the banging. We're slow right now, so Gull can handle things for a day or two. And I feel like a little camping."

"Then camp somewhere else."

"I'm going with the horse. You'd better get your gear."

She dismounted, looped the reins around the fence. "I'll give you a fair price for him. Then he's my horse."

"You'll give me a fair price when we get back. Consider it a test drive. If you're not happy with him after, no charge for the rental."

"I don't want company."

"I'm not looking to be company. I'm just going with the horse."

She swore, shoved at her hat. The longer this went on, she realized, the more she wanted that damn horse. "Fine. You keep up or I leave you behind. You'd better have your own tent, your own gear, your own food, because I'm not sharing. And keep your hands to yourself, this isn't a ride down memory lane."

"Same goes."

HE DIDN'T KNOW why he was doing it. All the reasons he gave were true enough, but they weren't the why. The simple fact was he didn't particularly want to be with her for an hour, much less a day or two—it was just easier to steer clear.

But he didn't like the idea of her going by herself.

Stupid reason, he admitted as they rode in silence. She could go where she wanted and when. He couldn't stop her if he'd wanted to. And she could have gone without him knowing about it, and if he hadn't known about it he wouldn't have thought about it. And wondered if she was okay.

So when he looked at it that way, it was easier to go than to stay.

In any case, the impulsive trip had some clear advantage. The first was the blessed quiet. He could hear the wind whisper through the trees, and the clomp of hooves on snowy ground, the creak of leather.

For a day or two he wouldn't have to think. About payroll, overhead, grooming, feeding, his grandfather's health, his grandmother's mood.

He could do what he hadn't had the time, and maybe not the inclination, to do since he'd come back to South Dakota.

He could just be.

They rode for a full hour without a word between them before she pulled up and he came up alongside her.

"This is stupid. You're stupid. Go away."

"Have you got a problem breathing the same air as I do?"

"You can breathe all the air you want." She waved a hand in a circle. "There are miles of air. I just don't see the point in this."

"There is no point. We're just going in the same direction."

"You don't know where I'm going."

"You're going up to the grassland where you saw the cougar take down the buffalo calf. The same place, more or less, we found the body."

Her eyes sharpened. "How do you know that?"

"People talk to me whether I want them to or not. They talk to me about *you* whether I want them to or not. That's where you usually go when you go on your own."

She shifted, seemed to struggle. "Have you been back since?"

"Yeah, I've been back."

She clucked to Rocky to get him moving again. "I guess you know they never found whoever did it."

"He might've done others."

"What? What others?"

"Two in Wyoming, one in Idaho. Solo female hikers. The second one two years after Melinda Barrett. Another thirteen months later. The last six months after that."

"How do you know?"

"I was a cop." He shrugged. "I looked into it. Ran like crimes, did some work on it. Blow to the head, stabbing, remote areas. He takes their pack, ID, jewelry. Leaves them for the animals. The others are open and unsolved. Then it stopped, after four killings, it stopped. Which means he's moved on to other types of kill, or he got busted for something else and he's inside. Or he's dead."

"Four," she said. "Four women. There must've been suspects or leads."

"Nothing that panned out, or stuck. I think he's inside, or dead. It's a long stretch without anything that matches his pattern."

"And people don't change that much. Not the basics," she added when he looked at her. "That's what killing is. It's basic. If it's the same killer, it's not because he knows the victim, right? Not especially. It's the type of victim—or prey. Female, alone, in a specific environment. His territory might range, but his prey didn't. When a predator is successful in its hunting, it continues."

She rode in silence for a moment, then went on when he didn't respond. "I thought, or convinced myself, that Melinda Barrett was some sort of accident. Or at least a onetime thing. Someone she knew, or someone who knew her, targeted her."

"You put a marker where we found her."

"It seemed there should be one. There should be something. I tagged a young male up there four years ago. He's moved on to Wyoming. That's where the camera went down a couple days ago. It's infrared, motion. We get a lot of hits. The animal cams, on the refuge and in the field, are popular on the website."

She caught herself. She hadn't meant to get into conversation with him. Not that it was, really. More of a monologue.

"You've sure gotten chatty over the years," she commented.

"You said you didn't want company."

"I didn't. Don't. But you're here."

So he'd make an attempt. "Do the cameras go out often?"

"They require regular maintenance. Weather, wildlife, the occasional hiker play hell with them." She stopped when they reached the stream. Snow lay in drifts and piles, crisscrossed with the tracks of animals who came to hunt or to drink.

"It's not memory lane," she repeated. "Just a good campsite. I'm going to unload before heading up."

It was upriver from the spot where they'd often had picnics. From where they'd first become lovers. He didn't mention it, as she knew it. Lillian Chance knew every foot of this territory as well as other women knew the contents of their closet.

Probably better than most. He unloaded as she did, making quick work of setting up his tent a good five yards from where she set hers.

The deliberate distance might have been the reason for the smirk on her face, but he didn't comment on it.

"So how's it going with the bunkhouse?" she asked when they were riding again. "Or does that fall into the area of none of my business?"

"It's coming along. I should be able to move in there real soon."

"Your valley condo?"

"Everybody gets their space, that's all."

"I know how that is. Before we built the cabin, anytime I'd come home for a stretch I'd start to feel like I was sixteen again. No matter how much room they give you, after a certain age, living with your parents—or grandparents—is just weird."

"What's weird is hearing the bed squeak and knowing your grandparents are having sex."

She choked and snorted laughter. "Oh, jeez. Thanks for that."

"Makeup sex," he added and made her choke again.

"Okay, stop." She looked over, and her quick, full-of-fun smile arrowed straight to his gut.

"You meant it that time."

"What? To stop?"

"The smile. You've been holding back."

"Maybe." She looked away, keeping those dark, seductive eyes straight ahead. "I'd say we don't know what to make of each other these days. It's awkward. Visiting's one thing, and we've hardly been in the same state at the same time since. Now we live in the same place, deal with some of the same people. I'm not used to living and working in close proximity with exes."

"Had many?"

She flicked him the quickest and coolest of glances from under the brim of her hat. "That would come under the heading of mind your own."

"Maybe we should make a list."

"Maybe we should."

They wound through the pines and birch as they had years before. But now the air was bright and bitter cold, and what they thought of was in the past, not in tomorrows.

"Cat's been through."

She pulled up her mount, as she had before. Coop had a flash of déjà vu—Lil in a red T-shirt and jeans, her hair loose under her hat. Her hand reaching out for his as they rode abreast.

This Lil with the long braid and the sheepskin jacket didn't reach for him. Instead she leaned over, studying the ground. But he caught a whiff of her hair, of the wild forest scent of her. "Deer, too. She's hunting."

"You're good, but you can't tell what sex the cat is by the tracks."

"Just playing the odds." All business now, she straightened in the saddle, those eyes keen as they scanned. "Lots of scratches on the trees. It's her area. We caught her on camera a few times before it went down. She's young. I'd say she hasn't had her mating season yet."

"So we're tracking a virgin cougar."

"She's probably about a year." Lil continued on, slowly now. "Subadult, just beginning to venture out without her mother. She lacks experience. I could get lucky with her. She's just what I'm looking for. She might be a descendant of the one I saw all those years ago. Maybe Baby's cousin."

"Baby."

"The cougar at the refuge. I found him and his littermates in this sector. It'd be interesting if their mothers were littermates."

"I'm sure there's family resemblance."

"DNA, Coop, the same as cops use. It's an interest of mine. How they range, cross paths, come together to mate. How the females might be drawn back to their old lairs, birthplaces. It's interesting."

She stopped again, on the verge of the grassland. "Deer, elk, buffalo. It's like a smorgasbord," she said, gesturing at the tracks in the snow. "Which is why I might get lucky."

She swung off the horse and approached a rough wood box. Coop heard her muttering and cursing as he tethered his own horse. "The camera's not broken." She picked a smashed padlock out of the snow. "And it wasn't the weather or the fauna. Some joker." She shoved the broken lock in her pocket and crouched to open the top of the box.

"Playing tricks. Smash the lock, open it up, and turn off the camera."

Coop studied the box, the camera in it. "How much does one of those run?"

"This one? About six hundred. And yeah, I don't know why he didn't take it either. Just screwing around."

Maybe, Coop thought. But it had gotten her up here, and would've gotten her up here alone if he hadn't impulsively come along.

He wandered away as she reset the camera, then called her base on her radio phone.

He couldn't track or read signs with her skill, no point in pretending otherwise. But he could see the boot prints, coming and going. Crossing the grassland, going into the trees on the other side.

From the size of the boot, the length of the stride, he'd estimate the vandal—if that's what he was—at about six feet, with a boot size between ten and twelve. But he'd need more than eyeballing to be sure he was even in the ballpark.

He scanned the flatland, the trees, the brush, the rocks. There was, he knew, a lot of backcountry, some park, some private. A lot of places someone could camp without crossing paths with anyone else.

Cats weren't the only species who stalked and ambushed.

"Camera's back up." She studied the tracks as Cooper had. "He's at home up here," she commented, then turned to walk to a weathered green tarp staked to the ground. "I hope he didn't mess with the cage."

She unhooked the tarp, flung it back. The cage was intact, but for the door she'd packed on the horse. "We remove the door, just in case somebody tries to use it, or an animal's curious enough to get in, then can't get out. I leave one up here because I've had luck in this section. Easier than hauling the cage up every time. Not much human traffic up here through the winter."

She jerked her chin. "He came from the same direction we did, on foot, at least for the last half mile."

"I got that much myself. From behind the camera."

"I guess he's shy. Since you're here, you might as well help me set this up."

He hauled the cage while she retrieved the door. On the edge of the grassland he watched her attach it with quick, practiced efficiency. She checked the trap several times, then baited it with bloody hunks of beef.

She noted the time, nodded. "A little more than two hours before dusk. If she's hunting here, the bait should bring her in."

She washed the blood off her hands with snow, put her gloves on. "We can watch from camp."

"Can we?"

She grinned. "I have the technology."

They started back toward the campsite, but she veered off—as he'd suspected she would—to follow the human trail.

"He's crossing into the park," she said. "If he keeps going in this direction, he's going to hit the trailhead. Alone and on foot."

"We can follow it in, but eventually you're going to lose the origin in other traffic."

"No point anyway. He didn't go back this way. He went on. Probably one of those survivalist types, or extreme hikers. Search and Rescue's pulled two small groups out this winter. Dad told me. People think they know what it is—the wilderness, the winter. But they don't. Most just don't. He does, I think. Even stride, steady pace. He knows."

"You should report the camera."

"For what? Officer, somebody broke my ten-dollar padlock and turned off my camera. Organize a posse."

"It doesn't hurt to have it on record."

"You've been away too long. By the time I get back home, my staff would've told the delivery guy and the volunteers, who'll mention it to their boss, neighbor, coworker, and so on. It's already on record. South Dakota–style."

But she turned in the saddle, looked back the way they'd come.

Back at camp she unpacked a small laptop, sat on her pop-up stool, and set to work. Coop stayed in his area, turned on his camp stove, and made coffee. He'd forgotten the small pleasure of that, of brewing a pot of coffee over a camp stove, the extra kick from the taste of it. He sat enjoying it, watching while the water in the stream fought and shoved its way over rocks and ice.

From Lil's neighborhood it was business, as far as he could tell. She spoke on the radio phone, working with someone on coordinates and data.

"If you share that coffee so I don't have to make some right this minute, I'll share my beef stew." She glanced over his way. "It's not from a can. It's my mother's."

He sipped his coffee, glanced her way, and said nothing.

"I know what I said, but it's stupid. Plus, I'm finished being annoyed with you. For now."

She set the laptop on the stool after she rose, and went to her saddlebags for the sealed bag of stew. "It's a good trade."

He couldn't argue with that. In any case, he wanted to see what she was doing on the computer. He poured a second cup of coffee, doctored it as he remembered she liked it, then walked it over to her campsite.

They drank coffee standing on the snowy banks of the stream.

"The computer's linked with the camera. I'll get a signal and a picture when and if it activates."

"Fancy."

"Lucius rigged it. He's our resident nerd genius. He can get a message to your grandparents if you want to check on them. But I told him to call them, or have Tansy call, and let them know we're camped. Weather's holding, so we should be good."

She turned her head. Their eyes met, held. Something knocked hard and loud in his heart before she turned away. "It's good coffee," she said. "I'm going to settle my horse, then I'll heat up that stew."

She walked away and left him by the stream.

SHE DIDN'T WANT to feel this way. It annoyed her, frustrated her that she couldn't just block what she didn't want, just refuse it.

What was it about him? That hint of sad and mad, still there, still under the surface of him, just pulled at her.

Her feelings, she reminded herself. Her problem.

Was this how Jean-Paul felt? she wondered. Wanting, needing, and never quite getting the real thing in return? She should have every square inch of her ass kicked for making anyone else feel this helpless.

Maybe knowing she was still in love with Cooper Sullivan was her ass-kicking. God knew, it was painful.

A pity she didn't have Jean-Paul's option to go, just leave. Her life was here, roots, work, heart. So she'd just have to deal with it.

With her horse fed and watered, she heated the stew.

Dusk floated down as she carried the plate over to him.

"Should be hot enough. I've got work, so . . . ."

"Fine. Thanks." He took the plate, went back to reading his book by the dying light and the glow of his stove.

In the twilight, mule deer came to drink downstream. Lil could see their movements and shadows, hear the rustles and hoof strikes. She glanced at the computer, but there was no movement—yet—on the grassland.

When the moon rose, she took the computer and her lantern into her tent. Alone—she felt more alone with Coop there than she would have by herself—she listened to the night, to the wild. With the night music came the call of the hunter, the scream of the hunted. She heard her horse blow, whinny lightly to Coop's.

The air was full of sound, she thought. But the two humans in it exchanged not a single word.

SHE AWOKE JUST before dawn, sure the computer had signaled. But a glance showed her only a blank screen. She sat up slowly, ears tuned. There was movement outside the tent, stealthy and human. In the dark, Lil visualized her drug gun and her rifle. She made the decision, and reached out to take the drug gun.

She opened her tent slowly, scanned through the opening. Even in the dark, she recognized the shadow as Cooper. Still, she kept the gun as she slid out of the tent.

"What is it?"

He held up a hand to silence her, used it to gesture her back into her tent. Ignoring that, she moved toward him.

"What?" she said again.

"Somebody was out here. That direction."

"Could've been an animal."

"It wasn't. He must've heard me inside the tent, opening it. He took off, and fast. What the hell is that for?"

She glanced down at the tranquilizer gun. "For immunizing. Including humans, if necessary. I heard you out here, but I couldn't be sure it was you."

"Could've been an animal."

She hissed out a breath. "Okay, yes, you probably know the difference as well as I do. What the hell is that for?" she demanded, pointing at the 9mm in his hand.

"For immunizing."

"Jesus, Cooper."

Rather than respond, he went back to his tent, came out with a flashlight. He handed it to her. "Read the tracks."

She shone the light on the snow. "Okay, that's you, likely moving off from the campsite to empty your bladder."

"You'd be right about that."

"And that's another set of tracks, coming from across the stream, cutting this way. Walking. Heading north, that's at a run, or at least a good lope." She huffed out a breath. "Poacher, maybe. Somebody looking to set up a hunting stand, spotted the campsite. But hell, the tracks look like the ones up by the cage. Could still be a poacher. Just one who likes to screw around."

"Maybe."

"You probably still think like a cop, or a PI, so everyone's a suspect. And you're probably thinking I'd have had trouble if you weren't here."

"Wow, now you're a mind reader."

"I know how it goes. Believe me, you wouldn't be thrilled to take a hit with one of these tranqs. And believe me, I can handle myself. I've been handling myself for a long time." She paused just long enough to make sure that sank in. "But I appreciate the advantage of numbers. I'm not a fool."

"Then you're asking yourself how he moved so fast, and straight for the trail, in the dark. Moon's set. It's getting lighter now, but it was pitch."

"His eyes adjusted or he has infrared. Probably the latter if he's scouting a hunting site in the dark. He knows what he's doing. I'll report it, but—"

She broke off at the beep inside her tent. Forgetting everything else, she dashed back, dived inside. "There she is! Son of a bitch. You must be my good-luck charm. I didn't expect to get a look, not really. There's that beauty," she murmured as she watched the young cougar scenting the air at the far end of the grassland. "Coop, come see this. Come on."

She shifted to give him an angle on the screen when he eased in. "She's got the scent of the bait. Stalking, keeping to the shadows and the brush. Secretive. She can see in the dark, keen eyes. The cage is an unknown, but inside it? That scent. God, she's beautiful. Look at her."

She seemed to swim across the snow, bellying down.

Then she was up, and Lil caught her breath at the flash of speed, the *power*. Leap, bound, streak. Even as the trap sprang, the cat had the bait in her jaws.

"We got her. We got her!" On a triumphant laugh, Lil grabbed Coop's arm. "Did you see how—"

She turned her head. Her mouth nearly collided with his in the close confines of the tent. She felt the heat from him, saw the glint of his eyes, those ice blue eyes. For an instant, just an instant, the memory of him, of them, flooded her.

Then she moved back, out of the danger zone. "I need to get my gear. It's nearly dawn. It'll be light enough to see the trail soon."

She picked up the radio phone. "You'll have to excuse me. I need to make a call."

9

Since she had more to pack up and deal with than he did, Coop fried up some bacon, made coffee. By the time she'd made her calls, gotten her gear, he'd put a trail breakfast together and set his campsite to rights. He was saddling his horse when she came over to saddle her own.

"What are you going to do with her?"

"Immobilize. With the drug gun I brought, I can get within two feet of her, inject a dart into her without hurting her. I'll take blood and hair samples, gauge her weight, age, size, and so on. Fit her with a radio collar. Thanks," she added, obviously distracted when he handed her a mug of coffee. "I plan on giving her a small dose, but it'll keep her out a couple of hours, so I'll have to stand by until she comes out of it, recovers. Until she's recovered fully from the drug, she's vulnerable. It's a good day's work, but if things go well, by noon she'll be on her way, and I'll have what I came for."

"And what does all that give you?"

"You mean besides satisfaction?" As the sun pinked the rims of the eastern hills, she swung into the saddle. "Information. The cougar's listed as a near-threatened species. Most people, I'm talking people who live and travel in known cougar territories, never see one."

"Most people wouldn't be you." He mounted, offered her one of the bacon biscuits he'd put together.

"No, they wouldn't." She looked at the biscuit, then at him. "You made breakfast. Now I feel guilty about bitching about you coming along."

"That's a nice side benefit."

"Anyway"—she took a bite as they turned the horses toward the trail—"most of the sightings reported turn out to be bobcat, or the occasional pet. People buy exotic cats—and we get calls every month from someone who did, and doesn't know what the hell to do now that Fuzzy isn't a cute little kitten anymore." She took another bite. "But mostly, people see a bobcat and think—holy shit, cougar. And even on the rare occasion it is holy shit, cougar, most people don't understand it isn't looking for man meat."

"There was a woman right in Deadwood a year or so ago who almost had one join her in her hot tub."

"Yeah, that was cool." Lil polished off the biscuit. "The point that might be missed is it wasn't interested in her—didn't attack. It was stalking deer and ended up on her back deck at the same time she was having her soak. It took a look at her, probably thought, Not dinner—went away. We encroach, Coop, and you don't want to get me started on my conservation riff, believe me. But we do. So we have to learn how to live with them, protect the species. They don't want to be around us. They don't want to be around one another unless it's time to mate. They're solitary, and while they interact with others higher on the apex in some habitats, we're their only predator once they reach maturity."

"Might make me think twice about putting in a hot tub."

She laughed. "One's unlikely to join you. They can swim, but they don't much care for it. The girl up there's wondering how the hell she got trapped? She's got about another eight, nine years if she hits the average life span for a female in the wild. She'll mate every couple of years, have a litter, again on average of three. Two of those three will likely die before their first year. She'll feed them, defend them to the death, teach them to hunt. She'll love them until it's time to let them go. She might range a hundred and fifty square miles of territory during her life span."

"And you'll track that with the radio collar."

"Where she goes, and when, how she gets there, how long it takes. When she mates. I'm doing a generational study. I've already tagged two generations through Baby's littermate and a subadult male I captured and tagged last year in the canyon. I'll start another with this one."

They moved into an easy trot when the trail allowed. "Don't you already know everything there is to know about cougars by this point?"

"You never know it all. Biology and behavior, ecological role, distribution and habitat, even mythology. It adds to the wealth, and the more there is, the better we know how to preserve the species. Plus, funding. Contributors like to see and hear and know cool stuff. I give the new girl up there a name, put a shot of her on the Web page, and add her to the Track-A-Cat section. Funding. And by exploiting her, in a sense, I add to the coffers going to protect, study, and understand her and her kind. Plus, I want to know."

She looked his way. "And tell the truth, it's a great way to start the morning."

"I've had worse."

"Fresh air, a good horse under you, miles of what people pay good money for in art books, and an interesting job to do. It's a good deal." She cocked her head. "Even for an urbanite."

"The city's not better or worse. It's just different."

"Do you miss it? Your work there?"

"I'm doing what I want. Just like you."

"It counts. Being able to do what you want. You're good at it. The horses," she added. "You always were." She leaned over to stroke her gelding's neck. "We're still going to dicker over the price for this one, but you were right. Rocky suits me."

She frowned, slowed. "There's our friend again." She gestured at the tracks. "He cut across, picked up the trail here. Long strides. Not running but moving fast. What the hell is he up to?" Something tripped in her heart. "He's heading toward the grassland. Toward the cougar."

Even as she spoke, the scream ripped and echoed. "He's there. He's up there." She pushed the horse into a gallop.

The scream echoed again, full of fury. And the third, high and sharp, cut off with the snapping report of a gunshot.

"No!" She rode half blind, dragging at the reins to steer around trees, clinging, pushing as her mount raced through the snowpack.

She slapped out at Coop when he pulled up alongside and grabbed her reins. "Let go. Get off! He shot her. He shot her."

"If he did you can't change it." Shortening Rocky's reins, he kept his voice low to calm the horses. "There's somebody up there, armed. You're not rushing up, risking breaking that horse's leg and your neck in the bargain. Stop. Think."

"He's already got a good fifteen, twenty minutes on us. She's trapped. I have to—"

"Stop. Think. Use your phone. Call this in."

"If you think I'm just going to sit here while—"

"You're going to call it in." His voice was as cold and flat as his eyes. "And we're going to follow the tracks. We're going to take it one step at a time. Call your people, see if the camera's still up. Have them report the gunshot. Then you're going to stay behind me, because I'm the one with a real gun. That's it. Do it now."

She might have argued with the tone, she might have argued with the orders. But he was right about the camera. She pulled her phone out while Coop took the lead. "I've got a rifle if I need it," she told him.

She reached a sleepy-voiced Tansy. "Hey, Lil. Where—"

"Check the camera. Number eleven. The one I fixed yesterday. Check it now."

"Sure. I've been watching since you called. I went out to check on the animals, brought Eric back with me so. . . . Hell, it's down again. Are—"

"Listen to me. Cooper and I are about twenty minutes from the site. Somebody's up there, been up there. There was a shot."

"Oh, my God. You don't think—"

"I need you to put the police and game warden on alert. We'll know in about twenty minutes. Get Matt on call. If she's wounded I'll get her in. We may need an airlift for that."

"I'll take care of it. Stay in contact, Lil, and be careful." The line clicked dead before Lil could respond.

"We can move faster than this," Lil insisted.

"Yeah, and we can move right into the crosshairs. It's not how I want to spend my morning. We don't know who's up there, or what he has in mind. What we know is he has a weapon, and he's had time to run, or find cover and lie in wait."

Or he could have doubled back, Coop thought, and even now could be setting himself up for some human target practice. He couldn't be sure, so he couldn't follow the urge to *immobilize* Lil and tie her to a damn tree while he went on without her.

"We'd better go on foot from here." He turned his head, met her eyes. "It'll be quieter, and we make smaller targets. Take your knife, the drug gun, the phone. Anything happens, you run. You know the territory better than anyone else. Get lost, call for help, and stay lost until it comes. Clear?"

"This isn't New York. You're not a cop anymore."

His gaze was frigid. "And this isn't a bag-and-tag anymore either. How much time do you want to waste arguing with somebody who's bigger than you are?"

She dismounted because he was right, and loaded a small pack with what she felt she needed. She kept the tranquilizer gun in her hand.

"Behind me," he ordered. "Single file."

He moved quickly, covering ground. She kept pace as he knew she would. Then he stopped, pulled out his field glasses, and using the brush for cover, scanned the grassland up ahead.

"Can you see the cage?"

"Hold on."

He could see trampled snow, the line of trees, the jut of boulders. Countless opportunities for cover.

He scanned over. The angle was poor, but he could see part of the cage, part of the cat. And the blood on the snow.

"I can't get a good look from here. But she's down."

Lil closed her eyes for a moment. Even so, he watched grief rush over her face. "We'll cut over, come up behind the cage. It's better cover."

"Okay."

It took longer, and the way was a battle with incline, knee-deep snow, rough and slippery ground.

She shoved through brush, accepted Coop's hand for a boost when she needed it.

And on the bright, crisp air, she scented blood. She scented death.

"I'm going out to her." Lil's voice held calm and nothing else. "He'd have heard us coming if he stuck around. He'd have had time to circle around, take cover, and pick us off if that's what he wanted. He shot a trapped animal. He's a coward. He's gone."

"Can you help her?"

"I doubt it, but I'm going out to her. He could've shot you last night, the minute you stepped out of the tent."

"I go first. Nonnegotiable."

"I don't care. Go on, then. I need to get to her."

Stupid, he told himself. A risk that solved nothing. But he thought of helping Lil set up the cage, how he'd watched with her as the trap sprang.

He couldn't leave the cat there.

"Maybe you should fire a couple of rounds, so he knows we're armed, too."

"He might take that as a challenge." He glanced back at her. "You're thinking it's easier to kill a trapped animal, or an animal anyway, than it is a human being. It's a mistake to think that. It depends on who's doing the shooting. Stay back, and stay down until I tell you."

He stepped into the open.

For a moment his skin was alive, his muscles tight and tensed. He'd been shot once, and it wasn't an experience he wanted to repeat.

Overhead a hawk circled and cried. He watched the trees. A movement brought his weapon up. The mule deer waded through the snow, leading the way for the herd that came behind.

He turned and walked to the cage.

He hadn't expected her to stay once he moved, and of course, she didn't. She stepped around him, knelt on the frozen ground.

"Would you turn the camera on? If he didn't wreck it, that is. We need to document this."

In the cage, the cat lay on her side. Blood and gore from the heat of the shot soiled the ground. She buried the urge to open the cage, to stroke, to mourn, to weep. Instead, she contacted her base.

"Tansy, we're bringing the camera back up. The female's been shot. A head wound. She's gone."

"Oh, Lil."

"Make the calls, and make a copy of the video. We need the authorities here, and transportation to get her out."

"I'll take care of it right now. I'm so sorry, Lil."

"Yeah. Me too."

She clicked off, looked over at Coop. "The camera?"

"Just turned off, like before."

"There's a short, restricted hunting season on cougar. We're outside that now. And this is private land, posted land. He had no right."

Though her voice remained steady, firm, she'd gone very pale, so her eyes shone like black pools.

"Even if she hadn't been caged, defenseless, he had no right. I understand hunting. For food, as a sport, the arguments for ecological balance as we take over more and more habitat areas. But this wasn't hunting. This was murder. He shot a caged animal. And I put her in the cage. I put her there."

"You're not stupid enough to blame yourself."

"No." Those eyes kindled now with pure rage. "The bastard who walked up to the cage and put a bullet in her head's to blame. But I'm a factor. I'm the reason he could."

She sat back on her haunches, took a breath. "It looks like he came up the trail, crossed to the camera, disabled it. He circled the cage, took a look at her, stirred her up. She gave her warning call. He kept her stirred up. Maybe it was more exciting that way, who knows. Then he shot her. Fairly close range, I'd guess. But I don't know for sure. Can't tell. We'll do an autopsy, recover the bullet. The police will take it and tell us what kind of gun he used."

"A handgun from the sound of it. Small-caliber from the look of the wound."

"You'd know more about that, I suppose."

She did what she needed to do now, and he said nothing about the integrity of a crime scene when she opened the cage. She laid her hand on the ruined head of the young female who by her estimation had lived only one full year. Who'd learned to hunt and ranged free. Who kept to her secret places and avoided company.

She stroked. And when her shoulders began to tremble she rose to walk out of camera range. Because he had nothing else to offer, Coop went to her, turned her, held her while she wept. And wept.

She was dry-eyed and professional when the authorities arrived. He knew the county sheriff slightly, but imagined Lil had known him most of her life.

He'd be in his early thirties, Coop judged. Tough-bodied, tough-faced, sturdy in his Wolverines as he assessed. His name was William Johannsen, but like most who knew him, Lil called him Willy.

While he spoke to Lil, Coop watched a deputy take pictures of the scene, the cage, the tracks. He saw, too, Willy lay a hand on Lil's shoulder, give it a pat before he stepped away and headed in Coop's direction.

"Mr. Sullivan." Willy paused, stood beside Coop and looked at the dead cat. "That's a terrible, cowardly thing. You hunt?"

"No. Never got the taste for it."

"I get a buck every season. I like being outdoors, pitting myself against their instincts. My wife makes a good venison stew. Never hunted cougar. My pa, he's a hunt-it-eat-it man, and taught me the same. Don't fancy chowing down on cougar. Well, cold out here. Got some wind going. Lil says you've got horses standing down yonder."

"Yeah. I'd like to get to them."

"I'll walk you down a ways. Said she called her pa, and he's on his way to meet you back where the two of you camped last night. Help you load up."

"She needs to go with the cougar."

"Yeah." Willy nodded. "I'll walk down some with you and you can tell me what's what. I need more, I'll get it from you later on, after you've had a chance to get back. Warmed up."

"All right. Give me a minute."

Without waiting for assent, Coop went back to Lil. Unlike Willy, he didn't give her a comforting pat. Her eyes were dry when they met his. Dry, and a little distant. "I'll get the horses, meet Joe back at the campsite. We'll get your gear to you."

"I'm grateful, Coop. I don't know what I'd've done if you hadn't been along."

"Handled it. I'll be by later."

"You don't need to—"

"I'll be by later."

With that, he walked away, and Willy fell into step with him.

"So you were with the police back east."

"I was."

"Went into private, I hear."

"I did."

"I recall when you used to come out as a boy, visit with your grandfolks. Good people."

"They are."

Willy's lips twitched, and his stride was steady on the trail. "I heard how Gull Nodock, who works for you now, gave you a chaw one day and you about puked yourself inside out."

The faintest hint of humor touched Coop's mouth. "Gull never gets tired of telling that one."

"It's a good one. Why don't you just give me the run-down, Mr. Sullivan. You don't need me telling you what I need to know, seeing as you were police."

"Cooper, or Coop. Lil and I started out yesterday morning. Around eight, maybe just after eight. We unloaded some of the gear at the campsite, by the stream, and got up here before eleven. Close to eleven, I think."

"Good time."

"Good horses, and she knows the trail. She's got that camera up there. Somebody broke the lock on its cover, switched it off. She said it went down a couple days ago. She reset it. We saw the tracks left by whoever did it. Looks like around a size eleven to me."

Willy nodded, adjusted his Stetson. "We'll be checking on that."

"We set up the cage, and baited it, and we were back at camp before two. She worked, I read, we had a meal, turned in. Five-twenty this morning, I heard somebody moving around. I got my gun. He was already running when I got out of the tent. I heard him more than saw him, but I got a glimpse. I'd guess about six feet tall, male. Most likely male just from the way he moved, the basic shape. He had on a backpack, and a cap. Gimmecap style. Couldn't tell you age, race, hair color. I just got the shape, the movement as he ran, then he was in the trees. He moved fast."

"Black as ink that time of day."

"Yeah. Maybe he had infrared goggles. I only saw him from behind, but he moved like a fucking gazelle. Fast, fluid. Between the two of us, Lil woke up. Not long after, she got the signal the trap had sprung. It took us a good thirty minutes, maybe closer to forty to pack up, for her to contact her base. And we spent some time looking at the cat on her computer. He had a good lead on us. Neither one of us considered he'd head up there, do that."

"Why would you?"

They'd reached the horses, and Willy gave Coop's mare a friendly rub.

"We had light by then, but we didn't hurry. Then she spotted the tracks. We were about halfway between the camp and the cage, and she spotted them."

"Got an eye for it, Lil does," Willy commented in his mild way.

"He'd circled around, crossed back to the trail, and headed up. We heard the cat scream, the way they do."

"Hell of a sound."

"Third time it screamed, we heard the shot." He detailed the rest, adding the times.

"There's no exit wound," Coop added. "It's going to be small-caliber. Compact handgun, maybe a thirty-eight. The kind somebody could carry easily under his jacket. Wouldn't weigh him down on a hike, wouldn't show if he ran into anybody on the trail. Just another guy out loving nature."

"We take something like this serious around here. You can count on that. I'm going to let you get on. If I need to talk to you again, I know where to find you. You keep an eye out on the way down, Coop."

"You can count on that." Coop mounted, took the reins of Lil's horse from Willy.

The trip back alone gave him time to think.

It was no coincidence that the camera had been tampered with, an intruder had chosen their campsite, the cougar Lil had trapped had been shot.

Common denominator? Lillian Chance.

She needed to have that spelled out for her, and she needed to take whatever precautions she could.

She assumed it was easier for a man to kill a caged animal than a human.

Coop didn't agree.

He didn't know William Johannsen well, and prior to now hadn't had any professional dealings with him. But his impression had been one of competence and a cool head. He expected the man would do all that could and should be done in the investigation.

And Coop figured unless Willy was really lucky, he'd get nowhere.

Whoever had killed Lil's cougar knew exactly what he was doing and exactly how to do it. The question was why.

Someone with a grudge against Lil personally, or with a vendetta against the refuge? Maybe both, as Lil was the refuge in most people's minds. An extremist on either side of the environmental/conservation issue was a possibility.

Someone who knew the area, knew how to live in the wild for stretches, go unnoticed. A local maybe, Coop mused, or someone with local ties.

Maybe he'd tug on a few old connections and see if there'd been any similar incidents in the last few years. Or, he admitted, he could just ask Lil. No doubt she'd know or could find out faster than he could.

Of course that blew to hell the idea of keeping his distance. He'd already blown that, he admitted, when he'd jumped on going with her on this trip. So who was he kidding?

He wasn't going to stay away from her. He'd known that, however much he'd tried to deny it, the minute she'd opened the door to that cabin. The instant he'd seen her again.

Maybe it was just unfinished business. He wasn't one for leaving things unresolved. Lil was . . . a loose end, he decided. If he couldn't cut it off, he had to tie it off. Screw the guy she wasn't exactly engaged to.

There was still something there. He'd felt it from her. He'd seen it in her eyes. However long it had been since he'd seen her, been with her, he knew her eyes.

He dreamed of them.

He knew what he'd seen in them that morning in her tent, while on the computer screen the young cougar hissed in the cage. If he'd touched her then, he'd have taken her then. As simple as that.

They weren't going to get through this new phase of their lives, what-ever the hell it was, until they'd gotten past the old feelings, the old connection, the old needs. Maybe once they had, they could be friends again. Maybe they couldn't. But standing in place wasn't going to cut it.

And she was in trouble. She might not believe it, or admit it, but somebody meant to hurt her. Whatever they were to each other, whatever they weren't, he wasn't going to let that happen.

As the camp came into view, Coop slowed. He flicked back his coat and rested a hand on the butt of his gun.

Long precise slashes ran down the length of both tents. Bedrolls lay sodden in the icy stream, along with the cookstove he'd used that morning to fry bacon, make coffee. The shirt Lil had worn the day before lay spread out on the snow. Coop would've made book that the blood that smeared it had come from the cougar.

He dismounted, tethered the horses, then opened Lil's saddlebag to find the camera he'd seen her put in that morning.

He documented the scene from various angles, took close-ups of the shirt, the tents, the items in the stream, the boot prints that weren't his, weren't Lil's.

Best he could do, he thought before digging out a plastic bag that would stand for an evidence bag. With his gloves on, he bagged Lil's shirt, sealed the bag, and wished only for a pen or marker to note down the time, date, and his initials.

He heard the approach of a horse, thought of Joe. Coop stowed the shirt in his own saddlebag, laid a hand back on his weapon. He let it drop when the horse and rider came into view.

"She's fine." Coop called it out first. "She's with the county sheriff. She's fine, Joe."

"Okay." Still mounted, Joe surveyed the campsite. "You two didn't have a drunken party and do this."

"He had to come back, double around again while we were up above. It's quick work. Down and dirty. Probably took him ten minutes tops."

"Why?"

"Well, that's a question."

"It's one I'm asking you, Cooper." Joe slid off the saddle, held the reins in a hand Coop imagined was white at the knuckles under his riding gloves. "I'm not an idealist. I know people do fuck-all. But I don't understand this. You'd have a better idea on it. You'd have thought about it."

Lies often served a purpose, Coop knew. But he wouldn't lie to Joe. "Somebody's got it in for Lil, but I don't have the answers. You'd have a better idea, or she would. I haven't been part of her life for a long time. I don't know what's going on with her, not under the surface."

"But you'll find out."

"The police are on this, Joe. Willy strikes me as somebody who gets things done. I took pictures of all this, and I'll turn them over." He thought of the bloodstained shirt, but kept that to himself. A father, already scared, already sick with worry, didn't need more.

"Willy will do his job, and he'll do his best. But he's not going to be thinking about this, and about Lil, every minute of the day. I'm asking you, Coop. I'm asking you to help me. To help Lil. To look out for her."

"I'll talk to her. I'll do what I can."

Satisfied, Joe nodded. "I guess we'd better clean this up."

"No. We'll call it in, and leave it. He probably didn't leave anything behind, but we'll leave it for the cops to go through."

"You'd know best." On a shaky breath, Joe pulled off his hat, ran a gloved hand through his hair once, twice. "Jesus, Cooper. Jesus. I'm worried about my girl."

So am I, Coop thought. So am I.

10

Lil shut down her emotions to assist Matt in the autopsy. One of the deputies stood by, going clammy green during the procedure. Under other circumstances, the poor man's reaction would have amused her a little.

But the blood on her hands was partially her fault. No one would ever be able to convince her otherwise.

Still, the scientist in her collected blood and hair samples from the dead as she'd planned to from the living. She'd analyze, and have the data for her files, for her papers, for the program.

When the vet removed the bullet, she held out the stainless-steel dish. It rang, almost cheerfully, when Matt dropped it in. The deputy bagged it, sealed it, logged it in their presence.

"Looks like a thirty-two," he said, and swallowed. "I'm going to see that this gets to Sheriff Johannsen. Ah, you verify this as cause of death, right, Dr. Wainwright?"

"A bullet in the brain usually is. No other injuries or insults. I'm going to open her up, complete the exam. But you're holding what killed this animal."

"Yes, sir."

"We'll send a full report to the sheriff's office," Lil told him. "All the documentation."

"I'll go on, then." He bolted.

Matt exchanged forceps for scalpel. "Given her weight, height, her teeth, I'd put the age of this female between twelve and fifteen months." He looked to Lil for confirmation.

"Yes. She's not pregnant—though you'll verify—nor does she show signs of having given birth recently. It's unlikely she mated this fall, being too young at that time to come into season. All visual indications are she was in good health."

"Lil, you don't have to do this, you don't have to be in here for this."

"Yes I do." She made herself cold, and watched Matt make the first precise line of the Y cut.

When it was done, all the data recorded, all the conclusions made, her eyes were gritty, her throat raw. Stress and grief made an uneasy marriage in her stomach. She washed her hands thoroughly, repeatedly, before going into the office.

The minute he saw her, Lucius's eyes filled.

"I'm sorry. I can't seem to pull it together."

"It's all right. It's a hard day."

"I didn't know if you'd want me to put anything up on the site. Any sort of statement or . . ."

"I don't know." She rubbed her hands over her face. Her mind simply hadn't gone there. "Maybe we should. Yes, maybe we should. She was murdered. People should know about her, what happened to her."

"I can write something up for you to look over."

"Yeah, do that, Lucius."

Mary Blunt, sturdy of body, sensible of mind, rose from her desk to pour hot water into a mug. "It's tea. Drink it," she ordered, and she pushed it into Lil's hand. "Then go home for a while. There's nothing you have to do. It's nearly closing time. Why don't I come over, fix you something to eat?"

"Couldn't right now, Mary, but thanks. Matt's doing the paperwork, putting the file together. Can you take it to Willy on your way home?"

"Sure I can." Mary, hazel eyes full of concern over the silver rims of her cheaters, gave Lil a brief one-armed hug. "They'll find that motherless coward, Lil. Don't you worry."

"I'm counting on it." She drank the tea because it was there, and because Mary was watching to see that she did.

"We've got that Boy Scout field trip coming in next week. I can reschedule if you want more time."

"No, let's try to keep it business as usual."

"All right, then. I did some grant research, and put some possibilities together. You can look them over, see if you want me to take any of them further."

"All right."

"Tomorrow," Mary said firmly, and took the empty mug. "Now, go home. We'll close up."

"I'm going to check on everybody first."

"Tansy and the interns, some volunteers saw to the feedings."

"I'll just . . . check. Go on home." She glanced over at Lucius to include him. "As soon as Matt's finished, close up and go home."

When she stepped outside, she saw Farley coming from the direction of the stables. He raised a hand in salute. "I brought your new horse, and your gear. Gave her a good rubdown, some extra grain."

"Farley, you're a godsend."

"You'd do the same." He stopped in front of her, gave her arm a little pat and rub. "Hell of a thing, Lil."

"Yes, it is."

"Anything need doing?" He squinted into the gathering twilight. "Your dad said I should stay as long as you need. He thought maybe I should bunk down here for the night."

"You don't need to do that, Farley."

"Well, I'd say it was more he said I'd be bunking down here for the night rather than I should." Farley gave her his appealingly goofy grin. "I'll use the cot back in the stables."

"There's a better one in the offices. Use that. I'll talk to your boss, but we'll let this ride tonight."

"He'll sleep better."

"That's why we're letting it ride. The fact is, I'll probably sleep better, too, knowing you're close by. I'll make you some supper."

"No need. Your ma packed me plenty. Wouldn't hurt to give them a call." He shifted in his worn-at-the-heels boots. "Just saying."

"I will."

"Ah, is Tansy inside?"

"No. She must be out here somewhere." The little light in his eye made her want to sigh again. It was so damn sweet. "Maybe you could take a look around for her, tell her we're going to close a little early. If the animals have been checked, she can go on home."

"I'll do that. You take it easy, now, Lil. If you need anything tonight, you just give me a holler."

"I will."

She turned toward the small-cat area. She stopped by each habitat to help remind herself why she was doing this, what she hoped to do. Most of the animals they sheltered, they studied, would be dead otherwise. Euthanized or disposed of by owners, killed in the wild they were too old or handicapped to survive. They had a life here, protection, and as much freedom as could be allowed. They served to educate, to fascinate, to draw funds to help maintain the whole.

It mattered. Intellectually she knew it mattered. But her heart was so sore it wasn't the intellect that needed reinforcement.

Baby waited for her, the engine purr in his throat. She crouched, leaning her head against the cage so he could bump his to it in greeting.

She looked beyond him to where the two other cougars they'd taken in tore into their evening meal. Only Baby would leave his favorite chicken dinner for her.

And in his brilliant eyes, she took comfort.

IT TOOK FARLEY a while to find her, but his heart gave a few extra beats when he did. Tansy sat on one of the benches—and for once she was alone, watching the big old tiger (imagine a tiger living right in the valley!) wash his face.

Just like a house cat would, Farley thought, licking at his paws, rubbing them on his face.

He wanted to think of something clever to say, something smart and funny. He didn't think he was clever when it came to words mostwise anyhow. And he got his tongue tangled and stuck when he was within speaking distance of Tansy Spurge.

She was about the prettiest thing he'd ever seen, and he wanted her for his own so bad it hurt in the belly.

He knew all that dark, curly hair of hers was soft, and kinda springy to the touch. He'd managed to get his hands on it once. He knew the skin of her hands was smooth and soft, but he wondered if her face would be the same. That pretty, golden brown face. He hadn't had the nerve to try to touch that yet.

But he was working up to it.

She was smarter than he was, no question. He'd finished high school because Joe and Jenna laid that down as law. But Tansy had all kinds of education on him and those fancy college degrees. He liked that about her, too, how the smart of her showed in her eyes. The goodness in them right there with it.

He'd seen how she was with animals. Gentle. Farley didn't hold with causing an animal harm.

And with all that, she was so damn sexy his blood started humming in his head—and other places—whenever he got within ten feet of her.

Like right now.

He squared his shoulders, wished he wasn't so damned skinny.

"He sure keeps himself clean and tidy, doesn't he?" While he was building up the gumption to sit beside her, Farley stopped by the cage to watch the old boy wash.

He'd touched Boris once, too, when Tansy'd had him under to help Matt clean what was left of his teeth. It sure was a *big* experience, letting your hands walk right over a jungle cat.

"He's feeling good today. Had a good appetite. I worried if he'd last the winter, sweet old thing, when he had that kidney infection. But he just keeps going."

The words were easy, casual-like, but he knew—had made a study on—her tones. He heard the tears before he saw them.

"Ah, now."

"Sorry." She waved a hand. "We're all having a rough day. I was mad, just mad, for most of it. Then I sat down here, and . . ." She shrugged, waved again.

He didn't need gumption to sit beside her. He'd only needed the tears. "I had a dog run over about five years ago. Hadn't had him long either. Just a few months. I cried like a baby right on the side of the road."

He put his arm around her shoulders and just sat with her, watching the tiger.

"I didn't want to see Lil again until I settled down. She doesn't need me crying on her shoulder."

"Mine's right here."

Though he'd offered, sincerely, in the spirit of friendship, his heart took that extra beat again when she tipped her head to his shoulder.

"I saw Lil." He spoke quickly now before his mind went blank with the thrill. "She said to tell you she's closing a little early, sending every-body on."

"She shouldn't be alone."

"I'm staying tonight. I'll bunk in the second cabin."

"Good. That's good. I'll feel better knowing that. It's nice of you, Farley, to—"

She tipped her face up and his tipped over. And in that moment, lost in her eyes, the comfort became an embrace. "Holy God, Tansy," he managed, and pressed his mouth to hers.

Soft. Sweet. He thought she tasted like warm cherries, and now that he was close enough he could smell her skin, and that had warm in it, too.

He thought a man would never be cold, not a day in his life, if he could kiss her.

She leaned into him, he felt her come in. It made him feel strong and sure.

Then she pulled away, fast. "Farley, this isn't— We can't do this."

"Didn't mean to. Not just that way." He couldn't help himself and stroked a hand over her hair. "I didn't mean to take advantage of the situation."

"It's all right. It's fine."

Her voice was jumpy, and her eyes were wide. It made him smile. "It was fine. I've been thinking about kissing you for so long I can't remember how long it is. Now I guess I'll be thinking about kissing you again."

"Well, don't." Her voice jumped again, as if he'd poked her with a stick. "You can't. We can't."

She got to her feet. So did he, but more slowly. "I think you like me."

She flushed—God that was pretty—and started twisting the buttons on her coat. "Of course I like you."

"What I mean to say is, I think you think about kissing me sometimes, too. I've got a powerful yen for you, Tansy. Maybe you don't have the same, but I think you've got a little one any way."

She pulled her coat together, still twisting at buttons. "I'm not . . . that isn't . . ."

"It's about the first time I've seen you all flustered up. Maybe I should kiss you again."

The button-twisting hand slapped right out onto his chest. "We're not

going to do this. You have to accept that. You should be looking at—
having a yen for—girls your own age."

His smile widened. "You didn't say you didn't have one for me. What
we need to do is for me to take you out to dinner. Dancing maybe. Do
this proper."

"We're not doing anything."

She got a line between her eyebrows—he'd liked to have kissed it—
and her voice firmed up. He just kept smiling.

"I mean it." Exasperated now, she pointed the index fingers of both
hands at him. "I'm going to check in with Lil, then I'm going home.
And— Oh, wipe that stupid smile off your face."

She spun around, stalked away.

Her temper turned his smile into a mile-wide grin.

He'd kissed Tansy Spurge, he thought. And before she'd gotten her
dander up, she'd kissed him right back.

LIL TOOK THREE extra-strength Tylenol for the stress headache and
topped it off with a long, blistering shower. Dressed in flannels, thick
socks, and a comfortably tattered University of North Dakota sweatshirt,
she added logs to the flames in her compact fireplace.

Heat, she thought. She couldn't seem to get enough of it. She kept
the lights blazing, too. She wasn't ready for the dark yet. She gave some
thought to food, but couldn't work up the energy or the appetite.

She'd called her parents, so that was crossed off the list. She'd reassured them, promised to lock her doors, and reminded them she had a
refuge loaded with early warning signals.

She'd work. She had articles to write, grant proposals to complete.
No, she'd do laundry. No point in letting it pile up.

Maybe she should upload her photos. Or check the webcams.

Or, or, or.

She paced like a cat in a cage.

The sound of the truck had her pivoting toward the door. The staff had been gone nearly two hours now, and Mary would have locked the gate across the access road behind her. They all had keys, but . . . given the circumstances, wouldn't whoever might have forgotten something, wanted something, needed something have called first to alert her?

Baby gave a warning cry, and in the big-cat area, the old lioness roared. Lil grabbed her rifle. Farley beat her outside by a step.

In contrast to her thudding heart, his voice was calm as a spring breeze. "Why don't you go on back inside, Lil, while I see who . . . Okay." He shifted the shotgun he'd carried out, angled the barrel down. "That's Coop's rig."

Farley lifted a hand in greeting as the truck eased to a stop, and Coop climbed out.

"This is a hell of a welcoming committee." Coop glanced at the guns, then over to where the animals let the newcomer know they were on alert.

"They set up a ruckus," Farley commented. "Sure is something hearing those big jungle cats carry on, isn't it? Well." He gave Coop a nod. "I'll be seeing you."

"How did you get in the gate?" Lil demanded when Farley had slipped back inside.

"Your father gave me his key. Lot of keys floating around, from what I understand. A lock's not much good if everybody's got a key."

"Staff members have keys." She knew her voice lashed out in defense because she'd been frightened. Really frightened for a moment. "Otherwise somebody'd have to open it every damn morning before anybody else could get in. You should've called. If you came by to check on me, I could've told you and saved you the trip."

"It's not that long a trip." He stepped up on the porch, handed her a covered dish. "My grandmother sent it. Chicken and dumplings." He picked up the rifle she'd leaned against the rail and walked into the cabin without invitation.

Setting her teeth, Lil went in behind him. "It was nice of her to trouble, and I appreciate you bringing it by, but—"

"Jesus, Lil, it's like a furnace in here."

"I was cold." It was warmer than it needed to be now, but it was her damn house. "Hey look, there's no need for you to stay," she began as he stripped off his coat. "I'm covered here, as you can plainly see. It's been a long day for both of us."

"Yeah. And I'm hungry." He took the dish back from her, then strolled toward the back of the cabin to her kitchen.

She hissed under her breath, but hospitality had been ingrained since childhood. Visitors, even unwelcome ones, were to be given food and drink.

He'd already turned on her oven, and he stuck the dish inside as she came in. As if, she thought, *she* were the guest.

"It's still warm. Won't take long to heat it through. Got a beer?"

And visitors, she thought resentfully, should wait to be *offered* food and drink. She yanked open the refrigerator, pulled out two bottles of Coors.

Coop twisted off the cap, handed it to her. "Nice place." He leaned back, enjoying the first cold sip as he took a quick survey. Though the kitchen was compact, there were plenty of glass-fronted cabinets and open shelves, a good section of slate-colored counter. A little table tucked in the corner in front of a built-in bench provided eating space.

"You do any cooking?"

"When I want to eat."

He nodded. "That's about how it is for me. The kitchen in the bunkhouse'll be about this size when it's done."

"What are you doing here, Cooper?"

"Having a beer. In about twenty minutes, I'll be having a bowl of chicken and dumplings."

"Don't be thick."

Watching her, he lifted his beer. "There's two things. Maybe it's three. After what happened today I wanted to see how you were, and how you were set up here. Next, Joe asked me to look out for you, and I told him I would."

"For God's sake."

"I told him I would," Coop repeated, "so we'll both have to deal with that. Last—maybe last—you might think because of the way things turned out with us, you don't matter. You'd be wrong."

"The way things turned out isn't the point. It's the way things are." *That,* she thought, was essential to remember. "If thinking you're looking out for me eases my parents' minds, that's fine, that's good. But I don't need you looking out for me. That rifle out there's loaded, and I know how to use it."

"Ever aimed a gun at a man?"

"Not so far. Have you?"

"It's a different matter when you have," he said by way of answer. "It's a different matter than that when you know you can pull the trigger. You're in trouble, Lil."

"What happened today doesn't mean—"

"He'd been back to the campsite while we were up with the cougar. He used a knife on the tents, tossed some of the gear in the stream."

She took a breath, long and slow, so fear didn't get through again. "Nobody told me."

"I said I would. He dug out the shirt you'd had on the day before and smeared blood on it. That's personal."

Her legs jellied on her, so she stepped back, lowered to the bench. "That doesn't make any sense."

"It doesn't have to. We're going to sit here, eat some of Lucy's famous chicken and dumplings. I'm going to ask you questions and you're going to answer them."

"Why isn't Willy asking me questions?"

"He will. But I'll be asking them tonight. Where's the French guy?"

"Who?" Struggling to take it in, she scooped the fingers of both hands through her hair. "Jean-Paul? He's . . . in India. I think. Why?"

"Any trouble between the two of you?"

She stared at him. It took her a moment to realize he wasn't asking out of personal interest, but as a kind of de facto cop. "If you're fishing around, thinking Jean-Paul had anything to do with this, you need to cut bait. He'd never kill a caged animal, and he'd never do anything to hurt me. He's a good man, and he loves me. Or did."

"Did?"

"We're not together anymore." Reminding herself it wasn't personal, she pressed her fingers to her eyes. "We haven't been since right before I left for South America. It wasn't acrimonious, and he's in India, on assignment."

"All right." It was easy enough to verify. "Is there anyone else? Someone you're involved with, or who wants to be involved?"

"I'm not sleeping with anyone," she said flatly, "and no one's made any moves on me. I don't see why this is about me, personally."

"Your camera, your cougar, your shirt."

"The camera is refuge property, the cougar wasn't mine. She wasn't anyone's but herself. And the shirt could've been yours just as easily."

"But it wasn't. Have you pissed off anyone lately?"

She angled her head, raised her eyebrows. "Only you."

"I've got a solid alibi." He turned, got bowls down.

It annoyed her, the way he took over, the way he made himself at home. So she sat where she was and let him hunt for hot pads, for spoons. *He* didn't seem annoyed, she realized. He just found what he needed then went about the business of getting the meal in bowls.

"You had to go through some red tape to put this place together," he continued. "Licenses, zoning."

"Paperwork, politicking, paying fees. I had the land, thanks to my father, and was able to buy a little more after we were set up."

"Not everybody wanted you to succeed. Who bucked you?"

"There was some resistance on every level, local, county, state. But I'd done all the research. I'd been laying the groundwork for years. I spoke at town meetings, went to Rapid City, and into Pierre. I spoke to National Park reps and rangers. I know how to glad-hand when I have to, and I'm good at it."

"No doubt." He set the bowls on the table, joined her on the bench. "But—"

"We had to deal with people who worried about one of the exotic cats getting loose, and diseases. We allayed that by letting people come in, watch the process when we were laying it out, building it. And we gave them a chance to ask questions. We work with the schools and with 4-H, with other youth groups, and offer educational programs, on-site and on the Internet. We offer incentives. It works."

"Not arguing. But?"

She sighed. "There are always some, and you have extremes on both sides. People who think an animal is either domesticated or prey. And people who think of animals in the wild as gods. Untouchable. That it's wrong to interfere with what they see as the natural order."

"*Star Trek*'s prime directive."

He got a smile out of her for the first time that evening. "Yeah, in a way. Some who see a zoo as a prison rather than a habitat. And some are. I've seen terrible conditions. Animals living in filth, with disease, and horribly mistreated. But most are run well, with very strong protocols. We're a refuge, and a refuge must be just that. A safe place. And that means the people who run it are responsible for the health and well-being of the animals in it—and are responsible for their safety and the safety of the community."

"You get threats?"

"We report, and keep a file, on the more extreme letters and e-mails. We screen the website. And yeah, we've had a few incidents here over the years with people who came to start trouble."

"Which you documented?"

"Yes."

"You can get me a copy of the file then."

"What is this, Coop, a busman's holiday?"

He turned his head until their eyes met. "I caged that cougar, too."

She nodded, poked at a dumpling. "You were right about the gun. It looks like it was a thirty-two. And I didn't think that much of it at the time, but Matt—our vet—he said he thought somebody was on the property one night while I was in Peru, when he bunked here. Someone always stays on-site through the night, so while I was gone, they switched off. The animals got riled up, middle of the night. He came out to check, but he didn't see anything."

"When was this?"

"A couple nights before I got back. It could've been an animal, and probably was. The fencing is primarily to keep our animals contained, but it also keeps other animals out. They can be a source of contamination, so we're careful."

"Okay, but they'd be around other animals in the wild so—"

"They're not in the wild," she said shortly. "We re-create, but they're enclosed. We've changed their environment. Other animals—birds, rodents, insects—all potentially carry parasites or disease. It's why all the food is so carefully processed before feeding, why we clean and disinfect the enclosures, why we do regular physical exams, take samples routinely. Vaccinate, treat, add nutrients to their diet. They're not in the wild," she repeated. "And that makes us responsible for them, in every way."

"All right." He'd thought he'd understood what she was doing here, but saw now he only understood the more obvious pieces. "Did you find anything off the night the vet thought someone—or something—was out there?"

"No. None of the animals, the equipment, the cages were messed with. I looked around, but it had snowed since, and my people had been all over, so there was no real chance of finding tracks or a trail—human or animal."

"Do you have a list of all your staff, the volunteers?"

"Sure. But it's not one of ours."

"Lil, you were gone for six months. Do you know, personally, every volunteer who comes in here to toss raw meat at the cats?"

"We don't toss—" She broke off, shook her head. "We screen. We use locals as much as we can, and have a volunteer program. Levels," she explained. "Most of the volunteers do grunt work. Help with the food, the cleaning, shelve supplies. Unless they've had some experience, reached the top level, other than the petting zoo, volunteers don't handle the animals. The exception would be the veterinary assistants, who donate their time and help with exams and surgeries."

"I've seen the kids around here handling them."

"Interns, not volunteers. We take interns from universities, students who are going into the field. We help train, help teach. They're here for some hands-on experience."

"You keep drugs."

Weary, she rubbed the back of her neck. "Yes. The drugs are in Medical, locked in the drug cabinet. Matt, Mary, Tansy, and I have keys. Even the vet assistants don't have access to them. Though you'd have to be jonesing pretty hard to want anything in there, we inventory weekly."

It was enough for now, he thought. She'd had enough for now. "It's good chicken," he said, and took another bite.

"It really is."

"Want another beer?"

"No."

He rose, poured them both tall glasses of water.

"Were you a good cop?" she asked him.

"I did okay."

"Why'd you quit? And don't tell me to mind my own business when you're trashing around in the middle of mine."

"I needed a change." He considered a moment, then decided to tell her. "There was a woman in my squad. Dory. A good cop, a good friend. A friend," he repeated. "There was never anything between us but that. She was married, for one thing, and for another, there just wasn't anything like that. But when the marriage went south, her husband decided there was."

He paused, and when she said nothing, drank, then continued. "We were working a case, and one night after shift we grabbed a meal together to talk it through. I guess he was watching, waiting for his moment. I never felt it coming," he said quietly. "Never got that hum, and she never let on how bad it was, not even to me."

"What happened?"

"He came around the corner, firing. She went down so fast, fell against me. Maybe saved my life because of the way she fell back against me. He caught me in the side, barely caught me. In and out."

"Shot? You were shot?"

"In and out, not much more than a graze." He didn't dismiss it. No, he never dismissed it. A few inches the other way, a whole different story. "She was taking me down with her. People were screaming, scattering, diving for cover. The glass shattered. A bullet hit the window of the restaurant.

"I remember what it sounded like, when the bullets were going into her, into the glass. I got to my weapon. I got to it as we were going down, as she was taking me down with her. She was already dead, and he kept putting bullets into her. I put five into him."

His eyes met Lil's now, and they were ice blue in color, in expression. She thought: This is the change. More than anything else, this is what marked him.

"I remember every one of them. Two mid-body as I was falling, three more—right hip, leg, abdomen—after I hit the sidewalk. It all took less than thirty seconds. Some asshole recorded it on his cell phone."

It had seemed so much longer, eons longer. And the jumpy video hadn't captured the way Dory's body had jerked against his, or the feel of her blood flooding over his hands.

"He emptied his clip. Two bullets went through the glass, one went into me. The rest, he put into her."

Coop paused, drank some water. "So I needed a change."

Her chest was full to aching as she put her hand over his. She could see it, so clearly. Hear it—the shots, the screams, the breaking glass. "Your grandparents don't know. They never said anything about this, so they don't know."

"No. I wasn't hurt that bad. Treat and release. A few stitches. They didn't know Dory, so why tell them? It was a good shoot. I didn't get any trouble over it, not with Dory dead on the sidewalk, all the witnesses, and that asshole's phone recording. But I couldn't be a cop anymore, couldn't work out of the squad, couldn't do it. Besides"—he shrugged now—"there's more money in private."

She'd said that, hadn't she? Casually, carelessly when she'd seen him again. How she wished she could take it back. "Did you have someone? When it happened, did you have someone there for you?"

"I didn't want anyone for a while."

Because she understood, she nodded, said nothing. Then he turned his hand over, laced his fingers with hers. "And when I did, I thought about calling you."

Her hand flexed, a little jerk of surprise. "You could have."

"Maybe."

"There's no maybe, Coop. I'd have listened. I'd've come to New York to listen if you'd needed or wanted it."

"Yeah. I guess that's why I didn't call you."

"How does that make sense?" she wondered.

"There are a lot of contradictions and twists when it comes to you and me, Lil." He brushed his thumb, lightly, over the inside of her wrist. "I thought about staying here tonight, talking you into bed."

"You couldn't."

"We both know I could." He tightened his grip on her hand until she looked at him. "Sooner or later, I will. But tonight, the timing's off. Timing counts."

All her softer feelings hardened. "I'm not here for your convenience, Cooper."

"There's nothing convenient about you, Lil." His free hand snaked up, gripped the back of her neck. And his mouth, hot, desperate, familiar, captured hers.

For the moment he held her, panic, excitement, need fought a short and vicious little war inside her.

"There's nothing convenient about that," he muttered when he released her.

He rose, took their empty bowls to the sink.

"Lock up after me," he ordered, and left her.

PART TWO

HEAD

The head is always the dupe of the heart.

—LA ROCHEFOUCAULD

II

March bit like a tiger, stalking from the north to spring in a killing leap over the hills and valleys. Snow and ice plunged out of the sky, cracking tree limbs with their weight, downing power lines, and turning roads into treachery.

At the refuge, Lil and any of the staff or volunteers who could make it trudged, plowed, and shoveled while the relentless wind blew mountainous drifts into frigid ranges.

The animals retired to their dens, wandering out when the mood struck them to watch the humans shiver and swear. Bundled to the eyeballs, Lil crossed paths with Tansy.

"How's our girl?" Lil asked, thinking of the lioness.

"Weathering this better than I am. I want a hot, tropical beach. I want the smell of sea and sunscreen. I want a mai tai."

"Will you settle for hot coffee and a cookie?"

"Sold." As they plodded their way toward Lil's cabin, Tansy gave her friend a sidelong look. "You don't smell like sea and sunscreen."

"Neither would you if you'd been shoveling snow and shit."

"And we're the smart girls," Tansy commented. "Makes you wonder, doesn't it?"

"Even smart girls shovel shit. It should be a bumper sticker." Lil stomped and scraped off snow, and felt her muscles quiver in response when the first shot of warmth inside the cabin hit her. "We got through the worst of it," she said as she and Tansy stripped off gloves, hats, coats, scarves. "We'll haul the dung over to the farm first chance. Nothing like shit for farming. And I'm going to insist this is the last ice storm of the season. Spring, with its flash flooding and acres of mud, can't be far off."

"Joy."

Lil headed back to the kitchen to start coffee. "You've been Miss Cranky Scientist the last few days."

"I'm tired of winter." Scowling, Tansy dug a tube of ChapStick out of her pocket and smeared it on.

"I hear that. But I hear something else, too." Lil opened a cupboard, pulled out her stash of Milano cookies, handed Tansy the bag. "And call me crazy, but I suspect the something else has a penis."

Tansy gave her a droll look, and took a cookie. "I know a lot of some-things with penises."

"Me too. They're freaking everywhere." Warm, and happy for a cookie break, Lil leaned back while the coffee brewed. "I have this theory. Want to hear it?"

"I'm eating your cookies, so I guess I'm obligated to."

"Good. The penis is here to stay, so those of us without them must learn to appreciate, exploit, ignore, and/or utilize them, depending on our own needs and goals."

Tansy poked out her bottom lip as she nodded. "It's a good theory."

"It is." Lil got down mugs, poured the coffee for both of them. "As we've elected to work in what is still a male-dominated field, the ratio of us v. them may demand that we appreciate, exploit, ignore, and/or utilize more often than those of our species who have not elected to work in this field."

"Are you correlating hard data or will you conduct an empirical study?"

"At this point, it's still in the observation/speculation phase. However, I do have, on some authority, the identity of the penis which is, I believe, playing a part in making you Miss Cranky Scientist."

"Oh, really?" Tansy got a spoon and dumped three doses of sugar in her coffee. "Who would the authority be?"

"My mom. She misses little. I'm informed that while I was away the spark quotient between you and a certain Farley Pucket increased."

"Farley's barely twenty-five."

"That would make you a cougar," Lil said and grinned.

"Oh, shut up. I'm not dating him, sleeping with him, encouraging him."

"Because he's twenty-five? Actually, I think he's twenty-six. And that makes him—good God—*four* years younger than you are." In wild reaction—and with some theatrics—Lil pressed the back of her hand to her lips. "Horrors! You're a cradle robber!"

"It's not funny."

Sobering, Lil lifted her eyebrows. She didn't mind the embarrassed flush on Tansy's cheeks—what were friends for if not to embarrass friends?—but she did mind, very much, the unhappiness in those big, dark eyes.

"No, apparently it's not. Tans, you're seriously unwrapped because you're a few years older? If the ages were reversed you wouldn't blink."

"But they're not, and I don't *care* if it's not logical. I'm the older woman. The older *black* woman, for God's sake, Lil. In South Dakota. It's not going to happen."

"So no problem if Farley was thirty-something and black?"

Tansy pointed a finger. "I told you I didn't care if it was logical."

Lil pointed a finger right back. "Good thing, because it just isn't. Let's put that aside for a minute."

"It's key."

"I'm putting away the key for a minute. Do you have feelings for him?

Because I admit I thought it was just a little lusty deal. Long winter, close quarters, healthy, consenting adults. I figured the two of you just had a maybe-we-should-fool-around thing going. Which I was going to rag you about mercilessly because, well, it's Farley. He's sort of my honorary lit—brother."

"See, you were going to say little brother." Tansy shook her fingers in the air. "*Little* brother!"

"Key is put away, Tansy. Obviously, this is more than a you've-got-a-nice-ass-on-you-cowboy-and-I'm-looking-for-a-little-tussle."

"I checked out his ass, sure. It's my inalienable right as a female. But never with the idea of a *tussle*. What a stupid word."

"Oh, I see, you never thought about having—insert stupid word—with Farley. Excuse me while I get the fire extinguisher. Your pants are smoking."

"I may have speculated on stupid wording with Farley, but never with any intent to follow through. It's another inalienable right." Exasperated, Tansy tossed up her hands. "We both checked out the ass of Greg the Adonis Grad Student when he volunteered for a month last summer. We didn't jump that fine ass."

"It was fine," Lil said, remembering. "Plus he had that whole six-pack ab thing going. And the shoulders."

"Yeah. Shoulders."

They both fell into reverent silence for a moment.

"God, I miss sex," Lil said with a sigh.

"Tell me."

"Aha! So why aren't you having it with Farley?"

"You won't trap me that way, Dr. Chance."

"Oh, won't I? You're not having it with Farley because he's not just another hot body like Greg the Adonis Grad Student. You're not having it with Farley because you have feelings involved."

"I . . ." Tansy opened her mouth, then hissed. "Damn it. Okay. All right, I do have them. I don't even know how it started. He'd come around to help out sometimes, and sure I'd think, Cute guy. He is a cute guy, and sweet. Cute and sweet and funny, so we'd talk or he'd give me a hand, and somewhere along the line I started feeling this buzz. He'd come around and, whew, lots of buzzing in there. And . . . well, I'm not stupid, but an experienced woman of thirty years."

"Yeah, yeah."

"I caught the way he'd look at me. So I knew he had the buzz going on, too. I didn't think much of it at first. Just: What do you know, I've got the hots for the cute cowboy. But it wouldn't go away, and it got buzzier. Then last week, the bad day," she said, and Lil nodded, "I was feeling sad and sorry, and he sat with me. He kissed me. I kissed him right back before I realized what I was doing. I stopped, and I told him it wasn't going to happen again. He just kept grinning at me. He says, and I quote, he's got 'a powerful yen' for me. Who talks like that? It's put me in a mood."

She dug for another cookie. "I can't get that damn grin out of my head."

"Okay. You're not going to like what I have to say, but . . ." Lil put her index finger against her thumb, and flicked it sharply dead center of Tansy's forehead.

"Ow!"

"Stupid. You're taking the path of stupid, so get off of it. A handful of years and a skin color aren't reasons to turn away from someone you care about, and who cares about you."

"People who say skin color doesn't matter are usually white."

"Well, ow right back at you."

"I mean it, Lil. Mixed relationships are still difficult in a lot of the world."

"News flash. Relationships are still difficult in all of the world."

"Exactly. So why add layers to the difficulty?"

"Because love's precious. That part's simple. It's getting it and keeping it that's hard. You've never been in a serious relationship."

"Not fair. I was with Thomas for more than a year."

"You liked, respected, and lusted for each other. You spoke the same language, but you were never serious, Tansy. Not this-is-the-one sort of serious. I know what it's like to be with a nice guy you're comfortable with and never think of him as the one. And I know what it's like to know the one. I had that with Coop, and he broke my heart. Still, I'd rather have my heart broken than never look and know."

"You say that, but you're not the only one with theories. Mine is you've never gotten over him."

"No, I never have."

Tansy lifted her hands. "How can you handle it?"

"I'm still figuring that out. The bad day was, apparently, a day for a shift in status. He brought me chicken and dumplings. And he kissed me. It's not a buzz with me, Tansy. It's a flood, that pours in and fills me up." She laid a hand on her heart, rubbed. "I don't know what's going to happen. If I sleep with him again, will it help me tread water until I can finally get to solid ground? Or will it just take me under? I don't know, but I'm not going to pretend the odds aren't strong that I'll be finding out."

Steadier for having said it out loud, Lil set her mug down, smiled. "I've got a powerful yen for him."

"You're—what was your word? Unwrapped. You're unwrapped over the man who walked away from you and broke your heart. And I'm un-wrapped over a farmhand with a rubber-band grin."

"And we're the smart girls."

"Yeah. We're the smart girls," Tansy agreed. "Even when we're idiots."

COOP WORKED WITH the pretty buckskin mare he'd trained over the winter. She had, in his estimation, a sweet heart, a strong back, and a lazy disposition. She'd be happy to snooze in the stall, paddock, or field most of the day. She'd go if you insisted, if she was sure you really meant it.

She didn't nip, she didn't kick, and she would eat an apple out of your hand with a polite delicacy that was undeniably female.

He thought she'd do well with children. He named her Little Sis.

Business was slow in these last stubborn weeks of bitter winter. It gave him time—too much of it—to catch up on paperwork, clean the stalls, organize his new home.

And think about Lil.

He knew she had her hands full. Word got back to him through his grandparents—from her parents, from Farley, from Gull.

She'd come by once, he'd heard, to return his grandmother's dish, and visit awhile. And she'd come by when he'd been in town, doing a stint in the storefront office.

He wondered if that had been accident or design on her part.

He'd given her space, but he was about done with that now. Those loose ends were still dangling. The time was coming to knot them off.

He started to walk Little Sis toward the barn. "You worked good today," he told her. "We'll get you brushed down, and maybe there'll be an apple in it for you."

He'd have sworn her ears twitched at the word "apple." Just as he'd have sworn he heard her sigh when he changed direction and steered her toward the house when he saw the county sheriff step out of the back door.

"That's a pretty girl."

"She is."

Standing, legs spread, Willy squinted up at the sky. "The way the weather's clearing up, you'll have her and the rest under the tourists and on the trails before long."

Coop had to smile. "This is one of the few places I know where eighteen inches of snowpack and drifts taller than me would be considered clearing up, weather-wise."

"Yeah, haven't gotten anything falling since the last storm. Clearing up. Spare me a minute, Coop?"

"Sure." Coop dismounted, looped the mare's reins around the porch rail. Hardly necessary, he thought. She wouldn't go anywhere she wasn't told to go.

"I've just come from seeing Lil over at the refuge, and figured I owed you a stop-by."

Coop could see it clearly enough in the man's face. "To tell me you're hitting dead ends."

"To tell you that. Fact is, what we got is a dead cougar, a thirty-two slug, a buncha tracks in the snow, and a vague description of someone you saw in the dark. We've been giving it a push, but there's not much to move along."

"You got copies of her threat file?"

"Yeah, and we've been following up on that. I rode out and spoke personal to a couple of men who went by the refuge a few months back and gave them some trouble. Don't fit the physical, either of them. One's got a wife swears he was home that night, and through the morning—and he was at work nine on the dot in Sturgis. That's verified. The other runs damn near three hundred pounds. I don't think you'd've mistaken him."

"No."

"I talked to a couple rangers I know, and they'll be keeping an eye out at the park, spreading the word. But I'm going to tell you like I had to tell Lil, we're going to need a serious run of luck to tie this up. I gotta figure whoever it was is gone. Nobody with a lick of sense would've stayed up there when that storm came in. We'll keep doing what we can do, but I wanted to tell her straight. And you, too."

"There are a lot of places a man could wait out a storm. In the hills and in the valley. If he had some experience, some provisions, or some luck."

"That's a fact. We made some calls, checking if somebody who looked like they'd come off the trail moved into one of the motels or hotels around here. We didn't get anything. Her camera's been up and running since, and nobody's seen anybody around the refuge—or the Chance place—who shouldn't be around."

"It sounds like you've covered everything you could cover."

"Doesn't close the book on it, though. Open book keeps my palms itchy." Willy stood a moment, looking out at the snow, the sky. "Well.

Good to see Sam up and around. I hope I'm tough as him when I get his age. If you think of anything I need to know, I'll be around to hear it."

"I appreciate you coming by."

Willy nodded, gave Little Sis a pat on her flank. "Pretty girl. You take care, Coop."

He would, Coop thought. But what he needed to take care of was at the refuge.

He dealt with the horse, so Little Sis got her rubdown and her apple. He took care of the rest of the chores, ones as routine to him now as dressing every morning. Because there would be coffee hot and fresh, he went into his grandmother's kitchen.

His grandfather walked in, without his cane. Coop fought down the urge to comment, especially when Sam gave him a quick scowl.

"I'm still going to use it when I go outside, or if my leg gives me trouble. I'm just testing things, that's all."

"Stubborn old goat," Lucy said as she came out of the laundry room with a basket full of whites.

"That makes two of us." Sam limped over, took the basket, and while Coop held his breath limped away again to set it on a chair. "Now." His face actually flushed with pleasure as he turned, winked at Coop. "Why don't you get the menfolks some coffee, woman?"

Lucy folded her lips, but not before the quick smile escaped. "Oh, sit down."

Sam let out a quiet sigh as he sat. "I smell a chicken roasting." He scented the air like a wolf. "Heard a rumor about mashed potatoes. You ought to help me eat that, Coop, before this woman fattens me up like a pig before the roast."

"Actually, I have something to do. But if you hear somebody sneaking around in here later tonight, you'll know it's me coming after the leftovers."

"I can make you up some, put it over next door for you," Lucy offered.

The bunkhouse had become "next door."

"Don't worry about that. I can fend for myself."

"Well." She set coffee in front of both of them, then ran her hand along Coop's shoulder. "It looks nice over there, but I wish you'd take another look up in the attic. I know you could use more furniture."

"I can only sit in one chair at a time, Grandma. I wanted to tell you the mare—Little Sis—is coming along."

"I saw you working her." Lucy poured the water she had simmering in the kettle to make the tea she preferred that time of day. "She's got a sweet way."

"I think she'll be good with kids, especially if they don't want to get anywhere fast. I was hoping you'd take her out a couple times, Grandma. See how she feels to you."

"I'll take her out tomorrow." She hesitated a moment before turning to her husband. "Why don't you ride out with me, Sam? We haven't had a ride in a while."

"If the boy can spare the pair of us."

"I think I can manage," Coop told him. He finished off his coffee and pushed to his feet. "I'm going to get cleaned up. Do you need anything before I go?"

"I think we can manage," Lucy said with a smile. "You going out?"

"Yeah. I've got something to take care of."

Lucy lifted her eyebrows at Sam when the door closed behind Coop. "I'll give you two to one that something has big brown eyes."

"Lucille, I don't take sucker bets."

STREAKS AND SMEARS of red shimmered over the western sky, and the light dipped soft into twilight. The world was vast and white, a land caught in the clutched fist of winter.

He'd heard people talking about spring—his grandparents, Gull, people in town, but nothing he saw gave any indication they'd turned a corner toward daffodils and robins. Then again, he thought, as he pulled up to the gates of the refuge, he'd never spent a winter in the Black Hills before this one.

A few days at Christmas didn't come close to the whole shot, he mused, as he got out to unlock the gate with the copy of the key he'd had made from Joe's. The wind whistled and skipped along the road and sent the pines whooshing. The scent of pine and snow and horse would forever say winter in the hills to him.

He got back into the truck, drove through the gate. Stopped, got out to close and relock it. And wondered how much an automatic gate with a frigging keypad ran. Plus a couple of security cameras for the entrance.

He'd have to check on what kind of alarm system she had installed.

If he could make a copy of the key, so could half the county. The other half could just hike around, circle back, and stroll onto refuge land on a whim.

Fences and gates didn't keep people out if they wanted in.

He followed the road back and slowed at the first turn, the turn that brought the cabins into view. Smoke pumped out of Lil's chimney, and lights glowed against the window glass. Paths leading from the split-log cabin led to the second cabin, to the habitat areas, to the education center and commissary, and around to where he understood they stored equipment, dry feed, supplies.

He assumed she had enough sense to lock her doors, just as he assumed she was smart and aware enough to understand there were countless ways onto the land, to those doors, for anyone who had the skills and patience to travel the hills and trails.

He skirted the small visitors' parking area and pulled up by her truck.

The animals announced him, but their calls seemed almost casual to his ear. It wasn't full dark yet, and from what he could see of the habitat most of the inhabitants had chosen their dens.

Casual or not, Lil was at the door before he'd gained the cabin porch.

She stood in a black sweater and worn jeans, scarred boots, with her hair pulled back in a thick black waterfall. He wouldn't have described her stance or her expression as friendly.

"You're going to have to give my father back his key."

"I did." He stepped onto the porch, looked into her very annoyed eyes. "Which should give you a slice of clue on just how much security that gate gives you."

"It's served its purpose up till now."

"Now's the point. You need a more secure, automatic gate with a code and camera."

"Oh, really? Well, I'll get right on that as soon as I have a few thousand extra piled up, and nothing else to do with it but beef up a gate that is essentially a symbol and a deterrent. Unless you're going to suggest I build a security wall around more than two dozen acres of land while I'm at it. Maybe post sentries."

"If you're going to have a deterrent, it might as well deter. Since I'm standing here, yours didn't do such a good job. Listen, I've been outside most of the day, and I'm tired of freezing my ass off."

He stepped forward, and since she didn't move out of the doorway simply cupped his hands under her elbows, lifted her up, over. Inside, he plunked her down again and closed the door.

"Jesus, Cooper." It was hard to form actual words when her jaw kept wanting to drop. "What's *with* you?"

"I want a beer."

"I bet you have some back at your own place. If not, there are several places to buy beer in town. Go there. Do that."

"And despite the fact you're bitchy and unfriendly, I want to talk to you. You're here, and there's probably beer."

He started back to the kitchen. "Why are you here alone?"

"Because this is my house, this is my place, because I wanted to be alone."

He glanced at the table, noted the laptop, a scatter of files, and a glass of red wine. He picked up the bottle on the counter, approved the label, and allowed himself a change of mind.

He got a wineglass out of one of her cabinets.

"Just make yourself the hell at home."

"Willy came by to see me." He poured himself a glass of wine, sampled it, then set the glass down to strip off his coat.

"Then I assume we both got the same information, and there's nothing to talk about. I'm working, Coop."

"You're frustrated and you're pissed off. I don't blame you. The fact is, they don't have much to work with, and none of the lines of investigation are going anywhere. That doesn't mean they stop, just that they might have to change the angle."

He picked up the wine again, glanced around the room while he drank. "Don't you eat?"

"Yes, often when I'm hungry. Let's just say I appreciate you coming by to reassure me the wheels of justice are turning, and add that I'm aware Willy is doing and will do his best. There. We talked."

"Do you have a reason to be pissed at me, or is it just in general?"

"We've had some long and very physical days around here. I'm on deadline on an article I'm writing. Writing articles helps pay for that wine you're drinking, among other things. I've just been told that it's very unlikely that whoever shot a cougar that I caged will be identified or apprehended. You waltz in here when I'm trying to work and help yourself to the wine this article will help replace. So we'll say it's in general with a special section just for you."

"I didn't waltz." He turned and opened the refrigerator. "Shit, Lil," he said after a short exam, "even I do better than this."

"What the hell do you think you're doing?"

"Finding something to fix for dinner."

"Get out of my refrigerator."

In response, he simply opened the freezer. "Figures. Bunch of girl frozen meals. Well, at least there's frozen pizza."

He thought he could hear her teeth grinding all the way across the room. It was, he admitted, oddly satisfying.

"In about two minutes I'm going to get my rifle and shoot you in the ass."

"No you're not. But in about fifteen minutes, according to the directions on this box, you'll be eating pizza. It might help your mood. You get some itinerant volunteers," he continued as he switched on the oven. "Some one- or two-timers."

Annoyance didn't seem to work. She tried sulking. "So?"

"It's a good way to scope out the setup here, the staff, the routines, the layout. A lot of the farms and businesses around here do the same. Hire somebody on in season, a few days, a few weeks, whatever works. I'm going to do the same in another month or so."

He put the unboxed pizza in, set the timer.

"What difference does it make? Willy thinks he's done and gone."

"Willy could be right. Or he could be wrong. If a man knew what he was doing, and wanted to, he could make a nice shelter for himself in the hills. They're pocketed with caves."

"You're not making me feel any better."

"I want you to be careful. If you feel too much better, you won't be." He brought the bottle over, topped off her wine. "What's the article about?"

She picked up the wine, scowled into it, then sipped. "I'm not going to sleep with you."

"You're writing about that? Can I read it?"

"I'm not going to sleep with you," she repeated, "until when and *if* I decide otherwise. Tossing a frozen pizza in the oven isn't going to make me feel warm and fuzzy about you."

"If I was after warm and fuzzy, I'd get a puppy. I'm going to sleep with you, Lil. But you can take some time to get used to the idea."

"You had me once, Cooper, and you could've kept me. You dumped me."

His expression flattened out. "We remember it different."

"If you think we can just go back—"

"I don't. I don't want to go back. But I'm looking at you, Lil, and I know we're not done. You know it, too."

He sat on the bench with her, sipped his wine, and poked at the photos she had fanned out beside the files. "Is this South America?"

"Yeah."

"What's it like going places like that?"

"Exciting. Challenging."

He nodded. "And now you'll write a story about going to the Andes to track cougar."

"Yeah."

"Then where?"

"Where what?"

"Where will you go?"

"I don't know. I don't have any plans right now. This trip was the big one for me. What I got out of it personally, professionally, what I can generate from it with articles, papers, lectures. The research, the findings." She moved her shoulders. "I can channel a lot of that into benefits for the refuge. The refuge is the priority."

He set the photos back down to look at her. "It's good to have priorities."

He moved in slowly, giving her time—this time—to resist or decide. She didn't speak, didn't try to stop him, only watched him the way she might a coiled snake.

Warily.

He caught her chin in a light grip, and took her mouth.

She wouldn't have said he was gentle, or tender. No, she wouldn't have called the kiss, the tone, the intent either of those. But there wasn't the rough fire he'd shown her before. This time, he kissed her like a man who'd decided to take his time. Who was confident he could.

And though his fingers were easy on her face, she knew—didn't he intend she would?—that they could tighten at his whim. That he could plunder instead of seduce.

And knowing it sparked excitement in her blood.

Hadn't she always preferred the wild to the tame?

He felt her give, just a little. Just a little more. Her lips moved against his, warmed and softened, and her breath hummed low in her throat.

He eased away as slowly as he'd eased to her. "No," he said, "we're not done." The oven timer dinged, and he smiled. "But the pizza is."

12

He'd spent worse nights, Coop thought, as he added logs to the fire in Lil's living room. But it had been a lot of years since he'd made do with a chilly room and a lumpy sofa. And even then, he hadn't had the additional discomfort of knowing the woman he wanted slept one floor above.

His choice, he reminded himself. She'd told him to go; he'd refused. So he'd gotten a blanket, a pillow, and a sofa six inches too short for him. And it had very likely been for nothing.

She was probably right. She was perfectly safe on her own, in her cabin. Locked doors and a loaded rifle were solid safety factors.

But once he'd told her he intended to stay, he hadn't been able to back down.

And it was damn weird, he mused, as he walked back to the kitchen to put on coffee, to be wakened in the dark by a jungle cat's roar.

Damn weird.

He supposed she was used to it, as he hadn't heard her stir, even when he'd been compelled to pull on his boots and go out to check.

The only things he'd discovered were she needed more security lights, and that even if a man knew there were sturdy barriers, the roars and growls in the dark could send an atavistic finger of fear up his spine.

She was stirring now, he thought. He'd heard her footsteps above, and the clink of the pipes as she turned on the shower.

It would be light soon, another frigid, white-drenched dawn. Her people would be heading in, and he had his own work to see to.

He hunted up eggs and bread, a frying pan. She might not agree, but he figured she owed him a hot breakfast for the guard duty. He was slapping a couple of fried egg sandwiches together when she walked in. She'd bundled her hair up, wore a flannel shirt over a thermal. And looked no more pleased to see him this morning than she had the night before.

"We need some ground rules," she began.

"Fine. Write me up a list. I've got to get to work. I made two if you want the other," he added as he wrapped his sandwich in a napkin.

"You can't just come here and take over."

"Put that at the top of the list," he suggested as she followed him into the living room. He passed the sandwich from hand to hand as he shrugged on his coat. "You smell good."

"You need to respect my privacy, and get it through your head I don't need or want a guard dog."

"Uh-huh." He settled his hat on his head. "You're going to need to bring in more firewood. I'll see you later."

"Coop. Damn it!"

He turned at the door. "You matter. Deal with it."

He bit into his sandwich as he strode to his truck.

She was right about the ground rules, he thought. Most things worked better with rules, or guidelines anyway. There was right and there was wrong, and a big, wide mass of gray between them. Still, it was best to know which shades of gray worked for any particular situation.

She was entitled to set some rules, as long as she understood he'd be exploring the gray.

He ate his egg sandwich as he drove the looping road to the gate, and setting rules, guidelines, and the mystery of just what he wanted from Lil aside, he mentally arranged what he had to do that day.

Stock to be fed, stalls mucked out. Then getting his grandparents out on horseback would be an accomplishment. He needed to get into town for some supplies, do some paperwork at the storefront. If they didn't have customers who wanted a trail guide, he'd get Gull to work on some of the tack.

He wanted to work out a basic plan, cost analysis, and feasibility of adding pony rides to the business. Take a few horses like Little Sis, he mused, walk them around a fenced track for a half hour, and you could . . .

His mind switched off business and to alert.

The corpse was draped over the gate. Below it, blood stained the hardpack of snow. A couple of vultures were already pecking for breakfast while more circled overhead.

Coop hit the horn to scatter the birds as he slowed to scan the trees and brush, the road beyond the gate. In the dim, early light, his head-lights washed over the dead wolf, turned its dead eyes eerily green.

Coop leaned over, opened his glove compartment, and took out his 9mm and his flashlight. Climbing out of the truck, he shined the light on the ground. There were footprints, of course. His own would be among them from the night before, when he'd opened the gate.

He saw none he judged as newer than his own on the inside. That, he supposed was something. Still, he walked in his own tracks to reach the wolf.

It had taken two shots—one mid-body, one head—to bring the wolf down, as far as Coop could see on a visual. The body was cold to the touch, and the small blood pool frozen.

It told him the message had been delivered several hours before.

He flipped the safety back on his gun, pushed it into his pocket. As he dug for his phone he heard the hum of an approaching car. Though he doubted the messenger would be back so soon, or travel in a vehicle, Coop slid his hand into his pocket and over the grip of his gun.

The light had gone misty gray with dawn, and in the eastern sky the red rose and spread. He walked back, cut his headlights, and standing at the gate saw his instinct had been right. The four-wheel drive slowed. He held up a hand to stop them, to keep them as far back from the gate as he could manage when they made the turn.

He recognized the man who got out the passenger side by sight, but not name. "Keep back from the gate," Coop ordered.

Tansy climbed out the other side and stood holding the door handle as if for support. "Oh, my God."

"You want to keep back," he repeated.

"Lil."

"She's fine," Coop told Tansy. "I just left her up at the cabin. I need you to call the sheriff—Willy. Get back in the car and call. Tell him somebody left a dead wolf at the gate. Two bullet holes that I can see. I want you to wait in the car, don't touch anything. You." He pointed to the man.

"Uh, Eric. I'm an intern. I just—"

"In the car, stay. The vultures come back, hit the horn. I'm going to go get Lil."

"We've got some volunteers coming in this morning." Tansy took a breath that huffed out a fog, then another, shorter, smoother. "And the other interns. They should be here soon."

"If they come before I get back, keep them away from the gate."

He got back into his truck, backed up until he came to one of the pull-offs. He did a quick three-point turn and pushed for speed.

She was already outside, standing on the path that led from her cabin to the offices. Her hands moved to her hips even as the scowl moved over her face.

"What now? Mornings are busy times around here."

"You need to come with me."

The scowl faded. She didn't question him. There was enough in the tone, in his eyes to tell her there was trouble.

"Get a camera," he called out when she started toward the truck. "Digital. Make it fast."

Again, she asked no questions but set off toward the cabin at a run. She was back in under two minutes, with the camera and her rifle.

"Tell me," she said when she jumped in the truck.

"There's a dead wolf hanging over your gate."

She sucked in a breath, and out of the corner of his eye he saw her hand tighten on the barrel of the rifle. But her voice stayed calm.

"Shot? Like the cougar?"

"It took two shots, that I can see. Not much blood, and it's cold. He killed it somewhere else, hauled it down. It doesn't look like he got in, or tried. But I didn't look that close. A couple of your people pulled up right after I found it. They're calling the sheriff."

"Son of a bitch. What's the damn point in— Wait!" Alarm ringing in her words, she pushed up straight in the seat. "Go back, go back. What if he's using this to lure us away? If he got inside? The animals, they're helpless. Go back, Coop."

"Nearly at the gate. I'll drop you off. I'll go back."

"Hurry. Hurry." When he braked at the gate, she turned. "Wait for me," she demanded and jumped out. "Eric!"

She circled wide of the wolf—smart girl—and Coop watched Eric get out of the car on the other side. "Catch this! Catch it. Get the best pictures you can of the wolf, the gate, of everything. Wait for the sheriff."

"Where are you—"

She scrambled back in Coop's truck, slammed the door on Eric's question. *"Move!"*

He punched the gas, shot back in reverse, and went with the fish-tail when he whipped into the turn. When he blasted the horn, she jumped, then stared at him. "On the off chance you're right, and he hears us coming, he'll book. This isn't about confrontation." Not yet, Coop thought. Not yet. "It's about harassment."

"Why off chance?"

"It's unlikely he knew I was here last night, or I'd be leaving before your people got here. Otherwise, they'd be the ones to find the wolf, and they'd have come in, come up to tell you. Everybody'd be here, not at the gate."

"Okay, okay, that's a point." But she didn't breathe easily until she saw the first habitats, heard the usual calls and clamor of morning.

"I need to check them, all of them. If you take that direction, just follow the path, I'll take this side and circle around, then we—"

"No." He pulled up, stopped. "Off chance," he repeated. "And I'm not risking him getting you alone."

She lifted the rifle she had across her knees, but Cooper shook his head.

"Together." And when they'd finished, he thought, he'd check both cabins, all the outbuildings.

"They'll think I'm coming to visit, so there's going to be some annoyance when I don't."

There were grumbles and hisses, and a few protesting calls as they walked by. She moved briskly as each visual confirmation eased the painful thud of her heart. That heart stuttered a moment when she scanned Baby's enclosure. Then she looked up—she knew his games—and found him standing on the thick branch of his tree.

His leap down was gorgeous and full of fun. When he purred, she gave in and ducked under the barrier. "Soon," she murmured. "We'll play a little soon." She stroked his fur through the fence, then laughed when he rose on high hind legs, pressed closer so she could use her fingers to tickle his belly. "Soon," she repeated.

His disappointment rumbled in his throat as she stepped back behind the rail. She shrugged when Coop stared at her.

"He's a special case."

"Didn't I hear disapproval, even some derision, in your voice when you talked about people who buy exotic pets?"

"He's not a pet. Do you see me fitting him with a jeweled collar and leading him around on a leash?"

"That would be the one you call Baby."

"You pay more attention than I think. He's been at the refuge since he was a kitten, by his own choice. They're okay," she added. "If someone unknown was around they'd make some noise. But I have to check anyway. We've got a group coming in this morning, a youth group. And we've got two cats with ingrown claws that need to be seen to. Plus the interns have a few hundred pounds of meat to process in the commissary. We've got a routine, Coop. We can't let this interfere with the health of the animals or the running of the refuge. If we don't have tours, our budget dips. And you've got a business to run, animals to feed."

"Check the rest on your cameras. Let's go through the offices. If they're clear, you can set up there, check your animals."

"Willy's going to let us open the gates, isn't he? Let my people in."

"Shouldn't be long."

"I didn't get a good look at the wolf. It was good size, so I'd say full-grown. To take one down like that . . . Maybe it wasn't with a pack. A lone wolf's easier prey. He wants me upset, off-balance, to throw this place into upheaval. I took my share of psych courses," she said when Coop only studied her face. "I know what he's doing. Not why, but what. I could lose some volunteers, even some interns over this sort of thing. Our intern program is essential, so I'm going to be doing some fast, hard talking at our emergency staff meeting today."

She unlocked the cabin that held the offices. Coop nudged her aside, pushed the door open. The area appeared to be clear. He stepped in, swept it, then moved from space to space to do the same.

"Stay in here, use the computer. I'll check the other buildings. Give me the keys."

She said nothing, only passed them to him. When he left her she sat and waited for the computer to boot up.

She'd known he'd been a cop. But she'd never *seen* him be one until today.

He'd thought he understood what went on in the refuge. But he realized he hadn't considered the full extent of the work even after Lil had given him an overview. The commissary alone was an eye-opener, with its enormous coolers and freezers, its massive amounts of meat, and the equipment required for processing it, handling it, hauling it.

The stables held three horses, including the one he'd sold her. Since he was there, he saw to their feeding and watering, and marked off both chores on the chart posted on the wall.

He checked the equipment shed, the garage, and the long, low cabin posted as the education center. He took a quick scan of the displays inside, the photographs, the pelts, teeth, skulls, bones—where the hell did she get those?

Fascinating, he thought as he checked both restrooms, and each stall inside. He walked through the small attached gift shop with its stuffed animals, T-shirts, sweatshirts, caps, postcards, and posters. Everything tidy and organized.

She'd built something here. Saw to the details, the angles. And all of it, he knew, all of it, for the animals.

As he backtracked he heard the sound of cars, and headed around to meet the sheriff.

"Everything's fine here. She's in the offices," he said to Tansy, then turned to Willy.

"Looks like he decided to hole up after all," Willy said. "We can't be sure it wasn't somebody else, and they just happened to pick that gate. Or somebody got the bright idea because of the cougar. But the fact is hunting wolves is illegal around here, and people know it. Know the trouble they'll get into for it. Now, a farmer shooting one that's after his lifestock's one thing. But I know every farmer in this county, and I can't see any one of them hauling the body up here like this. Even the ones who think Lil's a little on the odd side."

"The bullets in that wolf are going to be from the same gun that shot the cougar."

"Yeah, I expect they are." With a nod, Willy folded his lips tight. "I'm going to be talking to the Park Service, and the state boys. You might do some talking yourself. Maybe somebody going on the trail, using your outfit or one of the others, saw somebody, saw something."

He looked over as Lil came out. "Morning. Sorry about this trouble. Your vet around?"

"He'll be here shortly."

"I'm going to leave a man, same as before. We're going to do what we can, Lil."

"I know, but there's not much you can do." She came down the steps. "One cougar, one wolf. It's bad, but it's a hard world. And those two species may be romanticized in other places, but not here, not where they might wander down from the hills and take down a man's cattle or ravage a henhouse. I understand that, Willy, I live in reality. My reality is I have thirty-six animals, not including the horses, spread over about thirty-two acres of habitat and facilities. And I'm afraid he's going to decide to bring it here, that's what he hinted at today. And he's going to kill one of the animals that live here, that I brought here. Or worse, one of the people who work here, who I brought here."

"I don't know what I can say to ease your mind."

"There's nothing, that's where he's holding the advantage right now. My mind can't be eased. But we have work to do here. We'll keep doing it. I've got six interns who need to finish our program. There's a group of eight- to twelve-year-olds coming in this morning, in about two hours, to take the tour and a session in the education center. If you tell me you don't think those kids will be safe, I'll cancel."

"I've got no reason to think a man who kills a wild animal's going to start taking potshots at kids, Lil."

"Okay. Then we'll all just do whatever we can do. You should go," she said to Coop. "You have your own business, your own animals to see to."

"I'll be back. You may want to make up that list."

She looked blank for a moment, then shook her head. "That's not my top priority just now."

"Your choice."

"Yes. It will be. Thanks, Willy."

Willy pursed his lips as she went back in the office. "I have a feeling the two of you were talking about something other than a dead wolf. Since I do, I'm thinking you'll be staying here tonight."

"That's right."

"I feel better knowing that. Meanwhile, I'm going to have some men scout around the area, check the other gates, look for weak spots. He's holed up somewhere," Willy muttered, looking out toward the hills.

LIL KNEW word would spread, and quickly, so it didn't surprise her when her parents arrived. She walked away from the immobilized tiger to the habitat fence. "Just an ingrown claw. It's a common problem." She reached up to touch the fingers her mother slid through the fence. "I'm sorry you have to be worried."

"You talked about going down to Florida for a couple weeks, working with that panther refuge. You should do that."

"For a few days," Lil corrected. "Next winter. I can't go now. I especially can't go now."

"You could come back home until they find him."

"Who do I put here in my place? Mom, who do I tell I'm too afraid to stay here, so you do it?"

"Anybody who isn't my baby." Jenna gave Lil's fingers a squeeze. "But you can't, and you won't."

"Cooper stayed here last night?" Joe asked her.

"He slept on the living room sofa. He wouldn't leave, and now I'm forced to be grateful he wouldn't let me kick him out of my own house. I have any number of people pushing to stay. We're taking all the precautions we can, I promise. I'm going to order more cameras, use them for security. I've looked at alarm systems, but we just can't afford the type that would cover the place. No," she said even as Joe started to speak. "You know you can't afford it either."

"What I can't afford is anything happening to my daughter."

"I'm going to make sure nothing does." She glanced back to where Matt worked on the tiger. "I need to finish up here."

"We'll go back to the compound, see if anyone can use some extra hands."

"Always."

FROM HIS POSITION on high ground, through the lenses of his field glasses, he watched the family group. Observing prey was essential, learning the habits, the territory, the dynamics, strengths. Weaknesses.

Patience was another essential. He could admit that the—occasional—lack of it was one of his weaknesses. Temper had been another. Temper had cost him eighteen months inside when it had pushed him to beat a man half to death in a bar.

But he'd learned to control his temper, to remain calm and objective. To use the kill for personal satisfaction.

Never in heat, never in rage. Cold and cool.

The cougar had been impulse. It was there, and he'd wanted to know what it was like to kill the wild thing eye-to-eye. He'd been disappointed. The lack of challenge, the lack of *the hunt* equaled no personal satisfaction.

It had, he was forced to admit, brought him a mild sense of shame.

He'd had to offset that by letting his temper out—just a little—and destroying the camp. But he'd done so precisely, and that was important. He'd done so in a way that sent a message.

Lil. Lillian. Dr. Chance. She was so interesting. He'd always thought so. Look at her with her family unit—there, a definite weakness.

It might be satisfying to use that against her. Fear added to the thrill of the hunt. He wanted her to fear. He'd learned how much more it meant when the fear came with it. And he believed it would be more exciting to scent hers, as he'd seen she didn't fear easily.

He would make her fear.

He respected her, and her bloodline. Even if she did not respect her ancestry. She defiled it with this place, these cages where the free and wild were imprisoned. This sacred place of his people—and hers.

Yes, he would make her fear.

She'd be an excellent addition to his count. His biggest prize to date.

He replaced his binoculars, shimmied back from the ridge before he rose. He hefted his light pack, and stood in the late-winter sunlight, fingering the necklace of bear teeth around his neck. The single thing he'd kept of his father's.

His father had taught him of the ancestry, and the betrayals. He'd taught him how to hunt and how to live on the holy land. How to take what he needed without remorse, without regret.

He wondered what he would take, and keep, from Lil after the kill.

Satisfied with the day's scouting, he began his hike back to his den, where he would plan the next step of the game.

13

Lil was about to prep for the evening feeding when Farley arrived. He came on horseback, looking like a man who could sit easy all day in the saddle if that was required.

It struck her, as it never had before, how alike he and Coop were in that single area. A couple of city kids who'd morphed into cowboys. Who looked, when they were in the saddle, as if they'd been born there.

And there, she supposed, the similarity ended. Farley was open and easygoing, Coop closed and difficult.

Or maybe that was just her perspective on them.

She turned to Lucius.

"Why don't you go keep an eye on things in the commissary? I'll be right along."

She walked over to meet Farley and give his horse Hobo a pat on the cheek. "Hello, boys."

"Hi there, Lil. Got ya something." He pulled the clutch of pink-and-white daisies peeking their tops out of his saddlebag.

Pleasure and surprise bloomed in equal parts. "You brought me flowers?"

"I thought maybe you could use a little brightening up."

She looked at them—sweet, fresh, and yes, bright. And she smiled. Smiling, she crooked her finger to signal him to lean over.

His rubber grin stretched when she planted a loud kiss on his cheek. Then she cocked an eyebrow. "Are those daffodils I see sticking out of your saddlebag?"

"Sure look like daffodils to me."

Lil patted his ankle affectionately. "She's touring a group who came in a while ago. The father's a big fan of *Deadwood*. The TV thing. So they made the trip to see it, after doing Rushmore, and heard about us in town. He thought the kids would get a charge."

"Bet they will."

"They'd be about halfway around now, if you want to catch up."

"Guess I will. Lil, I can bunk here tonight if you want."

"Thanks, Farley, but I'm covered."

"Yeah, I heard." His cheeks pinked a little when she stared at him. "I mean to say Joe said how Coop was likely staying around. To keep an eye out. It eases your pa's mind knowing that," he added.

"Which is why I'm allowing it. Tell Tansy we're about to start the evening feeding. The family from Omaha is going to get more bang for their buck."

"I'll do that."

"Farley?" She gave Hobo another rub as she looked up into Farley's face. "You and Tansy are two of my favorite people in the world. You're family to me, so I'm going to say what I think."

His face went carefully blank. "All right, Lil."

"Good luck."

His smile flickered, then expanded. "I guess I need it."

He trotted off, bolstered. He set store by Lil's opinion, so her approval—it seemed approval to him—meant a lot. Whistling a little, he traveled the loop of the path out of the compound and around the first enclosures.

The ground rose and fell as nature would have it. Outcroppings of rocks jutted up—some had been there since God knew, and some Lil had put in. Trees speared and spread, offering shade and opportunities for climbing, for scratching. Even as he rode by, one of the bobcats stretched out, sharpening his claws on the bark of a pine.

He spotted the trolley they used for groups around the bend and across the flat, but resisted the urge to nudge Hobo into a gallop. When he reached them they stood outside the tiger habitat watching the big cat yawn, roll, and stretch in a way that told Farley he'd just awakened from a nap.

Probably knew it was coming on suppertime.

"Howdy, folks." He tapped a finger to the brim of his hat. "Lil said I should tell you it's feeding time," he told Tansy.

"Thank you, Farley. Excluding those in the petting zoo, the animals here at the refuge are nocturnal. We feed them in the evening, as it reinforces their natural hunting instincts."

She used what Farley thought of as her "official" voice. He could listen to it all day long.

"We process hundreds of pounds of meat every week in our commissary. The staff and interns prepare the meat, primarily chicken, which is generously donated by Hanson's Foods. You really timed your visit well today, because watching feeding time is an experience. You'll see firsthand the power of the animals here at Chance Wildlife Refuge."

"Mister? Can I ride on your horse?"

Farley looked down at a girl of about eight, pretty as a sunbeam in her pink hooded coat.

"If your folks say so, you can sit up here with me, and I'll walk you around. Hobo's a gentle one, ma'am," he said to the mother.

"Please! *Please!* I'd rather ride on the horse than watch the lions and stuff eat chicken."

There was a short debate. Farley stayed out of it and gave himself the pleasure of watching Tansy tell the boy—about twelve, Farley supposed—how tigers stalked and ambushed.

In the end, the girl had her way and squeezed onto Hobo in front of Farley. "This is a *lot* more fun. Can you make him go really fast?"

"I could. But I expect if I did your ma would have my hide."

"What's a hide?"

He chuckled. "My skin. She'd skin me if I did that after I promised to go easy."

"I wish I had a horse." She leaned forward to brush her hand over Hobo's mane. "Do you get to ride all the time? Every day?"

"I guess I do."

The little girl sighed. "You're so lucky."

Behind her, Farley nodded. "I am. I'm lucky all right."

Since the girl—Cassie—couldn't have been less interested in the feeding, Farley got the okay to show her around on the horse. Hobo, steady as Gibraltar, placidly clopped the path while the animals screamed, growled, roared, and howled.

As twilight fell, Farley waved goodbye.

"That was nice of you, Farley." Tansy watched the minivan head down the road. "Taking the time and trouble to entertain her."

"It wasn't any trouble. Easier to walk a horse around than haul all that meat, which I'd've felt obliged to help do if I hadn't been occupied."

He pulled the daffodils out of his bag. "These are for you."

She stared at the bright yellow trumpets. He wondered if she knew how clearly everything showed on her face, the surprise and the pleasure—and the worry. "Oh, Farley. You shouldn't—"

"You had a rough start this morning. I'm hoping you let me give you a better end to the day. Why don't you come out with me, Tansy?"

"Farley, I told you we're not going to get involved like that. We're friends, and that's all. We're not going to date."

It took some effort not to smile. She was still using her "official" voice. "Then why don't you let me buy you a burger, like a friend would when his friend has a hard day. Just take your mind off things, that's all."

"I'm not sure that's—"

"Just a hamburger, Tansy, to save you from having to fix a meal or figure out where to get one for yourself. Nothing more than that."

She gave him a long look, with that line digging in between her eyebrows. "Just a burger?"

"Well, maybe some fries. Doesn't seem like a burger without the fries."

"Okay. Okay, Farley, I'll meet you in town. In about an hour. How about Mustang Sally's?"

"That's fine." Since he didn't want to push his luck, he swung into the saddle. "I'll see you later."

He rode away, with a big grin on his face and a loud *yee-haw* in his heart.

In the office she shared with Tansy, Lil sat with her foot on the desk and her eyes on the ceiling. She glanced over when Tansy came in, smiled at the daffodils. "Pretty."

"I don't want any remarks." She clipped out the words. "It was just a nice gesture from a friend. Something to cheer me up."

Lil debated for a moment, then decided if you couldn't screw with your friends, who could you screw with? "I know. He brought me daisies."

Tansy's face fell. "He did?" She recovered, smiled toothily. "Well, there, you see? Just a nice gesture. It doesn't mean anything but that."

"Absolutely not. You ought to put them in water. The wet paper towels and plastic wrap only hold them for so long."

"I will. I'm going to go home, if there's nothing urgent. Long day. The interns are finishing up, so I'll give Eric—and whoever needs it—a lift back to town."

"Sure. Lucius is working on something. He said he'd probably be another twenty minutes, which in Lucius time means another hour. He can lock up."

"After this morning that doesn't seem good enough."

"I know, but it's what we can do."

Worry clouded her eyes. "Cooper's coming back, staying the night?"

"Apparently I'm outvoted on that. And no comments there, either. Tit for tat."

Tansy held up her free hand. "Not a word."

"I can hear what you're thinking, and will ignore it. Meanwhile, one thing. I just got off the phone with a woman outside of Butte. She has an eighteen-month-old melanistic jaguar, born in captivity and purchased by her as an exotic pet."

"Spotted or black?"

"Black. She's had it since it was a kit. A female, named Cleopatra. A couple of days ago, Cleo was, apparently, feeling both frisky and peckish and ate Pierre, a teacup poodle."

"Oops."

"Yes, big oops for little Pierre. The owner is hysterical, her husband is furious. Pierre belonged to his mother, who was visiting from Phoenix. He's laid down the law, and Cleo must go."

"Where would we put her?"

"There's a question. I'm working on it. We could provide a temporary habitat by fencing off a section of Sheba's area. She's not using all her area anyway. Rarely leaves the den or the immediate vicinity."

"Can we afford it?"

"I'm working on that, too." Leaning back, Lil tapped a pencil on the edge of her desk. "I think Cleo's owner can be persuaded to make a nice, fat donation to ensure Cleo's happiness and well-being."

"Define 'nice and fat.'"

"I'm hoping for ten thousand."

"I like the way you hope."

"It's not an impossible dream," Lil told her. "I just Googled the owners. They're rolling in it. They're ready to pay all expenses and fees to get her here, the transportation, the cost of sending a team to Montana for her—and indicated there would be a prize in the box if we could move quickly. I asked her to give me a day to consider the logistics."

Lil's eyes lit up as she tossed the pencil down. "A black jaguar, Tansy. Young, healthy. We could breed her. And God knows she'd be happier and better off here than on some ranch in Montana. We have most of the materials we need for a temporary habitat. In the spring, when the ground's thawed, we can expand, put in a permanent one."

"You've already decided."

"I don't see how we can resist. I think I can get the cat and five figures out of this. I think I can make this woman so happy and grateful we may end up with a valuable supporter. I'm going to think about it more. You do the same. We'll talk about it in the morning, and decide."

"Okay. I bet she's beautiful."

Lil tapped her computer screen, so Tansy skirted around the desk. "She e-mailed me pictures. We'll get the rhinestone collar off her. She's gorgeous. Look at those eyes. I've seen them in the wild. They're dramatic and mysterious and a little spooky. She'd be an amazing addition. She needs a refuge. She can't be introduced to the wild. We can give her a good home here."

Tansy patted Lil's shoulder. "Oh, yeah, you *think* about it more. See you in the morning."

It was full dark by the time Lil left the office. When she stepped out and spotted Coop's truck, she hunched her shoulders. She hadn't heard him drive up. Too involved, she admitted as she crossed the compound, with refreshing herself on jaguars, working out the logistics of transportation and habitat. They'd need a vet to clear her, Lil thought. She couldn't trust the word of the owner on that. Still, if the cat had any medical problems it might be even more important to give her sanctuary.

She'd wheedle money out of Cleo's owner. She was good at wheedling donations. It might have been far from her favorite part of the job, but she was good at it.

She stepped inside.

A fire crackled cheerfully in the hearth. Coop sat on the sofa, his feet on her coffee table, a beer in his hand. With the other he worked on a notebook computer on his lap.

She shut the front door with a little more force than necessary. He didn't bother to look up.

"Your mother sent over a chunk of ham, some sort of potatoes, and I think it might be artichokes."

"I can make my own food, you know. I just haven't had a chance to get to the store for supplies in the last few days."

"Uh-huh. I brought over a six-pack if you want a beer."

"Coop, this can't . . . This is wrong in so many ways." She pulled off her coat, tossed it aside. "You can't just *live* here."

"I'm not. I've got my own place. I'm just sleeping here for a while."

"And how long is a while? How long do you plan to sleep on my sofa?"

He sent her a lazy glance as he took a pull of his beer. "Until you loosen up and let me into your bed."

"Oh, well, if that's all, let's go. Come on, let's hit the sheets. Then we can both get back to our regularly scheduled lives."

"Okay. Just give me a minute to finish this up."

She clamped her hands on her head, paced a circle. "Fuck," she said. "Fuck, fuck, fuck."

"I might've put it more delicately than that."

She stopped, then squatted on the other side of the coffee table. "Cooper."

He took another sip of his beer. "Lillian."

She shut her eyes a moment because there had to be some sense, some shade of sanity in the chaos murking up her brain. "This arrangement is awkward and unnecessary, and just weird."

"Why?"

"Why? Why? Because we have a history, because we had a . . . thing. You do realize that everyone in the damn county figures we're sleeping together again."

"I don't think everyone in the county knows either one of us, or cares. And so what?"

She had to scramble for an answer to that. "Maybe I want to sleep with somebody else, and you're in the way."

Coop took a long, slow pull from the beer this time. "Then where is he?"

"Okay, forget that one. Just forget that one."

"Happy to. It's got to be your turn to put the meal on."

"See?" She jabbed a finger in the air. "*There.* What is this 'turn' crap? This is *my* house. Mine, mine, mine. And I come in to find you on *my* sofa, with your feet on *my* coffee table, drinking *my* beer—"

"I bought the beer."

"You're deliberately missing the point."

"I got the point. You don't like me being here. The point you're missing is I don't care. You're not staying here alone until this trouble is resolved. I told Joe I'd look out for you. That's it, Lil."

"If it makes you feel any better I can arrange for an intern to stay in the next cabin."

The faintest trace of impatience flickered over his face. "Would the average age of your interns be maybe twenty? I wonder why the idea of some skinny college kid as your backup doesn't ease my mind. You'd save yourself from aggravation if you just accept that I'm going to be around until this is settled. Did you make that list?"

"Until" was the sticking point, wasn't it? she thought. He'd be around until . . . he was finished, he decided to move on again, he found something or someone else.

"Lil?"

"What?"

"Did you make that list?"

"What list?" When he smirked, it came back to her. "No, I didn't make any damn list. I had a few other minor things on my mind today." Though she knew it was a kind of surrender, she dropped down to sit on the floor. "We took two thirty-two slugs out of the gray wolf."

"I heard."

"They have to run ballistics, but we all know it was the same gun, used by the same man."

"That's your good news. You'd have more to worry about if you had two shooters."

"I hadn't thought of it that way. Well, whoopee."

"You need better security."

"I'm working on it. More cameras, lights, alarms. The health and safety of my animals is priority, but I can't just reach in my pocket and pull out the money to pay for all that."

He hitched up, reached in his pocket, and took out a check. "Donation."

She smiled a little. Damn it, he was being considerate and kind—and she was being nothing but bitchy. "And all are gratefully accepted, but I priced some of the equipment and systems today so . . ."

She glanced at the check. Her brain simply froze. She blinked, blinked again, but the number of zeros remained the same. "What the hell is this?"

"I thought we'd established it's a donation. Are you going to heat up that food your mother sent?"

"Where the hell did you get this kind of money? And you can't just give it away like this. Is this a real check?"

"It's family money. Trust fund. My father's kept it locked down as much as he could, but it's been trickling in every five years or so."

"Trickle." She whispered the word. "In my world this is a lot more than a trickle."

"He'll have to let loose of another payment when I hit thirty-five. He can hold the rest back until I'm forty, and he will. It pisses him off he can't break the trust altogether and stiff me. I'm a big disappointment to him, on every level. But since that's mutual, we deal with it."

The gleam the donation put in her eyes dulled into sympathy. "I'm sorry. I'm sorry things never got any better between you and your father. I haven't even asked about that, or your mother."

"She's married again. Third time. This one seems solid. He's a decent guy, and from the outside, anyway, it looks like she's happy."

"I know they came out to visit. I was doing fieldwork so I wasn't here. I know it meant a lot to Sam and Lucy."

"She flew out when he got hurt. Surprised me," Coop admitted. "I think it surprised everyone, including her."

"I didn't know. So much has been going on since I got back from Peru. I've missed a lot of details. It's better, then? You and your mother?"

"It's never going to be Norman Rockwell, but we deal with each other when we see each other."

"That's good." She looked back at the check. "I want this. We could really use this. But it's a lot. More than I was going to pry out of the jaguar lady, and that was going to give me happy dreams tonight."

"Jaguar lady?"

Lil just shook her head. "This is a major contribution. The sort I usually have to go begging for."

"I have a lot of money. More than I need. You're a tax write-off, which'll make my accountant happy."

"Well, if it makes your accountant happy. Thank you, more than I can say." She gave his boot, still resting on her table, a friendly pat. "You're entitled to a number of fabulous prizes. A stuffed cougar, an official Chance Wildlife Refuge T-shirt, *and* mug. A subscription to our newsletter, and free admission to the refuge, the education center, and all facilities for . . . with this amount the rest of your natural life."

"Wrap 'em up. You can use the strings attached to the check."

"Uh-oh."

"They're simple. You use it for security. I'll help you pick the system. It's something I know. If there's anything left after that, go crazy. But you use that to secure the compound, and as much of the refuge as possible."

"Since I didn't have this in my hand five minutes ago, I can live with those strings. I do need a new habitat. A home for the panther. Melanistic jaguar from Butte."

"What the hell is 'melanistic,' and when did they get jaguars, unless you're talking about ones with engines, in Montana?"

"'Melanistic' means black or nearly black pigmentation, though black jaguars can produce spotted young. And there are no jaguars in the wild in Montana anymore. They may be making a comeback, but in the U.S. jaguars are bred in captivity. I have a woman in Butte who wants us to adopt her cat because it ate the dog."

Coop studied Lil's face for a long moment. "I think I need another beer."

She sighed. "I'll heat up dinner and explain." She pushed to her feet, then stopped herself. She waved the check in the air. "See? I'm heating up dinner."

"No, you're just standing there talking about it."

"You give me a big, fat donation and I'm heating up dinner, forgetting to be annoyed that you're squatting like a homesteader in my living room."

"There aren't those kinds of strings on that check, Lil. I told you clearly the ones that were."

"You don't have to put strings on it for them to be there. Damn it."

"Here, give it back. I'll tear it up."

"No way in hell." She stuffed it in her back pocket. "But we do have to set boundaries, Coop. Ground rules. I can't live like this. It's too unsettled and stressful."

"Write them up. We'll negotiate."

"Here's one. If you're going to eat here, whoever makes the food or heats up the food or whatever, the other cleans up after. That's basic roommate dynamic."

"Fine."

"Did you ever have one? After college and the academy, I mean."

"You want to know if I ever lived with a woman. No. Not officially."

Because he'd seen through her very thin smoke screen, she said nothing else, but went back to heat up her mother's care package.

Since it made for easy conversation, she told him about Cleo while they ate.

"She's lucky it ate a dog and not a toddler."

"Actually, that's true enough. Cleo may—and probably did—start out playing. Then instinct took over. Wild can be trained, and they can learn, but they can't and won't be tamed. Rhinestone collars and satin pillows don't make a pet out of the wild, even when they're born and raised in captivity. We'll bring her in, give her a big splash on the website. A new animal always generates more hits, more donations."

"Will you include her taste for pups in her bio?"

"I think we'll leave that out. What were you working on? On your laptop?"

"Spreadsheets. Just basic outlay, income, projections."

"Really?"

"You sound surprised I'd know what a spreadsheet is. I ran my own business for five years."

"I know. I guess it's one of those gaps I still haven't jumped. Private investigating. Is it anything like TV? I know I asked before, but you were being snotty when you answered."

"I recall being honest. No, it's not like TV, or not much. It's a lot of legwork and sitting-on-your-ass work. Talking to people, computer checks, documenting."

"But still, solving crimes?"

Amusement at her hopeful tone warmed those ice blue eyes. "That's TV. We handled a lot of insurance claims, checking them for fraud. Divorces. Surveilling cheating spouses. Missing persons."

"You found missing people? That's important, Coop."

"Not everyone who's missing wants to be found. So it's relative. And it's done. Now it's horses, feed, vet bills, farrier bills, tack, insurance, crops. They need a full-time hand at the farm. They need a Farley."

She jabbed her fork at him. "You can't have Farley."

"If I tried to take him, he'd turn me down anyway. He's in love with your parents."

"Among others. He's got his eye on Tansy."

"Tansy?" Coop considered it. "She's hot. Farley's . . ."—he searched for a word—"affable."

"And charming and reliable, and very, very cute. He flusters her. I've known Tansy since we were eighteen. I've never seen her flustered by a man."

Intrigued, Coop angled his head. "You're rooting for Farley."

"Mentally I'm shaking pom-poms and doing C jumps."

"Interesting image." He drew his loosely closed fist down her braid. "When's the last time you were flustered, Lil?"

Since the answer was *right now,* she slid off the bench, and took the plates to the sink. "I've got too much going on to be flustered. Dishes are yours. I'm going up. I need to finish my article."

He caught her hand as she passed, yanked enough to throw her off balance so he could pull her across his lap. He took her braid again—no loose fist this time—and tugged so her lips lined with his. Took her mouth.

Irritated at being caught off-guard, she pushed, twisted. He was much stronger, his body a lot tougher than it had been once upon a time.

And his mouth, his hands, considerably more skilled.

Lust wrapped around irritation. Need lit a fire to the mix.

Then he softened the kiss, enough to add a layer of sweetness that bruised her heart.

"'Night, Lil." He murmured it against her mouth before drawing back.

She pushed to her feet. "No physical or sexual contact. That's a rule."

"I'm not going to agree to that one. Pick another."

"It's not right, Coop. It's not fair."

"I don't know if it's right or not. I don't care if it's fair." His tone was the equivalent of a shrug. "I want you. I know how to do without what I want, and I know how to go after what I want. It's about deciding."

"And where am I in this decision?"

"You'll have to figure that out for yourself."

"You're not going to do this to me. You're not going to break my heart again."

"I never broke your heart."

"If you believe that you're either seriously stupid or emotionally stunted. Don't bother me anymore tonight. Don't bother me."

She strode away, up the stairs, into her bedroom, where she shut— and locked—the door.

14

Lil waited until she heard Coop start his truck in the morning before she came downstairs. The delay put her a little behind, but the lack of stress made it worthwhile.

She'd done a lot of work, and a lot of thinking, locked in her room through the night. Clearheaded work, she decided. Clearheaded thinking.

She smelled the coffee before she reached the kitchen, and could—clearheadedly—consider that a benefit of having him stay overnight. There *were* benefits, and she'd weighed them against the difficulties.

Her kitchen was clean. The man was no slob. And the coffee was hot and strong, just as she liked it. Alone in the quiet, she zapped a bowl of instant oatmeal, shoveled it in. Dawn lifted the light when she'd finished, and interns and staff began to arrive for the day's work.

Enclosures and stalls needed to be mucked out, and the enclosures disinfected. Interns would collect samples of scat from each animal, which would be tested for parasites.

Always, Lil mused as she manned a hose, a fun job.

According to her daily chart, it was time for Xena's leg to be examined, which meant immobilizing the old wolf and transporting her to Medical. While she was out, they'd give her a full exam and take blood samples.

The little zoo animals required feeding and tending, and fresh hay laid. Horses needed feed and water, exercise, and grooming. The sheer physical labor of a routine morning at the refuge sweated out any lingering tension.

By mid-morning she had assigned some interns to inventory the fencing, the poles, and other materials needed to create a viable temporary habitat for the jaguar before Lil went into the office to contact Butte.

When she'd done all the plans and preparations she could, she went out to find Tansy.

"Elementary school field trip," Tansy told her, gesturing to the kids being herded down the path. "I put Eric and Jolie on them. They work well together. The fact is, Lil, Eric's one of the best interns we've had in the program."

"I agree. He's smart, willing to work, and he's not afraid to ask questions."

"He wants to stay another term. He's already contacted his professors to ask if they'd clear it."

"We've never had a second-term intern. Could be useful." Lil considered. "He could help with training the newbies, and we could put his own training up a notch or two. If he can make it work with the university, I'll clear it."

"Good. We'll be switching over very soon. Lose this group, start over with the next." Tansy tipped her head. "You don't look like you got much sleep."

"I didn't. Because I was working, fiddling and finagling, plotting and planning. I've got to head into town shortly, and deposit this."

She pulled the check out of her pocket, held it by the corners, tipped it back and forth as if it danced.

"What—is that— Holy shit!"

Tansy threw her arms around Lil, and the two of them bounced in a circle. "Lil, this is amazing and wonderful and out of the blue. Coop?

How many sexual favors did you have to offer and/or provide? Does he have that kind of money?"

"I didn't offer and/or provide any sexual favors. But for this kind of dough, I would have. And yes, apparently he does have this kind of money. Who knew?"

"Does he have more? We can both offer and/or provide. I'm in."

"We'll keep that in reserve." Because it still dazzled her, Lil studied all the zeros again. "I've spent this about ten times in my head overnight. I've got prices on security systems, security lights, cameras. New gates. We'll see how far it goes. And to add to it, Montana is donating ten grand, with the stipulation we use at least part of it to build Cleo a spiffy new home in the spring."

"When it rains, it freaking monsoons."

"My mother always says life's made up of cycles, of checks and balances. I like to think this is to balance out the horrible. Matt spoke with the vet in Butte, and we're good there. I'm dealing with the permits, documentation, the paperwork, the logistics."

"Jesus, Lil, we're getting a jag. We're actually getting a black jaguar."

"And I need you to go to Montana and bring Cleo to her new home."

"Sure, but you always go to check out the animals."

"I can't leave now, Tans, not even for the two or three days this'll take." She scanned the compound, the humans and animals. "I can't take the chance that something could happen while I was gone. And since this is moving so quickly, I want to be here to help with the temporary habitat, and finalize plans for the permanent one. I've arranged for the crate and the box truck."

"Problem there would be I've never driven one of those rigs."

"You won't be driving. You'll be in charge of the cat. Her safety—public safety—her health. It's about a seven-hour drive—eight, tops. Farley will handle the rig."

"Oh, Lil."

"Big picture, Tansy. He can handle the truck, and he's a top-level volunteer. He's the best one for it, and he's got enough experience help-

ing around here to assist you in any way you might need. I don't antici-
pate any problems."

"Your big picture's logical. But what about the yen? What about that?"

Lil knew exactly how to play it. She widened her eyes. "Are you telling
me you can't handle Farley and his yen?"

"No. Not exactly." Trapped, Tansy hissed out a breath. "Damn it."

"You could be there in six hours if it goes well," Lil continued, talking fast, "check out Cleo, charm and reassure the owner. Spend the
night, load her up the next morning, and be back here before feeding time."

Now, shamelessly, Lil added the big guns. "I can't do it myself, Tansy,
so I need you to do me this really big favor."

"Of course I will. But it's a situation."

"Then why did you have dinner with him last night?"

Scowling, Tansy stuffed her hands in her coat pockets. "How do you
know I did?"

"Because interns eat, too, and talk."

"It was just a burger."

"And this is just transport. I'll put everything together for you before
the end of the day, and you can go over any medical stuff you feel you
might need to with Matt. You can leave in the morning. If you get here
by six, you can get an early start."

"You've already talked to Farley."

"Yeah. He's bringing the rig over here tonight."

"Tell him to plan on leaving at five A.M. It'll give us a good jump on
the day."

"Done. God, Tansy, you're bringing home a jag. Now I'm going into
town to swell our coffers before I deplete them."

SHE HAD a number of errands to run in Deadwood. The bank, the store,
the contractor, the post office. Since it would save time later, she loaded
up at the feed-and-grain.

She saved Coop for last, since she saw his truck outside the stables they kept on the edge of town.

She took the folder with the information and specs she'd gotten off the Internet and went into the smell of horses and leather and hay.

She found him in the third stall, sitting on a stool as he wrapped the right foreleg of a chestnut gelding.

"Is he all right?"

Coop nodded, his hands steady and competent. "Just a little strain."

"I had some business in town, and thought I'd drop this off when I saw your truck. I got information on a couple of security systems I think would work for us. I'll leave it on the bench out here."

"Go ahead. I made a call earlier. Contact I have in the business. I like their system, and he'd shave a little off the cost for me." He named the system.

"That's one of the two I have in the folder."

"It's a good one. If you go with that, he'll give us the contact for the closest rep out here. They'll come out, help you design and install."

"All right. Let's just go with them."

"I'll give him a call when I'm done here, have him contact you."

"I appreciate it. I've also got an official letter of thanks from the refuge acknowledging your generous donation. Your accountant may want that on file. And Farley will be staying overnight in the compound."

He looked over then. "Okay."

"I'll let you get back to work."

"Lil. We have more to talk about."

"I guess we do. Sooner or later."

SHE WAS UP to see Tansy and Farley off in the cold dark. Farley's easy cheer started her day with a smile, despite the occasional dirty look from Tansy.

"Try to avoid speeding tickets, especially coming back."

"Don't worry."

"And call me when you get there, or if you run into any problems, or—"

"Maybe you should remind me not to leave the keys in the rig and to chew my food thoroughly before swallowing."

She poked a finger in his belly. "Don't speed—too much—and stay in contact. That's all I have to say."

"Then let's roll. You all set, Tansy?"

"Yes." She sent him a brisk, businesslike nod.

And he sent Lil a grin and a wink.

Knowing both of them, Lil would've laid odds the wink would cut through the businesslike before the first sixty miles.

Waving, she stood and listened to the diminishing sound of the truck as it curved toward the main road.

It occurred to her that for the first time since she and Coop had camped she was fully alone in the compound. For another two hours—give or take—she had it all to herself.

"Just you and me, guys," she murmured.

She listened to the carol of her old lion, who often called out to the night before dawn struck. In those acres of sanctuary, the wild was awake and alive.

And hers, she thought, as much as they could be.

She looked up, happy to see the night sky brilliant with stars. The air was apple-crisp, the stars like jewels, and Boris's roar joined Sheba's.

In that moment, Lil, realized, she couldn't have been more content.

A sane woman would go back to bed for an hour—or at least go inside in the warmth and have another cup of coffee, maybe a leisurely breakfast. But she didn't want bed, or indoors. No, she wanted the night, the stars, her animals, and this small slice of solitude.

She went in to fill a go-cup with coffee, grabbed a flashlight, shoved her cell phone in her pocket out of habit.

She'd walk her land, she decided, her place. Wander the habitat trails before the sun rose, before it wasn't all hers again.

As she stepped outside, a sudden, high *beep-beep-beep* stopped her in her tracks. Cage door alarm, she thought, as her pulse jumped. The coffee splattered when she dropped it to streak down the steps, to race to the other cabin.

"Which one, which one?" She booted up Lucius's computer on the run, grabbed a drug gun and darts from Medical. Afraid of what she might find—or not find—she stuffed extra tranquilizers into her pocket.

She hit the switch for the path lights, the emergency lights, then rushed to the computer to call up a camera scan.

"Could be a blip, could be nothing. Could be . . . Oh, God."

The tiger's cage stood wide open. In the yellow glare of the emergency lights she saw a blood trail across the path and into the brush. And there the shadow of the cat, the glint of his eyes against the dark.

Go now, go fast, she ordered herself. If she waited she might lose him. Even at his age, he could travel fast, travel far. Across the valley, into the hills, into the forest, where there were people, hikers, farmers, campers.

Go now.

She sucked in her breath like a diver about to take the plunge, then stepped outside.

The alone, so appealing only moments before, now pulsed with fear. The air beat with it, matching the pounding of her heart, and stabbed at her throat like tiny, vicious needles with each breath. The steady beep of the cage alarm stirred the other animals, so roars, howls, screams broke across the compound and echoed toward the sky. That would help, she told herself, help mask the sound of her approach.

The cat knew her, but that made no difference. He was a wild and dangerous thing, more so out of containment and on a blood trail. More, the blood trail meant the cat wasn't the only predator who could spring. She knew she might be stalked even as she stalked the cat.

She had to shut down the fear and ordered herself to ignore the rush of blood in her ears, the knock of her own heart, the snake of sweat slithering down her back. Her job—her responsibility—was to immobilize the cat. Quickly, cleanly.

She called on every instinct, every hour of training and experience. She knew the ground— better, in fact, than her quarry did. She forced herself to move slowly, to use caution, to *listen*.

She shifted direction. The route would take longer but would bring her upwind. If, as she believed, her tiger was busy with the bait that had drawn him from his cage, the route, the noise would be to her advantage.

She moved through the backwash of the lights, into shadows and back again. Gauging her ground, the distance, shutting her mind to everything but reaching the cat, immobilizing him.

She heard, under the calls from the habitats, a sound she knew well. Fang and claw rending flesh, the crunch of bone, and the low rumble of the cat as it tore through the meat.

Sweat slid down her temples, wormed down her sides as she angled again. The cat lay low, feasting. For a clear shot, one that injected the dart into large muscle, she'd have to step out into the open, stand in his line of sight.

Lil gripped the drug gun, moved sideways, and came out of the trees a bare six feet from him.

The cat lifted its head, and he growled. Blood from the nearly decimated elk calf smeared his snout, dripped from fangs. Eyes glinted at her, gold and feral.

She fired, struck him behind the shoulder, and prepared to fire again as he roared in rage. He twitched and shook, trying to dislodge the dart. She took a step back, and another, testing the placement of each foot before giving it her weight.

And he watched her, dipping his head back to the bloody meat while she counted off the time in her mind, while she listened to the thunder rumbling in his throat.

Though her fear screamed *Run!*, she knew running would spark his instinct to chase, to attack. So slowly, her muscles quivering, she continued the careful retreat. Get in his enclosure, she thought still ticking off the seconds in her mind, close the door. Inside, too far to make the shot, but close enough, maybe, to reach safety until the drug took him under.

Or to take a second shot if he went for her.

He should be under, going under. Goddamn it, go down. Don't make me give you another dose. She heard the ragged whoosh of her own breath as he snarled again at her inching retreat, and readied to squeeze her trembling finger on the trigger as he bunched to spring.

Terror was bright. Bright and cold. She'd never make the cage.

But even as he gathered himself, his front legs buckled. Lil eased back a step, then another, maintaining distance, *seeing* the enclosure in her mind, as the tiger staggered. It sprawled, the feral glint fading from its eyes. She kept the drug gun aimed as she changed her angle and moved back into the shadows, the cover of trees.

She wouldn't retreat to the enclosure now. The tiger was no longer the threat.

Nothing moved. The night birds had gone quiet, and the morning calls had yet to begin. She scented animal, and blood and her own clammy sweat.

If another hunted, she prayed he'd gone to ground. Though she crouched, made herself small, she knew if he was there, if he was armed, she was vulnerable.

But she wouldn't, couldn't leave her defenseless tiger alone. With her free hand she dug in her pocket for her cell phone.

Following instinct again, she called Coop.

"Yeah?"

"There's been a break-in here. I need you to come, quick as you can. Don't call my parents."

"Are you hurt?"

"No. It's under control, but I need you to come."

"Fifteen minutes," he said, and hung up.

She made a second call to the sheriff, then went to check the big cat. Satisfied his respiration was normal, she went into the light again, and down to the path. She checked the cage door, studied the damaged lock, the baited trail.

She pivoted at a sound, searched the path, the brush, the trees for movement before she realized the sound came from her. Her breath was whooshing in and out, short, hard gasps, and the hand that held the drug gun shook violently.

"Okay, okay, good thing I waited until it was done to fall apart. Okay."

She bent from the waist, braced her hands on her knees to try to get her breath back. Even her legs were quivering, she realized, and tipping her wrist, she saw with some shock that only sixteen minutes had passed since the alarm sounded.

Minutes, not hours, not days. A handful of minutes only.

She made herself straighten. Whoever had broken the lock, baited the tiger out of containment would be gone now. Logic demanded it. If he'd stayed to watch, he'd have seen her immobilize the cat, make the calls. If he was smart, and he was, he'd know she'd called for help, called the police. He'd want to be well away before that help arrived.

Back to his hole, back to his lair.

"Stay away from what's mine," she called out, more in fury than in any hopes he would hear. "I'll find you. I swear to God I'll find you."

She paced the path, checking the near cages, and counted off the minutes. When another ten had passed, she risked leaving the unconscious cat. She made the dash back to the compound, into the equipment shed to load the harness and sling into one of the carts. Even as she backed the cart out of the shed, she heard the truck roaring on the road. Lil leaped out of the cart, waved her arms to signal Coop when his headlights slashed over her.

"I want to move fast. I'll explain. Just get in the cart."

He didn't waste time, didn't ask questions until they were both back in the cart and she was speeding toward the habitats. "What happened?"

"Somebody got inside, compromised the lock on the tiger's cage, baited a trail to lure him out. He's okay. I tranquilized him."

"*He's* okay?"

"Yes. My priority right now is to get him back inside, to get him contained and the door secured. I called Willy, but let's not get into all the whys and hows. I want the cat back inside before the interns get here, if possible. I don't want a bunch of college kids freaking on me."

She stopped the cart, jumped out. "I can't move him by myself. He weighs close to five hundred pounds. I'm going to rig up this harness, and we'll back the cart up as close to him as we can. The two of us should be able to lift him on."

"How long will he be out?"

"About four hours. I gave him a strong dose. Coop, it'll be easier to tell the interns if he's secured than if they start coming in and see this."

He looked as she did at what remained of the young elk, at the blood smearing the tiger's muzzle.

"Let's get it done. Then, Lil, I've got a lot to say to you."

They worked to rig the harness on the unconscious tiger. "I bet this is something you'd never thought you'd be doing."

"There are a lot of things I never thought I'd do. I'll get the cart."

He backed it over the plantings that lined the far end of the path, over the river rock, into brush. "We could rig these cables to drag him across."

"I'm not dragging him." She checked his respiration, his pupils. "He's old and it's rough ground. He didn't do anything wrong, and I'm not having him hurt. We've used this method before, for transferring them from the habitat to Medical, but it takes two people."

Three or four, she thought, would've been a hell of a lot easier and faster.

"A tiger is the biggest of the four big cats," she said as she hooked the cables to the harness. "He's Siberian, he's protected. He's twelve, and did time in a circus, in a second-rate zoo. He was sick when we got him, four years ago. Okay, okay, you're sure the brake's locked."

"I'm not an idiot."

"Sorry. You need to run that winch while I run this one. Try to keep him level, Coop. When he's up, I can maneuver him on the cart. Ready?"

When he nodded, they both began to crank. As the harness lifted, she watched, eagle-eyed—to be sure the cat was secure, the harness holding. "A little more, just a little more. I'm going to lock my side down, move him in. I may need you to give me more play. There you go, there you go," she muttered as she guided the harness over the cart. "Ease your side down, Coop, ease it down a few inches."

It took time, and some finesse, but they transferred the cat to the cart, drove it into the enclosure. The first streaks of dawn bloomed as they lowered the tiger to the mouth of his den.

"His respiration's good, and his pupils are reactive," she stated as she crouched to do another quick exam. "I want Matt to run a full diagnostic on him. The bait might have been doctored."

"You need a new lock, Lil."

"I got one out of the equipment shed. I've got one in my pocket. It'll do for now."

"Let's go."

"Yeah. Yeah." She stroked a hand over the cat's head, down its flank, then rose. Outside, she snapped a new lock on the chain securing the cage door. "The interns and staff are going to be coming along soon. So will the police. I need, really need, coffee. Coffee and a minute to breathe."

He said nothing while she drove the cart back to the shed. As he started toward the cabin with her, he lifted his chin toward the headlights far down her road. "You're not going to get that chance to breathe."

"I still want the coffee, which is smarter than the three fingers of whiskey I really want. Did you relock the gate?"

"No, it wasn't at the top of my to-do list this morning."

"I guess not. I think it's the law." She nearly managed a smile with it. "One more favor? Will you wait for him while I get that coffee? I'll get you one, too."

"Make it quick."

Funny, she thought, as she paused inside her own kitchen, her hands were shaking again. She took a moment to splash cold water on her face in the kitchen sink before filling two insulated mugs with black coffee.

When she went back out Coop was standing with Willy and two deputies.

"You doing all right, Lil?" Willy asked her.

"Better now. But Jesus, Willy, this son of a bitch has to be crazy. If that cat had gotten away from here, away from me . . . God knows."

"I need to take a look at things. What time did the alarm go off?"

"About a quarter after five. I'd just glanced at the clock before I left my cabin, and I'd only gotten as far as the porch when it sounded." She walked with them, leading the way. "Tansy and Farley left pretty much on the dot of five, maybe a minute or two after. Tansy was anxious to get started."

"You're sure on that? It was about five-thirty when you called me, and that was after you'd put the tiger down."

"I'm sure. I knew where to find him. I'd switched on the computer, the cameras when I went in for the drug gun. I saw the cage open, I saw the cat, so I knew where to go. It didn't take long, only seemed like a year or two."

"Did you maybe give a passing thought to calling me first?" Willy demanded.

"I had to move fast. I couldn't wait, risk losing the cat. If he'd left the compound . . . They can move damn fast when they want, and by the time you'd have gotten here . . . He needed to be contained as quickly as possible."

"All the same, Lil, any more trouble, I want you to call me before you do anything else. And I'd think you'd know better than to go walking all over a crime scene, Coop."

"You're right."

Willy puffed out his cheeks. "It'd be more satisfying if you'd argue a little." Willy paused before they hit the blood trail. "Get some pictures," he told one of the deputies. "Of the broken lock over there, too."

"I left it where I found it," Lil said. "And kept out of the tracks as much as I could. We didn't touch the bait. The tiger'd only had ten minutes or so on it when I got to him, but he'd torn in pretty good from what I could see. It was a small elk."

"You'll do me a favor and stay here." He signaled to his men and moved into the brush in the tracks of the cart.

"He's a little bit pissed." Lil sighed. "I guess you are, too."

"Good guess."

"I did exactly what I thought had to be done, what I still think had to be done. Know had to be. But . . . The interns are coming," she said as she heard the trucks. "I need to go deal with them. I appreciate you coming so fast, Coop. Appreciate everything you did."

"Save it, and see how grateful you are once you and I are finished with this. I'll wait for Willy here."

"Okay." She'd handled an escaped tiger, Lil thought, as she headed back. She could handle an angry man.

BY SEVEN-THIRTY in the morning, Lil felt as though she'd put in a full and brutal day. The emergency staff meeting left her with a headache and a clutch of uneasy interns. She had no doubt that if turnover hadn't been only days away, some would have quit and walked away. Though she wanted to assist Matt with his exam of Boris, and the tests, she assigned interns. The work would keep them busy and focused. And reinforce the fact that everything was under control. Others she put to work on the temporary enclosure, and had no doubt there would be several pairs of eyes tracking warily over habitats throughout the day.

"A couple of them are going to be calling in sick tomorrow," Lucius said when he and Lil were alone.

"Yeah. And the ones who do will never make it in the field. In research, labs, classrooms, but not fieldwork."

With a sheepish smile, Lucius raised his hand.

"You're planning to be sick tomorrow?"

"No, but I spend most of my time right in here. I can guarantee I wouldn't have gone out armed with a drug gun to hunt me down a Siberian tiger. You had to be scared fully shitless, Lil. I know you relayed all this at the meeting as if it was almost routine, but this is me."

"Fully shitless," she acknowledged. "But more scared I wouldn't get him tranquilized and contained. My God, Lucius, the damage he might have done if he'd gotten away from us. I'd never be able to live with it."

"You weren't the one who let him out, Lil."

Didn't matter, she thought as she went back outside. She'd learned a lesson, a vital one. Whatever the cost, she'd have the very best security available, and as quickly as it could be arranged.

She met Willy and Coop on their way back from what she supposed they considered a crime scene.

"We've got what's left of that carcass bagged, and we'll test it, in case it was doctored," Willy said. "I've sent the men to follow the tracks. I'll be calling in more."

"Good."

"I'm going to need a full statement from you, both of you," he added to Coop. "Why don't we talk in your place, Lil?"

"All right."

At her kitchen table, over more mugs of coffee, she went over every detail.

"Who knew you were going to be here alone once Farley left this morning?"

"I don't know, Will. I'd guess word got out that he was driving with Tansy to Montana this morning. I had arrangements to make, and I didn't make them on the down low. But I don't know if that's relevant. If Farley had been here, everything would've gone about the same way it did. Except I wouldn't have had to call Coop to help me get Boris back in his enclosure."

"The fact is the cage door opened a few minutes after they left, and almost two hours before any of your people were scheduled to get here. Now, maybe that was just luck, or maybe somebody's keeping track."

She'd thought of that, of exactly that. "He'd have to know we have alarm signals on the cages we keep activated unless we're working in them. Otherwise, it would be getting the tiger out, baiting him out that was the goal here. It could've been another two hours, easily, before anyone noticed the door was open, and by that time, Boris might have roamed off, or just as easily gone back inside, to his den. His home. If I can't be sure, and this is an animal I've worked with—this is what I *know*—whoever's doing this couldn't know."

"You've been here for about five years now," Willy said. "I've never had a report from you on anyone trying to get one of your animals out."

"No. It's never happened before. I'm not saying it's a coincidence, just that the purpose might have been to get one of the big cats out and cause havoc."

Willy nodded, assured she understood him. "I'm going to coordinate a manhunt with the park service. I can't tell you what to do, as sheriff, Lil, but I'm telling you as your friend I don't want you here alone. Not even for an hour."

"She won't be," Coop put in.

"I won't argue that. I don't intend for anyone, including me, to be alone here until this man's found and put away. I'm going to contact a security company this morning and arrange for the best system I can manage. Willy, my parents live less than a mile from here. Believe me when I say I'm not taking any chances, any, on this ever happening again."

"I do believe you. But you're a lot closer than a mile to those enclosures, and I've got a fondness for you. I had a painful crush on her when I was sixteen," he said to Coop. "If you tell my wife I said that I'll say you're a dirty liar."

He pushed to his feet. "I went around, took a good look. All your enclosures are secure. I'm not going to shut you down. I could," he added when Lil made a strangled sound in her throat. "And you could try to get that overturned, and we'd end up on opposite sides here. I want you to make that call about the new security, and I want you to keep me updated on it. I got a fondness for you, Lil, but I've also got people to protect."

"Understood. We haven't violated a single ordinance or safety measure since we brought in the first cat."

"I know that, honey. I do. And I bring my kids here two or three times a year. I want to keep bringing them." The gesture both casual and affectionate, he reached out to pat her head. "I'm going to go. I want you to remember I'm the first call you make from here on out."

She sat where she was, stewing. "I suppose you have plenty to say now," she suggested when she and Coop were alone.

"You should've stayed inside and waited for help. Two people with drug guns are better than one. And you're going to say there wasn't time for that."

"There wasn't. How much do you know about tigers as a species, and Siberians as a subspecies?"

"They're big, have stripes, and I'd have to assume come from Siberia."

"Actually, the correct name for the subspecies is Amur—Siberian's the name commonly used, and it's misleading, as they live in the far east of Russia."

"Well, now that we've cleared that up."

"I'm just trying to make you see it. It's fiercely territorial. It stalks and ambushes, and can reach a speed of thirty-five miles an hour, maybe forty."

She took a breath, easy in and out as the idea still made her belly quake. "Even an old guy like Boris can book when he wants. It's strong, and can carry a prey of, say, a hundred pounds and still leap a six-foot fence. Man isn't its usual prey, but according to most accepted records, tigers have killed more humans than any other cat."

"You seem to be making my point for me, Lil."

"No. No. Listen." She dragged at her hair. "Most man-eaters are older—which Boris is—often going for a man because they're easier to take down than larger prey. It's solitary and secretive, like most cats, and if interested in man meat would hunt in sparsely populated areas. Its size and its strength mean it can kill smaller prey instantly."

Desperate to make him understand, she squeezed her hand on his on the table. "If I'd waited, that cat could've been miles away, or it could've wandered into my parents' backyard. Your grandparents' front pasture. It could've roamed to where the Silverson kids catch the bus for school. All while I was sitting inside, waiting for someone to help."

"You wouldn't have had to wait if you hadn't been alone."

"Do you want me to admit I underestimated this bastard? I did." Both passion and apology shone in her eyes. "I was wrong. Horribly wrong, and that mistake could've cost lives. I never expected anything like this, never anticipated it. Damn it, Coop, did you? You know damn well I was taking precautions, because I made a point of telling you about the security systems I'd looked at."

"That's right, when you came by to make sure I knew you'd have Farley here, so I wasn't needed."

As her head started to pound, she dropped her gaze. "It made sense for Farley to be here, since they were leaving from here this morning. That's all there was to it."

"Bullshit. For Christsake, Lil, do you think I'd put wanting you in bed above wanting you safe?"

"No. Of course I don't." She looked at him again. "I don't. Coop, I called you. I called you even before I called Willy."

"Because I was closer, handier, and you didn't want your parents scared."

She heard the bitterness, and couldn't blame him for it. "That's all true, but also because I knew I could count on you. I knew, without any question, I could count on you to help me."

"You can, and to make sure you don't forget it, sex is now off the table."

"Sorry?"

"*You're* sorry?" Some of the temper—at least its sharp, leading edge—seemed to have dulled when he shook his head at her.

"Yes. No. I mean I don't know what *you* mean."

"Simple. Sex is out of the equation. I won't touch you. I won't ask you. And I'll be here from dusk to dawn, every day. If I can't be, someone else will be. I've got to go get caught up," he said as he rose. "You'd better talk to your parents about this before someone else does."

15

He could've taken her out as easily as he had the elk calf, just aim and down she'd go. The tiger would've gone for her then, oh, yeah. A shot in the leg, he mused, playing it out in his head. Not a kill shot, just something to take her down. Would the tiger have traded elk for woman?

He'd put money on it.

And wouldn't *that* have been something to see?

But it wasn't the game of choice. Plus it had been so interesting and entertaining to watch her. She'd surprised him, he had to admit it, even with what he knew of her. What he'd observed. He hadn't expected her to act so quickly, so decisively, or to stalk the cat so expertly.

He'd left her—life and death—and the rest of the game up to fate. And the cat.

She'd shown courage, which he admired, and a cool head. If for no other reason, those traits, and his interest in them, had kept her alive for another day.

Most of the others he'd hunted had been pathetically easy. The first had been an accident really. Just an impulse, just circumstances. But the incident had, in a very real sense, defined him. Given him a purpose he'd never had, and a means to honor his bloodline.

He'd found his life with death.

Now this last phase of the hunt raised the stakes considerably. This added such a *zing*. When the time came, she'd give him some real competition, some real satisfaction. No question about it. Better, certainly, than the couple of countrified deputies tromping around trying to follow his trail.

He could take them out, too. So easily. He'd backtracked, circled around behind, and studied them as he might study some deer strayed from the herd. He could take them both out and be a mile away before anyone knew the difference.

It had tempted him.

He had sighted one, then the other, in the scope of the rifle he carried with him today, and made little popping sounds to mime the shot. He'd killed men before, but he preferred the female.

Females were, in nearly every species, the fiercer hunter.

He had let them live, primarily because two dead deputies would bring others swarming over the hills. That could spoil the main hunt. He didn't want to lose his primary target or be forced to leave his territory before he was done.

Patience, he reminded himself, and he slipped away as silently as a shadow from the sun.

TELLING HER PARENTS and allaying their fears—or trying to—left Lil exhausted. When she contacted the security company, from her parents' kitchen in a further attempt to calm those waters, the receptionist put her through, immediately, to the head of the company.

Ten minutes later, she hung up, turned to her parents. "Did you get any of that?"

"Someone's coming out to work with you on a security system."

"Not someone," she corrected her father—"the head guy. He was expecting my call because Coop contacted him a half hour ago and gave him the rundown. He's getting on a plane today. He'll be here this afternoon."

"How soon can they install what you need?" her mother demanded.

"I don't know. We'll find out. Meanwhile, there are cops and rangers out looking for this guy. I'm not going to be careless, and I promise, I won't be alone in the compound again. Not even for ten minutes. I'm sorry. I'm so sorry I didn't consider he might do something like this. I thought he might try to hurt one of the animals, but I never thought he'd risk letting one out. I need to get back to the compound. The interns and staff need to see me there, need to see me going through the daily routines."

"Joe, go with her."

"Mom—"

Jenna's eyes flashed. It took no more than that to have Lil swallowing her protest. "Lillian, I haven't told you what to do in a long time. But I'm telling you now. Your father's going with you, and he's staying with you until he's satisfied that *I'll* be satisfied you're as safe as possible. That's the final word on it."

"It's just . . . I've already stolen Farley from you for two days."

"I'm perfectly capable of handling this farm. I said it's my final word. Look at my face." Narrowing those heated eyes, Jenna pointed a finger at her jaw. "This is my final-word face."

"Let's go, Lil. Your mother's final word is law. You know that as well as I do." He leaned down, kissed his wife. "Don't worry."

"I'll worry less now."

Giving up, Lil waited while her father got his coat, and said nothing when he unlocked his rifle from its case. She got behind the wheel of her truck, sent him a look before she turned to drive away. "How come you don't have to go with me every time I head out to the field? Did I see you in Nepal? You know I've tracked tigers, in the wild, for collaring programs."

"Somebody wasn't trying to arrange it so the tiger was tracking you, were they?"

"Okay, your point. Anyway, I could use you with the construction of the new enclosure." With a sniff, Lil pushed her sunglasses on, then folded her arms. "Don't think you're getting a free lunch out of this."

"I'll remind you about lunch around noon. If I'm working, I'd better get a sandwich."

It made her laugh, and when she reached over, Joe took her hand and gave it a squeeze.

COOP HELPED OUTFIT a group of eight men for a scheduled three-day trip. The group from Fargo put the package together as a bachelor's party. Which, Coop reflected, made a change from a strip club. They ragged on each other constantly in the way of old friends, and were hauling enough beer to float down the trail. Since the horses were his, he checked their camping gear, their kits and supplies—and satisfied himself that everything was in good order.

With Gull, he watched them trot to the trailhead, and wondered how they'd have reacted if he'd mentioned there might be a psychopath roaming the hills. He suspected they'd have gone on their merry way regardless, and took some relief that their plans would take them well away from the refuge.

"They'd do fine," Gull told him. "That Jake? He's been coming around every year for the six years I've been working the outfit with your grandpa. He knows what he's doing."

"They're going to get shit-faced tonight."

"Yah," Gull said, mimicking their accent. "You betcha. Anyhow, we could use more groups like that." Gull watched their progress from under the brim of his battered brown hat. "We'll be getting them now that it's coming on spring."

"It may be coming on spring, but those boys are going to freeze their dicks off tonight pissing out that beer."

Gull grinned. "Well, yeah. Hope it thaws out for the groom before the honeymoon. So, boss, I got that guided in another hour. Family trail ride. The pa runs a good two-eighty. I was going to put him up on Sasquash."

"He's good to go. Do you have any plans for tonight, Gull?"

"Can't say I do." Gull's grin widened with his wink. "You asking me on a date, boss?"

"I'm too shy," Coop said, and it made Gull guffaw. "Lil's had some trouble over at her place."

"I heard about it."

"She could use some help, if a man didn't mind freezing his dick off."

Gull gave his crotch a subtle pat. "South Dakota peckers don't freeze so easy as a drunk's from Fargo."

"Must be from all the jerking off," Coop mused, and put Gull in stitches again. "Can you take a turn at guard duty over there tonight? Say two to six?"

"Sure, boss, I can do that. Need anybody else?"

No hesitation, Coop thought. No complaint. "I could use two more men who you trust not to shoot themselves, or anybody else."

"I'll see what I can do about that. I'll think on it. I guess I'll go see about getting those box lunches for this guided."

"I'll check them in when they get here."

When they parted ways, Coop went to the storefront. The old desk faced the window and gave him a view of Deadwood that wasn't quite what he imagined Calamity Jane and Wild Bill had seen in their day. Still, it maintained its Western flavor, with its awnings and architecture and old-timey lampposts. Its *feel,* he supposed, as the town spread and climbed its way up the hills. Cowboys mixed with the tourists; saloons cozied up to souvenir shops.

And a man could find a game of poker or blackjack day or night if he wanted to gamble. But the proprietors weren't likely to murder a man in the back room and feed him to the pigs.

Progress.

He dealt with the paperwork, the forms and waivers, so he could move the family group along when they arrived. And so he could carve some time for his own devices.

He pulled a ginger ale out of the cold box, since he'd buzzed his blood on coffee that morning. People passed by, and some likely glanced in. They'd see a man going about his business, keyboarding on a computer that, to Coop's mind, desperately needed replacing.

He opened Lil's file. He might not be an investigator anymore, but that didn't mean he'd forgotten how to investigate. He'd have preferred being sure her list of staff, interns, and volunteers was complete. But he had enough to keep him busy. The staff, past and current, hadn't netted him a thing. He probably knew more about all of them now than some would be comfortable with, but he knew more about a lot of people than most were comfortable with.

Though Jean-Paul had not technically been staff, Coop had done a run on him. Broken relationships were petri dishes waiting to brew trouble. He knew the French guy had been married and divorced in his early twenties. It was likely Lil had that information, and since it didn't seem to be relevant, Coop simply filed it away. He found no criminal, and a current address in Los Angeles.

Stay there, Coop thought.

He'd uncovered a few criminal brushes on staff, but nothing more violent than the vet having a scuffle during a protest on animal testing fifteen years earlier.

The former interns comprised a bigger chunk. They were a diverse group, economically, geographically, academically. He followed some through college, grad school, into careers. A quick scan showed Coop that a high percentage of interns Lil had trained pursued careers somewhere in the field.

He found some scrapes with the law as he picked his way through. Drugs, DUIs, a couple of assaults and/or destruction of property—usually connected to drugs or alcohol.

Those would earn a closer look.

He did the same with the volunteers—any whose names actually made it into the files, he thought, annoyed.

He culled out any who'd lived in or moved to the Dakotas. Proximity could be a factor, and he believed whoever was harassing Lil knew the hills as well as she did.

In the tedious way it demanded, he cross-referenced the assaults, the drug busts, the DUIs with geography, and got a single hit.

Ethan Richard Howe, age thirty-one. A trespassing hit in Sturgis, and that was close, when he'd been twenty, charges dropped. Carrying a concealed weapon—.22 revolver—without a license two years later in Wyoming. And an assault that looked like a bar fight and had put him inside for a year and a half in Montana at the ripe old age of twenty-five.

Early release, time off for good behavior. And, thought the former cop, to move inmates out as others moved in.

Three hits, Coop mused, one for being where he didn't belong, one for a weapon, and the last for violence. He'd give Howe a closer look.

He started to move on, then had to break as the Dobsons arrived—Tom, Sherry, and their two teenage daughters—for check-in.

He knew his job and it was more than getting forms signed, more than making sure the customers could actually sit a horse. He chatted with the father, gave little back stories on each of the horses. Took time as if he had an endless supply of it in his pockets.

"It's a good, easy trail," he assured Sherry, who seemed more nervous than excited. "There's nothing like seeing the hills on horseback."

"But we'll be back well before dark."

"Gull will have you back by four."

"You hear about people getting lost."

"Now, Sherry," Tom began.

"Gull grew up here," Coop assured her. "He knows the trails, and so do the horses. You couldn't be in better hands."

"I haven't been on horseback in ten years." Sherry stepped onto the mounting block Coop provided. "I'm going to ache in places I forgot I had."

"You can get a good massage right here in town, if you're interested."

She glanced back at Coop, and for the first time a little light gleamed in her eyes. "Really?"

"I can book you one, if you're interested. Maybe for five o'clock?"

"You can do that?"

"Happy to."

"Five o'clock massage. I don't suppose I could get a hot stone?"

"Sure. Fifty or eighty minutes?"

"Eighty. My day just got a lot better. Thank you, Mr. Sullivan."

"My pleasure, ma'am. You have a nice ride."

He went in, booked the massage, wrote up the particulars. The business would get a referral fee, which didn't hurt. Then he shifted gears and went back to Lil's file.

He started a new run on the women. He leaned toward a man in this case, but he knew better than to discount the female. He hadn't gotten a good enough look that early morning to be absolutely certain. In any case, a woman might be the connection.

He worked his way through the ginger ale and half the ham sandwich his grandmother had packed him. He couldn't stop her from packing his lunch, and had to admit he didn't try very hard.

It was nice to have someone who'd take the time, take the trouble.

Marriages, divorces, kids, degrees. One of the earlier interns in the program now lived in Nairobi, another was a vet specializing in exotic animals in L.A.

And another, he noted as his instincts hummed, had vanished.

Carolyn Lee Roderick, age twenty-three, missing for eight months and a handful of days. Last seen in Denali National Park, where she'd been doing fieldwork.

He followed the hum and dug out what he could on Carolyn Roderick.

AT THE REFUGE, Lil shook hands with Brad Dromburg, the owner of Safe and Secure. He was a beanpole of a man, obviously comfortable in his Levi's and Rockports, with a close-cropped head of dark blond hair and green eyes. He had an easy smile, a firm hand, and a voice with just a hint of Brooklyn.

"I appreciate you coming all this way, and so quickly."

"Coop tugged the line. Is he around?"

"No. I—"

"He said he'd try to make it by. Some place you've got here, Ms. Chance." He stood, hands on his hips, studying the habitats, the compound. "Some place. How long have you been in operation?"

"Six years this May."

He gestured over where some of her interns had set the poles for the new habitat. "Expanding?"

"We're acquiring a melanistic jaguar."

"Is that so? Coop said you've had a little trouble. Someone compromised one of the cages?"

"The tiger enclosure, yes."

"That would be a little trouble, all right. Maybe you could walk me around, give me a feel for the place. And what you have in mind."

He asked questions, made notes on a PDA, and showed no particular nerves when he walked up to the enclosures to study the doors, the locks.

"That's a big boy there," he said when Boris rolled over to stretch in front of his den.

"Yes. All four hundred and eighty-six pounds of him."

"It took a lot of balls or stupidity to open that cage, middle of the night, gamble that big boy's going to go after the bait and not the live meal."

"It would, but the fresh kill would be more appealing. Boris was trapped, illegally from what I can dig up, when he was around a year old.

He's been in captivity ever since, and he's used to the scent of human. He's fed in the evening, to continue to stimulate the hunt by night instincts, but he's used to being fed."

"And he didn't go far."

"No, fortunately. He followed the blood trail to the bait and settled in for his unexpected predawn snack."

"Takes some balls to come out here and shoot a mickey into him."

"Necessity is often the mother of balls, so to speak."

He smiled, stepped back. "I don't mind saying I'm glad he's in there and I'm out here. So that's four gates, including the one for public access during operating hours. And a lot of open land."

"I can't fence off the entire property. Even if I could, it would be a logistical nightmare. There are trails running through the hills that cross this land, my father's, others'. We're posted private around the perimeter, and the gates tend to stop people. My priority is securing the compound, the habitats. I need to keep my animals safe, Mr. Dromburg, and keep everyone safe from my animals."

"That's Brad. I've got some ideas on that, and I'm going to work something up. One of the things I'm going to recommend are motion sensors set outside the enclosures. Far enough that the animals won't set them off, but anyone approaching the enclosure would."

She felt her budget wince in pain. "How many would I need?"

"I'll figure that for you. You want more lights. Sensor goes off, alarm kicks on, lights flood this place. An intruder's going to think twice about trying for a cage at that point. Then there's the locks themselves, and that goes for your gates as well as your cages. Interesting situation," he added. "Challenging."

"And—sorry I have to be crass here—expensive."

"I'm going to work out two or three systems I think would work for you, and I'll give you an estimate on each. It'll be a chunk of change, I won't lie to you, but getting it at cost's going to save you some serious moolah."

"At cost? I'm confused."

"It's for Coop."

"No, it's for me."

"Coop made the call. He wants this place wired up, we wire it up. At cost."

"Brad, this place runs on donations, funding, charity, generosity. I'm not going to turn yours down, but why would you do all this and not make a profit?"

"I wouldn't have a business if it wasn't for Coop. He calls, it's cost. And speak of the devil." Brad's face lit up as Coop started down the path toward them.

They didn't shake hands. Instead they greeted each other with the one-armed, backslapping hug men favored. "I wanted to be here sooner, but I got hung up. How was the flight?"

"It's a long one. Jesus, Coop, it's good to see you."

"And I have to give you a job before you come out. Have you been around?"

"Yeah, your lady gave me the tour."

Lil opened her mouth, then shut it. No point in breaking up the re-union by pointing out she wasn't Coop's "lady."

"You'll have to excuse me. It's feeding time."

"Seriously?" Brad asked.

He looked like a kid, she thought, who'd just been shown the biggest cookie in the jar. "Why don't I get you both a beer, and you can watch the show?"

Brad rocked on his heels as Lil walked away. "She's sexier than her picture."

"It was an old picture."

"Seeing her in the flesh, I'd say the chances of you coming back to New York are slim to none."

"They started out slim to none, and she wasn't why I moved here."

"Maybe not, but I haven't seen many better reasons to stay." Brad looked over the habitats, up to the hills. "Hell of a long way from New York."

"How long can you stay?"

"I've got to fly back tonight, so we'll have to keep it to the one beer. I had to shuffle some things to get out here today. But I'll draw up a couple of options in the next day or two. I'll get them to you, and I'll make sure I'm back when we do the install. We'll lock it down for you, Coop."

"I'm counting on it."

Lil stayed busy, and out of Coop's way. Old friends, to her way of thinking, needed time to catch up.

She and Coop had been friends once. Maybe they could be again. Maybe this pang she felt was just missing him, just missing her friend.

If they couldn't go back, they could move forward. It seemed he was making the effort, so how could she do less?

She finished up in her office just as Coop walked in. "Brad had to go. He said to tell you goodbye, and he'd have plans for you to look over within the next few days."

"Well. For a day that started out as bad as this one, it's ending well. I just got off the phone with Tansy. Cleo is as advertised. Gorgeous, healthy, and she'll be ready to travel tomorrow. Cooper, Brad said he'd be doing the security system at cost."

"Yeah, that's the deal."

"We should all have such generous friends."

"He likes to think he owes me. I like to let him."

"My IOUs are piling up in your hat."

"No they're not. I don't want an accounting." Irritation darkened his face as he took another step toward her desk. "You were the best friend I ever had. For a good part of my life you were one of the few people I could trust or count on. It made a difference to me. In me. Don't," he said when her eyes welled.

"I won't." But she rose and walked to the window to look out until she had control. "You made a difference, too. I've missed you, missed having you for a friend. And here you are. I'm in trouble and I don't know why, and here you are."

"I have a possible line on that. On the trouble."

She turned. "What? What line?"

"An intern named Carolyn Roderick. Do you remember her?"

"Ah, wait." Lil closed her eyes, tried to think. "Yes, yes, I think . . . Two years ago. I think nearly two years ago. A summer session—after she'd graduated? Maybe after, I'm not sure. She was bright and motivated. I'd have to pull the records for more detail, but I remember she was a hard worker, serious conservationist disciple. Pretty."

"She's missing," he said flatly. "She's been missing for about eight months."

"Missing? What happened? Where? Do you know?"

"Alaska. Denali National Park. She was doing fieldwork with a group of grad students. One morning, she just wasn't in camp. Initially they thought she'd just wandered off a little to take some pictures. But she didn't come back. They looked for her. They called in the rangers and Search and Rescue. They never found a trace of her."

"I did fieldwork in Denali my senior year. It's extraordinary, and it's immense. A lot of places to get lost if you're careless."

"A lot of places to be taken."

"Taken?"

"When they started to worry, her teammates looked in her tent more carefully. Her camera was there, her notebooks, her tape recorder, her GPS. None of them believed she'd wander off that way, with nothing but her jacket and boots and the clothes on her back."

"You think she was abducted."

"She had a boyfriend, someone she met while she was here, in South Dakota. According to the friends I've managed to track down so far, nobody really knew him. He kept to himself. But they shared a passion for the wilderness, for hiking, for camping. It went sour and she broke things off a couple months before the Alaska trip. Ugly breakup, reportedly. She called the cops; he skipped. His name is Ethan Howe, and he volunteered here. He also did a little time for an assault. I'm checking on that."

It crowded in her mind, beat there until she rubbed her temple to quiet it. "Why do you think this connects to what's happening here, now?"

"He used to brag about how he'd lived on the land for months at a time. He liked to claim he was a direct descendant of a Sioux chief, one who lived in the Black Hills. Sacred ground to his people."

"If half the people who claimed to be a direct descendant of a Sioux chief or 'princess' actually were . . ." Lil rubbed her forehead now. She knew this, something about this. "I remember him, vaguely. I think. I just can't get a clear picture."

"He talked about this place, how he'd helped out here when Carolyn was an intern. She's missing, and I can't find anything on him. Nobody's seen him since the breakup."

She dropped her hand, and in one moment of weakness wished she didn't understand him. "You think she's dead. You think he abducted her, and killed her. And he's come back here, because of the refuge. Or me."

He didn't soften it. Soft wouldn't help her. "I think she's dead, and he's responsible. I think he's here, living off the land. Your land. It's the only solid connection I've been able to make. We'll run him down, get a line on him. Then we'll know who we're dealing with."

16

Tansy took another sip of truly crappy wine while a debatably crappy band slammed out what she thought of as "Ye-haw Country" from behind a barrier of chicken wire.

The clientele—a mix of bikers and cowboys and the women who loved them—looked perfectly capable of throwing beer bottles and plastic dishes of indigestible nachos at the stage but so far hadn't worked up the energy.

A number of people were dancing, which she supposed boded well for the band, and their laundry bill.

She'd lived in what she, affectionately, thought of as the Wild West for a full five years now, not counting her years in college. And there were moments, such as these, when she still felt like a tourist.

"You sure you don't want a beer?"

She glanced over at Farley, and thought he looked perfectly at home here. In fact, she'd never seen him anywhere he didn't look perfectly at home.

"I should've listened to you and opted for beer in the first place." She took another tiny sip of wine. "But it's too late now. Besides, I'm going to head back."

"One dance."

"You said one drink."

"One drink, one dance," he said as he took her hand, tugged her off the bar stool.

"One." She agreed because they were already on the dance floor. In any case, they'd both put in a long day, so one drink, one dance seemed reasonable.

Until he put his arms around her. Until her body was locked tight to his, and his eyes smiled down at her. "I've been wanting to dance with you a long time."

Keep it light, she warned herself, even as her insides went soft and jittery at the same time. Keep it nice and easy. "Well, you're good at it."

"Jenna taught me."

"Really?"

"When I was about seventeen, I guess, she told me most girls like to dance, and a smart guy learned how to move on the dance floor. So she taught me."

"She did a good job." He could move all right, she thought. Smooth as butter. And he had her heart doing a little flip when he spun her out, and back again. He did a quick turn, slid her under his raised arm, leading her around until her back was to him, pressed close again.

She knew she fumbled some—he was a hell of a lot better than she was—but she let out a breathless laugh as he turned her again so they were face-to-face and she was shuffling backward.

Damn it, the guy had *moves.* "I guess I need Jenna lessons."

"She's a good teacher. I think we dance pretty well together, seeing it's the first time out."

"Maybe."

"You come dancing with me back home, Tansy, and we'll do better."

Her answer was the slightest shake of her head, and when the music stopped, she deliberately stepped back to break the contact before the next song started. "I really need to get back, and make sure I've got everything in order. We're getting an early start tomorrow."

"Okay." He took her hand as they returned to the table.

"You don't have to go. You should stay, enjoy the music." And I should go, she thought, and take a long, cold shower.

"Even if you weren't the prettiest woman in the room, I'd be walking you back just like I walked you over."

It was only a few minutes at a brisk walk from the bar to the motel they were using, but she knew him well enough not to argue. He had, Tansy knew, an unbendable code about certain things—undoubtedly Jenna-taught as well. A man walked a woman to her door, and that was that.

But she stuck her hands in her jacket pockets before one of them ended up caught in his.

"Lil's going to be happy when she sees that big cat," Farley commented.

"She's going to be ecstatic. She's a beauty, no question about it. I hope she handles the drive without any trouble. Anyway, Lil said the temporary enclosure will be ready for her, and the permanent one's already started."

"Lil doesn't wait for flies to land."

"Never has." She hunched inside her coat, as the short walk was still a cold one. Farley's arm came around her shoulders, easing her against him.

"You're shivering some."

Not just from the cold now, she thought. "Ah . . . I think if we plan to pick up Cleo by seven, that's early enough."

"We'll get gassed up first. Cut back on stops. We head out of here 'round six, that'd give us time to fuel up, get us some breakfast."

"Works for me." She spoke brightly while waging a small, violent war against her own hormones. "I can meet you at the diner. We'll check out first, and go right from there?"

"We could do that." He skimmed a hand down her back as they crossed the motel parking lot on foot. "Or we could walk over to breakfast together."

"You can knock on my door in the morning," she said as she dug out her room key.

"I don't want to knock on your door. I want you to let me come in." When she looked up, he turned her as smoothly as he had when they'd danced, so she was caught between him and the door. "Let me come in, Tansy, and be with you."

"Farley, that's not—"

His mouth found hers. He had a way of kissing her that had common sense, good intentions, firm resolve all slipping away. Despite sense, intention, and resolve, she was kissing him back.

Oh, hell, oh, *damn,* she thought, even as her arms locked around him. That rubber-band mouth of his was so good at kissing.

"It can't go anywhere," she told him.

"It could go to the other side of this door for right now. Let me come in." He took the key from her, slid it into the lock, and kept his eyes on hers. "Say yes."

No formed solidly in her mind, but it didn't come out of her mouth. "It's going to be like the drink and the dance. One time. You have to understand that."

He smiled at her, turned the knob.

LATER, AFTER MORE than one time, Tansy stared up at the dark ceiling. Okay, she told herself, she'd just had sex with Farley Pucket—twice. What the hell was she going to do now?

Best, she decided, to think of it as an out-of-town exception. Just something that happened. She was, after all, a mature, sophisticated, and experienced woman.

All she had to do was ignore that the sex had been incredible, both times. That he had a way of making her feel as if she were the only woman who existed. And that it wasn't just her hormones losing the battle, but her heart.

No, she had to remember she was older and wiser, and it was up to her to put things right.

"Farley, we need to talk about this. We need to understand that when we get back, this isn't going to happen again."

He linked his fingers with hers, brought them to his lips. Rubbed them there. "Well now, Tansy, I guess I need to be honest and tell you I'm going to do what I can to see it does. I've had a lot of good things happen to me, but being with you? It's the best."

She made herself sit up, cautiously bringing the sheet with her so he didn't get any ideas. "We don't exactly work together, but you do volunteer at the refuge. Lil's my closest friend."

"That's all true." He sat up, too, his eyes quiet on her face. "But what's that got to do with me being in love with you?"

"Oh. Love. Don't say love." Panic ticked at the back of her throat.

"But I do love you." Reaching out, he brushed his hand over her hair. "And I know you have feelings for me."

"Of course I do. We wouldn't be here, like this, if I didn't. But that doesn't mean—"

"I think they're strong feelings."

"All right, yes. I'll cop to that. But Farley, let's be realistic. I'm several years older than you are. We're in different decades, for God's sake."

"In a few years we'll be in the same decade for a while." Amusement showed clearly on his face. "But I don't want to wait that long to be with you."

On a huff of breath, she reached over and switched on the bedside lamp. "Farley, look at me. I'm a thirty-year-old black woman."

He cocked his head, studied her as she'd asked. "More caramel. Jenna makes these caramel apples in the fall. They're all golden brown and sweet on the outside, and just a little tart in. I love those caramel apples. I love the color of your skin, Tansy, but the color of your skin's not why I love you."

It made her shiver. It made her weak. Not just the words, but the look of him when he said them.

"You're smarter than me."

"No, Farley."

"Sure you are. It was the smarter that made me nervous around you for a while. Too nervous to ask you to come out with me. I like that you're smart, and how sometimes you and Lil will get talking about things and I can't understand the half of it. Then I thought, Well hell, it's not like I'm stupid."

"You're not stupid," she murmured, undone by him. "Not any-where near stupid. You're steady and clever and kind. If things were different—"

"Some things you can't change." He took her hand again, so the con-trasting tones showed in the light. "And some things, Tansy, make the different not mean one damn. Like this."

He drew her to him, laid his lips on hers, and showed her.

IT FELT STRANGE knowing people with guns patrolled the edges of her compound. Strange even, at her own insistence, knowing she was one of them. Her animals prowled and called. The night was their time. And more, the scent of man, the glow of the lights kept them stirred up.

She spent more time with Baby, to his obvious delight, and the love in his eyes when he looked at her steadied her nerves. When she stood or paced or drank yet another mug of coffee, she outlined long- and short-range plans to keep her mind occupied and off the reason she stood and paced and drank yet another mug of coffee.

They would get through this, and that was that as far as she was con-cerned. If the person causing the trouble was this Ethan Howe, they'd find him, and they'd stop him.

She remembered him a little better now. She'd had to go back, look up Carolyn's files, refresh herself on the reports and data in order to get a clear picture of the student. But once she had, she'd been able to re-form one of the men who'd come around a few times to lend a hand, to flirt with Carolyn.

Above average height, she thought, slim build, strong back. Nothing special about him that she could recall. Not a lot to say, other than his claim to be descended not just from any warrior but from Crazy Horse himself.

Lil remembered being mildly amused by his insistence on that, and largely dismissing it, and him. She didn't think she and this Ethan had exchanged over two dozen words. Still, hadn't most of them had to do with the land, the sanctity of it, and *their* duty to honor it because of their bloodline?

She'd dismissed that, too, had considered him just another harmless oddball. But she remembered now that she'd felt him watching her. Or did she remember that because of hindsight, because of nerves? Was she projecting?

Maybe Tansy would remember him more clearly.

And maybe he had nothing to do with what was happening. But Coop's instincts said he did. She trusted those instincts. Whatever problems they had with their personal lives, she trusted Coop's instincts absolutely.

That, she supposed, was also a matter of her own instincts.

She shifted her stance, rolled her shoulders, as they wanted to stiffen up from her stint in the cold. At least the overcast sky kept some of the heat in, she mused. But she'd have preferred the stars and the moon.

In the harsh glow of the emergency lights, she watched Gull head in her direction. He gave her a wide salute. She expected the gesture was a precaution, to make certain she recognized him.

"Hey there, Gull."

"Lil. Coop said I should take over for you here."

"I'm grateful, Gull, for what you're doing."

"You'd do the same for me. Never been out here at night like this."

He scanned the habitats. "It's kind of cool, I guess. Doesn't look like those animals are getting much sleep."

"They're nocturnal. And they're curious what all the people are doing out here in the dark. Losing sleep and drinking too much coffee mostly. He's not coming back around here tonight."

"Maybe he's not because all these people are out here losing sleep and drinking too much coffee."

"That's a good point."

"Go on, get inside, Lil. I've got this now. Unless you want to wander over and visit with Jesse. Like old times."

She gave him a light punch in the arm. "I don't think Rae would like that," she said, referring to her old sort-of boyfriend's wife.

"What happens at the refuge," Gull deadpanned, "stays at the refuge."

She headed back, chuckling. She saw others moving toward their trucks or cars as friends and neighbors came to stand in their places. Voices carried, so she heard jokes, sleepy laughs, calls of good night.

She quickened her pace when she spotted her parents. "You said you were going to use the cabin and get some sleep," she said to her mother.

"I said that so you'd stop nagging me. Now I'm going home to get some sleep. You do the same." She gave Lil a pat on the cheek with a gloved hand. "I know this is a bad reason, but it's good to see people come out to help this way. Take me home, Joe. I'm tired."

"You get some sleep." Joe tapped a finger on Lil's nose. "We'll talk tomorrow."

No doubt about that, Lil thought as they separated. They'd keep close tabs on her until this was resolved. It's the way they worked. And if the situation were reversed, it would be the way she'd work.

Inside, she stowed her rifle, then peeled off her outdoor gear. She glanced at the steps, thought about bed. Too restless, she decided. Too much coffee in the bloodstream.

She set a fire in the hearth, got it going. If Coop didn't want one, he could bank it down. But at least it added more warmth and cheer to his temporary sleeping arrangements.

She wandered back to the kitchen, thought about making some tea. And decided she was too impatient to wait for the water to boil. Instead she poured half a glass of wine, hoping it would counteract the caffeine.

She could work, she considered. She could spend an hour at the computer until the edge wore off. But the idea of sitting still didn't appeal either.

Then she heard the front door open and knew she'd been waiting for that. For him.

When she came back into the living room he was sitting down, pulling off his boots. He looked, she thought, alert, awake, his eyes clear as they met hers.

"I figured you'd be upstairs by now."

"Too much coffee."

He made a vague sound of agreement, and took off the second boot.

"Maybe I'm feeling as restless as the animals. I'm not used to having people around this time of night either. I can't settle." She walked to the window, stared out.

"I'd suggest a couple hands of gin rummy, but I'm not in the mood."

She glanced back at him over her shoulder. "And I'm in your way. I could try solitaire."

"You could also try turning off the lights and closing your eyes."

"That would be the sensible thing." She swallowed the last of the wine, set the glass aside. "I'll go up, let you get some sleep." She started toward the stairs, stopped, turned back. He hadn't moved. "What if I want sex on the table?"

"You want to have sex on the table?"

"You said sex was off the table. Maybe I want it back on. Maybe I don't want to sleep alone tonight. You're here; I'm here. We're friends. That's established, right? We're friends."

"We always were."

"So that's all it is. Friends, and not being alone. Giving each other something to take the edge off."

"Reasonable. Maybe I'm too tired."

Her lips curved. "Like hell."

"Maybe I'm not."

But he stayed where he was, watching her. Waiting.

"You said you wouldn't touch me. I'm asking you to set that rule or provision, or however you think of it, aside. Come up with me, come to bed with me, stay with me. I need to shut my mind off, Coop, that's the God's truth. I need some peace of mind. A few hours of it. Do me a favor."

He stepped to her. "Doing you a favor's standing out in the cold until two in the morning. Taking you to bed?" He reached up, ran his hand down her braid. "Doesn't qualify. Don't tell me you need peace of mind, Lil. Tell me you want me."

"I do. I do want you. I'll probably regret it tomorrow."

"Yeah, but it'll be too late." He pulled her in, captured her mouth with his. "It's already too late."

He turned toward the steps, then gripped her hips, boosting her up so she wrapped her legs around his waist, her arms around his neck.

Maybe it had always been too late, she thought as he carted her upstairs, and she let her lips roam his face as she had once, long before. Back in time, the familiar. Like closing a circle, she told herself. It didn't have to be any more than that.

She pressed her cheek to his, sighed. "Feel better already."

At the bedroom he turned, pressing her back to the door. And those eyes, the ice blue that had always snagged her heart, caught hers. "A hot bath makes you feel better. This is more, Lil. We'll both have to deal with that."

When his mouth took hers it wasn't for comfort, or to soothe, but to ignite. So that slow simmer, never fully banked, came roaring back to full, furious flame.

Peace of mind? Had she thought she would find peace here, with him? There would be no peace with the war raging between them, inside her. Engulfed, she gave herself to it, and to him.

Maybe this time the battle would be done, and that constant flame inside her finally, finally burned out.

The need rose up, riding along her skin, filling her breasts, her belly with heat. Familiar, perhaps. But more and less than what had been. Had his hands been so sure, his mouth so urgent?

She was still wound around him when he strode to the bed. The lights from the compound slanted through the slats of her blinds, thin bars of light that fell over the bed, over her when he set her on the edge. A kind of cage, she supposed. Well, she walked into it willingly.

He gripped her boot, tugged. She heard herself laugh, nervous joy, as he pulled off the other. Then he reached down to unbutton her flannel shirt.

"Unbraid your hair." He drew the shirt off. "Please."

She lifted her arms, slid the tie at the end of her braid onto her wrist out of habit, and loosened her braid as he took off his shirt.

"No, I'll do that," he said as she started to comb her fingers through her hair.

"I'd think about your hair, the way it feels and smells, the way it looks after I've had my hands in it. All that midnight hair."

He wrapped her hair around his fist, tugged so that her face tipped up to his. The gesture, the flare of heat in his eyes spoke as much of temper as passion. "I'd see you when you weren't there. Like a damn ghost. A glimpse in a crowd, a tease out of the corner of my eye, disappearing around a corner. You were everywhere."

She started to shake her head, but he tightened his grip. For an instant she saw that anger flash, then he released her hair. "Now you're here," he said, and drew the thermal shirt over her head.

"I've been here."

No, he thought. No. But she was here now. Aroused, a little annoyed, just as he was. To please himself, to pleasure her, he traced his fingers down her collarbone, over the subtle swell of her breasts. The girl he'd known had been a willow stem. She'd bloomed without him.

She shivered at his touch; he'd wanted her to.

Then he pressed the heel of his hand to her forehead, gave her a light shove onto her back. And made her laugh again.

"Mr. Smooth," she said, then he was on her, his body pressing her into the mattress. "You've put on a few pounds."

"You too."

"Really?"

"In interesting places."

She smiled a little, and combed her fingers through his hair as he had with hers. "Well, it's been a while."

"I think I remember how everything works. How you work."

He brushed his lips to hers, a teasing, then a sinking, sinking until it was drowning deep. His hands were on her, reminding her what it had been, confusing her with what it was now.

Strong, hard, working hands, sliding over her, pressing, molding until her breath quickened, until past and present were one brilliant blur over her senses.

He flipped open her bra, tugged it aside, and had her—hands and mouth, teeth and tongue—so quickened breaths became gasps, gasps became moans. She dragged at his thermal, yanking it up and away, impatient now to feel him. Strong back, ridges of muscle. New and fascinating.

He'd been a boy, just a boy really, when last she'd touched him like this. It was a man under her hands now, a man whose body pressed down on hers.

In the dark, barred with light, they rediscovered each other. A curve, an angle, a new point of pleasure. Her fingers skimmed over a scar that hadn't been there before. And she whispered his name as his lips raced frantically down her body.

She quivered when he unbuttoned her jeans, hitched her hips up to help him pull them away. Rolled with him over the bed as they hurried to strip off every barrier.

Outside one of the cats called out, a wild thing prowling the dark. He took her there, into the dark, and what was wild in her cried out, released in harsh and primitive pleasure.

She moved for him, and with him, her eyes a gleam in the shadows. Everything he'd found and lost, everything he'd lived without was here. Right here. His senses swam with her, a rush of woman, all scent and skin, all wet and warm. The beat of her heart against his hungry mouth, the slide of her skin under his desperate hands.

He pushed her over, felt her rise and break, then gather again.

His name. She said his name over and over.

His name when he drove into her. He held, held himself on that whippy edge, filled and surrounded, entrapped until they were both trembling. Then it was all movement, mad, mindless. And when she broke again, he shattered with her.

She wanted to curl up against him, just fit her body against his like two pieces of a puzzle. Instead she lay quiet, willing herself to hold on to the pleasure, and the peace that had finally come with it.

She could sleep. If she closed her eyes, let her mind shut down, she could sleep. Whatever needed to be said or dealt with could be said or dealt with in the morning.

"You're cold."

Was she?

Before her brain could connect with her body he'd shifted her up and over. When had he packed on all the muscle? she wondered. He tugged the sheet and comforter over her, then drew her against him.

She started to stiffen—to ease away, a little at least. Didn't she need some room, some sort of distance? But he held her there, curled her in exactly where she'd wanted to be.

"Go to sleep," he said.

And too tired, too undone, to argue, she did just that.

SHE WOKE BEFORE SUNRISE, stayed very still. His arms had stayed around her, and hers had gone around him in the brief hours of the night.

Why, she wondered, did something that basic, that human, break her heart?

Comfort, she reminded herself. In the end, he'd given her the comfort she'd needed. And maybe she'd given him some in return.

It didn't have to be more than that.

She'd loved him all of her life, and there was no point in trying to convince herself that would ever change. But sex was just an elemental act, and in their case a kind of gift between friends.

Single, consenting, healthy adult friends.

She was strong, smart, and self-aware enough to accept that—and keep it that way. The first step, she thought, was to untangle herself from him and get out of bed.

She started to ease away, as cautiously as she might if she'd been wrapped around a sleeping cobra. She'd barely gained an inch when his eyes opened and beamed straight into hers.

"Sorry." She wasn't sure why she whispered—it just seemed the reasonable thing to do. "Didn't mean to wake you. I've got to get started."

He kept her close, only lifted her hand, turning her wrist to look at the luminous dial of her watch. "Yeah, I guess we both do. In a couple minutes."

Before she could react he rolled over, and was inside her.

He took his time. After that first shock of possession, he went slow. Long, lazy strokes that left her both weak and giddy. Helpless she floated up, felt herself all but shimmer. Pressing her face to the side of his throat, she let go.

She sighed, lingering longer than was wise.

"I guess I owe you breakfast."

"I never argue with breakfast."

She made herself turn away, made the effort to keep her voice light. "I'll go start the coffee if you want to grab the shower first."

"Sure."

She grabbed a robe, pulling it on as she hurried out.

She avoided looking at herself in the mirror and concentrated on the practicalities. Strong black coffee and what she thought of as a full farm breakfast. Maybe she didn't have any appetite, but she would damn well eat. No one would know she was sick with love. Again.

Better to focus on the positive, she reminded herself. She'd gotten more rest in four hours than she'd had in days. And surely that buzzing sexual tension between her and Coop would diminish now.

The deed was done. They'd both survived. They'd both move on.

Bacon sizzled in the cast-iron skillet while she warmed biscuits in the oven. He liked his eggs over easy, she remembered. At least he had.

By the time he came down, smelling of her soap, she was breaking eggs into the pan. He poured his coffee, topped her mug off, then leaned against the counter and watched her.

"What?"

"You look good. It's nice to look at you over my morning coffee." He glanced at the bacon she had draining, then the hash browns sizzling with the eggs. "Guess you're hungry."

"I figured I owed you the full shot."

"I appreciate the breakfast, but I'm not looking for payment."

"All the same. Anyway, I hope I can get that alarm system installed soon. I can't expect people to keep guarding the place like it was Fort Apache. Everyone's got their own to see to, including you."

"Look at me."

She glanced over as she flipped the eggs. "Why don't you sit down? This is about ready."

"If you're thinking about stepping back, think again."

With hands remarkably steady, she scooped out the hash browns. "Sex isn't a ball and chain, Coop. I step where I want."

"No, you don't. Not anymore."

"Anymore? I never—" She put up a hand as if to stop herself. "I'm not getting into this. I've got too much to deal with today."

"It's not going away, Lil, and neither am I."

"You were gone for over ten years. You've been back for a few months. Do you think, really think, everything just picks up where you want it to, for as long as you want it?"

"Do you want to hear what I think and what I want? Are you ready to hear it?"

"No, actually, I don't, and I'm not." She didn't think her heart could bear it. Not now. "I'm not interested in a discussion, debate, or rehash. We can be friends, or you can push until we're not. That's up to you. If what happened between us ruins our friendship, Cooper, I'll be sorry. Really sorry."

"I'm not looking for a fuck buddy, Lil."

She let out a breath. "Okay, then."

He took a step toward her, she took one back. And the door opened.

"'Morning. I wanted to let you know . . ." Gull wasn't the quickest off the mark, but even he could sense bad timing. "Sorry to interrupt."

"You're not," Lil said quickly. "In fact, you're right on time. Coop was about to have breakfast. You can keep him company and have some yourself."

"Oh, well, I don't want to—"

"Grab some coffee." She began dishing up two plates. "I've got to go up and get dressed. Everybody okay out there?"

"Yeah. Yeah. Um . . ."

"Have a seat and dig in. I'll be back down in a few minutes." She picked up her coffee, walked out without looking back.

Gull cleared his throat. "Sorry, boss."

"Not your fault," Coop muttered.

17

She didn't come back down in a few minutes. In fact, she didn't go back to the kitchen at all. She showered, dressed, then let herself out the front of the cabin.

Avoidance? No question, Lil admitted. But she couldn't afford to bog down her mind, her heart, her spirit. The interns were her full responsibility until Tansy got back—and when she did, they'd have another cat.

She kept herself busy checking the temporary enclosure and working with the crew on the permanent habitat.

Sunny skies and rising temperatures meant she could work in shirt-sleeves for a change. It also meant more snowmelt, more mud. As fickle March headed for capricious April, the dawning of spring would bring more patrons—and more on-site donations.

For her morning break, she visited Baby, pleasing them both with a long play period with lots of scratching, rubbing, and petting.

"I swear, that one's just a big house cat." Mary shook her head as Lil came out of the enclosure, double-checked the locks. "Less arrogant than my tabby, come to it."

"Your tabby couldn't rip out your jugular if he turned."

"Got me there. Can't see that one turning. He's been a sweetheart since day one. Pretty day, isn't it?" With her hands on her hips, Mary turned her face up to the bold blue of the sky. "I got bulbs sprouting up in my yard. Crocus blooming, too."

"I'm ready for spring. Good and ready."

Lil took the path around, wanting to check all the animals. Mary fell into step beside her.

In their yard, the bobcats rolled and wrestled together like a couple of boys on holiday, while perched in her tree, the lynx watched them with what might have been disdain.

"I know the jaguar and the new security system are going to take a big bite out of the budget. We're okay, aren't we, Mary?"

"We're okay. Donations were a little slow this winter, except for that whopper Coop gave us. That one put us far and away over last year's first quarter."

"Now we worry about the second quarter."

"Lucius and I are brainstorming on some fundraising ploys. And we'll start clicking along here with the warmer weather."

"I'm worried the trouble we've been having will keep people away, and cut hard into entrance fees and on-site donations. Word gets around." Reality, Lil knew, came in dollars and cents. "We'll have two new animals, with Xena and Cleo, to feed, house, and care for. I'd hoped to be able to hire at least a part-time veterinary assistant for Matt this summer. I'm not sure we'll be able to stretch the budget for it now."

"Willy needs to catch that son of a bitch, and soon. Matt's overworked, but so is everybody else around here. That's the way it is. We're okay, Lil, and we're going to stay okay. Now, how are you?"

"I'm fine. I'm good."

"Well, if you ask me—which you didn't, but I'm telling you anyway—you look stressed. And speaking of overworked, what you need is a day off. A *real* day off. And a date."

"A date?"

"Yes, a date." Clearly exasperated, Mary rolled her eyes. "You remember what a date is. Dinner, the movies, dancing. You haven't taken a full day off since you got back, and however much you enjoyed that trip to South America, I know you worked every damn day there, too."

"I like to work."

"That may be, but a day off and a date would do you good. You ought to get your ma and drive into Rapid City for the day. Do some shopping, get your nails done, then come back and have that good-looking Cooper Sullivan buy you a steak dinner, take you dancing, then parking afterward."

"Mary."

"If I were thirty years younger and single, I'd damn well see to it he bought me a steak dinner, and the rest of it." Mary gave Lil a hard, somewhat impatient squeeze. "I worry about you, honey."

"Don't. Don't worry."

"Take a day off. Well, break's over." She checked her watch. "Tansy and Farley ought to be rolling up in a couple hours. Then we'll have some excitement."

She didn't want a day off, Lil thought when Mary walked away. She didn't want to go shopping—very much. Or to get her nails done. She looked at her nails, winced. Okay, maybe she could use a manicure, but she didn't have any lectures, appearances, or events scheduled. No fundraising drums to beat. When she needed to, she cleaned up very well.

And if she wanted a steak dinner, she could buy her own. The last thing she needed was a date with Coop, which would complicate a situation she'd already complicated with sex.

Completely her fault, she admitted.

He'd been right about one thing that morning. She had to deal with it. Why hadn't she made that list?

She stopped in front of the tiger's enclosure. He lay at the entrance of his den, eyes half shut. Not dozing, not yet, Lil thought. His tail switched lazily, and Lil could see awareness in those slitted eyes.

"Not still mad at me, are you?" Lil leaned on the rail, watched Boris's ears flick. "I had to do it. I don't want anything to happen to you, or for anything to happen because of you. Not our fault, Boris, but we'd be responsible."

Boris made a rumbling that sounded so much like reluctant agreement, Lil smiled. "You're beautiful. Big, beautiful boy." Lil let out a sigh. "I guess my break's over, too."

She straightened to stare out across the enclosures, the trees, the hills. And she thought it didn't seem as if there could be a thing wrong in the world on a day like this.

HE MUNCHED ON his second Ho Ho. He *could* live off the land, but didn't see any reason to deny himself a few pleasures from the Outside. In any case, he'd stolen the box of snack cakes from a campsite, so technically he was living off the land as he ate them. He'd also confiscated a bag of potato rolls and a six-pack of Heineken.

He limited himself to one beer every two days. A hunter couldn't let alcohol slow his brain, even for an hour. So he only drank the single beer at bedtime.

Drinking had been his weak spot—he could admit it—just like it had been his daddy's. Just, as his daddy had often said, like it was for their people. Liquor was only one more weapon the white man had used against them.

Drinking had gotten him in trouble, brought him to the attention of the white man's law.

But he did love the taste of a cold beer.

He wouldn't deny himself. He would simply control himself.

He'd learned that on his own. Of all the things his father had taught him, control hadn't been one of them.

It was a matter of control, he thought. Just as letting the campers live had been a matter of control, and power. Killing them would have been fish-in-barrel time, and that wasn't worth his skill. He had considered killing three of the four, then hunting down the last.

It never hurt to practice.

But taking out four campers would have the cops and rangers covering the hills like ants. Not that he couldn't evade them, as his forefathers had for so long. One day he would be a one-man war party, hunting and killing those who desecrated the land at his whim and his will.

One day they would speak his name with fear and reverence.

But for now he had bigger fish to fry, fish that weren't in the barrel.

He took out his field glasses to scan the compound below. His pride still surged from his observation of the guards placed around the perimeters through the night.

Because of him.

His prey scented him, and feared. Nothing he'd done before had given him such satisfaction.

How easy, and how exciting, it would have been to have taken them out. All of them. Moving silent as a ghost, slitting throats, one by one, blood warm and wet on his hands.

All that game bagged in one night.

And what would his prize have felt in the morning, when she'd come out of the cabin to see the carnage he'd left behind?

Would she have run, run screaming in terror?

He loved it when they ran, when they screamed. And more, when they had no breath left to scream.

But he'd snapped control firmly into place. It wasn't time.

He could send her a message, he considered. Yes, he could. Something that made it very personal. The more there was at stake, the deeper the competition when the time came.

He didn't just want her fear—fear was easy to come by.

He watched her for another moment as she crossed the compound toward the cabin that held the offices.

No, not just her fear, he thought, lowering the glasses, licking chocolate off his fingers. He wanted her *involved* as none of the others had been. As none of the others had deserved.

He turned away, and hitching his pack on his shoulders, began a circular hike back to his den, whistling a tune.

When the lone hiker, puffing a bit, crossed his path, he smiled.

"Lost?" he asked.

"No. Not exactly. Glad to see a friendly face, though. I was on Crow Peak, heading toward the summit. I think I got off the mark a little." He pulled a bottle of water out of his belt harness. "I guess I should've stuck with one of the easier trails. It's been a while."

"Mmm-hmm." This one looked healthy enough, fit enough. And lost, just enough. "You're making the trip alone?"

"Yeah. The wife headed back at the junction. I'da done the same except she said I couldn't do the seven miles. You know how it is. Gotta prove them wrong."

"I'm heading that way myself. I can get you back on track."

"That'd be great. Wouldn't mind the company either. Jim Tyler," he said, offering a hand. "From St. Paul."

"Ethan Swift Cat."

"Nice to meet you. You from around here?"

"That's right, I'm from around."

He started off, leading Jim Tyler from St. Paul farther off the trail, away from the blazes on pines, the signs, the posts, and deeper into the wilderness. He kept the pace moderate. Didn't want to wear Jim out before the games began. He watched for signs of others, and listened to the man talk about his wife, his kids, his business—real estate—back in St. Paul.

He pointed out tracks to keep the man entertained, waited while Jim took pictures with a nice little digital Canon.

"You're better than my guidebook," Jim said with real pleasure. "Wait until I show off these pictures, and my wife sees what she missed. I'm lucky I ran into you."

"Lucky." He gave Jim a big smile as he pulled out his revolver.

"Run, rabbit," he said, grinning. "Run."

LIL RUSHED OUT of the cabin when Farley pulled in. Staff, volunteers, interns dropped what they were doing to hurry over. Before Farley came to a full stop, Lil boosted herself onto the running board on Tansy's side and grinned at her friend.

"How'd it go?"

"Fine. Good. She's getting a little restless back there. As if she knew we were getting close. You're going to be very happy with her, Lil. She's a beauty."

"You have all her medical records?" Matt asked her.

"Yeah, and I spoke with her vet personally. She's got a clean bill of health. She'd had some intestinal problems a few months ago. Her owner liked to feed her chocolate truffles—I swear. Godiva truffles, and Beluga caviar on special occasions. Apparently Cleo's very fond of dark chocolate with hazelnut filling, and caviar on lightly browned toast points."

"Good God," was Matt's response.

"She's left the high life, but I think she'll adjust." Lil forced herself not to climb right on in and take a look. "Take her on over to the tempo-rary, Farley. Let's get her out of the cage, and into her new home. I bet she'd like to stretch her legs."

She glanced over to where two of the interns continued a tour for a small group. "Annie," she said to the young woman at her shoulder. "Why don't you go tell that group to head over toward the enclosure. This should be a real treat for them."

She rode with them, standing on the running board. "We were expect-ing you about an hour ago," she commented.

Tansy shifted in her seat. "We, ah, left a little later than we'd planned."

"No problems?"

"No. No." Tansy stared straight ahead. "No problems. Cleo handled the drive just fine. Slept through most of it. I've got all the paperwork if you want to go over it after she's settled."

Lil's first look at the cat took her breath away. Sleek, muscular, her eyes tawny glints, Cleo sat in her travel cage like royalty on a throne.

She eyed the humans, with what struck Lil as a gaze of pure superior-ity, and let out her coughing roar in case they didn't fully understand who was boss.

Lil approached the cage so the jaguar could get her scent. "Hello, Cleo. Yes, you're gorgeous. Strong, powerful, and you know it. But I'm alpha here. No more Godivas or poodles on the menu."

The cat tracked her with those exotic eyes as she circled. "Let's get her out. Keep your hands away from the bars. Her favored killing method may be to pierce the skull, but she won't quibble at taking a good swipe of a careless hand or arm. I don't want any trips to the infirmary. And don't let her taste for chocolate fool you. She's got powerful jaws, arguably the most powerful of all felids."

They lowered the cage by the lift, and as the tourist group took snapshots, positioned it at the entrance to the enclosure.

Cleo grumbled in her throat, displeased, Lil concluded, with the crowd, the scent of them, the scent of other animals. Across the compound the lion roared.

Lil lifted the cage door, locked it open, stepped back.

The cat sniffed the air as she scanned the space, the tree, the boulders, the fencing. And the other animals beyond.

Her tail switched as the lioness prowled along their shared fenceline and marked her territory.

"This melanistic, or black, female jaguar hasn't reached maturity," Lil began for the benefit of the tourists. "She gets her color from a dominant allele—a unique pairing of genes. But she does have rosettes—spots— that can be seen if you're close enough. She's one of the four big cats, along with the lion, the tiger, and the leopard."

As she spoke, she studied Cleo's reactions.

"As you can see, while young, she has a compact, muscular body."

"It looks sort of like a leopard."

Lil nodded at one of the men in the group. "You're right. Physically she looks like a leopard, though she'll be bigger and stockier in build. Behaviorally, she's more like the tiger—and like the tiger, actually enjoys swimming."

Cleo inched toward the opening of the cage. Lil stayed where she was, kept very still, and continued to talk. "And like the tiger, the female kicks the male to the curb after giving birth."

That got a little laugh from the tour group as they angled for more pictures.

"She's a stalk-and-ambush hunter, and no other species comes close to her abilities there. In the wild, she's an apex predator, top of the food chain. Only man preys on her. Because of deforestation and encroachment and fragmentation of its habitats and poaching, jaguar populations are declining. The species is considered Near Threatened. Conservation efforts will help preserve her species, which in turn will help preserve other, smaller-range species."

Crouched, the jaguar stepped out, nosing both ground and air. When she'd cleared it, Lil lowered the door on the enclosure, locked it.

The crowd applauded.

"She'll be protected here," Lil added. "Cared for by the staff, interns, and volunteers of Chance Wildlife Refuge, and through," lest they forget, Lil thought, "the donations of our patrons and visitors. She'll have a good life here, and may have it for over twenty years."

She watched the black cat belly through the grass, nosing it, nosing the air, then rising to stalk. Squatting to pee, marking her territory as the lion marked hers.

She paced and circled, and even when she stopped to drink from her trough, Lil saw her muscles quivering.

She continued to pace, to prowl, sending out that hoarse roar. When she rose on her hind legs to sharpen her front claws on her tree, Lil felt her own muscles quiver at the beauty of the cat's lines, the power of her build.

She watched, even when the others drifted away, she watched for nearly an hour. And smiled when Cleo leaped into the tree to spread her muscular body over a thick branch.

"Welcome home, Cleo," she said aloud.

She left the new guest alone and went back to the office to check the paperwork.

She looked in on Matt first to find him reading the new addition's medical records. "Everything as advertised?"

"Healthy female melanistic jaguar, who has not yet come into estrus. She's had regular exams, the proper inoculations. Her diet has been somewhat suspect. Tansy brought blood samples, but I'll want to examine her myself."

"Understood. Let's give her a day or two to adjust to her new environment before we put any more stress on her. I can get you some scat and urine without too much trouble if you want to start sooner."

"Sooner the better."

"I'll take care of it."

Lil walked to the office she shared with Tansy, and shut the door.

Tansy looked up from the keyboard. "Everything okay?"

"We'll get into that in a minute. First, what's up with you?"

"Nothing. I don't want to talk about it now. I want to talk about it later," Tansy decided. "With alcohol."

"Okay, after tonight's feeding. We'll have some wine and a debriefing. But here's what you have to know now."

Lil sat and filled Tansy in on what had happened during her trip.

"My God, Lil. My God. You could've been seriously hurt. You could've been killed." Tansy shut her eyes. "If one of the kids—"

"Middle of the night. The kids aren't here. We're taking steps. Every step we can. With the new alarm system the animals, the staff, everyone will be protected. I should've dug into the coffers for an updated system before."

"It did the job, Lil. It did the job until some crazy person came around. You have to be crazy to open the enclosure that way. Whoever did it could've ended up as fresh meat just as easily as that elk. The cops can't find him? Any trace of him?"

"Not so far. Coop thinks he has a line on who it is. Tansy, Carolyn Roderick—you remember her?"

"Sure. What does she have to do with this?"

"She's missing. She's been missing for months, disappeared from a group working in Alaska."

"Missing? Oh, no. Her family. I talked to her mother a couple of times when Carolyn was here."

"She had a boyfriend—an ex. He came around here when she interned."

"The mountain-man type—Ed? No, not Ed."

"Ethan."

"Right, Ethan, of the I'm-descended-from-Crazy-Horse blather."

"You remembered that faster than I did," Lil replied.

"I had dinner with Carolyn and some of the other interns a few times, and he'd come along or show up. Full of himself and his proud heritage, which came off as bullshit to me. But she liked it, liked him. He brought her wildflowers, did some volunteering. Took her dancing. She was smitten.

"It went bad between them. She broke it off, and people Coop contacted said they thought he was violent." Lil got them both bottles of water. "I remembered, after I looked through her file, how he'd gone around claiming to be Sioux, and how he bragged about living in the wild for long stretches of time, like—well—Crazy Horse. Had a hard-on for the Park Service. Claimed this area was sacred ground."

"You think it's him? The one who killed the cougar and wolf? Why would he come back here and harass you?"

"I don't know. But he's vanished, too. Coop hasn't been able to locate him. Yet. If there's anything more you can remember about him, anything at all, you should tell Coop and Willy."

"I will. I'll think about it. God, you think he did something to Carolyn?"

"I wish I didn't think that." Thinking it made her feel sick and sad, and guilty. "I'm not sure if I'm actually remembering or if I just have the heebies, but I feel like he was a little spooky. Like I'm remembering him watching me. A lot. And maybe didn't think anything of it at the time, as some of the volunteers and interns tend to watch me. They want to see what I'm doing, and how I do it. You know."

"Sure."

"And now I'm feeling like that wasn't the feeling I got when he watched me. That maybe I felt something slightly off, but dismissed it."

"I don't remember him that well. I just thought he was a bullshitter, but he helped out around here and seemed focused on charming Carolyn."

"Okay."

"What else can I do?"

"Talk to the interns, keep them steady. I've told them everything I can, and I've contacted the universities for the incomings. I figured full disclosure. I don't believe any of them are in any danger, and we have to keep the refuge running normally. Still, full disclosure. And that's bound to make some of them jumpy."

"Okay. Most of them are going to be over at the commissary, processing for the evening feeding. I'll go over, get a gauge."

"That'd be good."

"We'll talk later." Tansy rose. "Do you want me to stay here tonight?"

Coward, Lil told herself when she nearly agreed. But the agreement wouldn't be due to fear of some maniac prowling the hills. It would be due to avoidance of Cooper Sullivan.

"No. We're covered here. I'd rather stick with routine as much as we can."

Lucius tapped on her doorjamb as Tansy went out. "I e-mailed you pictures of Cleo, and a kind of montage we took as we were transferring her. I can get them on the Web page whenever you approve."

"I'll take a look." Focus, she ordered herself, and she shifted gears into work mode. "I'll write something up to go with the montage. We'll want something on her specifically, the jag in general, and some behind-the-scenes stuff. Then put her up on the Adopt page. Did Mary see about getting the black jag toy for that donation, and for the gift shop?"

"I think she's got some possibles e-mailed to you."

"Okay. I'll get on it."

"Want the door shut?"

"No, open is fine."

She dug up a soft drink for the hit of caffeine, then dug into work.

It took her through feeding time, and she still wasn't quite satisfied. She copied the work and photos to a thumb drive, stuck it in her pocket. She'd give it another pass at home, after a solid break. Come to it fresh.

Contributors, she knew, wanted info, but they also wanted a story. A new animal meant new interest, and she intended to exploit that. She cleaned up other paperwork while twilight filled with the sounds of feeding.

She came out, locked up as the last of the interns left for the day. Eventually, she thought, she'd have enough in the budget to build the dorm. Housing for the interns, their own kitchen. Two years down the road, by her estimation, with the hit on the budget with the proposed security system, the expense of building a new enclosure.

She found Tansy in the living room with a bottle of wine and a bag of corn chips. "Alcohol and salt." Tansy toasted her. "It's what I need."

"Food of the gods." Lil tossed her jacket, her hat aside, poured her own glass. "You look tired."

"I guess I didn't get much sleep last night." Tansy took a long gulp of wine. "Because I was busy having sex with Farley."

"Oh." Lil decided that bulletin required sitting down. "Okay. Yes, this is news best served with adult beverages. Wow."

"Really, really good sex." Brows knit, Tansy bit into a chip. "Now what am I supposed to do?"

"Ah, have more?"

"Oh, good God, Lil, what have I done? I knew better, but it just happened." She knocked back a slug of wine. "Four times."

"Four? Four times in one night. Jeez. Here's to Farley."

"It's not a joke."

"No, it's a serious accomplishment."

"Lil."

"Tansy. You're a grown-up, he's a grown-up."

"He thinks he's in love with me." Tansy crunched on chips. "Do you know what he said to me last night?"

"Before or after sex?"

"After, damn it. And also before. I'm trying, really trying to be sensible and fair and realistic."

"And naked."

"Shut up. Then he looks at me. Man, he sure can look at me."

Tansy told her everything Farley said, nearly word for word.

"Oh." She couldn't help it. Lil pressed a hand to her heart. "That's beautiful. And so Farley, so completely and beautifully Farley."

"I know it. I know, but Lil, this morning, over breakfast in this diner, I'm fumbling around, trying to . . . I don't know slow it down, calm it down. Be *sensible*. He just keeps smiling at me."

"Well, four times puts a smile on a guy's face."

"Stop it! He says, 'I'm going to marry you, Tansy, but you can take some time to get used to it first.'"

"Wow." Lil's jaw dropped before she managed to close it and take another drink. "Well. I repeat, Wow."

"It doesn't matter what I say. He just smiles and nods, and when we go outside, he gets ahold of me again and kisses my brains out. I felt them leak out of my ears. I think I lost half my brain in Montana."

"Have you set the date?"

"Will you *stop* it! You're not helping."

"Sorry, Tans, but you're sitting there, stress-eating Fritos and telling me a good man, a really good man, loves you and wants you. A man you had multiple orgasms with—I assume."

"Yes, multiple was a factor. He's very . . . attentive and energetic."

"Now you're just bragging."

"Some. God, Lil, he's sincere and sweet and just a little scary. I'm messed up over this, over him."

"Which would be a first. I like that you're in love with him, and all I can think is good. It's good. All I can be is happy, and a little bit jealous."

"I shouldn't have slept with him," Tansy continued. "Now I've complicated it even more, because before I could think I just had the hots for him, but now I know I have the hots for him, *and* I'm crazy about him. Why do we do that? Why do we end up sleeping with them?"

"I don't know. I slept with Coop."

Tansy ate another chip, washed it down with wine. "I thought you'd hold out longer."

"So did I," Lil admitted. "Now we're mad at each other. I think. Or I snapped and snarled at him this morning. Which I knew, even as I was doing it, was ninety percent defense and ten percent truth."

"He broke your heart."

"Into countless pieces. Farley's incapable of doing that to you."

Tansy's deep, dark eyes went soft. "I could break his."

"Yes, you could. Will you?"

"I don't know, that's the problem. I don't want to. He's not what I was looking for. When I thought about what I might be looking for, down the road, it sure wasn't a skinny white cowboy."

"I don't think we get to choose as much as we tell ourselves we choose." Thoughtfully, Lil dug into the bag of chips. "If I could pick, it would be Jean-Paul. He's a better choice for me. But he wasn't the one, and I couldn't make him the one. So I ended up hurting him even though I didn't want to."

"Now I'm depressed."

"Sorry. No more talk of broken hearts." Deliberately Lil shook herself as if shedding a weight. "Let's talk about sex with Farley. Spare no details."

"No." Amused, Tansy pointed at her. "At least not on one glass of wine. And since I'm driving, no more for me. I'm going home and I'm going to think about something else. Anything else. You'll be all right here?"

"There's half a dozen armed men outside."

"Good. But I meant regarding Cooper."

Lil blew out a breath. "I'm going to take the late shift, thereby avoiding that problem, as he'll take first duty. It's not a solution but it's a plan. Tansy, just one question. Don't think first, just answer. Are you in love with Farley? Not just crazy about, but in love with."

"I think I am. Now I'm even more depressed." She pushed to her feet. "I'm going home to brood."

"Good luck with that. I'll see you tomorrow."

Alone, Lil fixed herself a sandwich and a short pot of coffee. She sat at her kitchen table, eating her dinner and polishing her pieces for the website.

She braced, every muscle on alert, when the door opened. Then relaxed again when her mother came in. "I told you not to come tonight."

"Your father's here, I'm here. Live with it." At home, Jenna opened the fridge, sighed once at the contents, then took out a bottle of water. "You're working, and I'm interrupting."

"It's all right. I'm just fine-tuning some articles for the Web page, on our new princess."

"I saw her. Lil, she's beautiful. So elegant and mysterious. She'll be a huge draw for you."

"I think so. And she'll be happy here. Plenty of room once we finish her permanent habitat. The right diet, the right care. I'm going to look into breeding her next year."

Jenna nodded, sat. "This is probably nothing."

"Oh-oh."

"You know Alan Tobias, the ranger."

"Sure. He brings his kids here."

"He's helping out tonight."

"That's nice of him. I should go out and thank him."

"Yes, at some point. He told us there's a hiker missing."

"For how long?"

"He was due back around four. His wife didn't start worrying, seriously, until five."

"Well, it's barely eight."

"And dark. He's not answering his cell phone."

Nerves jangled, but she spoke calmly. "Reception's spotty. You know that."

"I do, and it's probably nothing. He probably got turned around a little, and he may end up having a lousy night if he doesn't make it back to a trailhead soon. But Lil, he was hiking Crow Peak, and that's not all that far from where you trapped the cougar with Coop."

"It's a full-day hike to the summit and back, and it's not an easy trail. If he's not experienced, it would take longer, probably longer than he allowed. Why was he hiking alone?"

"I don't know. I don't have all the details." Jenna glanced toward the window, and the dark. "They're looking for him."

"I'm sure they'll find him."

"They've looked for the man who shot your cougar, the man who came here. They haven't found him."

"He doesn't want to be found," Lil pointed out. "This hiker does."

"They're calling for rain before morning. Hard rain." Jenna looked back toward the window. "You can smell it coming. I have a sick feeling about this, Lil. A sick feeling in the pit of my stomach that more than hard rain's coming."

18

The rain came, and came hard. At dawn, Lil dragged herself back into the house, hung her slicker up to dry, pulled off her soaked and muddy boots.

She wanted to grab another hour's sleep. Two if she could manage it, then spend a couple days in a hot shower and eat like a lumberjack.

As of dawn, the hiker—James Tyler of St. Paul, according to her sources—hadn't been found. She hoped the worst that happened was he'd spent an even more miserable night than she had.

She moved quietly in her bare feet out of the kitchen and toward the stairs. But when she glanced at the living room, the sofa was empty. Gone home, she assumed. She hadn't seen his truck, but then in the driving rain she hadn't seen much of anything. Relaxing, she climbed the stairs.

Set the alarm, she told herself. Ninety minutes would be a good compromise. Then bed. Warm, soft, dry bed.

When she stepped into her room she saw that warm, soft, dry bed was already occupied.

She gritted her teeth against the curse that sprang to her tongue, but when she started to back out, Coop's eyes opened.

"I'm not sleeping on the damn couch."

"Fine. It's morning, so you can get up and go. You can make coffee if you want it, but be quiet. I need some sleep." She stalked across the bedroom to the bath, and shut the door, firmly.

So, shower first, she thought. She'd sleep better for it. Nice hot shower, then bed. No big deal. And no reason the man shouldn't make use of the bed after standing out in the dark for several hours.

She stripped off, leaving her clothes in a puddle on the floor, then switched the shower on, full and hot as she could stand. She actually moaned when she stepped in and felt the heat beat through her chilled skin to her chilled bones.

She hissed when the curtain flicked back. "Goddamn it!"

"I want a shower."

"It's *my* shower."

He simply stepped in behind her. "Plenty of room, plenty of water."

She shoved her wet hair out of her face. "You go too far, Cooper."

"Too far would be putting my hands on you, which I won't."

"I'm tired. I'm not going to argue with you."

"Good. I'm not in the mood for an argument." He pumped out some of the shower gel, soaped up. "We're going to get some flooding with this rain."

She just let the water beat over her head. She didn't want conversation either.

She stepped out first, wrapped her body in a towel, wrapped her hair in another. In the bedroom she pulled on flannel pants and a T-shirt, then sat on the side of the bed to set her alarm.

He came out, damp hair, jeans, and a shirt he hadn't bothered to button. "Did they find the hiker?"

"No. Not yet. Not when I came in."

He nodded, then sat to pull on socks, watching as she slid into the bed he'd left warm for her. "Your hair's wet."

"I don't care. I'm tired."

"I know." He rose, went to the bed. Leaning over, he pressed his lips to hers, as gently as he might to a sleepy child. "I'll be back later."

He trailed a finger down her cheek before he walked to the door. "It wasn't just sex, Lil. It never was."

She kept her eyes closed, listened to him go down. Waited until she'd heard the front door open, then shut behind him.

And gave in to the turmoil he managed to set off inside her. As the rain pounded, she cried herself to sleep.

IT RAINED THROUGH the morning, canceling scheduled trail rides and rentals. Coop dealt with the stock at the farm, and gave up cursing the rain and wind after the first hour.

No point.

With his grandfather set cleaning and repairing tack, and his grand-mother hip-deep in paperwork—both in the warm and dry—he loaded two more horses into the trailer.

"Plenty of shelter in the hills," Lucy said as she packed up a lunch for Coop. "I pray that poor man found some. God knows how they'll find him in this weather."

"We've got six horses out with volunteers. I'll take these into town in case they want more. Flash floods are going to be a problem."

"So much trouble. Too much. It comes down like the rain."

"It'll clear. If they need more men on the search, I'll let you know. Otherwise, I'll be back in a few hours."

"You'll be staying at Lil's again tonight."

He stopped, one hand on the door. "Yes. Until this is settled."

"And you and Lil?" She gave him her keen, no-nonsense look. "Are you going to settle that, too?"

"Working on it."

"I don't know what happened between you all those years ago, and

I'm not asking. But if you love that girl, stop wasting time. I'd like to see you settled and happy. And, damn it, I'd like some babies around here."

He rubbed the back of his neck. "That might be jumping the gun."

"Not from where I'm standing. If you go with the search party, you take a rifle."

She handed him the sack holding his lunch, then laid her hands on his cheeks. "You take care of my boy, because he's precious to me."

"Don't worry."

Nothing to worry about, he thought as he dealt with the miserable drive into Deadwood. He wasn't the one being stalked, or the one lost somewhere in the hills. All he was doing was what came next. Provide the horses, and another pair of eyes if they were needed. And for Lil? All he could do was be there.

Did he love her?

He'd always loved her. He'd done what came next there, too, and lived without her. And look where she'd landed. Exactly where she wanted to be—needed to be. Doing what she'd dreamed of doing. She'd made her mark, and in his way so had he.

Now, well, he'd just keep doing what came next. The problem was, he didn't know where he stood with her.

Friend? Occasional lover? A port in the storm?

Screw that. It wasn't enough this time around, not for him. So he'd push, because that came next as he saw it. Then both of them would see where he stood.

In the meantime, he'd do whatever it took to protect her. She'd just have to deal with it.

Gull came out of the stables as Coop pulled up. Water poured off the brim of his hat, sluiced down the shine of his slicker as he helped unload the horses.

"Haven't found him yet," Gull shouted over the thunder of the rain. "No way to track in this mess. Got flooding between the snowmelt and the rain. It's bad up there, boss."

"They're going to need more horses." Coop looked toward the black and angry sky. Even if choppers could go up, what the hell could they see in this? Ground search, such as it was, would be the best bet.

"They're working on coordinating or some such on his cell phone. Trying to find the signal." Gull led his horse into a dry stall. "I don't know how they're doing there. But if you don't need me, I figure I can replace somebody who's been out in this long enough."

"Take whichever mount you want and check in. You keep in touch with me, Gull."

"Will do. He's got any sense he's holed up in a cave on high ground. Don't know if he's got any sense. Everybody else, so I hear, who was up on a trail or camping, they're accounted for. Just this guy from St. Paul."

"It's a long time to be lost in this weather."

"Damn right. Word is they haven't found the first sign of him yet." As he spoke, Gull saddled a big bay gelding. "Couple day-trippers saw him, even had a word or two with him at the junction on Crow Peak. They took the spur trail south, and he was headed north to the summit, so he said. But that was before noon yesterday."

"Did they see anybody else?"

"At the junction, yeah, and on the spur trail. But not heading to the summit. He went on his own."

"Then let's hope he has sense. If they need more relief, you let them know I'm around. And you keep in touch."

Coop drove over to the office, brewed a pot of coffee. Until he was called on, he intended to find out more about Ethan Howe.

He booted up the computer and picked up the phone.

He spent the next hour bouncing between cops and investigators in Alaska, North Dakota, New York, slowly, tediously filling in a few blanks. He talked to Howe's parole officer and former landlords and added a few names to his call list.

As far as known companions, they were few and far between. The man was a loner, a drifter, preferred low-population areas, and as far as

Coop could discern, had rarely stayed in one place more than six months at a time. Usually camping. Occasionally motels or weekly rooms. Paid in cash.

Employment sketchy. Day laborer, ranch hand, trail guide.

Kept to himself. Quiet. Hard worker, but unreliable. Came and went.

Coop dug deeper, followed the dots to a bar in Wise River, Montana.

Spinning wheels, he thought as he made the call. Chasing my own tail. Might as well throw a dart at a map.

"Bender's."

"I'm looking for the owner or manager."

"I'm Charlie Bender. This is my place."

"Was it your place four years ago, July and August?"

"Been my place sixteen years. What's the problem?"

"Mr. Bender, I'm Cooper Sullivan. I'm a private investigator licensed in New York."

"Then why are you calling from South Dakota? I got caller ID, buddy."

"I'm in South Dakota. I'll give you my license number if you want to check it out." He might've sold his business, but his license was still good. "I'm trying to find someone who worked for you for a couple months the summer of '05."

"Who?"

"Ethan Howe."

"Don't ring, right off. Four years is a space of time, and I get a lot of people in and out of here. Why do you want him?"

"He may be connected to a missing-person's case I'm working on. He'd've been late twenties," Coop began and gave a description.

"Sounds like everybody else."

"He'd have been fresh out of prison for assault."

"Still not cutting him out of the herd."

"He claims he's part Sioux, likes to brag about his mountain-man skills. Keeps to himself, but he's very polite and charming with the ladies. At least initially."

"Chief. We called him Chief mostly because he talked about being blood kin to Crazy Horse after he'd had a couple beers. Just another asshole. I recollect he wore what he said was a bear-tooth necklace—talked about how he and his pa hunted bear and other bullshit. He worked good enough when he was here, but it wasn't for long. Then he took off with my best waitress."

"Got a name on her?"

"Yeah. Molly Pickens. She worked for me four years before Chief came along. Then she lit out with him, and I was short two people. Had to drag my wife in to wait tables, and I heard about it for weeks. So I remember."

"Do you know how I can get in touch with Molly?"

"Haven't seen or heard of her since that August."

Coop felt a buzz at the back of his skull. "Does she have family? Friends? Someone I can get in touch with?"

"Look, buddy, I don't keep tabs on people. She came in here looking for work. I gave her work. She got on fine with the rest, the customers. Minded her own business, and I minded mine."

"Where was she from?"

"Christ, you're a nosy bastard. Back east somewhere. Said once she'd had enough of her old man—couldn't say if that was husband or father—and hit the road. She never gave me any trouble, till she took up with Chief."

"She left you without notice. Did she take her things?"

"Didn't have much. Packed up some clothes and such, cleared out her bank account, and took off in her old Ford Bronco."

"Did she like the outdoors? Hiking, camping?"

"What the fuck? Are you looking for him or her?"

"Right now? Both of them."

Bender heaved out an audible breath. "Now that you mention it, she liked being out and about. She was a good, strong girl. Liked to go off, take photographs in the park on her days off. Wanted to be a photographer, she said. She picked up some extra money selling photographs to tourists. I expect she landed on her feet somewhere."

Coop wasn't so sure of it. He worked Bender for more details, scrawling notes.

When he'd compiled everything, he sat back, shut his eyes, let his mind turn it over. Patterns, he thought. Patterns and circles and cycles. They were always there if you looked for them.

He shut everything down and went to see Willy.

The sheriff's face was pasty with exhaustion, his eyes bloodshot, and his voice like the bottom of a gravel pit. "Caught something." He sneezed heroically into a red bandanna. "Goddamn spring. Came back down from the search about a half hour ago." He lifted a thick white mug. "Cup-a-Soup. Can't taste a damn thing, but my ma always says you down chicken soup for a cold. I'm downing."

"You haven't found him."

Willy shook his head. "A man can barely find his own pecker out in this mess. Supposed to let up tomorrow. That poor bastard's alive, he's miserable." He drank, wincing. "Throat feels like my tonsils took sandpaper to it. It's only been a day. He didn't get hurt or dead, and he holed up out of the rain, he'll do okay. He had pack food. Energy bars, water, trail mix, and the like. Wouldn't starve. We're mostly worried he'd get caught in a flash and drown."

"Do you need more hands up there?"

"We got it covered. The fact is I'm worried somebody else is going to drown or fall off a damn cliff. Two on the search team had to be brought out. Got a broken ankle and what we thought was a heart attack. Just indigestion, it turns out. If we need to go up again tomorrow, we'll need fresh horses."

"You'll have them. Willy—"

He broke off when a woman came to the door. "Sheriff."

"Mrs. Tyler. Come right in here and sit down." Wheezing, Willy got to his feet to lead her to a chair. "Now, you shouldn't oughta be out in this weather."

"I can't just sit in the hotel room. I'm going crazy. I need to know what's going on. I need to know *something*."

"We're doing everything we can. We've got a lot of men looking for your husband, Mrs. Tyler. Men who know the trails, who've done plenty of search-and-rescues before. You told me your husband was a sensible man."

"Usually."

She dashed a hand over her brimming eyes. From the look of them, Coop doubted she'd closed them for more than an hour since her husband had gone missing.

"He should've had more sense than to insist on making that hike." She rocked in the chair as if the movement would help keep her calm. "He hasn't hiked on much more than his own treadmill in five years."

"Kept in shape, you said."

"Yes. I should've gone with him." Biting her lip, she rocked a little faster, a little harder. "I shouldn't have let him go by himself. I just didn't want to spend all day tromping around. I wanted to rent horses, but Jim, he's nervous around horses. I thought I could talk him into coming back with me when we got to that junction. I was so annoyed when he wouldn't. I snapped at him. The last thing I did was snap at him. Oh, my God."

Willy let her weep, signaling Coop to stay and pulling up a chair so he could pat the woman's arm.

"I know you're scared, and I wish I had more to tell you, more that would ease your mind."

"His phone. You said they'd try to track his cell phone."

"I did. They did. We can't find the signal. Could be the battery's dead."

"He'd have called. He'd have tried to call." While her voice trembled, she mopped at her face with a tissue. "He wouldn't want me worried. We charged our phones full before we started that morning. They said there's flooding. On the news, they said."

"He's a sensible man. A sensible man sticks to high ground. We haven't found him, Mrs. Tyler, but we haven't found any signs to indicate anything happened to him. Let's hold on to that for now."

"I'm trying."

"I'm going to have somebody take you back to the hotel. If you want, I can have someone stay with you, if you don't want to be alone."

"No. No, I'll be all right. I haven't called my boys—our sons. I was so sure he'd be back this morning, and now . . . it's twenty-four hours since he should've been back. I think I have to call our boys."

"You know best."

"Jim just got it into his head he wanted to make this trip. Wild Bill, Calamity Jane, Crazy Horse, the Black Hills. We've got a three-year-old grandson, and another coming. He said we should practice taking them on hikes. He bought all new gear."

"And you said he'd packed everything the guides recommended," Will began as he led her out. "He had a map, a flashlight . . ."

Coop walked to the window to watch the rain hammer the ground. He waited until Willy came back and then shut the office door.

"Another night up there isn't going to do Jim Tyler any good."

Coop turned around. "If he ran into Ethan Howe, he might not have a second night."

"Who's Ethan Howe?"

Coop told him everything he knew, giving the information in a quick, concise report as he'd been trained to do as a cop, as an investigator.

"It's a loose connection to Lil and her animals, but it's a connection," Willy allowed. "But as far as you know, or she remembers, this Howe and Lil never had any trouble, any hard words?"

"She barely remembered him, and then only because of the intern. He's trouble, Willy. A drifter, a loner, stays off the grid—except for one serious bust. He'd been drinking. Slipped up there. Otherwise, he keeps his head down when he's around people. He likes to talk about his Native American connection, but he blends. He's got that temper, and that self-importance, his weak points."

"I know a lot of people who have both of those."

"Enough of a temper, according to her friends and family, to scare off this Carolyn Roderick," Coop added. "She was a type, like the one from Montana. Athletic, pretty, strong, single. Molly Pickens emptied her bank account and left with him."

Willy sat back with his white mug of soup, nodded as he sipped. "Of her own free will."

"And that's the last I can find her, when she left with him, of her own free will. There's no credit card activity since that August, and up until then she used a MasterCard, regularly. She's never renewed her driver's license. Hasn't filed taxes. She left Columbus, Ohio, in '96. She was eighteen. Rumors of an abusive father, who didn't file a missing-person's report. She left a paper trail. I've picked up some of it. But when she left with Ethan Howe, nothing. No trail."

Willy took a thoughtful breath that came out as a wheeze. "You think he killed that waitress, and the intern."

"Damn right I do."

"And you think he's the same one who's been causing this trouble for Lil."

"He connects, and she fits his type."

"And if Tyler crossed paths with him . . ."

"Maybe he doesn't want to be seen, doesn't want some guy going back and talking about this man he met on the trail. Or Tyler stumbled over his campsite, found him poaching. Or maybe he just likes to kill. There's more."

"Jesus." Willy pinched the bridge of his nose. "Let's have it, then."

"Melinda Barrett. Age twenty."

Willy's forehead creased. "That's the girl you and Lil found."

"Strong, pretty, athletic. Alone on the trail. I'm betting she was his first. He'd've been about the same age. There've been others." Coop dropped a folder on Willy's desk. "I copied my file for you."

Willy stared, not at the file, but at Cooper. "Jumping Jesus, Coop, you're talking serial killer. You're talking about a dozen years of killing."

"Which stopped, as far as I've been able to determine, during the year and a half Howe was in prison. The problem with tying the first killing to the others I tracked, the like crimes, was the wide time lag between. But when you add in missing persons, bodies that weren't found, by chance or by his design? It plays then."

Willy looked down at the file, started to speak, then broke into a hacking cough. He waved his hand until he'd caught his breath. "God-damn spring," he complained. "I'll look at what you've got. I'll read through it, and I'm going to want to talk to you about it after—one way or the other."

He took a last swallow of his now lukewarm soup. "Want a job?"

"I've got one, thanks."

Willy smiled. "Cop's in the blood."

"I just want my horses, that's the fact. But in this case, I've got a vested interest. He doesn't get a chance to touch Lil. He doesn't get that chance." Coop got to his feet. "That's where I'll be, most likely, when you're ready to talk this through."

He went home to toss fresh clothes in a duffel. He glanced around the converted bunkhouse and figured he'd spent less time sleeping there than he had on Lil's couch. Or in her bed.

That's the way it had to be, he decided, and trudged through the re-lentless rain to toss the duffel in his truck before going back to the farmhouse.

He sat his grandparents down at the kitchen table and told them everything.

When he'd finished, Lucy rose, went to the cupboard, and got out a bottle of whiskey. She poured three short glasses.

Sitting, she tossed hers back without a blink or hiss.

"Have you told Jenna and Joe?"

"I'm going by there on the way to Lil's. I can't prove—"

"You don't have to prove," Sam said before he could finish. "It's what you believe. That's enough. We'll pray you're wrong about this man they're looking for. We'll pray you're wrong about that, and he just got lost, got himself a good soaking and a good scare."

"While you're praying I want you to stay inside. The stock's fed and bedded down. I'll be back around first light. You stay in, doors and windows locked, and the shotgun close. I need you to promise." He pressed, and pressed hard when he recognized the stubborn set of his grandfather's jaw. "If you don't give me your word on that, I can't leave. I can't look after Lil."

"Putting the squeeze on me," Sam muttered.

"Yes, sir. I am."

"You got my word on it, if that's what it takes."

"All right. If you hear anything, feel anything off, you call me, and you call the police. You don't think twice, you just call, and don't worry about false alarms. I need your word on that, too, your promise, or I'm getting a couple of men to guard the place."

"You think he'll come here?" Lucy demanded.

"No, I don't. I think he's on a mission. I don't think he's going to come here because here isn't part of the plan. But I'm not leaving without your word. Maybe he'll want some supplies, or a dry place to sleep. He's a psychopath. I'm not going to try to predict what he might do. I'm not taking any chances with either of you."

"You go on to Lil's," Sam told him. "You've got our word on all of it." He looked at his wife, and she nodded. "Joe and Jenna are probably on their way over there, or will be soon enough. You can talk to them over there. Meanwhile I'll call them myself, in case they're home. I'll tell them what you told us."

Nodding, Coop picked up the whiskey and drank. And stared into the glass. "Everything that means anything to me is here. In this house, with Joe and Jenna, at Lil's. That's everything there is."

Lucy reached over, laid her hand over his. "Tell her."

He looked up, looked at her and thought about the morning conversation. He smiled a little, and gave her the same answer. "Working on it."

BY THE TIME he got to Lil's, feeding time was in full swing. He'd watched the process before, but never in a violent rain. Staff hustled around in black slickers, hauling and carting enormous hampers of food—whole chickens, slabs of beef, tubs of game, all processed in the commissary. Hundreds of pounds of it, he estimated, all cleaned, prepared, transported every evening.

Tons of fortified feed, grain, bales of hay, hauled, poured and spread night after night, whatever the weather.

He considered offering a hand, but he wouldn't know what the hell he was doing. Besides, he'd had enough of the wet for now, and would have more than his share of it later.

He carried the tub of beef stew his grandmother had pressed on him into the cabin. He'd be more useful, he decided, putting a meal on the table.

He opened a bottle of red, let it sit to breathe while he heated the stew and buttermilk biscuits.

It was oddly relaxing, to work in the cozy kitchen with the rain beating on the roof and windows, with the sound of the wild rising with the dark. He took two candles from her living room, set them on the table, lit them.

By the time she came in, drenched and surly of eye, he'd set the table and heated the stew and biscuits through and was pouring a glass of wine.

"I can cook my own damn dinner."

"Go ahead. More stew for me."

"They're going to start installing the new security tomorrow, weather permitting. Then we can stop this insanity."

"That's good. Want some wine?"

"It's *my* wine."

"Actually, I brought it with me."

"I have my own."

"Suit yourself." He watched her as he took the first sip. "This is pretty nice."

She dropped down on the bench, gave the candles the evil eye. "Is this supposed to be romantic?"

"No. It's supposed to be a backup if the power goes out."

"We have a generator."

"Takes a minute to kick on. Blow them out if they bother you."

She huffed, but not at the flames. "I hate that you can do this. Be all casual and reasonable when I'm feeling bitchy."

He poured a second glass of wine, took it over, and set it on the table. "Drink the damn wine, bitch. Is that better?"

She sighed, nearly smiled. "Maybe a little."

"It's some job, feeding that zoo in this rain."

"They have to eat. And, yes, it is." She scrubbed her hands over her face. "I'm tired. I'm edgy. And I'm hungry, so that stew—which I'm assuming is Lucy's doing—is welcome. I haven't written out a list, but I have it in my head, and we need to discuss things. I changed things. My choice, my move, my doing. I'm sorry if it was a mistake, if it affects our friendship. I don't want that."

"You changed things the first time around, too. Your choice, your move, your doing."

"I guess that's true."

"It can't always be your way, Lil."

"I'm not talking about my way, or your way. Besides, it sure as hell hasn't been all my way. I just want to put us back on solid ground, Coop. So—"

"We may need to wait to get into all of that. I need to tell you what else I've found out about Ethan Howe."

"The man you think abducted Carolyn Roderick."

"Yeah. And the man I think abducted other women, killed other women. The man I think killed Melinda Barrett."

She went very still. "Why do you think he killed her? That was nearly twelve years ago."

"We're going to eat, and I'm going to tell you. And Lil? If there's anything on that mental list of yours that gets in the way of me being here, of me making sure nothing happens to you, you'd better scratch it off now."

"I'm not about to refuse any help that protects me, my staff, my family, my animals. Any of it. But you're not responsible for me, Cooper."

"Responsibility has nothing to do with it."

He set the stew, the biscuits on the table. Candlelight flickered between them as he sat and told her of murder.

19

She heard him out, saying little as he related facts, wove them into theory. She tried, again, to get a clear picture in her mind of the man Coop spoke of. But all she could form was vague outlines, smudged details, like a faded pencil sketch.

He'd meant nothing to her, made no real impression. They'd had only a few conversations when he'd come to volunteer or see Carolyn.

"I remember him asking me about my ancestry, the Lakota Sioux bloodline. It's the sort of thing people I don't know ask fairly regularly. We use it in my bio because it sparks interest, and it shows that my family's lived here, in the hills, for generations. But he wanted more specifics, and told me he was Sioux, descended from Crazy Horse."

She lifted her hands. "You get that, too. Some people want to claim the heritage, and since they do, why not go for the gold, so to speak? I didn't pay that much attention, because the Crazy Horse or Sitting Bull claim is usually an eye-roller for me."

"So you dismissed that, and him."

"I was probably polite. I don't make a habit of insulting people, especially volunteers or potential donors. But I didn't offer to buy him a beer and talk about our ancestors."

"You dismissed him," Coop repeated. "Politely."

She blew out an annoyed breath. "Probably. I just don't remember that well. He was ordinary, mildly irritating but only because he seemed more interested in asking me about that sort of thing than about the refuge. Coop, I have dozens of conversations any given week with people I don't know and don't remember well."

"Most of them don't kill people. Try harder."

She pressed her fingers to her eyes, thinking, thinking, trying to put herself back to that summer, that brief period. Hot, she thought. It was hot that summer, and insects—the parasites and diseases they could carry—were something they battled constantly.

Cleaning, disinfecting. They'd had an injured marmot. Or was that the summer before?

The smells. Sweat, dung, sunscreen.

Lots of tourists. The summer was prime for that.

She got a vague picture of standing in an enclosure, giving it a second rinsing after cleaning and disinfecting. Explaining to him? Yes, explaining to him about the procedures and protocols for providing safe, clean, healthy environments for the animals.

"The cougar's enclosure," she murmured. "I'd cleaned their toys. The blue ball Baby especially liked, the orange pylon, the red ball. All cleaned and stacked while I rinsed, and I explained all the steps to the daily cleanings. And . . ."

She struggled, but still couldn't really *see* him. Just another guy in boots, cowboy hat, jeans. But . . .

"At some point he asked if I thought I was reclaiming sacred land for my people and their spirit guides—the animals. I was busy. I'm not sure exactly what I said. Probably that I was more interested in protecting the actual animals, and educating people, than spirit guides."

Coop nodded. "So you dismissed him again."

"Damn it." She dragged a hand through her hair. "Now I sound like a bitch. I *wasn't* bitchy about it. He was helping out. I wouldn't have been bitchy. And what I said isn't even entirely true. The cougar's mine. Spirit guide or talisman, or whatever you choose to call it. But it's private, it's personal. I don't trade off it."

"Do you remember anything else? What he said, or did? How he reacted?"

"We were busy. Chichi was sick—the leopard we lost that fall. She was old and sick, and I was distracted. I don't know, honestly, whether it's hindsight or I'm projecting now that I know all this, but I didn't particularly like him. He'd just sort of pop up out of nowhere. Just be there. He spent a lot of time around the enclosures, watching the animals, and me."

"You? Specifically?"

"It feels like that now. But people do—it's my place. I'm in charge and the refuge carries my name. Except . . . Baby didn't like him. I'd forgotten that. Baby likes attention, but he wouldn't come to the fence when this guy was around. He wouldn't purr. In fact, a couple of times he charged the enclosure fence when Ethan was around. And that's not Baby's normal behavior. He's not aggressive, and he likes people."

"But he didn't like this one."

"I guess not. Otherwise, Ethan wasn't here that much or that long, and we didn't interact much. He didn't wear a bear-tooth necklace or anything like that. I would've noticed, and remembered."

"It would've stood out in a place like this. Animal refuge. You'd have noted it, commented." Coop studied her face. "You wouldn't have liked it."

"You're right about that. Coop, do you seriously think this man has killed all these people? That he's the one who killed Melinda Barrett?"

"No proof. All of this is circumstantial. It's speculation."

"That's not what I asked. Is it what you really think?"

"Yeah. Why aren't you afraid?"

"I am." The shudder caught her unexpectedly as if to prove it. "But being afraid doesn't help. I need to talk to my parents. They need to know."

"My grandfather's taking care of that. I thought they'd be here."

"I asked them to stay home tonight. I used guilt," she added with a tight smile. "You're worried about me? How about me being worried about you? I'll worry if you don't get a decent night's sleep, and so on. My father put in six hours on the search today. My mother rode fence, they brought Jerry Tobias in to ride with her, and he hasn't ridden fence in five years. Now I wish I hadn't said anything. If they were here, they'd be tired, but I'd know they were okay."

"Call them. You'll feel better."

She nodded. "If you're right, he's been killing since he was basically a boy. I can't understand what drives someone to that, to make death his life's work."

Coop sat back, scanning her face. "That's exactly what it is. His life's work. You may not understand what makes him, but you understand that. I got some background. He spent some time in the system as a kid. Bounced from his parents to foster homes and back again. His father did some time, small time. Knocked him and his mother around off and on. She never pressed charges. They moved around a lot. Then he's off the grid for a while. It looks like they did itinerant work, around here, in Wyoming, Montana. His old man got busted for poaching right here in the national forest."

"Here?"

"When Ethan would've been about fifteen. No record of the mother at that time."

"I could have met him," she murmured. "I don't remember him, but it's possible. Or passed him in town or on the trail when we went hiking."

"Or he might've seen you. Your family. Maybe he and his father came by looking for work."

"I don't remember." She sighed, irritated with herself, and got up to dig up some crackers. She pulled a hunk of cheddar out of the fridge while she talked. "My parents don't hire drifters as a rule. I think that policy was mostly because of me. They're generous, but they're protective. They wouldn't have hired strangers, especially not when I was about thirteen and we're talking about a man and his mid-teenage boy."

She paused, worked up a smile as she set the quick snack on the table. "And I'd remember a fifteen-year-old boy who worked around the farm when I was that age. I was just really starting to find boys interesting."

"In any case, from what I've been able to put together Ethan took off right around that time, and that's when I lose him for a couple years. I picked him up when he got work as a trail guide in Wyoming. He'd've been eighteen. He lasted six months. Took off with one of the horses, some gear and provisions."

"A man doesn't steal a horse when he's going to hit the road. He steals it when he's going to hit the trail."

With a nod that might've been approval, Coop topped a cracker with cheese, then handed it to her. "You might've made a half-decent cop."

"It's just plain logic, but what about his parents? Maybe if we were able to talk to them we'd get a clearer picture."

"His father died eight years ago in Oshoto. Complications from a lifetime of alcohol abuse. I can't find anything on the mother. Nothing for the last seventeen years. The last I had, she cashed her paycheck in Cody, Wyoming, where she worked as kitchen help in a diner. Nobody remembers her. Seventeen years," he said with a shrug. "But up until then she worked. A few weeks, a few months, some space between jobs. But she picked up jobs wherever they were. Then she didn't."

"You think she's dead."

"People who are motivated enough, afraid enough, figure out how to hide. She could've changed her name. Hell, she could've moved to Mexico and gotten remarried and is at this moment bouncing a fat, happy grandkid on her knee. But I figure, yeah, she's dead. Had an accident, or maybe her husband tuned her up once too often."

"He'd have been just a boy. This Ethan. If that happened, if he saw that happen . . ."

His face went hard, went cold. "That's what his lawyer will say. The poor, abused boy, damaged, broken by an alcoholic father and a passive mother. Sure, he killed all those people, but he's not responsible. Screw that."

"Learned behavior isn't just for animals. I'm not arguing the point, Coop. In my head, killing is a clear choice. But everything you're telling me says he was predisposed, then he made choices that brought him his life's work. If all this is true, a lot of people are dead, and those who loved them grieving because of those choices. I don't feel sorry for him."

"Good," he said shortly. "Don't."

"I don't feel sorry for him," she repeated, "but I think I understand him better. Do you think he stalked the others, taunted them the way he is me?"

"Barrett looked like a killing of opportunity, of impulse. Molly Pickens, by her boss's account, went off with him of her own volition. But Carolyn Roderick? I think there was some stalking, some taunting there. I'm going to say I think it depends on how well he knows his quarry. And how invested he is."

"If Jim Tyler's dead, at his hand, that would be another impulse killing."

"Or a form of release. None of the women whose bodies were discovered had been raped. No sign of sexual assault, no torture or mutilation. It's the kill that gets him off."

"I can't quite see that as the glass is half full. Anyway, what he's been doing has put me, put everyone on alert. It's made it close to impossible for him to get to me, or to mine. So . . ." She read Coop's face perfectly. "Which makes it—me—more of a challenge?"

"Maybe. If I'm right, this is at least his fourth time here, in this area. He may have been here other times. When he didn't make contact with you, or when you were away. He could've picked up work around here, on one of the farms, one of the outfits. He knows the territory."

"So do I."

"He knows that, too. If he just wanted to kill you, you'd be dead."

The cool, flat way he said it brought on another shudder. "Now that boosts my confidence."

"He could've picked you off the night he let the tiger out. Or any other time you were here alone, he could've kicked in the door, and taken you out. You ride over to your parents, he ambushes you. Lots of scenarios, but he doesn't do any of that. Yet."

She picked up her wine, took a slow sip. "You're trying to scare me."

"Damn right I am."

"Unnecessary. I'm scared enough, and I intend to be careful."

"You could take another trip. There has to be somewhere else you could work for a few weeks, a couple months."

"Sure. I'm practically renowned. And he could find out where I am, follow me, go after me somewhere I'm not as familiar with my territory. Or he could just wait me out, wait until I start to relax. And you've already thought of all that, too."

"Maybe a better than halfway decent cop," he acknowledged. "Yeah, I've thought of it. But I've also thought of the odds of tracking him down while you're somewhere else. I like the odds."

"I'm not leaving, Coop."

"What if I could arrange for your parents to be somewhere else for a few weeks, too."

She set her wine down, tapped her fingers on the table. "That's low, using them."

"I'll use whatever it takes to keep you safe."

She rose then, walked over to start a pot of coffee. "I'm not leaving," she repeated. "I won't be run off my own place, one I built. I won't leave my staff, my animals vulnerable while I hide out. You know that, or you don't know me."

"It was worth a try."

"You put a lot of time and work into this."

"You want a bill?"

She glanced back. "I'm not trying to make you mad. I was before, hoping you'd get pissed off and go, give me some space. I don't know what to do about you, Coop, that's a fact. I just don't. I know we need to have all that out, but it's not the time. Not enough time," she corrected. "I need to call my parents, and take my shift outside."

"There are enough people out there. You don't need to take a shift. You're worn out, Lil. It shows."

"First you boost my confidence, now my ego." She got out a thermos. "I guess that's what friends are for."

"Take the night off."

"Would you? Could you, in my place? I'm not going to get any sleep anyway."

"I could shoot you with the drug gun. That'd get you a few hours."

"What are friends for?" he said when she laughed.

She filled the thermos, took it to him. "Here you go. I'll be out after I call home."

He got up, set the thermos on the table to take her arms. "Look at me. I'm never going to let anything happen to you."

"Then we've got nothing to worry about."

He laid his lips on hers, a brush, a rub. And her heart rolled over in her chest. "Or given that we've got other things to worry about. Take the coffee."

He pulled on his rain gear first, then picked up the thermos. "I'm not sleeping on the couch."

"No."

She sighed when he went out. Choices, she thought again. It seemed she was making hers.

LIL STATIONED HERSELF and wandered along the fenceline of the small-cat area. Despite the rain, Baby and his companions played stalk-and-ambush with the big red ball. The bobcats raced each other up a tree, making a lot of mock growls and snarls. She suspected if it hadn't been for the floodlights, the sounds, scents, sights of humans, the cats would have settled down out of the rain.

Across the habitat, the newest addition sent out the occasional bark-ing roar, as if to say she didn't know where the hell she was, as yet, but she was pretty damn important.

"It's like they're having a party."

She smiled at Farley as he stepped up beside her to watch. "I guess they are. They appreciate an audience. I feel stupid out here tonight," she told him. "Nobody's going to troop down here in all this mess to bother me."

"Seems to me that's just when you have to be most careful. When you figure you're safe."

"Oh, well. Want some coffee?" She offered her thermos.

"I had some already, but I can't say no." He poured himself a little. "I'm figuring Tansy told you about things."

"She did." She waited until he'd glanced over. "I think she's pretty lucky."

His smile spread slowly. "Feels good you'd say so."

"Two of my favorite people become each other's favorite people? There's no downside for me."

"She thinks I'm going through a phase. Well, she wants to think that. Maybe she'll keep thinking it until we have a couple of kids."

She choked on a gulp of coffee. "Jesus, Farley, when you finally move, you move like a damn cheetah."

"When you find what you want, what's right, you might as well get going. I love her, Lil. She's all flustered up about it, and how she feels about me. I don't mind that so much. It's kind of flattering, really."

He drank coffee while the rain dripped from the brim of his hat. "Anyways, I'm hoping you'll do me a favor."

"I talked to her, Farley. Told her I thought you were perfect for her."

"That's nice to hear, too. But that's not the favor. I was hoping you'd go with me and help me pick out a ring. I don't know anything about that kind of thing. I don't want to get the wrong kind."

For a moment Lil could only stare. "Farley, I . . . Just like that?

Seriously? You're going to buy a ring and ask her to marry you? Just like that?"

"I already told her I love her and I'm going to marry her. I got her into bed." Even in the dark she could see he flushed a little. "I don't mean to talk out of school on that, but you said she told you. I want to get her what she'd like, and you'd have a good idea. Wouldn't you?"

"I guess I would. I've never shopped for an engagement ring, but I think I know what she'd like if I saw it. Holy shit, Farley."

"You think we could find the right one in Deadwood? Otherwise, I could drive us on into Rapid City."

"Let's try Deadwood. We should . . . I can't get over it." She studied him through the curtain of rain. "Farley." With a laugh, she boosted up to her toes and gave him a smacking kiss. "Have you told Mom and Dad?"

"Jenna cried. The good kind of crying. She's the one who said I should ask you to go with me for the ring. I made them promise not to say anything until it's all done. You won't say anything, Lil?"

"Lips. Sealed."

"I wanted to talk to them first. Sort of— I don't know . . . it sounds dumbass."

"What?"

He shifted on his long, grasshopper legs. "Get their blessing, I guess."

"It doesn't sound dumbass. You're a prize, Farley, I swear to God. How come you didn't fall for me?"

He grinned, ducked his head a little. "Lil. You're all but practically my sister."

"Can I ask you something, Farley?"

"Sure."

She began to walk with him, at a pace that would've been a stroll in the rain but for the guns both carried. "You had it rough as a kid."

"Plenty do."

"I know. I think I'm more aware of that because I didn't. I had it pretty damn perfect. When you took off on your own, you were still a kid."

"I can't say I felt like one."

"Why did you? Decide to leave, I mean. It's a big, scary step. Even when the familiar's crap, it's still the familiar."

"She was a hard woman to live with, and I got tired of living with strangers, then being put back with her and whoever she'd taken up with. I can't remember many nights there wasn't yelling or fighting going on. Sometimes she'd start it up, sometimes the man she was with would. Either way, I'd end up bleeding sooner or later. I thought about taking a bat to this one guy once, after he slapped us both around. But he was a big man, and I was afraid he'd get it away from me and bash me with it."

He pulled up short. "God, Lil, you're not thinking I'd hurt Tansy, that I'd do her that way?"

"Not in a million years, Farley. It's something else I'm trying to figure out, trying to get a handle on. You were broke when you got out here, and hungry and just a boy. But there was no meanness in you. My parents would've seen it. They may be soft touches, but they have good instincts. You didn't steal or brawl or cheat your way here. You could have."

"I'd've been no better than what I left, then, would I?"

"You chose to be better than what you left."

"God's truth is, Lil, Jenna and Joe saved me. I don't know where I'd've ended up, or if I'd've made it there in one piece without them taking me in."

"I guess we were all lucky that day you stuck out your thumb and my father drove by. This man, the one we think is out there, he had it rough as a kid."

"So what? He's not a kid now, is he?"

She shook her head. It was simple Farley logic—and while she appreciated it, Lil knew people were a lot more complicated as a rule.

Just after two, she went inside. She stowed her rifle and went upstairs. She still had some nice lingerie from her Jean-Paul days. But it seemed wrong to wear for Coop what she'd worn for another man.

Instead she changed into her usual sleeping garb of flannel pants and a T-shirt, then sat on the side of the bed to brush out her hair.

Tired? she thought. Yes, she was tired, but also aware. She wanted him to come to her, wanted to be with him after a long and difficult day. To make love with him while the rain drummed and night crept toward morning.

She wanted something bright in her life, and if it was a complicated shine, it was better than the dull and the dark.

She heard him come in, and rose to put her brush back on her dresser. Letting her mind drift, she walked back to turn down the bed. And turned to face him as he came in.

"We need to talk," she said. "A lot has to be said. But it's two in the morning. Talk's for the daylight. I just want to go to bed with you. I just want to feel, to know there's something good and strong after a day that's been so bleak."

"Then we'll talk in the daylight."

He came to her then, tunneled his fingers through her hair, tipped her head back. His lips met hers with a tenderness, a patience she'd forgotten he could give.

Here was the sweet they'd once shared.

She lay down with him on cool, smooth sheets, and opened body, mind, and heart. Slow and soft, as if he knew she needed . . . tending. Tension slipped away, swept back by pleasure. His hands glided over her, hard palms, a gentle touch. On a contented sigh, she turned her head as his lips explored her throat, her jaw.

No need to rush, to take and take, not this time. This was silk and velvet, warm and smooth. Not just sensation now, not just desires met, but *feelings*. She slid his shirt away, traced her fingers over the scar at his side.

"I don't know if I could have stood it if—"

"Shh." He brought her hand to his lips, kissed her fingers, then her mouth. "Don't think. Don't worry."

Tonight he could give her peace, and take some for himself. Tonight he wanted to show her love as much as passion. More. Tonight they would savor each other. Skin, sighs, scents.

She smelled of the rain, somehow both dark and fresh. Tasted of it. He drew her clothes away, touching, tasting the newly exposed flesh, lingering when she shivered.

Scars crossed her, too. Scars that hadn't been there when they'd first become lovers and all that lovely skin had been unmarred. Now she bore the marks of her work. Just as, he supposed, the scar left by a bullet had been a mark of his.

They were not what they had been, either of them. And yet she was still the only woman he'd ever wanted.

How many times had he dreamed of this, of loving Lil through the night? Of having her hands run over him, of having her body move with his.

She rolled, shifted to trail her lips over his chest, to bring them back to his and sink, sink, sink into the kiss while her hair fell around him in dark curtains. Beneath her hands, her lips, his heart tripped and stumbled. He rose up to wrap his arms around her, to rock and hold as his mouth found her breast.

Here pleasure was thick, movement slow, and every nerve alive.

She watched him as she took him into her, watched as her breath caught, then shuddered out again. Her lips came to his, trembling in the kiss. Then her body bowed, her eyes drifted shut.

She rode, gently, gently, drawing out every drop of pleasure. Slow and silky, so the beauty of it had tears rising in her throat. Even as her body released, her heart filled.

She let her head rest on his shoulder as she drifted down again. He turned his face into the side of her throat. "Lil," he said. "God, Lil."

"Don't say anything. Please don't." If he did, she might say too much. She had no defenses now. She eased back to touch his cheek. "Talk's for daylight," she repeated.

"All right. There'll be daylight soon enough."

He lay down with her, drew her close. "I need to leave before dawn," he told her. "But I'll be back. We need to have some alone time, Lil. Uninterrupted time."

"There's so much going on. I can't think straight."

"Not true. You think straighter than anyone I know."

Not about you, she admitted silently. Never about you. "The rain's slowing down. Tomorrow's supposed to be clear. We'll work things out tomorrow. In the daylight."

But the daylight brought death.

20

ull found Jim Tyler. It was more luck than skill that brought him, his brother Jesse, and one of the greener deputies to the bend of the swollen waters of Spearfish Creek. They were walking their horses through the mud on a morning hazed with fog like a window steamed from a shower. The water, churning from the rain and snowmelt, beat like a drum, and above its rush thick tendrils of mist wound in long gray ribbons.

They were well off the logical route Tyler would have taken to the summit of Crow Peak and back to the trailhead. But the search had spread out through the tree-covered slopes of the canyon, with small groups combing the rocky high ground and the brown, deadwood shale of the low.

Gull hadn't expected to find anything, and felt a little guilty about enjoying the meandering ride. Spring was beginning to show her skirts, and the rain teased out the green he loved in the hills. A jay shot—a blue bullet through the mists—while the chickadees chattered like children in a playground.

Rain had stirred up the waters, enlivened them, but there were still places the creek was as clear as gin in a short glass.

He hoped he got himself a tour group soon who wanted to fish so he could spend some time reeling in trout. Gull figured he had the best job in the whole damn world.

"That man got himself all the way over here from the marked trail, he's got no more sense of direction than a blind woodpecker," Jesse said. "Wasting our time."

Gull glanced over at his brother. "Nice day to waste it. Besides, could be he got turned around in the storm, in the dark. Zig insteada zag, and he kept going the wrong way, he might've come this far off."

"Maybe if the idiot'd find a rock and sit still somebody'd find his sorry ass." Jesse shifted in the saddle. He spent a lot more time shoeing horses than riding them, and *his* sorry ass was sore. "I can't take much more time riding around looking for somebody hasn't got the sense to get found."

The deputy, Cy Fletcher—the baby brother of the girl who owned the first pair of breasts Gull had ever got his hands on—scratched his belly. "I say we follow the creek another little while, then we'll circle back around."

"Fine by me." Gull agreed.

"Can't see shit on a stick in this fog," Jesse complained.

"Sun'll burn it off." Gull shrugged. "It's breaking through here and there already. What the hell better you got to do, Jesse?"

"Got a living to earn, don't I? I don't got some lazy-ass job where I ride around with numbnut tourists all damn day."

It was a bone of contention between the brothers, and they poked each other about it as the sun strengthened and the fog thinned. As they approached one of the little falls, the drop and tumble of water made shouting insults at his brother over the noise too much trouble.

Gull settled down to enjoy the ride again, and thought about the whitewater outfits who'd start gearing up soon. Weather might turn again, he thought, more snow was every bit as likely as daffodils, but people sure did like to strap themselves into rubber rafts and shoot down the creek.

He didn't get the appeal.

Riding now, or fishing, that made sense. If he could find a woman who appreciated both, and had a nice pair on her, he'd marry her in a New York minute.

He took a deep, satisfied breath of the fresh and warming air, and grinned happily as a trout leaped. It flashed, shiny as the good silver his ma used for Christmas dinner, then plopped back into the busy water.

His eye followed the ripples all the way to the foaming white of the falls. He squinted, and the hair on the back of his neck stood up.

"I think there's something down there, down in the falls there."

"I don't see dick."

"You don't see dick doesn't mean I don't." Ignoring his brother, Gull guided his mount closer to the bank.

"You end up in that water, I ain't coming in after you."

It was probably just a rock, Gull thought, and then he'd feel like a numbnut and have to suffer Jesse's ragging for the rest of the ride. But it didn't look like a rock. It looked like the front half of a boot.

"I think that's a boot. You see that, Cy?"

"I can't tell." Cy peered with eyes shaded by his hat and not especially interested. "Probably a rock."

"I think it's a boot."

"Alert the freaking media," Jesse proclaimed, boosting up a little to rub at his worn-out ass. "Some asshole camper lost a boot in Spearfish Creek."

"If some asshole camper lost a boot in the creek, why's it just there? How come it's not floating off, pushed along by the falls? Asshole," Gull muttered as he dug out his binoculars.

"'Cause it's a freaking rock. Or it's some asshole's boot that's stuck on a freaking rock. Hell with this. I gotta piss."

As he stared through the glasses, Gull's face went pale as wax. "Oh, Jesus. Mother of God. I think there's somebody in that boot. Holy shit, Jess. I can see something under the water."

"Oh, bullshit, Gull."

Gull lowered the glasses, stared at his brother. "Do I look like I'm bullshitting?"

Studying his brother's face, Jesse set his teeth. "I guess we'd better get a closer look."

They tethered the horses.

Gull looked at the deputy—the scrawny build of him—and wished he didn't feel obliged. "I'm the best swimmer here. I'll go."

The breath Cy let out held both resignation and nerves. "It's my job."

"Might be your job," Jesse said, as he got his rope, "but Gull swims like a damn otter. Water's pretty rough, so we're going to get you secure. You're an asshole, Gull, but you're my brother and I'm not going to watch you drown."

Fighting off nerves, Gull stripped down to his jockeys, let his brother secure the rope around his waist. "I bet that water's pretty fucking cold."

"You're the one who had to go see something."

Since he couldn't argue with that one, Gull eased over the bank, picked his way over the rocks and shale, and stared at the fast water. He glanced back, reassured himself that his brother had the rope secured.

He went in. "Pretty fucking cold!" he shouted. "Give me some slack."

He swam against the fast water, imagined his toes going blue and just falling off. Even with the rope, he banged against the rocks, but pushed off them again.

He went under, pushing, pushing against the current, and in that gin-clear water, he saw he'd been right. Somebody was in the boots.

He surfaced again, choking, flailing. "Pull me back. Oh, holy bleeding Christ, pull me back."

Panic buzzed in his head, nausea churned in his belly. Slapping and clawing at the water, swallowing it, choking it out again, he relied on his brother to get him back to the bank.

He crawled onto a rock, heaved up water and his breakfast until he could only lie panting. "I saw him. I saw him. Oh, God, the fish've been at him. At his face."

"Call it in, Cy. Call it in." Jesse slid and slipped his way down to wrap a saddle blanket over his brother.

WORD SPREAD AS word did. Coop heard about Gull's discovery from three sources, with varying details, before Willy hunted him down at the stables.

"You'd've heard."

"Yeah. I'm going by to check up on Gull."

Willy nodded. His voice was still rough, but he was feeling better. "He's pretty shaken up. I'm going over to his place, get a formal statement down if you want to come along. The fact is, Coop, I'd appreciate if you did. Not just because he works for you. I've worked killings before, but nothing like this. We're going to have a lot of fingers in this pie. I'd like to have yours—unofficially."

"I'll follow you over. Did you notify Tyler's wife?"

Willy's mouth tightened. "Yeah. Worst part of it. I guess you did your share of notifications back east."

"Worst part of it," Coop agreed. "I've heard different versions. Do you have the cause of death?"

"Coroner has to give us that. He'd been in the water awhile—you know what happens. But it wasn't a fall, and it wasn't the damn fish that slit his throat. It wasn't either that weighed the body down. Flooding hadn't stirred it up, and Gull didn't have eyes like a damn hawk, God knows when we'd've found him."

"What did he use?"

"Nylon rope, rocks. Thing is, the way it was situated, it looked to me like the bastard had to get in the water to do it. Sick son of a bitch. Took his wallet, watch, pack, jacket, shirt. Left him with his pants and his boots."

"Must've been the wrong size. He'd have taken them otherwise. No point in wasting anything."

Gull had a little place on the other side of town, over a bar and grill. The narrow apartment smelled like him—horses and leather—and was furnished like a college dorm. With castoffs from his parents, his brother, and anyone else who wanted to upgrade a chair or table.

Jesse, despite his bitching about having to earn a living, answered the door. He hadn't been ten feet from his brother since he'd come out of Spearfish Creek.

"He's still a little shaky. I was thinking I'd haul him over to our ma, have her pat his head awhile."

"That might be just the thing," Willy said. "I'm going to get his statement now. I got yours, but could be you'll think of more."

"We got coffee on. He's been sucking on that Mountain Dew of his. Christ knows how he chokes that down, but that's what we've got."

"Wouldn't say no to coffee." Willy crossed over to where Gull sat on a saggy plaid couch, his head in his hands.

"I still see it in my head. Can't get it out."

"You did a hard thing today, Gull. You did the right thing."

"Can't help wishing somebody else'd seen that damn boot poking out of the water." He lifted his head, looked at Coop. "Hey, boss. I was going to come by, but . . ."

"Don't worry about it. Why don't you tell Willy everything. Just say it straight through. You'll feel steadier after."

"I told you," he said to Willy. "And the rangers, too." He blew out a breath, rubbed his face. "Okay. We were following the creek," he began.

Coop kept quiet, letting Willy ask the questions when they needed to be asked. He drank cowboy coffee while Gull purged himself of the details.

"You know how clear that water is. Even after the storm, it's good and clear. I went under, because I couldn't get a good look with the way the falls were beating down, foaming up. I got a good look then. His one leg had come up, you know. I guess the rain, the churning, worked it up. He didn't have a shirt on, just his pants and his boots. And the fish had been at him. His face . . ."

Gull's eyes watered up as he looked back at Coop. "I've never seen anything like it. It's not like the movies. It's not like anything else. I couldn't even say, for certain, it was him—the one we were looking for. Not from the picture we had. Because of the fish. I came up, but I swallowed a bunch of water. I guess I screamed like a girl under there and took a bunch in. I couldn't get my legs to move. Jesse and Cy had to pull me in with the rope."

He gave his brother a weak smile. "I got sick as two dogs—maybe not as sick as you did on a chaw, boss, but pretty damn sick. I guess I was pitiful enough Jesse didn't even rag me about it."

"I wanted to turn around," Jesse said. "Bitching and complaining. I said how that guy, the one Gull found dead, was an asshole. I'm sorry for it."

Outside, Willy puffed out his cheeks. "There's some distance between the trail and where Tyler ended up. A lot of area where he could've run into his killer."

"Do you think he got that far off the trail?"

"No, I don't. Not on his own if that's your meaning. Some, sure, but he had a map, he had his phone. I think he was driven that far, that's what I think."

"I'd agree with you. He didn't want the body found too soon, and he didn't want it found near his own territory. Drive the quarry away from your . . . habitat," he said, thinking of Lil. "Do the kill, the disposal, then go back to your own area."

"It would've taken time. Hours probably. The bastard got lucky with the rain."

"He can't stay lucky."

"Right now, we're looking for an unidentified subject. We can't tie Tyler's murder to what's happened at Lil's, or with the other murders you dug up. What I'm going to do is get Ethan Howe's picture out, as a Person of Interest. My boy Cy kept that scene preserved as best he could. He's green as a leaf of iceberg, but he's not stupid. We got pictures, and I don't think you'll squawk if I happen to slip you copies."

"I won't."

"Criminal Investigation Division's combing that scene now. They're not stupid either. If that bastard dropped so much as a toothpick, they'll find it. When we get a ballpark on the time of death, that'll help. We can do a couple of reconstruct scenarios. I'll listen to any thoughts you've got on it. I'm damned if somebody's going to get away with terrorizing one of my friends, and killing tourists."

"Then I'll give you a couple now. He's holed up. He's got a place, probably more than one, but one where he keeps the bulk of his supplies. He won't have much. He needs to travel light and often. When he needs something, or wants something, he steals it. Campers, vacation homes, empty houses. We know he's got at least one gun, so he needs ammo. He hunts for food, or pilfers campsites. And I think he keeps his ear to the ground. He's going to find out you found the body. The sensible thing to do would be to pull up stakes, head over into Wyoming, get lost for a while. But I don't think he's going to do that. He's got an agenda, and he isn't finished."

"We'll be searching, ground and air. If he shows the tip of his dick, we'll pull him in."

"Have you had any reports of anything stolen from campers, hikers, houses, stores?"

"There's always some. I'll look over everything for the last six months. Maybe you'd let me deputize you, for the short term."

"No. I don't want a badge again."

"One of these days, Coop, you and I are going to have to sit down over a beer so you can tell me why that is."

"Maybe. I need to get to Lil's."

"You swing by, pick up those pictures. Badge or not, I'm going to use you."

This time when Coop arrived at Lil's he wore his 9mm under his jacket. He carted his laptop, the files Willy had given him, and three spare clips into her cabin. After some debate, he shoved one of the clips into his pocket and stowed the other two in one of her dresser drawers.

And with an eyebrow cocked, drew out a short, silky black gown with very sheer lace in interesting places.

He wondered why she always seemed to wear flannel.

He poked at something red and virtually transparent, shook his head, and dropped the black number back into the drawer.

In the kitchen he set up his laptop on her table, dug a couple of bottles of water out of her supply, then went out to take a look at the progress on her security system.

He spent a little time with the head installer out of Rapid City, and made his escape after the man figured out he knew something about security—and before he could get roped into helping with the wiring.

The good weather brought people out, he noted. He counted three groups making the rounds of the habitat. And the big yellow school bus indicated there were more on the property. Education center, he surmised.

She was keeping busy, and that was good. It was also too bad, or so she might think. But there were only a few hours of daylight left—and they had an appointment.

He hooked her horse trailer to his truck, loaded the horse he'd sold her onto it. He chose the younger and larger of the horses left in the stable, then secured that one in the trailer.

It amused him that no one questioned him. Either he was too familiar or too forbidding, but the interns went about their business—and from across the compound, Tansy sent him a friendly wave.

A single question to a passing staff member gave him Lil's location as her office. He drove the trailer over to the cabin, then went in to get her.

"Coop." Mary gave him an absent nod of greeting from her desk. "She's on the phone, but I think she's wrapping it up." She glanced toward the office, lowered her voice. "Have you heard about the murder? Do you know if it's true?"

"Yeah, it's true."

"That poor man. His poor wife. Come out here for a little holiday, and go home a widow. Every time I think people are basically good and decent, something happens that convinces me too many of them are no damn good."

"You're right, both ways."

"That's the problem, isn't it? Oh, your friend—the alarm system man—he's been in touch."

"I talked to him. He should have you fully secured in another two days."

"Glad to hear it, and that's a shame, too. That we have to go to all this trouble and expense because some people are no damn good."

"It's the right investment."

"Well. There, she's off the line. Better get in there before she calls somebody else."

"Mary, do you have any problem with me taking Lil off for a couple hours?"

"Not if it's somewhere that doesn't involve work and worry, which is all she's been doing the last few weeks."

"That's a deal."

"Don't let her say no," Mary ordered, as he walked to Lil's office.

She sat angled toward her monitor, fingers on her keyboard.

He wondered if she had any idea how pale she was, or how shadowed her eyes.

"I've got a line on a tiger."

"Not a sentence you hear every day."

"Boris is lonely. Strip joint in Sioux City used a Bengal as part of an act."

"Did she strip?"

"Ha ha. No, they kept her caged, or chained. Finally got shut down for animal abuse. She's been declawed and drugged, and God knows. We're going to take her."

"Good, go get her."

"I'm working on having her brought to us. A lot of red tape to wind through. I'm pushing for donations. She's made some media outlets, and I can use it to beef things up. I just need to—"

"Come with me."

He watched her tense. "Is something wrong? Something else?"

"For the next hour or two, no. The tiger can wait. Everything can wait. We've got daylight."

"Cooper, I'm working. There's a busload of middle-schoolers in the ed center, a bunch of people roaming around hooking up alarms. Matt just finished sewing up a fawn that got clipped by a car, and I'm working on getting Delilah here by early next week."

"I assume Delilah's the tiger, not one of the dancers. I've got work of my own, Lil, and it'll be here when we get back. Let's go."

"Where? God, Coop, some poor man was killed and dumped in the Spearfish. I can't think about taking a walk with you and discussing . . . whatever."

"We're not walking. And I guess we do this the hard way." He came around the desk, pulled her up out of the chair, and boosted her over his shoulder.

"Oh, for God's sake." She gave his back a thump with her fist. "Cut it out. This is ridiculous. Don't! Don't you walk out of here with . . ."

He grabbed her hat on the way. "We'll be a few hours, Mary."

With her eyes laughing, Mary gave them a sober nod. "All right."

"You okay to close up if we're not back?"

"Not a problem."

"Stop it. This is *my* place. You don't tell my staff— Don't you step outside this building. Cooper, you're embarrassing both of us."

"I'm not embarrassed." He walked outside, continued toward the truck. "But you will be if you don't sit where I put you, because I'll just catch you and put you back again."

"You're just making me mad."

"I can live with that." He pulled open the passenger door, dumped her on the seat. "I mean it, Lil, I'll just haul you back." He reached across, hooked her seat belt, then dropped her hat in her lap. Ice-blue eyes met molten brown. "Stay where I put you."

"Oh, I'll stay. I'll stay because we're not having this out here. I'm not having more of a scene here."

"Good enough." He slammed the door, skirted the hood of the truck, then got behind the wheel. "We're going riding. We're not coming back until you've got some color back in your cheeks." He glanced over. "I'm not talking pissed-off color."

"Pissed-off is all you're going to get."

"We'll see." He headed down the road. "We'll drive to Rimrock. We could consider that neutral ground." And miles away from where Tyler's body had been found.

"What's the point of this?"

"The point is you need a break, and so do I. And Lil, we've put this off long enough."

"I decide when I need a break. Damn it, Coop, I don't know why you'd want to make me so mad. I've got enough going on without working in a fight with you—and we were fine. Just last night we were fine."

"You were too worn-out to get into this last night. I'd rather have you mad than almost in tears with the idea of *talking* to me."

"I've been talking to you plenty." She leaned her head back, shut her eyes. "Jesus Christ, Cooper, a man is dead. Dead. And you're pushing this? Talking about what? What's over and done?"

"That's right, a man's dead. And the one who did it has you in the crosshairs. You need help, but you don't trust me."

With sharp, jerky movements, she plucked the hat off her lap, set it on her head. "That's not true."

"You trust me to help you protect your place. You trust me enough to sleep with me. But you don't trust me down in the deep. We both know that."

He parked at the campground. Together, in silence, they unloaded the horses. "We can take the lower loop from here. It's shorter."

"I don't like being handled this way."

"I don't blame you. And I don't care."

She mounted, turned her horse toward the trailhead. "Maybe the women you got used to tolerate this kind of thing. I don't. I won't. You'll get your two hours because you're bigger and you're stronger—and because I'm not having this out in front of my staff, my interns, my guests. Then that's it, Cooper. That's it between us."

"You get some color in your cheeks, some worry out of your eyes, and we clear the air between us. After that, if you say that's it, that'll be it." He opened the cattle gate for her to pass through, then closed it behind them.

"You can tell me everything you know about what happened to James Tyler. I can't think about much else. I don't know how you could expect me to."

"Okay, we'll get that out of the way."

He laid it out for her, every detail he remembered, as they rode toward the rim of the canyon. He spoke of murder and death as the trail leveled out to wind through pines and quaking aspen where flickers swooped and darted among the trees.

"Is Gull all right?"

"He's going to see Tyler, the way he found him, every time he closes his eyes for a while. He'll lose sleep over it, have nightmares when he does sleep. Then it'll pass."

"Is that the way it was for you?"

"I saw Melinda Barrett for a long time. The first time I saw a body when I was in uniform, it was just as horrible. And then . . ." He shrugged.

"It becomes routine?"

"No. It becomes the job, but it's never routine."

"I still see her sometimes. Even before all this started up. I'd think it had gone away, then I'd wake up, cold and sweating, with her in my head." Calmer, she turned to look at him, so their eyes met. "We shared a hard thing at an early age. We shared a lot of things. You're wrong when you say I don't trust you. And you're wrong to think manhandling me is the way to get whatever it is you want."

"You're what I want, Lil. You're all I've ever wanted."

Color did indeed rush into her face as she whipped her head toward him. "Go to hell."

She kicked her horse into a trot.

PART THREE

SPIRIT

Nothing in the world is single;
All things by a law divine
In one spirit meet and mingle.
—PERCY BYSSHE SHELLEY

21

He thought: Shit. And let her take her distance. Maybe she'd blow off the steam of temper, maybe she wouldn't, but temper was better than exhaustion. She needed to ride, he thought, needed to just breathe awhile. The air filled with the scents of sage and juniper, while overhead an eagle circled on the hunt. He heard what he thought was the drumming of a grouse from a thicket of buckbrush that looked like it wanted to open its tight buds and bloom.

Mad or not, he knew she'd take it all in and be better for it.

She might not look up and watch the eagle, but she knew it was there.

When she finally slowed, he caught up with her. No, he decided, she hadn't blown off the steam. She rode on it every bit as much as she rode on Rocky.

"How can you say that to me?" she demanded. "All you've ever wanted? You left *me*. You broke my heart."

"We're remembering it differently, because I don't remember anybody leaving anybody. And you sure didn't act brokenhearted when we decided the long-distance deal wasn't working."

"When you decided. I came halfway to New York to see you, to be with you. I'd wanted to go all the way, to spend real time with you on your turf. In your place. But you wouldn't have that." Those dark eyes stabbed at him, lethal as knives. "I guess you figured it would be harder to dump me if I was sitting in your New York apartment."

"Jesus Christ, Lil, I didn't dump you." They wounded him, those eyes, spilled blood she couldn't see. "It wasn't like that."

"What the hell was it like, from your perspective? You told me you couldn't keep doing it, that you needed to concentrate on your own life, your own career."

"I said *we* couldn't, *we* needed."

"Oh, bullshit!" Rocky shied a bit, disturbed by the tone, the temper. She controlled him with no sign of effort or concern. "You had no right to speak for me or my feelings. Not then, not now."

"You sure as hell didn't say so at the time." His horse danced, as uneasy as Rocky. Coop steadied him, and would have turned so he and Lil were face-to-face. But she trotted off. Again. Setting his teeth, Coop nudged his mount to follow. "You agreed with me," he added, annoyed with the defensiveness in his tone once he'd caught up.

"What the hell was I supposed to do? Fling myself into your arms and beg you to stay with me, to love me?"

"Actually—"

"I drove all the way to that damn motel in Illinois, so excited. It felt like years since we'd seen each other, and I was worried you wouldn't like my hair, or my outfit. Stupid things. And I was *aching* to see you. Literally aching. Even my damn toes hurt."

"Lil—"

"And I knew the minute I saw you that something was wrong. You got there before I did—remember? I saw you crossing the parking lot, coming from that little diner."

Her voice changed. The anger leaked out of it as misery pushed in. Where the anger wounded him, the misery simply destroyed.

He said nothing, let her finish. Though he could've told her yes, he remembered. He remembered crossing that pothole of a parking lot, remembered the first instant he became aware of her. He remembered the thrill, the need, the despair.

All of it.

"You didn't see me, at first. And I knew. I tried to tell myself it was just nerves, seeing you again. It was just . . . you looked different. Tougher, harder."

"I was different. We both were by then."

"My feelings hadn't changed, not like yours."

"Wait a minute." He reached out to snag her bridle. "Wait a minute."

"We made love, almost the minute we closed the door of that motel room. And I knew you were going to end it. Do you think I couldn't tell you'd pulled away, pulled back?"

"I pulled back? How many times had you? Why had it been so long since we'd seen each other? There was always a project, a field trip, a—"

"You're blaming me?"

"There's no blame," he began, but she swung off her horse, stalked away.

Struggling for patience, he dismounted to tether both the horses. "You need to listen."

"I loved you. I loved you. You were the one, the only one. I'd have done anything for you, for us."

"That's part of the problem."

"Loving you was a problem?"

"That you'd have done anything. Lil, just—hold still, damn it." He gripped her shoulders when she would have walked away from him again. "You knew what you wanted to do with your life. You knew what you wanted, and you were doing it. Top of your class, honors and opportunities. You came alive, Lil. You were exactly where you needed to be, doing exactly what you needed to do. I couldn't be a part of that, and I sure as hell couldn't get in the way of it."

"Now you're claiming you dumped me and ripped my heart out for my own good? Is that how you choose to look at it?"

"That's how it was, how it is."

"I never got over you, you bastard." Anger and insult in every part of her—face, body, voice—she shoved at him. "You *ruined* me. You took something from me, and I could never get it back, never give it to anyone else. I hurt a good man, a very good man, because I couldn't love him, because I couldn't give him what he deserved to have and you'd thrown away. I tried. Jean-Paul was perfect for me, and I should've been able to make it work. But I couldn't, because he wasn't you. And he knew, he always knew. Now you want to stand there and tell me you left for my sake?"

"We were children, Lil. We were just kids."

"I didn't love you any less, or hurt any less, because I was nineteen."

"You were going somewhere. You were making a mark. I needed to make mine. So yeah, I did it for you, and for me. I had nothing to give you."

"Bullshit." She started to wrench away, but he yanked her back.

"I had nothing. I *was* nothing. I was broke, living from paycheck to paycheck—if I was lucky. Living in a dump because it was all I could afford, and moonlighting when I could get the extra work. I didn't get out here often because I didn't have the money for the trip."

"You said—"

"I lied. I said I was busy, or couldn't get time off. Mostly true, since I was working two jobs if I could get the extra work, and angling for over-time when I could get it. But that wasn't why I didn't come back more than I did. I sold the bike because I couldn't afford it. I sold blood to make rent some months."

"For God's sake, Coop, if things were that bad why didn't you—"

"Tap my grandparents? Because they'd already given me a start, and I wasn't going to take more money from them."

"You could've come home. You—"

"Come back here a failure, with barely enough to pay for a bus ticket? I needed to make myself into something, and you should understand that. There should've been money, a cut from my trust, when I turned twenty-one. I needed it, to get a decent place to live, to have a breather so I could work on the job and make that mark. My father tied it up. He was so pissed that I'd gone against his decisions, his plan for me. I had some money, what my grandparents gave me—what was left of it—my savings. He got my accounts frozen."

"How?"

"It's what he does. He knows people, he knows the system. Add that to the fact I'd screwed up in college, tossing money around like it was confetti. That's my fault, nobody else's, but I was young, stupid, in debt, and he had me by the balls. He figured I'd fall in line."

"Are you telling me your father cut you off financially, cut you off from even what was yours, because he wanted you to be a lawyer?"

"No." Maybe she'd never understand. "He did it because he wanted control, because he wouldn't—can't—tolerate anyone defying that control."

Since she was listening, Coop eased back. "Money's a weapon, and he knows how to use it. He'd release some of the funds if I . . . well, he had a list of conditions, and it doesn't matter now. I had to get a lawyer, and it took a lot of time and money. So even when I got what was mine, I owed a lot of it in legal fees. I couldn't let you come to New York and see the way I was living back then. I needed to put everything I had into the job. I needed to make detective, to prove I was good enough. And, Lil, you were flying. Getting articles published, traveling, making the dean's list. You were amazing."

"You should've told me. I had a right to know what was going on."

"And if I had? You'd have wanted me to come back, and maybe I would have. With nothing. I'd've hated it. And I'd have blamed you sooner or later. Or you'd have given it all up and come to New York. And we'd have hated each other sooner. If I'd told you, Lil, if I'd ask you to stick with me until I made something, there wouldn't be a Chance Wildlife Refuge. You wouldn't be who you are now. Neither would I."

"You made all the decisions."

"I'll cop to that. You agreed with them at the time."

"I said I did because all I had left was pride."

"Then you should understand that's all I had."

"You had me."

He wanted to touch her, just his fingertips on her face, something to smooth away the hurt in her eyes. But it wasn't the way.

"I needed to be someone, for myself. I needed something to be proud of. I spent the first twenty years of my life wanting my father to love me, to be proud of me. Just like my mother, I guess. He's got a way of making you want that approval, then withholding it so you want it more, and feel . . . less, because it never really comes. You don't know what that's like."

"No, I don't." She saw, so clearly, the boy she'd first met. Those eyes, those sad and mad eyes.

"I never knew what it was like to have someone care about me, for me, feel pride in me for anything until I came out here that summer to stay with my grandparents. After that, in some ways, it was even more important to get it from my own parents. From my father most of all. But I was never going to get it."

He shrugged that off, something over, something no longer important. "Realizing that changed things. Changed me. Maybe I did get harder, Lil, but I started going after what I wanted, not what he wanted. I was a good cop, and that mattered. When I couldn't be a cop anymore, I built up a business, and I was a good investigator. It was never about the money, though let me tell you it's damn, fucking hard not to have any, to be afraid you won't make the rent the second month running."

She stared out over the canyon where the rocks rose in silent power toward the deepening blue of the sky. "Did you think I wouldn't understand any of this?"

"I didn't understand half of it, and I didn't know how to tell you. I loved you, Lil. I've loved you every day of my life since I was eleven years old." He reached in his pocket, drew out the coin she'd given him at the end of their first summer. "I've carried you with me, every day of my life.

But there was a time I didn't think I deserved you. You can blame me for that, but the fact is we both had to make our way. We wouldn't have made it if we hadn't let each other go."

"You don't know that. And you didn't have the right to decide for me."

"I decided for me."

"And you can come back now, a decade later, when *you're* ready? I'm supposed to go along?"

"I thought you were happy—and believe me it sliced up a part of me when I'd think about you going on, doing what you wanted to do, without me. Every time I'd hear about you, it was about the name you were making for yourself, how you were building the refuge, or off to Africa or Alaska. The few times I saw you, you were always busy. Heading off somewhere."

"Because I couldn't stand being around you. It hurt. Goddamn it."

"You were engaged."

"I was never engaged. People assumed we were engaged. I lived with Jean-Paul, and we traveled together sometimes if our work coincided. I wanted to make a life. I wanted a family. But I couldn't make it work. Not with him, not with anyone."

"If it makes you feel any better, anytime I heard about him, or about you seeing someone else, it killed me. I had a lot of miserable nights and days, hours, years, wishing I hadn't done what I thought—still think—was the right thing. I figured you'd moved on, and half the time I hated you for it."

"I don't know what you want me to say, want me to do."

"Neither do I. But I'm saying to you I know who I am now, what I am, and I'm okay with it. I did what I needed to do, and now? I'm doing what I want to do. I'm going to give my grandparents the best I have, because that's what they always gave me. I'm going to give you the best I have, because I'm not letting you go again."

"You don't have me, Coop."

"Then I'll fix that until I do. If for now all I can do is help you, keep you safe, sleep with you, and make sure you know I'm not going anywhere, that's okay. Sooner or later you're going to be mine again."

"We're not who we were."

"We're more than we were. And who we are, Lil? Still fits."

"It's not all your decision this time."

"You still love me."

"Yes, I do." She faced him again, studied him with eyes that were both clear and unfathomable. "And I've lived a long time knowing love isn't enough. You hurt me, more than anyone else ever has, more than anyone else ever could. Knowing why? I'm not sure if it makes it better or worse. That's not an easy fix."

"I'm not looking for easy. I came out here because my grandparents needed me. And I was ready to let go. I expected to find you the next thing to married. I told myself I'd have to suck that up. I'd had my chance. The way I look at it, Lil, you had yours, too. Take your time if you need to. I'm not going anywhere."

"So you keep saying." She stepped back, started to turn toward the horses, but he took her arm, swung her back.

"I guess I'll have to, until you believe me. Here's one for you, Lil. Do you know how many ways love can hit you? So it makes you happy, or miserable? It makes you sick in the belly or hurt in the heart. It makes everything brighter and sharper, or blurs all the edges. It makes you feel like a king or a fool. Every way love can hit, it's hit me when it comes to you."

He drew her in to take her mouth, to give in to that endless ache while the wind swept the air with the perfume of sage.

"Loving you made a man out of me," he said when he let her go. "It's the man who came back for you."

"You still make my knees weak, and I still want your hands on me. But that's all I'm sure of."

"That's a start."

"I have to get back."

"You've got color in your cheeks, and you don't look so tired now."

"Well, yippee. That doesn't mean I'm not pissed off at the way you got me out here." She mounted her horse. "I'm pissed off at you in so many ways right now, on so many levels."

He studied her face as he swung into the saddle. "We never fought all that much the first time around. Too young and horny."

"No, we didn't fight so much because you weren't such an asshole."

"I don't think that's it."

"You're probably right. You were probably just as much of an asshole back then."

"You liked flowers. You always liked it when we'd go hiking or riding and the wildflowers were blooming. I'll have to get you some flowers."

"Oh, yeah, that'll make everything just fine." Her tone was as brittle as juniper in a drought. "I'm not one of your city women who can be bought off with a bunch of fancy roses."

"You don't know anything about my city women. Which probably sticks in your craw."

"Why should it? I've had plenty of men . . . bring me flowers since you."

"Okay, point for you on that."

"This isn't a game, or a joke, or a competition."

"No." But she was talking to him, and he considered that a check in the win column. "At this point, I have to believe it's just destiny. I worked pretty hard on my life without you. And here I am, right back where I started."

She said nothing while their horses waded through the high grass and back to the trailhead.

He waited until they'd loaded the horses, secured the tailgate. Behind the wheel, he started the engine and glanced at her profile. "I brought some of my things over. I'm going to be staying there, at least until they have Howe in custody. I'm going to bring some other things over tomorrow. I need a drawer, some closet space."

"You can have a drawer and the closet space. Just don't assume it means anything but that I'm willing to make it convenient for you, as I'm grateful for your help."

"And you like the sex."

"And I like the sex," she said, very coolly.

"I'll need to do some work while I'm staying at the cabin. If using the kitchen table doesn't work for you, I need somewhere else to set up my laptop."

"You can use the living room."

"All right."

"Are you not mentioning how James Tyler was killed because you think I can't handle it?"

"There were other things I wanted to talk about."

"I'm not fragile."

"No, but it's wearing on you. They'll have to wait for the autopsy, but from what Willy said, his throat was slit. He was stripped down to his pants and boots—so I figure his killer thought he could use the shirt and jacket, the cap he'd been wearing. His watch, his wallet. He probably destroyed the cell phone, or Tyler lost it along the way. The killer must have had the cord he used on him. He weighed the body down with rocks. Went to some time and trouble to get it in the river, in that spot, secure it. But the rain shifted things enough to bring it up to the point Gull spotted it."

"He's probably disposed of other bodies with more luck."

"Yeah, that would be my take."

"So if he's the one who killed Molly Pickens, he wasn't dead or in prison like you thought, or not in prison for the length of time you thought. He's just been mixing it up. Leaving some bodies for the animals, bodies that can be found or have been found. Hiding others."

"That's the way it looks."

She nodded slowly, the way he knew she did when she was reasoning something out. "And killers who do this, serial types, who troll and travel, who know how to hide and blend, who have some measure of control, they aren't always caught."

"You've been reading up."

"It's what I do when I need information. They end up with creative names—and maybe a feature film. Zodiac, Green River. Still, they usually need to taunt the police, or use the media. He doesn't."

"It's not about glory or acknowledgment. It's about the work. It's personal, and he gets his satisfaction from that. Every kill is proof he's better than the victim. Better than his father. He's proving something. I know what that's like."

"Did you become a cop to be a hero, Coop?"

His lips curved. "In the beginning? Yeah, probably. I was completely out of place during my short stint in college. Not just trying to find my place, but out of it. The only things I learned about the law were—I didn't want to be a lawyer, but the law itself was fascinating. So, law enforcement."

"Fighting crime in the urban canyons."

"I loved New York. Still do," he said easily. "And sure, I imagined I'd be hunting down bad guys, protecting the populace. I found out, fast, I'd be standing around a lot, sitting around, knocking on doors and doing paperwork. There's so much tedium in proportion to moments of absolute terror. I learned to be patient. I learned how to wait, and what it means to protect and serve. Then on 9/11, everything shifted."

She reached out, laid a hand over his, lightly, briefly. But it was all there in the touch. Comfort, sympathy, understanding. "We were all terrified until we knew you were safe."

"I wasn't on the roll that day. By the time I got down there, the second tower was gone. You just did what you had to, what you could."

"I was in class when we heard a plane had hit one of the towers. Nobody knew, not at first, what was happening. And then . . . everything stopped. There was nothing else but that."

He shook his head, because if he let them, the pictures would form in his mind again, of what he'd seen and done, and hadn't been able to do.

"I knew some of the cops who went in, some of the firefighters. People I'd worked with, or hung out with, played ball with. Gone. After that, I never thought I'd leave the job. It was like a mission then. My people, my city. But when Dory was killed, it switched off for me. Just like somebody cut the wire. I couldn't do it anymore. Losing that was the worst thing in my life next to losing you."

"You could've transferred to another place."

"That's what I did, in my own way. I needed to build something back, I guess. To make something out of the death and the grief. I don't know, Lil. I did what came next. It worked for me."

"You'd still be there if Sam hadn't had the accident."

"I don't know. The city came back, and so did I. I was done there, and I'd already put plans in place to come back before the accident."

"Before?"

"Yeah. I wanted the quiet."

"Considering what's happened, you haven't gotten what you wanted."

He looked over at her. "Not yet."

It was nearing dark by the time he turned onto her road. Long shadows at the end of a long day.

"I'm going to help with the feeding," she said. "Then I have some work to finish up."

"I've got some of my own." He reached over before she could open the door, and cupped the back of her neck in his hand. "I could say I'm sorry, but I'm not, because here you are. I could tell you I'll never hurt you again, but I will. What I can tell you is I'm going to love you for the rest of my life. Maybe that's not enough, but right now it's what I've got."

"And I'll tell you I need time to think, time to settle, and time to figure out what it is I want this time."

"I've got time. I have to run into town. Do you need any supplies?"

"No, we're good."

"I'll be back in an hour." He tugged her over, pressed his mouth to hers.

MAYBE WORK WAS a crutch, Lil admitted. Something to lean on, to help her limp along after a hard knock. It still had to be done. So she hauled food while the animals chorused. She watched Boris pounce on his dinner, rip at it. And thought, If things go well, he'll have company within the week.

Another notch in the refuge's belt, true enough, she mused. But more important, to her, another abused animal given sanctuary, freedom—as far as she could manage—and care.

"So how was your adventure?"

From the smile on Tansy's face, Lil concluded her friend had witnessed her humiliating exit earlier. And those who hadn't actually seen it had certainly heard of it.

She owed Coop for that one.

"Men are idiots."

"Often true, but we love them for it."

"He decided to do the caveman routine so he could tell me why he stabbed me in the heart back in the day. Manly pride and for my own good, and other *bullshit* reasons, which—natch—I was too young and starry-eyed to consider or *understand* at the time. Better to rip me to bloody pieces than to actually talk to me, right? Stupid bastard man."

"Wow."

"Did he ever consider what it did to me? How much it hurt? That I thought I wasn't enough for him, that he'd found someone else? That I've spent damn near half of my life trying to get the hell over him. And now he's back and, gee, Lil, it was all for you. I'm supposed to just jump and cheer, and be what, *grateful?*"

"I couldn't say. And probably shouldn't if I could."

"He's always loved me. Always will love me, and tra-la-la. So he hauls me off like I'm some package he can drop off and pick up on his whim, again *for my own good,* and dumps all this in my lap. If I were less civilized, I'd kick his ass for it."

"You don't look very civilized right at the moment."

She heaved out a breath. "Well, I am, so I can't. Plus, it would be sinking to his Neanderthal level. I'm a scientist. I have a doctorate. And you know what?"

"What, Dr. Chance?"

"Shut up. I was dealing with all this, with him, with me, with it before this. Now I don't know what the hell to think."

"He told you he loves you."

"That's not the point."

"Then what is? You love him. You told me when you and Jean-Paul called it a day it was because you were still in love with Coop."

"He hurt me, Tansy. He ripped me to pieces, again, just by telling me why he did it in the first place. And he doesn't see that. He doesn't *get* that."

Tansy put her arm around Lil, drew her against her side. "I do, honey. I really do."

"I can even understand, intellectually. If I step back and look at everything he said, objectively, I can nod sagely. Yes, of course, that's reasonable on this particular level. But I'm not objective. I can't be. I don't care about reasonable. I was so pitifully in love."

"You don't have to care about reasonable. You only have to care about how you feel. And if you love him, you'll forgive him, after he suffers."

"He should suffer," Lil stated. "I don't want to be fair and forgiving."

"Hell no. Why don't we go inside? I can make Men Suck margaritas. I can stay tonight, thereby avoiding my own idiot man. We'll get drunk and plot female world domination."

"That sounds so good. I could really use all of that. But he's coming back. Until we're secure here, that's the way it's going to be. I need to deal with it, somehow. Plus, I can't get drunk on Men Suck margaritas—though you do make the champions—because I have to work. I have to work because some asshole hauled me off for two hours."

She turned, wrapped her arms around Tansy. "God, God, there's a man dead, and his wife must be destroyed. And I'm standing here, feeling sorry for myself."

"You can't change what happened. None of it's your fault."

"I can think that, intellectually again. Not my fault, not my responsibility. But Tansy, my gut says differently. James Tyler was in the wrong place at the wrong time. And it was the wrong place and time because this maniac's focused on me. Not my fault, no. But."

"When you think like that, he scores points." Firmly, Tansy drew her away so their eyes met. "It's terrorism. It's psychological warfare. He's pushing at you. For him, Tyler wasn't any different than that cougar or that wolf. Just another animal to be bagged and used to get to you. Don't let him get to you."

"I know you're right." She wanted to say "but" again. Instead, she gave Tansy another hug. "You're awfully good for me. Even margarita-free."

"We're the smart girls."

"We are. Go on home, and deal with your own idiot man."

"I guess I have to."

Lil checked on the injured fawn—treated, fed, and secured in an area of the petting zoo. If she healed clean, they'd release her to the wild. If not . . . well, she'd have sanctuary here.

Time would tell.

She spent another hour in her office. She heard trucks leaving, trucks coming. Staff heading home, volunteer guards coming. Soon, she thought, the security system would be finished and she could stop imposing on neighbors and friends. Now she could only be grateful for them.

She went out, and spotted Gull immediately. "Gull, nobody expected you to come here tonight."

"I wouldn't be able to sleep anyway. It's better to be doing something." He might've looked a little peaked yet, but his eyes were healthy enough to be lethal. "I half hope that son of a bitch comes around here tonight."

"I know it's terrible, but because of you, his wife knows. She's not wondering anymore. If you hadn't found him, it would be worse. She'd still not know."

"Willy told me her boys came." His lips pressed together as he looked off and away. "Her sons came, so she's not alone."

"That's good. She shouldn't be alone." She gave his arm a rub before she walked on.

When she stepped inside the cabin, Coop was on the couch, his laptop on the coffee table. He turned something over, casually—too casually—as she stepped in.

A photograph, she thought, from the brief glimpse.

"I can make a sandwich," she said. "That's about all I have time for. I want to go take my shift outside."

"I picked up a pizza in town. It's in the oven on warm."

"Okay. That works, too."

"I'll finish up here. We'll grab a slice together, and take first shift."

"What are you working on?"

"Couple of things."

Annoyed with the nonresponse, she simply walked back to the kitchen.

There, on her table was a vase filled with yellow tulips. Because they made her eyes sting and her heart soften, she turned away to get plates down. She heard him come in as she dealt with the pizza.

"The flowers are pretty, thank you. They don't fix things."

"Pretty's good enough." He'd had to nag the woman who owned the flower shop to open back up and sell them to him. But pretty was good enough. "Do you want a beer?"

"No, I'll stick with water." She turned with two plates and nearly rammed him. "What?"

"We could take a break tomorrow. I could take you out to dinner, maybe a movie."

"Dates won't fix things either. And I don't feel right being away too long. Not now."

"Okay. Once the system's up and running, you can make dinner, and I'll rent a movie."

He took the plates, carried them to the table.

"Doesn't it matter how mad I am at you?"

"No. Or it doesn't matter as much as the fact that I love you. I've waited this long. I can wait until you stop being mad at me."

"It might be a really long wait."

"Well." He sat, picked up a slice. "Like I keep saying. I'm not going anywhere."

She sat down, picked up a slice of her own. "I'm still mad—plenty— but I'm too hungry to bother about it right now."

He smiled. "It's good pizza."

It was, she thought.

And, damn it, the tulips really were pretty.

22

In his cave, deep in the hills, he studied his take. He imagined the watch—decent, high middle-range—had been a birthday or Christmas present. He liked to imagine good old Jim opening it, expressing his pleasure and surprise, giving his wife—also very decent if she looked like the photo in the wallet—a thank-you kiss.

Six months, maybe a year down the road, he could pawn it if he needed some cash. Right now, thanks to good old Jim, he was flush with the $122.86 he'd taken out of Jim's pockets.

He'd also scored a Swiss Army knife—you could never have too many—a hotel key card, a half pack of Big Red gum, and a Canon Powershot digital camera.

He spent some time figuring out how to work it, then scrolling through the pictures Jim had taken that day. Mostly scenery, with a few shots of Deadwood, and a couple of the not-shabby Mrs. Jim.

He shut it off to preserve the battery, though Jim had considerately brought along a spare in his pack.

It was a good-quality pack, and brand-spanking-new. That would be handy down the road. Then there were the trail snacks, extra water, first-aid kit. He imagined Jim reading a hiking guide, making himself a checklist for what he should take on a day trip. Matches, bandages and gauze, Tylenol, a little notebook, a whistle, a trail map, and the hiking guide, of course.

None of that had done Jim any good, because he was an *amateur*. An *intruder*.

He'd been meat.

Spry though, he mused as he munched on some of Jim's trail mix. The fucker could run. Still, it had been so easy to herd the bastard along, to push him farther off the trail, to move him toward the river.

Good times.

He'd gotten a good shirt and a new jacket out of the match, too. A shame about the boots. The bastard had good Timberlands. And really small feet.

All in all, it had been a good hunt. He'd give Jim six out of ten. And the take was prime.

He'd considered the rain a bonus. No way the half-assed cops and rangers, the hayseed local yokels, would find any sign of good old Jim with the rain washing out the tracks.

He could have, he and those who'd come before him. Those who owned the holy ground.

It had saved him the time and trouble of backtracking, brushing out tracks, laying false trails. Not that he minded doing all that. It was part of the job, after all, and carried some satisfaction.

But when Nature offered you a gift, you took it with thanks.

The problem was, sometimes the gift was a booby prize.

Without the rain, the flooding, old Jim would've stayed where he'd been put—and for a good long while, too. He hadn't made a mistake there, no sir. Mistakes could cost you your life in the wild. That's why the old man had beat him bloody whenever he'd made one. He hadn't made a mistake. He'd loaded Jim down good and proper and tied him down strong under those falls. He'd taken his time. (Maybe not enough time, he thought in the secret part of his mind. Maybe he'd hurried it up because the hunt made him hungry. Maybe . . .)

He pushed those thoughts away. He didn't make mistakes.

So they'd found him.

He frowned at the handset he'd stolen weeks before. He'd heard them on their radios, scattered all over hell and back. He'd gotten a good laugh out of it, too.

Until that asshole got lucky.

Gull Nodock. Maybe he'd look up asshole Gull one of these days. He wouldn't be so damn lucky then.

But that would have to wait, unless the opportunity jumped up and bit him. It was thinking time now.

What he should likely do was pack it up, move on. Cross over into Wyoming and set up for a few weeks. Let things cool off. Asshole cops would take a dead tourist more seriously than a dead wolf or cat.

To his mind the wolf and the cat were worth a hell of a lot more than some fucker from St. Paul. The wolf, now, that had been a fair hunt. But the cat, he had had some bad moments over that cougar. Bad dreams about the cougar's spirit coming back and hunting him.

He'd just wanted to know what it was like, that's all, to kill something wild and free while it was caged up. He hadn't known it would feel so bad, or the spirit of the cat would haunt him.

Hunt him. In the dreams, under a full moon, it stalked him, and screamed as it leaped for his throat.

In dreams the spirit of the cougar he'd killed stared at him with cold eyes that left him shaking with sweat and waking with his heart pounding.

Like a baby, his father would've said. Like a girl. Sniveling and shaking and afraid of the dark.

Didn't matter, over and done, he reminded himself. And he'd given pretty Lil a good scare, hadn't he? Have to weigh the good against the bad there.

They'd be looking for him hard now, over good old Jim. It'd be prudent—like his old man used to say—it'd be prudent to put some miles between himself and the hunting ground.

He could come back for Lil, for their contest, a month from now, six months if the heat stayed on. Leave those cops and rangers chasing their tails.

The trouble was, he wouldn't be around to see it. No fun in that, no kick, no punch.

No point.

If he stayed, he'd feel them hunting him. Maybe he'd hunt them, too. Take a couple out along the way. Now, that would be worth the risk. And it was the risk that got the blood moving, wasn't it?

It was the risk that proved you weren't a baby, you weren't a girl. You weren't afraid of any goddamn thing. The risk, the hunt, the kill, they proved you were a man.

He didn't want to wait six months for Lil. He'd waited so long already.

He'd stay. This was his land now, as it was the land of his ancestors. No one would run him off it. He'd take his stand here. If he couldn't beat a bunch of uniforms, he wasn't worthy of the contest.

Here was his destiny, and whether she knew it or not, he was Lil's.

WORK IN THE compound moved efficiently, even more so to Lil's eye when Brad Dromburg arrived. He cracked no whips, pointed no fingers, but everything seemed to move faster when he was on-site.

Lil's only problem with the nearly completed system was the learning curve.

"You'll have some false alarms," Brad told her as he walked the paths with her. "My advice would be to limit access to the controls to your head staff, at least for now. The fewer people have your codes, know the routine, the less margin for error."

"We'll be fully operational by the end of the day?"

"Should be."

"That's fast work. Faster, I know, than usual—and smoother because you came out to oversee. It's a lot, Brad. I'm grateful."

"All part of the service. Plus I've had a few days of what we'll call a working vacation, a little time to catch up with a friend, and the best damn chicken and dumplings this side of heaven."

"Lucy's masterpiece." She stopped to stroke the sweet-eyed donkey who called to her before moving on again. "I have to say I was surprised you stayed at Coop's instead of a hotel."

"I can stay in a hotel anytime. Too many times. But how often does a city boy get to stay in a refitted bunkhouse on a horse farm?"

She glanced at him and laughed because he sounded very much like a kid who'd been given an unexpected holiday. "I guess not often."

"And it's given me some insight on why my friend and fellow urbanite traded the concrete canyons for the Black Hills. It's just like he always described," Brad added, looking off to the hills, green with the burgeoning spring.

"So he talked about it, about coming out here as a boy?"

"About how it looked, felt, smelled. What it was like to work with horses, fish with your father. It was clear that while he lived in New York, he considered this his home."

"Odd. I always thought he considered New York home."

"My take? New York was something Coop had to conquer. This was where he always felt . . . well, at peace. That sounds a little strong. The way he talked about out here, I thought he was romanticizing, putting the pretty touches on it the way you do when you remember something from childhood. I have to say I thought he was doing the same when he talked about you. I was wrong, in both cases."

"That's a nice compliment, but I imagine everyone romanticizes or demonizes their childhood to some extent. I can't imagine Coop had that much to say about me. And, wow, that was such obvious fishing," she added quickly. "Picture me packing up my rod and reel."

"He had plenty to say about you, when you were kids—when you weren't exactly kids anymore. He'd show me articles you'd written."

"Well." Baffled, Lil simply stared. "That must've been fascinating for the layman."

"Actually, they were. Into the Alaskan wilderness, deep in the Everglades, on the plains of Africa, the American West, the mysteries of Nepal. You've covered a lot of the world. And your articles on this place helped me with the security design."

He walked another moment in silence. "It's probably a violation of a buddy rule to tell you, but he carries a picture of you in his wallet."

"He stayed away. That was his choice."

"Can't argue with that. You never met his father, did you?"

"No."

"He's a cold son of a bitch. Hard and cold. I had some issues with my father off and on. But under that? I always knew I mattered to him. Just as Coop always knew the only part of him that mattered to his father was the name. Takes a while to build up self-esteem when the person who should love you unconditionally continually chips away at it."

Sad and mad, she thought. It would make you sad and mad. "I know it was hard for him. And hard for me, who has the best parents in the history of parents, to fully understand what it's like to go through it."

Still, she thought, *damn* it.

"But tell me, is it a guy thing? Separating yourself from people who love and value you, and fighting it out alone, continually butting head to head with those who don't love and value you?"

"How do you know you deserve to be loved and valued if you don't prove yourself?"

"A guy thing then."

"Could be. Then again, I'm standing here talking to a woman who recently spent six months in the Andes, a long way from the home fires. Work, sure," he said before she could respond. "Work you're dedicated to. But you don't travel with a safety net, do you? I imagine you've taken a lot of trips, spent a lot of time on your own because you needed to prove you'd earned your spot."

"That's annoyingly true."

"After his partner was killed and he was shot, he made an effort to reconcile with his mother."

Oh, she thought, then. Of course, then. It was perfectly Cooper Sullivan.

"It worked out pretty well," Brad continued. "He tried to mend some fences with his father."

"Did he?" she asked. "Yes, of course, he would have."

"That didn't work out. After, he built a very solid business for himself. It was a way to prove, if you ask me, that he didn't need the money from the trust to make his way."

"That would be something his father would say to him, I imagine. I've never met him, no, but I imagine him saying, when Coop tried to mend those fences, that he was nothing without the money. The family money. Money that had come from his father. Yes, I can hear him say that. Can imagine Cooper bound and determined to, again, prove him wrong."

"He did prove him wrong. More than once. But I'd say that was the point where Coop stopped needing his father's approval, on any level, in any way. He's never said, and probably wouldn't admit it, but I know him. And he's never stopped needing yours."

"He's never asked me what I thought, if I approved."

"Hasn't he?" Brad said lightly.

"I don't—" She turned at the shout, watched the van ease up in front of the first cabin. "That's our tiger."

"No shit, the strip-club tiger? Can I watch?"

"Sure, but she won't do a lap dance. We'll start her out in the enclosure," Lil began as they walked toward the van. "On the other side of the fencing we put up in Boris's. He's old, but he's feisty. She's young, but she's been declawed. And she's been chained or caged, drugged most of her life. She hasn't been around her own kind. We'll watch how they react to each other. I don't want either one of them hurt."

She stopped to introduce herself and shake hands with the driver and the wrangler. "Our office manager, Mary Blunt. Mary will take the paperwork. I'd like to see her."

Lil climbed into the cargo area, crouched so the dull eyes of the tiger met hers. Defeated, Lil thought, resigned. All the pride and ferocity sheared away by years of mistreatment.

"Hello, pretty girl," she murmured. "Hello, Delilah. Welcome to a whole new world. Let's take her home," she called out. "I'll ride back here with her."

She sat cross-legged on the floor of the van, cautiously pressed her palm to the bars. Delilah barely moved. "No one's ever going to hurt you again, or humiliate you. You have family now."

As they had with the pampered Cleo, they set the cage, locked open the door to the opening of the enclosure. Unlike Cleo, the tiger made no attempt to leave the cage.

Boris, on the other hand, prowled back to the fenceline, scenting the air. He marked his line, preening, Lil noted, as he hadn't done in a very long time. And puffing out his chest, he roared.

In her cage, Delilah's muscles twitched.

"Let's back off. She's nervous. There's food and water in the enclosure. And Boris is talking to her. She'll go in, in her own good time."

Lucius lowered his camera. "She looks kind of beaten down. You know, emotionally."

"We'll get Tansy to work with her. And if we need to, we'll bring in the shrink."

"You have a tiger shrink?" Brad asked, astonished.

"A behavioral psychologist. We've worked with him before, in extreme cases. I guess you could call him an exotic animal whisperer." She smiled. "Check him out on Animal Planet. But I think we'll be able to take care of her. She's tired and . . . her self-esteem's an issue. We'll just make sure she knows she's loved, valued, and safe here."

"I think the big guy there is smitten," Brad observed as Boris rubbed himself against the fence.

"He's been lonely. A male tiger mingles well with females. They're more chivalrous than lions." She moved back, sat on a bench. "I'll just keep an eye on them for a while."

"I'll go check on the progress on your gates. We should be able to test the system in another couple of hours."

After about a half hour, Tansy came to join her, and offer one of the two bottles of Diet Pepsi she'd brought out.

"They used cattle prods and Tasers on her," Tansy said.

"I know." Still watching the motionless cat, Lil sipped her soft drink. "She expects to be punished if she steps out of the cage. Sooner or later, she'll go after the food. If she doesn't, by tomorrow, we'll have to get her out. I'm hoping we won't. She needs to leave the cage on her own, and not be punished."

"Boris already has stars in his eyes."

"Yeah. It's sweet. She may respond to him, to the alpha, before she gives in to hunger. And she'll need to void. She's probably had to void in her cage before, but she won't want to, since there's a choice."

"The vet working with animal abuse treated her for an infected bladder, and had to pull two of her teeth. Matt's going over all the reports, and wants to examine her himself. But he feels, as you do, that she needs to be left alone for a while first. How are things between you and Coop?"

"We're in a kind of moratorium, I guess. We need to get this security up and running. Plus I think he's working with the police. He has files he doesn't want me to see. I'm leaving it alone for now."

"Like the tiger."

"As a metaphor for my relationship with Coop, it's not bad. It's fairly shaky, with the potential for a feral strike. I found two clips for his handgun in my lingerie drawer. Why the hell would he put them there?"

"I guess it's hard to forget where you put them. Your everyday stuff, or the fuck-me stuff?"

"The fuck-me stuff. It's mortifying. I was going to get rid of most of it. It's weird having it around. The Jean-Paul factor. He bought most of it, and enjoyed all of it."

"Clean it out. Buy your own."

"Yeah, I'm just not sure I want to invest in that area right now. It sends a signal."

"It does. I bought two extreme rip-this-off-me-big-boy nighties the other day. Online shopping is my friend. I'm still wondering why I didn't stop myself."

"Farley's going to swallow his tongue."

"I keep telling myself I'm going to break this off before it gets any deeper. Then I'm scoping out the spring line from Victoria's Secret. I am not well, Lil."

"You're in love, honey."

"I think it's just lust. Lust is good. No harm done. And it passes."

"Uh-huh. Just lust. You bet."

"All right, stop badgering me, you fiend. I know it's more than lust. I just haven't figured out how to handle it. So stop your insidious torture."

"All right, since you begged. Look. Look." Lil clamped a hand on Tansy's knee. "She's moving."

As they watched, Delilah bellied forward an inch, then another. Boris growled his encouragement. When she was halfway out, she went still as a statue again, and Lil feared she'd retreat. Then she quivered, bunched, and leaped on the whole chicken left on her concrete pad.

She gripped it in her paws, her head shifting as she scanned right, left, forward. Her eyes met Lil's.

Go on and eat, Lil thought. Go on, now.

She cocked her head, and still watching, sank her teeth into the meat.

She ripped and bolted the food. Lil squeezed her hand on Tansy. "Waiting for someone to lay into her. God, I wish I could take a cattle prod to those bastards in Sioux City."

"Right there with you. Poor girl. She could make herself sick."

But she kept it down. Rather than clean her paws, she slunk over to the trough, drank and drank.

On the other side of the fence, Boris rose on his hind legs, called to her. She kept low, kept subservient, but approached the fence to sniff at him. When he lowered, she scurried back to stand at the entrance to her cage.

To what, Lil knew, she thought of as safety. He called her again, insistently, until she bellied over to the fence, quivering, trembling as he sniffed her nose, her front paws.

When he licked her, Lil smiled. "We should've called him Romeo. Let's get the cage away, close her in. Boris will take it from here."

She checked her watch as she rose. "Excellent timing. I need to run into town."

"I thought we had our supply run."

"I've got to do some errands. And I want to swing by and see my parents. I'll be back before sundown."

SHE DIDN'T INTEND to stop by the Wilkses' stables, but she was early, and they were right there. In any case, it was irresistible when she spotted Coop leading a little girl around the paddock on a sturdy bay pony.

The kid looked as though she'd just been given the keys to the universe's biggest toy store. She bounced in the saddle, obviously incapable of being still, and her face under her pink cowgirl hat glowed like the summer sun.

As she stepped out of her truck, Lil heard the kid chattering away at Coop while her mother laughed and her father took pictures. Charmed, Lil walked over to the fence and leaned against it to watch.

Coop looked pretty damn pleased himself, she noted, giving the kid his attention, answering endless questions while the little horse plodded along patiently.

How old was the kid? she wondered. Four maybe? Long sunny pigtails twined down under the hat, and her jeans had colorful flowers embroidered on the hem.

Impossibly cute, Lil concluded. Then felt a hard, deep tug as Coop reached up to lift the girl out of the saddle.

She'd never really thought of him as a father. At one time she'd simply assumed they'd have a family together, but it had all been vague and silver-edged. Pretty dreams of "one day."

She thought of all the years between. They might have had a little girl.

He let the girl stroke and pet the horse, then fished a carrot out of a sack. He showed her how to hold it, and put the frothy icing on the kid's happy cake by allowing her to feed the pony.

Lil waited while he spoke with the parents, and saw him grin when the girl flung her arms around his legs in a hug.

"She'll remember you for the rest of her life," Lil commented when Coop came her way.

"The horse anyway. Nobody forgets their first."

"I didn't know you offered pony rides."

"It just happened. The kid was dying for it. Anyway, I've been thinking about opening that area up. Low overhead, nice profit. The father insisted on giving me a ten-dollar tip." He grinned again as he dug it out of his pocket. "Want to help me spend it?"

"Tempting, but I'm meeting somebody. You were good with the kid."

"She made it easy. And yeah, I've thought about it." When she lifted her brows in question, he laid his hands over hers on the top of the fence. "What kind of kids we might have made." He tightened his grip when she would have pulled back. "Your eyes. I've always been a sucker for your eyes. I wondered what kind of a father I'd make. I think I'd be okay. Now."

"I'm not going dewy-eyed over dream children, Coop."

"This is a good place to raise kids, the real kind. We both know that."

"You're taking a lot of big leaps. I'm sleeping with you because I want to sleep with you. But I have a lot of things to resolve, a lot to think through before it can be anything more than that, and what's turning out to be a tenuous friendship."

"I said I'd wait, and I will. That doesn't mean I'm not going to use whatever comes along to get you back. It occurs to me, Lil, I never had to work for you before. Could be interesting."

"I didn't come by to talk about this. God, you frustrate me." She yanked her hands from under his. "I wanted to tell you Brad thinks we'll have the security up and running by the end of the day."

"Okay. Good."

"I'm going to let everyone know we won't need patrols. That includes you."

"I'm there until Howe's in a cell."

"That's your choice. And I won't pretend I'd rather not stay in the compound alone at night. You can keep your drawer and your share of the closet. I'll sleep with you. For the rest, I don't know." She started to walk away, then stopped. "I want to know everything Willy's shared with you, because I know he's kept you up on the investigation, the manhunt. I want to see those files you've been so careful to keep away from me. You want a chance with me this time around, Coop? Then you'd better understand I expect to be trusted and respected. On every level. Good sex and yellow tulips aren't nearly enough."

FARLEY WAS PACING a trough in the sidewalk in front of the jewelry store when Lil arrived. "I didn't want to go in without you."

"I'm sorry I'm late. I got hung up."

"No problem." The hands in his pockets jingled loose change. "You're not late. I got here early."

"Nervous?"

"Some. I just want to make sure it's exactly the right one."

"Let's go find it."

There were a scatter of customers and a lot of glitter inside. Lil raised a hand in a wave to the clerk she knew, then hooked her arm through Farley's. "What did you have in mind?"

"That's why you're here."

"No, just tell me what you think."

"I . . . Well, it's gotta be special, and kind of different. I don't mean fussy or . . ."

"Unique."

"Yeah, unique. Like she is."

"So far, you're exactly right, according to her best friend." She drew him over to a display of engagement rings. "White or yellow gold?"

"Oh, shit, Lil." And he looked as panicked as if she'd asked if he'd prefer cyanide or arsenic in his coffee.

"Okay, that was a trick question. Given her coloring and her personality—and her appreciation for the unique—I think you should go with rose gold."

"What the hell is that?"

"Like this." She gestured to a band. "See, it's warm, and a little soft. Glows, I think, rather than glitters."

"It's still gold, right? I mean, it's good—it's not less, I don't know, important? It's got to be important."

"It's still gold. If you don't like it, then I'd go with yellow gold."

"I do like it. It's different, and it's, yeah, warm. Kinda rosy. Rose gold, ha, that's why."

"Relax, Farley, it's all good."

"Right."

"Just take a quick scan, pick the one that pops out to you first."

"Ah . . . That one? It's got that pretty round diamond in it."

"It's beautiful, but the trouble with that one is how it sticks up from the band." Lil held her thumb and index finger a little apart to show him what she meant. "Tansy works with her hands a lot, with the animals. That's going to catch."

"That makes sense. So she'll want something that doesn't stick up so high." He shoved up his hat to scratch his head. "There's not so many with this color, but still a lot to figure from. That one's nice, with the working on the band, but the diamond's kind of puny. I don't want to go on the cheap."

As Lil leaned forward for a better look, the clerk bounced up.

"Hey! Do you two have something to tell me?"

"We can't keep our great love for each other a secret any longer," Lil said and made Farley blush. "How are you, Ella?"

"Just fine. So you've dragged Farley in here for your cover? If you see what you want, I'll be glad to steer Coop to it when he comes in."

"What? No. No, no."

"Everybody's just waiting for the two of you to make an announcement."

"There is no announcement. Everybody's just . . . off." Flustered, she felt her own color rise. "I'm just here as consultant. Farley's in the market."

"Really?" Ella all but squealed it. "It's always the quiet types who run deep. Who's the lucky lady?"

"I haven't asked her yet, so . . ."

"It wouldn't be a certain exotic beauty I've seen you dancing with a time or two? The one who lives a couple blocks down, where your truck's been parked pretty regularly these past weeks?"

"Ah . . ." This time he shifted his feet.

"Oh, my God, it *is*! This is huge. Wait until I tell—"

"You can't. You can't tell anybody, Ella. I haven't asked her yet."

Ella laid a hand on her heart, held the other up to swear. "Not a word. We're experts at keeping secrets here. Though I may just pee my pants with this one if you don't ask her quick. Let's get down to business. Tell me what you have in mind."

"Lil thinks this rose gold."

"Oh, lovely choice for her." Ella unlocked the case, and began to set a small selection on a velvet pad.

They discussed, debated, with Lil helpfully trying on each contender. After considerable time and worry, he gave Lil a pained look. "You have to tell me if I'm wrong. I like this one here. I like how the band's wide—looks substantial, you know? And how the little diamond things ride up against the round one in the middle. She'll know she's got it on. She'll know I put it there."

Lil rose on her toes and kissed his cheek, as Ella stood behind the counter and sighed. "I was hoping you'd pick that one. She'll love it, Farley. It's just exactly right."

"Thank the Lord, 'cause I was starting to sweat."

"It's beautiful, Farley. Unusual, contemporary, and still romantic." Ella replaced the other rings. "What size does she wear?"

"Oh, well, hell."

"Around a six," Lil told her. "I'm a five, and we've traded rings before. Hers are a little bigger than mine. I wear hers on my middle finger. I think . . ." She picked up the ring and slid it on her middle finger. "This is about right."

"Must be fate. If it needs to be sized, you just bring her in with it, and we'll take care of it. Or she can exchange it if she sees something she likes better. I'm going to get the paperwork on it, Farley, and we'll do the deal."

Ella crooked her finger so he'd lean down. "And because I once let you kiss me behind the bleachers, I'm giving you fifteen percent off. You make sure you come back to me for the wedding bands."

"I wouldn't go anywhere else." He looked over at Lil, his eyes dazed. "I'm buying Tansy a ring. Don't do that," he said when Lil's eyes filled. "I'm afraid I'm going to water up myself."

She put her arms around him, laid her head on his chest while he patted her back. Choices, she thought, and chances. Some made the right choices, and made the best of their chances.

23

Farley followed her to the farm, so Lil experienced the sweetness of watching him show off the ring to her parents. There was backslapping, a few tears, and the promise to bring Tansy over for a family celebration once she'd accepted.

When Farley asked Joe to take a walk, undoubtedly to ask for man-to-man advice, Lil sat down with her mother.

"My God, he was a boy five minutes ago," Jenna said.

"You made a man out of him."

Jenna dabbed at her eyes. Again. "We gave him access to the tools so he could make a man out of himself. If Tansy breaks his heart I'm going to kick her ass to Pierre and back."

"Get in line. But I don't think she will. I don't think he'll let her. Farley's got a plan, some of which I imagine he's running by Dad right now. She's cooked."

"Think of the babies they'll make together. I know, I know." With a laugh, Jenna waved a hand. "Typical reaction. But I would love some babies around here. I've got the cradle your grandfather made for me, and I used for you, in the attic, just waiting. And I need to put all that on the back burner and think about wedding plans. I hope they let us throw the wedding. I'd love to get my hands into all that. Flowers and dresses and cakes and . . ." She trailed off.

"I haven't given you that."

"I made it sound just like that, and I didn't mean to. I don't have to tell you how proud we are of you, do I?"

"No, you don't. I had a plan once, and it didn't work out. So I made another plan, and it did. Now? I'm in a strange and complicated place. I could use some input."

"Cooper."

"It's always been Cooper. But it stopped being just that simple a long time ago."

"He hurt you so much." Leaning over, she cupped Lil's hand in both of hers. "Baby, I know."

"He took a piece out of me. Now he wants me to put it back, and I don't know if it can fit the way it did."

"It won't. It can't." Jenna gave her hand a squeeze before she leaned back. "That doesn't mean it won't fit another way. A better way. You love him, Lil. I know that, too."

"Love wasn't enough before. He told me—took his sweet time about telling me—why it wasn't enough."

As she related the story, she had to push out of her chair, walk to the window, open the front door for air. Move, just move while her mother sat quietly.

"For my own good, because he had something to prove, because he was broke, because he felt like a failure. What difference did any of that make? And besides all that, I deserved to know the reasons. I was part of that relationship. It's *not* a relationship if one person makes all the choices. Is it?"

"No, or not a balanced one. I understand what you're feeling, why you're angry."

"It's more than being angry, though. One of the biggest decisions of my life was made *for* me. And the reasons it was made kept from me?

How can I believe that won't happen again? And I won't build my life with someone who'd do that. I can't."

"No, you can't. Not you. And now I'm going to tell you something that may disappoint you. I'm sorry, so sorry, you were hurt. I hurt for you, Lil. I did. I felt your heartbreak inside my own. But I'm so grateful he did what he did."

Lil flinched, jerking back from the shock. "How can you say that? How can you mean that?"

"If he hadn't, you'd have given up everything you wanted—every passion you had—but him. If it had come down to him or your personal and professional goals, you were much too much in love to choose anything but him."

"Who's to say I couldn't have had both? Damn it! Where's the compromise, the working together?"

"Maybe you'd have made it, but the odds were so stacked against you. Oh, Lil," she said with such compassion Lil felt her eyes burn and tear. "You, not quite twenty and with the world opening up for you. Him almost two years older with his world narrowing and harsh. He needed to fight, and you needed to grow."

"So we were young. You were young when you and Dad married."

"Yes, and we were lucky. But we also wanted the same thing, even then. What we wanted was right here, and that gave us a better chance."

"So you think I should just shrug off the last ten years. All is forgiven, Coop, I'm yours?"

"I think you should take as much time as you need, and see if you can forgive him."

Lil let out a long breath as some of the pressure on her chest lifted.

"And I think while he had something to prove to himself before, this time he has to prove something to you. Make him. And while you're taking that time, ask yourself if you want to live the next ten years without him."

"He's changed, and who he's changed into . . . If I'd just met him, if there wasn't any history between us? I'd fall flat on my face. Knowing that is very scary. Knowing if I let myself fall flat, I'm giving him the power to rip another piece of me away."

"Aren't you tired, honey, of only getting close to men you know can't?"

"I don't know, honestly, if I did that deliberately or if it's because he's the only one who can." Lil rubbed her own arms as if to warm them. "Either way, it's another scary choice. And a lot to think about. I need to get back. I didn't mean to be gone this long."

"Important business." Jenna rose, laid her hands on Lil's shoulders. "You'll find your way, Lil. I know that absolutely. I need you to tell me if you're sure you don't need us to be there tonight."

"The system was nearly done when I left. If they ran into any glitches, I'll call. I promise. I may be confused about myself, about Coop, but I'm clear on the refuge. No chances taken."

"Good enough. Most people think he's gone. That he wouldn't stay in this area with the manhunt."

"I hope most people are right." She laid her cheek on Jenna's. "And I know we're not going to relax, not all the way, until he's caught. Don't you take chances either."

She stepped out on the porch, saw Farley and her father circling one of the outbuildings with the dogs pacing around them. "Tell Farley I'm pulling for him." She started for her truck, turned, walking backward as she studied how pretty her mother looked standing there on the porch of the old farmhouse. "He gave me yellow tulips."

And prettier yet, Lil thought, when she smiled.

"Did they work?"

"Better than I let him know. Talk about your typical reaction."

SHE GOT BACK before closing and found the new gate open. Still she glanced at the security camera, at the key swipe and code pad. They would, she thought, stop anyone from entering, in a vehicle, after closing. But you couldn't secure the hills.

She drove the road slowly, scanning the land, the trees.

She could find a way in, she mused. She knew every inch of the section, and could find a way to elude the security if she wanted to take the time and trouble.

But knowing that only made her more aware.

She let her gaze skim up as she drove. More cameras, positioned to pan the compound, the road. It would be hard to elude all of them. And the new lights would wash everything. No hiding in the dark, not once you were inside.

She pulled up in front of the cabin, pleased to see there were three separate groups making the tour of the habitats. She spotted Brad at the far western corner, talking to one of his installers. But her attention moved toward the newest member of the Chance family.

Everything in her lifted. Delilah lay against the fencing with Boris stretched on the other side. She made that her first stop.

The female didn't lift her head when Lil stepped up. She was crouched down, but her eyes opened. Still wary, Lil noted. She may very well always be wary of the human. But still, she'd found comfort in her own kind.

"I guess we'll be taking that barrier out sooner rather than later." She kept her voice easy, her movements slow. "Nice job, Boris. She needs a friend, so I'm counting on you to show her the ropes."

"Excuse me, miss?"

She glanced around to the group of four who stood behind the safety rail. "Yes?"

"You're really not supposed to be on that side."

She straightened, walked over to speak to the man who'd addressed her. "I'm Lil Chance." She offered a hand. "This is my place."

"Oh, sorry."

"No need. I was just checking on our newest addition. We don't have her plaque up yet. This is Delilah, and it's her first full day here. She's a Bengal," she began, and indulged in one of her rare guided tours.

By the time she'd finished and passed the new group on to a pair of interns, Brad was ready for her.

"You're online, Lil. Fully operational. I want to go over the whole system with you and your senior staff."

"I've let them know they may need to stay late tonight. I'd rather wait until closing, if that's okay with you."

"Not a problem, especially since Lucius said I could help with to-night's feeding—if you cleared it."

"It's a lot of work."

"I'd like to go back to New York and say I've fed a lion. I can dine out on that for a long time."

"Then you're on. I'll walk you through that, then you can walk us through the system." She turned back toward the habitat. "Even though I saw the design, I was afraid it was going to look intrusive, high-techy, and well, institutional. It doesn't. Everything's nicely camouflaged. It doesn't intrude."

"Aesthetics count, but so does efficiency. I think you're going to find we delivered both."

"I already do. Let me take you to the commissary."

AFTER FEEDING, AFTER closing, Lil worked through the controls of the security system, under Brad's tutelage. For the late staff meeting, she'd broken out the beer, provided a bucket of chicken and some sides. It might've been serious business, but there was no reason her people shouldn't enjoy it.

There'd been enough stress.

She went through sectors, then elements, switching on lights, alarms, locks, cutting them again, varying the camera view on the monitor.

"Aced it," Brad told her. "Not as fast as Lucius. He still holds the record."

"Geek," Tansy accused.

"And proud of it. Split screen, Lil, four views." Lucius bit into a drumstick, pushed his glasses back up his nose. "Let's see what you're made of."

"You think I can't do it?"

"I've got a buck says you can't first time out."

"I've got two she can," Tansy countered.

Lil rubbed her hands together, and quickly ran over the codes and sequence in her head. When four images appeared on-screen, she took a bow.

"Luck. I'll put five down Mary can't run the sequence."

Mary only sighed at Lucius. "I'd bet against me. Key cards, security codes. Next thing it'll be retinal scans." But she stepped up gamely. Inside thirty seconds, she had the alarms shrilling. "Damn it!"

"Thank God." Matt swiped a hand over his forehead. "That takes the pressure off me."

As Brad walked a frustrated Mary back through the drill, Lil eased over to Tansy. "You've got it. You can cut out any time."

"I want to run through it one more time. Besides"—she held up her paper plate—"potato salad. I'm not in a rush. What?" she said when Lil frowned at her.

"Nothing. Sorry. I was thinking of something else." Which would be the ring burning a hole in Farley's pocket. "You know, it's going to be quiet around here tonight. No guard duty."

"Well." Tansy wiggled her eyebrows when Coop came in. "In a manner of speaking. Maybe you should break out the sexy lingerie and give it one more wear."

Lil gave her an elbow bump. "Quiet."

She muffled a laugh as Mary managed to shut down the monitor. "It's going to be a while."

"If he could put the security on a spreadsheet, she'd kick ass."

"Meanwhile . . ." Lil eased a hip onto Lucius's desk, and nursed her beer.

It was full dark, with the three-quarter moon on the rise, when she saw off the last of her staff. She hoped they all managed the key card on the gate in the morning, but for now, she wanted a quick pass at some of the work she'd had to neglect during the day.

"I'll be by tomorrow," Brad told her. He lingered on the porch while Coop sat on the rail. "Work with Mary a little more, and make sure we don't have any glitches."

"I appreciate all you've done." She looked out toward the habitats, the streams of lights, the red blink of motion detectors. "It's a relief to know the animals are secure."

"You've got the local number if you have any problems. And you've got mine."

"I hope you'll come back, even if there aren't any problems."

"You can count on it."

"I'll see you tomorrow."

She went to her own cabin. Considering the time, she opted to make a pot of tea to get her through the hour or so of work she hoped to put in.

In the kitchen, on her rugged table, stood a vase of painted daisies. Pretty as a rainbow.

"Damn it."

Was she weak, was she simple, for going a little gooey inside? But really, was there any more direct hit than flowers on a woman's table put there by a man?

Just enjoy them, she ordered herself, as she put the kettle on. Just accept them for what they are. A nice gesture.

She made the tea, got a couple of cookies from her stash, then sat at the table with her laptop and the flowers.

She brought up her refuge e-mail first, as always amused by the letters from children, and pleased by the ones from potential donors asking for more details about certain programs.

She answered each in turn, and with equal attention.

She opened the next, caught her breath. Then slowly read it through a second time.

hello lil. long time no see at least for you. you've sure been doing a lot around the place, it gives me a good laugh to watch. i figure we'll get reacwainted. i figured on it being a surprize but seems like the locals figured out i was around. i'm haveing fun watching them chase there fat asses in the hills and will be leving a present for them soon. i have to say im sorry about the cougar but you never should of caged in that way so it's your fault it's dead. you think about that animels are free spirits and our ancesters knew it and respected them. you vialated the sacred trust i thougt about killing you for that back aways but i got sweet on carolyn. she was fine and she gave me a good game and died well. diing well is what counts. i think you will. when we are finished i will free all the animels you have put in prison. if you give me good game i will do it in your honer. stay well and strong so when we meet we will meet as equels. good old jim was good practise but you will be the mane event. i hope this gets to you ok i am not good with computers and have only borrowd this to send you this messag. yours truely ethan swift cat

Carefully she saved the post, copied it. She took a moment to make sure she had her breath, and her calm, before she walked out to get Coop.

She saw the taillights of Brad's rental car as Coop strolled toward the cabin porch. "Brad wanted to get back to the farm in time to sweet-talk my grandmother out of a piece of pie. He'll—" He broke off as she stepped into the light. "What happened?"

"He sent me an e-mail. You need to see it."

He moved fast, shifting her aside to go through the door and straight back to the kitchen, where he angled the laptop around to stand and read the message.

"Did you copy it?"

"Yes. It's saved to the hard drive and the thumb drive."

"We'll need hard copies, too. Do you recognize the e-mail address?"

"No."

"Should be easy to trace." He crossed over, picked up the phone.

Within a moment, she heard him giving Willy the details in a flat, expressionless voice that went with his face. "I'm going to forward it to you. Give me your e-mail." He scrawled it on the pad by the phone. "Got it."

He passed the phone to Lil on his way to the computer.

"Willy? Yes, I'm all right. Would you arrange for a drive-by? My parents." She glanced over at Coop as he tapped keys. "Coop's grandparents. I'd feel better if . . . Thanks. Yes, we will. Okay."

She hung up, barely stopped herself from twisting her hands together. "He said he'll trace the e-mail and check it out right away. He's going to call or come by as soon as he knows something."

"He knows he made a mistake with Tyler." Coop muttered it as if speaking to himself. "He knows we've identified him. How does he know? He's got a way to get information. A radio maybe. Or he risks coming into town to hear the local gossip."

Eyes narrowed, Coop reread the message. "Several places in town you can buy comp time, but . . . That's a stupid risk. We'd find the source, then find someone who'd seen him, talked to him. That gives us too much more. So a break-in's more likely. He sent it at nineteen thirty-eight. Waited for dark. Scoped out a house. Maybe one with a kid or a teenager. They tend to leave their computers on."

"He may have killed someone else. He may have murdered someone, more than one, just to send me that. Oh, God, Coop."

"We don't go there until we have to. Put it outside," he ordered, and coldly. "Focus on what we know, and what we know is he made another mistake. He came out of the shadows because he was compelled to connect with you. He learned we know who he is, so he felt free to make that connection, to communicate with you."

"But it's not *me*. It's his warped idea of me. He's talking to himself."

"That's exactly right. Keep going."

"He, ah . . ." She pressed a hand to her forehead, shoved it back through her hair. "He's uneducated, and unfamiliar with computers. It had to take him some time to write that much. He wanted me—his version of me—to know he's watching. He wanted to brag a little. He said he laughed at what we've done here. The new security. At the manhunt. He's confident neither will stop him from the goal. The game. He said Carolyn gave him a good game."

"And Tyler was practice. Everything points to his driving Tyler off the trail, way off, pushing him toward the river. Tyler was a healthy man, in good shape. And bigger, heftier than Howe. The conclusion would be Howe had a weapon. A knife doesn't work, not if Tyler managed to get any distance away. What's the game if you force-march some guy miles?"

She could see it now, the steps and the layers. And seeing it helped her stay calm. "We know he has a gun, and he knows the hills. He can track. He . . . he hunts."

"Yeah, you'd've held your own on the job. That's the game—the hunt. Pick the prey, stalk the prey, make the kill."

"And he's picked me because he believes I've violated sacred ground, sacred trust by building the refuge here. Because we share, in his head, the cougar as spirit guide. It's crazy."

"He also picked you because you know the land. You can track and hunt and elude. So you're a major prize."

"He might have come here before, for me, but Carolyn distracted him. She was young and pretty and attracted to him. She listened to his theories, certainly slept with him. And when she saw through enough to be afraid, or concerned, to break things off, he went after her instead. She became his prey."

Shaken, she lowered to the bench.

"It's not you, Lil. Not your fault."

"I know that, but she's still dead. Almost certainly dead. And there may be someone else dead tonight just so he could get his hands on a computer to send that to me. If he goes after anyone else, any of my people, I don't know what I'll do. I don't know."

"I'm less worried about that than I was.

"He's put you on notice," Coop said when she looked up at him. "He doesn't have to show you any more. Doesn't have to bait you or taunt you."

She took a breath. "Tell me. Is Brad staying at your grandparents' just because he likes Lucy's cooking, or did you ask him to so he could keep an eye on things there?"

"The cooking's a bonus." He got out a bottle of water, twisted the top off, and handed it to her.

She drank. "He's a good friend."

"Yeah, he is."

"I think . . ." She steadied herself with another long breath. "I think you can get an idea about someone by their friends."

"You need an idea when it comes to me, Lil?"

"I need an idea when it comes to ten years of you." She glanced toward the phone, wishing she could make it ring, make Willy call and tell her no one was hurt. No more death. "How do you stand waiting like this?"

"Because it's what comes next. This place is locked down. If he tries to come here, he'll trip an alarm. You're safe. You're with me. So I can wait."

Trying to keep her calm, she reached out, smoothed a finger over the petals of a daisy. "You brought me more flowers. What's that about?"

"I figure I owe you about a decade's worth of flowers. For fights, birthdays, whatever."

She studied his face, then went with impulse. "Give me your wallet."

"Why?"

She held out a hand. "You want to get back in my good graces? Hand it over."

Caught between amusement and puzzlement, he reached back to pull it out of his pocket. And she saw the gun at his hip.

"You're carrying a gun."

"I'm licensed." He passed her his wallet.

"You had clips in my drawer. They're not there anymore."

"Because I have a drawer all of my own now. Nice underwear, Lil. How come you never wear it?"

"Another man bought it for me." She smiled humorlessly when annoyance flickered over his face. "Or some of it. It didn't seem quite appropriate to use it on you."

"I'm here. He's not."

"And now, if I slipped that little red number on, for instance, it wouldn't pass through your mind as you're slipping it off me again, how he'd done the same?"

"Throw it out."

For very small, smug reasons, his clipped suggestion made her smile and mean it. "If I do, you'll know I'm ready to take you back—all the way back. What will you toss out for me, Coop?"

"Name it."

She shook her head and opened the wallet. For a time, for her own satisfaction, she studied his driver's license, the PI license. "You always took a good picture. Those Viking eyes, and the hints of trouble in them. Do you miss New York?"

"Yankee Stadium. I'll take you back for a game sometime. Then you'll see some real baseball."

With a shrug, she flipped through, and found the picture. She remembered when he'd taken it, the summer they'd become lovers. God, how young, she thought. How open and wildly happy. She sat by the stream, wildflowers spreading around her, the verdant green hills behind her. Her knees drawn up, her arms wrapped around them, and her hair free and tumbled over her shoulders.

"It's a favorite of mine. A memory of a perfect day, a perfect spot, the perfect girl. I loved you, Lil, with everything I had. I just didn't have enough."

"It was enough for her," she said quietly.

And the phone rang.

24

Willy followed up the phone call with a personal visit. Lil opened the gate for him by remote, and had a moment to think, At least, this is safer and easier. She'd switched from tea to coffee, and poured Willy a cup even as Coop went to the door to let him in.

She carried it to the living room, offered it to him.

"Thanks, Lil. I figured you'd want to hear the details in person. He used Mac Goodwin's account. You know the Goodwins, Lil, have the farm on 34."

"Yes, I went to school with Lisa." Lisa Greenwald then, she thought, a cheerleader, whom she'd disliked intensely because of Lisa's constant state of "perk." It made Lil's stomach twist just to think of how often she'd sneered at Lisa behind her back.

"I got a call from Mac not five minutes after I got yours. Reporting a break-in."

"Are they—"

"They're all right," he said, anticipating her. "They'd gone out for dinner and to their oldest boy's spring band concert. They got back and found the back door broken in. Did the smart thing, went right back out again and called me from the cell phone. Anyway, it seemed like too much coincidence, so I asked him if they had an e-mail account that matched the one I got from you. Sure enough."

"They weren't home. They weren't hurt." She sat then as her knees went shaky.

"They're fine. They've got a new pup since their old dog passed a few months back, and he was closed up in the laundry room. He's fine, too. I went by to talk to them, take a look at things. Left a deputy there to help Mac board up that door. It looks like he busted in, found the computer. Mac didn't shut it down before they left. Kids carrying on, he said, and just forgot. People do."

"Yes. People do. They went together all through high school. Mac and Lisa, Lisa and Mac. And got married the spring after graduation. They have two boys and a girl. The girl's still a baby."

Wasn't it funny, Lil thought, dazed, how much she knew about the once-detested Lisa.

"That's right, and they're all fine. The best they could tell on first look was he took some food supplies. Bread, canned goods, Pop-Tarts of all things, some beer and juice boxes. Left the kitchen in a state. Got the two hundred in cash Mac kept in his desk, and the money the kids had in their banks, and the hundred Lisa kept in the freezer."

He watched Lil's face, glanced at Coop, then just kept talking in that same easy way. "People don't seem to realize those are the first places any thief worth his salt is going to check. They need to take a second look when they're not so upset, to see if anything else is missing."

"Weapons?" Coop asked.

"Mac keeps his guns in a gun safe. Locked up tight. So that's a blessing. We got prints. We'll eliminate the Goodwins', and I'll go out on what I think's a damn sturdy limb and say we'll match the others to Ethan Howe. I'm planning to call the FBI in the morning."

He cocked his head at the expression that ran over Coop's face. "I don't much relish the idea of working with the feds, or having them take this investigation over, either. But the fact is it looks like we've got evidence that points to serial murder, and Lil got an e-mail threat. That's cybercrime. Added to it, it's a given that this fucker's—sorry, Lil—that his territory includes the national park. I'm going to fight for my stake in this, but I'm not going to worry about pecking order."

"When you match the prints, you need to plaster Howe's photo all over the media," Coop said. "Anybody coming into the area, using the trails, any of the locals, need to be able to ID him on sight."

"That's on the list."

"If he's using this aka, this Swift Cat, we might find something on it."

"Thirty-five miles per hour," Lil mumbled, then shook her head when Coop turned to her. "That's the peak for a cougar, and on a sprint. They can't run at that speed for any real distance. There are swifter cats. Much faster cats than the cougar. What I mean is . . ." She paused, pressed her fingers to her eyes to help line up her thoughts. "He doesn't really know the animal he claims is his spirit guide. And I think he gave me the name he's chosen because he believes we share that guide. I doubt he's used it before, or often."

"We'll do a little checking on it anyway." Willy set his coffee aside. "Lil, I know you've got your new alarms here, and the ex–New York City detective, but I can arrange for protection."

"Where? How? Willy, this guy covers ground fast, and he can and will go to ground and wait it out if I leave. He's watching this place, and he knows what's going on. The only chance you have of tracking him down is if he thinks I'm accessible."

"Lil gets volunteers and interns," Coop began. "There's no reason you couldn't put a couple of officers in soft clothes and have them go to work around here."

"I could fix that." Willy nodded. "Work with the state boys, with the park service. I think we could get a couple of men on-site."

"I'll take them," Lil agreed immediately. "I'm not being brave, Willy. I just don't want to go hide out, then have to face this all over again in six months, a year. Ever. I want it over."

"There'll be two men here in the morning. I'm going to start setting up what I can tonight. I'll check in with you tomorrow."

Lil caught the glance that passed between the men.

"I'll walk you out," Coop said.

"No you won't." Lil took his arm, held on. "If the two of you have something else to say about this, I'm entitled to know. Keeping information from me isn't protecting me. It's just pissing me off."

"I've placed Howe in Alaska at the time Carolyn Roderick went missing." Coop glanced at Lil. "It's just added weight. I tracked down a sporting goods store where the owner remembered him, and ID'd him through the picture I faxed him. He remembers him because Howe bought a Stryker crossbow, the full package with scope, carbon bolts, sling, and ammo for a thirty-two. He spent nearly two thousand, and paid cash. He talked about taking his girl hunting."

Lil made a little sound, thinking of Carolyn.

"I expanded my like-crime search after Tyler," Coop continued. "A body found in Montana four months later, male, mid-twenties, was left for the animals, and in bad shape. But the autopsy showed a leg wound— into the bone—the ME there concluded was from a bolt strike. If he still has the bow . . ."

"We could tie him up on the Roderick disappearance and the Montana murder," Willy concluded. "Odds are he does. That's a lot of cash."

"He got over three hundred from tonight's break-in, and what he took off of Tyler. It wouldn't take long, the way he works, to build up a cash supply."

"I'll add the bow and bolts to the APB. That's nice work, Coop."

"If you make enough calls, you can get lucky."

When they were alone, Lil went over to poke at the fire until the flames kicked up. She saw he'd brought his baseball bat, the one Sam had made him a lifetime ago. It stood propped against the wall.

Because this is home now, she thought. At least until we're done with this, he's home here.

And she couldn't think of that, not yet.

"It's harder to hide a crossbow than a handgun." She stood there, watching the flames rise. "He'd be more likely to carry the bow when he's specifically hunting. Maybe toward evening, or before dawn."

"Maybe."

"He didn't use a bow on the cougar. If he had it, if he'd used it, it would've given him more time to get away, cover his tracks. But he didn't use the bow."

"Because you wouldn't have heard the shot," Coop concluded. "Which is probably why he chose the gun."

"So I would hear it, and panic for the cat." She turned now, put her back to the light and the heat. "How much more do you know you haven't told me?"

"It's speculation."

"I want to see the files, the ones you put away whenever I come in."

"There's no point."

"There's every point."

"Damn it, Lil, what good is it going to do for you to look at photos of Tyler before and after they dragged him out of the river, after the fish had been at him? Or to read the details of an autopsy? What's the point in having that in your head?"

"Tyler was practice. I'm the main event," she said, quoting the e-mail. "If you're worried about my sensibilities, don't. No, I've never seen pictures of a body. But have you seen a lion spring out of the bush and take down an antelope? Not human, but take my word, it's not for the faint of heart. Stop protecting me, Coop."

"That's never going to happen, but I'll show you the files."

He unlocked a case, drew them out. "The photos won't help you. The ME determined the time of death somewhere between fifteen and eighteen hundred."

Lil sat, opened the file, and stared at the stark black-and-white photograph of James Tyler. "I hope to God his wife didn't see him like this."

"They'd have done what they could beforehand."

"Slitting his throat. That's personal, isn't it? From my vast police knowledge from *CSI* and so on."

"You have to get in close, make contact, get blood on your hands. A knife's generally more intimate than a bullet. He took Tyler from behind, going left to right. The body had cuts and bruises incurred perimortem, most likely from stumbling and slipping. The knees, hands, elbows."

"You said he died between three and six. Daylight hours, or just going to dusk on the later side of that. To get from the trail Tyler was seen on to that point of the river has to take several hours. Probably more if we agree he'd have driven Tyler over the roughest ground, the least likely areas where he'd have found help or another hiker. Tyler had a day pack. If you're running for your life, you'd shed weight, wouldn't you?"

"They didn't find his pack."

"I bet Ethan did."

"Agreed."

"And when he maneuvers Tyler to the right position, he doesn't shoot him. Not sporting. He comes in close for the personal kill."

She flipped through to the list of what the victim's wife stated Tyler had on him when he'd started for the summit. "It's a good haul," she added. "Victory spoils. He won't need the watch. He knows how to tell the time by the sky, by the feel of the air. Maybe he'll keep it as a trophy, or pawn it later on, a few states away, when he wants more cash."

She looked over. "He took something, some things from every victim you think he's responsible for, didn't he?"

"That's the way it looks. Jewelry, cash, supplies, articles of clothing. He's a scavenger. But not stupid enough to use any victim's credit cards or IDs. None of the MPs have had any account activity on their credit cards since they disappeared."

"No paper trail. Plus maybe he considers credit cards a white man's invention, a white man's weakness. I wonder if his parents had any credit cards. I'd bet not."

"You'd bet right. You're a smart one, Lil."

"We're the smart girls," she said absently. "But he buys a crossbow, not traditional Native American weaponry. He picks and chooses. He's full of shit, basically. Sacred ground, but he defiles it by hunting an unarmed man. For sport. For practice. If he really has Sioux blood, he's defiled that, too. He has no honor."

"The Sioux considered the Black Hills the sacred center of the world."

"*Axis mundi,*" Lil confirmed. "They considered—and still consider—the Black Hills the heart of all that is. Paha Sapa. Sacred ceremonies started in the spring. They'd follow the buffalo through the hills, forming a trail in the shape of a buffalo head. Sixty million acres of the hills were promised in treaty. But then they found gold. The treaty meant nothing, because the white man wanted the land, and the gold on it. The gold was worth more than honor, than the treaty, than the promise to respect what was sacred."

"But it's still under dispute."

"Been boning up on your history?" she asked. "Yeah, the U.S. took the land in 1877, in violation of the Treaty of Fort Laramie, and the Teton Sioux, the Lakota, never accepted that. Fast-forward a hundred years, and the Supreme Court ruled the Black Hills had been taken illegally, and ordered the government to pay the initial promised price plus interest. Over a hundred million, and they refused the settlement. They wanted the land back."

"It's accrued interest since then, and now stands at more than seven hundred million. I did my research."

"They won't take the money. It's a matter of honor. My great-grandfather was Sioux. My great-grandmother was white. I'm a product of that blending, and the generations since have certainly diluted the Sioux in me."

"But you understand honor, you understand refusing a hundred million dollars."

"Money isn't land, and land was taken." She narrowed her eyes. "If you think Ethan is into this because it's some sort of revenge for broken treaties, for the theft of sacred ground, I don't. It's not that deep. It's an excuse, and one that might make him think of himself as a warrior or a rebel. I doubt he knows the entire history. Bits and pieces maybe, and probably bastardized ones at that."

"No, he kills because he likes it. But he's chosen you, and this place, because it fits his idea of payback. That makes it more exciting, more satisfying. And his definition of honor's warped, but he has his own version. He won't pick you off when you're crossing the compound. It's not the game, it's not satisfying, and it doesn't complete the purpose."

"That's comforting."

"If I didn't believe that, you'd be locked up a thousand miles from here. Trying to be honest," he added when she frowned at him. "I've got a picture of him, a kind of profile, and it assures me he wants you to understand him, to face him, then to give him real competition. He'll wait for an opportunity, but he's getting impatient. The e-mail pushes it forward."

"It's a dare."

"Of sorts, and a declaration. I need your word, Lil, you won't let him goad you into that opportunity."

"You've got it."

"No argument? No qualifications?"

"No. I don't like hunting, and I know I wouldn't like being hunted. I don't need to prove anything to him, certainly not to myself by going out and doing a one-on-one with a homicidal maniac."

She went deeper into the files. "Maps. Okay, okay, we can work with this."

She rose, cleared everything else off the coffee table. "You've been busy," she said, noting he'd marked the map with incidents ascribed to Ethan Howe. "You're trying to triangulate locations where he might have his den."

"The sectors that seemed most likely have been searched."

"Next to impossible to cover every square foot, especially when you're looking for someone who knows how to move, and cover his trail. Here.

We found Melinda Barrett. Nearly twelve years ago. In that case, there was no indication he'd hunted her. No signs she'd run or been chased. The signs pointed to him following her up the trail. Stalking her, maybe. Or as likely just running into her. What set him off, made him kill her?"

"If the kill wasn't the goal, he might've wanted money or sex. They found some bruising on her biceps, the kind you'd get if someone gripped you hard and you tried to pull away. He knocks her back into the tree, with enough force to bash her head, open a wound. Bleeding."

"Blood. Maybe blood was enough. The wild scents blood, it spurs them." Lil nodded because she could see it, see how it might have been. "She fights, maybe screams, maybe insults him or his manhood in some way. He kills her—the knife, close-in, personal. If it was his first, it would have been a tremendous rush—and he was so young. A rush and a panic. Drag her off, leave her for the animals. He might have thought, probably thought, her death would be blamed on a cougar or a wolf attack."

"The next time we can confirm he came back, it was here. The refuge." Coop laid a finger on the map. "He made contact with you, tried to play on a shared heritage."

"And he met Carolyn."

"She finds him attractive, interesting, feeds his ego. And could probably tell him more about you, about the refuge. She meets a need, sex and pride, so he goes into her world. But it's not a good fit, and she begins to see him for what he is when he's out of his element. He follows her to Alaska, to close that door, to fulfill that need—stronger than sex—then winds his way back to you."

"And I'm in Peru. He has to wait."

"While he's waiting, he comes down at night, pays at least one visit."

"When Matt was here alone. Yes. And he disabled the camera, here. Only a few days before I was due back."

"Because he knew you were coming back. If someone else had gone to check it out, he'd have disabled it again. Until he got you."

"He assumed I'd come alone," she continued. "I like to go into the hills and camp alone. I'd planned to. He'd have been able to start the game if I had done that, and he might have won it. So I owe you."

"He probably thought he could take me out once he saw you had company. Eliminate me, take you. So I'd say we both owe countless nights on stakeouts and the ability to sleep light. Comes into camp here," Coop continued with his attention back on the map. "Heads back to camera site here, and doubles back to camp. Then it's to the main gate of the refuge to dump the wolf. Another pass at the refuge to let your tiger out."

"And to some point on the Crow Peak trail where he intercepted Tyler, to here, at this point by the river where he left him. Hits the Goodwin farm, which is about here. That's a lot of ground. The majority of it's in Spearfish, so he's at home here. Well, me too."

She glanced at her empty mug of coffee, wished more would magically appear. "Lots of caves," she added. "He has to have shelter, and I don't see him pitching a tent. He needs a den. Plenty of fish and game. His best cover, best ground would be in here." Lil drew a circle on the map with her finger. "It would take weeks to search that many acres, that many caves and hidey-holes."

"If you're entertaining the idea of going up as bait to draw him out, you can forget it."

"I entertained the idea for about two minutes. I think I could track him, or certainly have as good a chance as anyone they've got searching." She rubbed the back of her neck, where the lion's share of her stress had chosen to make camp. "And I've got a better chance of getting whoever's with me killed. So no, I'm not going to be bait."

"There should be a way to look at this and figure where he'll go next, or where he goes when he's done. There should be a pattern, but I don't see it."

She closed her eyes. "There has to be a way to goad him into coming out, to pull him into a trap instead of the other way around. But I can't see that either."

"Maybe you can't see it because you've had enough for one day."

"And you'd be willing to take my mind off this."

"The thought crossed my mind."

"In the interest of truth, I'll admit the thought crossed mine." She turned to him. "My mind's pretty busy, Coop. It's going to take some doing to distract me."

"I think I can handle it." Even as she reached out he rose, evading her.

"Straight upstairs, huh? I thought you might warm me up a little right here."

"We're not going upstairs." He turned off the lights so only the fire glowed, then moved to her little stereo and punched the button for the CD player. Music poured out, low and soulful.

"I didn't know I had any Percy Sledge."

"You didn't." He crossed back, took her hand to bring her to her feet. "I figured it might come in handy." He drew her in, and swayed. "We never did this much."

"No." She closed her eyes as Percy's magic voice told her what a man would do when he loved a woman. "We didn't do this much."

"We'll have to start." He turned his head to brush his lips over her temple. "Like the flowers. I owe you several years worth of dances."

She pressed her cheek to his. "We can't get them back, Coop."

"No, but we can fill them in." He ran his hands, up and down, up and down the tensed, tight muscles of her back. "Some nights I'd wake up and imagine you were there, in bed beside me. Some nights it was so real I could hear you breathing, I could smell your hair. Now some nights I wake up and you're in bed beside me, and there's this moment of panic when I hear you breathing, when I smell your hair, that I'm imagining it."

She squeezed her eyes tight. Was it her pain she felt, or his?

"I want you to believe in us again. In me. In this." He drew her back until his mouth found hers. And took her under, deep and breathless while they swayed in the gold shimmer of firelight.

"Tell me you love me. Just that."

Her heart trembled. "I do, but—"

"Just that," he repeated, and took her under again. "Just that. Tell me."

"I love you."

"I love you, Lil. You can't believe the words yet, so I'll just keep showing you until you can."

His hands skimmed up and down her sides. His mouth sampled and savored hers. And the heart that trembled for him began to beat for him, slow and thick.

Seduction. A soft kiss and sure hands. Easy, easy movements in golden light and velvet shadows. Quiet words whispered against her skin.

Surrender. Her body pliant against his. Her lips yielding to a gentle, patient assault. A long, long sigh of pleasure.

They lowered to the floor, kneeling, wrapped close.

Swayed there.

He drew her shirt away, then brought her hands to his lips, pressed them to her palms. Everything, he thought, she held everything he was in her hands. How could she not know?

Then he laid her palm on his heart, looked into her eyes. "It's yours. When you're ready to take it, to take me for what I am, it's yours."

He pulled her close so her hands were caught between them, and this time his mouth wasn't gentle, wasn't patient.

Need leaped inside her, alive and fierce, while his heart kicked its wild beat against her palms. He tugged her jeans open, and drove her roughly up and up, drove her higher even when she cried out.

When she went limp, when it seemed she melted to the floor, he covered her with his body. Took more.

His hands and mouth stripped her, left her raw and open, weak and dazzled. Her breath sobbed out, caught on a fresh cry when he thrust into her. He gripped her hands, held tight as her fingers curled with his.

"Look at me. Look at me. Lil."

She opened her eyes, saw his face washed in the reds and golds of firelight. Fierce and feral as that heartbeat. He plunged inside her until her vision blurred, until the slap of flesh to flesh was like music.

Until she'd given him everything.

She didn't object when he carried her upstairs. She didn't protest when he lay down with her and drew her close, his arms wrapped tight around her.

When he kissed her again it was like the first in the dance. Soft, sweet, seductive.

She closed her eyes and let herself dream.

IN THE MORNING, she rolled out of bed as he came out of the bath, hair still dripping.

"I thought you might sleep longer," he said.

"Can't. Full day."

"Yeah, me too. Some of your people should be here in about thirty minutes, right?"

"About. That's assuming they all remember how to work the new gate."

He crossed to her, skimmed a thumb down her cheek. "I can wait until some of them get here."

"I think I can handle myself alone for a half hour."

"I'll wait."

"Because you're worried about me or because you're hoping I'll use the time to fix you breakfast."

"Both." Now that thumb traced the line of her jaw. "I picked up bacon and eggs since you were out."

"Do you ever give a passing thought to cholesterol?"

"Not when I've got you talked into fixing me bacon and eggs."

"All right. I'll slap a couple biscuits together."

"I'll toss a couple steaks on the grill tonight. A trade-off."

"Sure, eggs, bacon, red meat. Screw the arteries."

He caught her hips, levered her up for a hard good-morning kiss. "So speaks the beef farmer's daughter."

She headed downstairs thinking it seemed almost normal, this talk of breakfast, of dinner plans, of full days. But it wasn't normal. Nothing was quite within that safe, normal zone.

She didn't need the scattered clothes on her living room floor to remind her.

She swept in there first, gathered them up to shove the whole armload into her laundry room.

Once the coffee got going she heated up a pan. Leaving the bacon sizzling, she opened the back door, stepped onto the porch to breathe in the morning air.

Dawn broke in the east, bringing the hills into soft silhouettes against the first light. Higher, higher still, the last stars were going out like candles.

She scented rain. Yes, she was a farmer's daughter, she thought. The rain would bring more wildflowers out, unfurl more leaves, and let her think about buying some plants for the compound.

Normal things.

She watched the sunrise and wondered how long he would wait. How long would he watch and wait and dream of death?

She stepped back in, closed the door. At the stove she drained bacon and broke eggs in the pan.

Normal things.

25

Tansy wasn't wearing the ring. Lil actually felt her spirits plummet; she'd been counting on some happy news. But when Tansy rushed over to where Lil and Baby were having their morning conversation, the ring finger of her left hand was bare.

Her eyes shining with distress, Tansy threw her arms around Lil and hugged hard.

Lil said, "Um."

"I started to call you last night. I was so upset. But then I thought you had enough to do and didn't need me adding to it."

"Upset? Oh, Tans." As the plummet became a dive, all Lil could do was return Tansy's crushing hug. "I know you can only feel what you feel, and you have to follow those feelings, but I hate that it upset you."

"Of course it upset me." Tansy pulled back, gave Lil a little shake. "Upset isn't even close to the mark when my best friend's being threatened. We're going to start screening your e-mail as of now. In fact, we screen all e-mails."

"E-mails?"

"Honey, did you take drugs this morning?"

"What? No! E-mails. The *e-mail*. Sorry, I saw you just drive up, so I didn't think you knew about it yet."

"Then what the hell did you think I was talking about?"

"Ah . . ." Flustered, Lil managed a weak laugh. "Got me there. I'm a little turned-around yet this morning. How did you find out so fast?"

"Farley and I ran into the sheriff last night after you called him about it. He—Willy—knew you were concerned about your parents, and wanted Farley to know what was going on. He went right home."

"*Farley* went right home?"

"Of course, Farley. Lil, maybe you should lie down awhile."

He didn't ask her, Lil realized as Tansy checked her brow for fever. Never had the chance to ask her. "No, I'm okay. Just a lot on my mind, and I'm trying to stick to routine. I think it'll help."

"What did it say? No." Tansy shook her head. "I'll read it for myself. I should've told you right away everyone's fine at your parents'. Farley called before I left this morning just to let me know."

"I've talked to them, but thanks. It's nice, you and Farley."

"It's weird, me and Farley. Nice and weird, I guess." She watched as Lil picked up the bright blue ball and winged it high over the fence, into the enclosure. Baby and his companions screamed in happy competition as they gave chase. "They're going to find him, Lil. They'll find him soon, and this will be over."

"I'm counting on it. Tansy, he mentioned Carolyn in the e-mail."

"Oh." Tansy's dark eyes sheened. "Oh, God."

"It sticks, right here, when I think about it." Lil fisted a hand at her sternum. "So, routine." She looked over to where Baby and his friends rolled and wrestled for the ball. "And comfort."

"There's always plenty of routine."

"You know what I'd like, Tansy? You know what would bring that comfort?"

"A hot fudge sundae?"

"That's a never-fail, but no. I'd like to be up there, hunting him down. I'd be comforted if I could be in the hills, tracking him."

"No."

"Can't do it." Lil shrugged, but her gaze stayed on the hills. "It would put others at risk. But it's something else that sticks right here. That I have to wait, just wait while others go after the person responsible for all this." She heaved out a breath. "I'm going around to check on Delilah and Boris."

"Lil," Tansy called after her. "You won't do anything stupid?"

"Me? And risk losing my smart-girl status? No. Routine," she repeated. "Just routine."

HE HAD A PLAN, and it was sweet. He believed it had come to him in a trance vision, and convinced himself his great ancestor in the form of a cougar guided him. He'd claimed Crazy Horse as his own for so long that the connection had become truth to him. The longer he remained in the hills, the truer it became.

This plan would take care and precision, but he was not a careless hunter.

He knew his ground, had his stand. He would lay the trail. He would gather the bait.

And when the time was right, spring the trap.

He scouted first, considering and rejecting several sites before settling on the shallow cave. It would do for his purposes, for the short term. Its location worked well, a kind of crossroads for his two main points.

It would serve as a holding cage.

Satisfied, he took a snaking route back toward park territory until he could ease onto a popular trail. He wore one of the jackets he'd stolen along the way, along with a pair of aviator sunglasses and a Chance Wildlife Refuge cap. A nice touch, he thought. Those and the beard he'd grown wouldn't fool any sharp-eyed cops for long, but it gave him a thrill to stay out in the open, to use good old Jim's little Canon to take photos.

He moved among them, he thought, but they didn't know him. He even made a point to talk to other hikers. Just another asshole, he thought, tromping around on sacred ground like he had a right.

Before he was done, everyone would know who he was, what he stood for. What he could do. He would be a legend.

He'd come to understand this was what he'd been born for. He'd never seen it prior to now, not clearly. No one had known his face, no one had known his name, not in all the years before. That, he realized, had to change for him to turn truly toward his destiny.

He could not, would not move on as he had in the past when he'd felt the hot breath of pursuit on the back of his neck, or feared—he could admit the fear now—capture. It was meant to be here, in these hills, on this land.

Live or die.

He was strong and wise and he was *right*. He believed he would live. He would win, and that victory would add his name to those who'd come before him.

Crazy Horse, Sitting Bull, Red Cloud.

Years before, before he had understood, he'd made sacrifice to this land. When the woman's blood had spilled, by his hand, it had begun. It had not been an accident, as he'd believed. He understood now his hand had been guided. And the cougar, his spirit guide, had blessed that offering. Had accepted it.

She had defiled that sacrifice. Lillian Chance. She'd come to the place of his sacrifice, *his* holy ground, where he'd become a man, a warrior, by spilling the blood of the woman. She'd brought the government there, in the form of the police.

She'd betrayed him.

It all made sense now, it all came clear.

It must be her blood now.

He traveled with a small group, merged with them as a helicopter buzzed overhead. Looking for him, he thought, and felt the pride fill his chest. When the group chose one of the many crossings over a narrow creek, he waved them off.

It was time to slip away again.

If he fulfilled his destiny, the *government* would surely have to disclose to the public what they'd stolen. And perhaps one day, the true people would erect a statue of him on that very land, as they had to Crazy Horse.

For now, the hunt and the blood would be their own reward.

He moved quickly, covering the ground—the rises, the flats, the high grass, the shallow creeks. Even with his speed and skill, it took most of the day to lay the false trail west toward the Wyoming border, leaving behind signs he thought, derisively, the blind could follow. He sweetened it with Jim Tyler's wallet before backtracking.

Once again he headed east through the pine-scented air.

Soon the moon would be full, and under that full moon, he would hunt.

LIL PERSONALLY PLANTED pansies in the bed across from Cleo's enclosure. They'd handle the frosts that weren't just likely but inevitable, and the spring snows that were more than probable for the next few weeks.

It felt good to get her hands in the dirt, and satisfying to see that splash of color. Since the jaguar watched her avidly, Lil crossed over to the path. "What do you think?"

Cleo appeared to have no particular bias against or liking for pansies. "If you're still waiting for some Godiva, you're doomed to disappointment."

The cat pressed her flank against the fence, rubbed back and forth. Interpreting, Lil went under the barricade. She watched Cleo's eyes as she approached, and watched them slit with pleasure when she stroked and scratched through the fencing.

"Miss that, don't you? No chocolate or poodles, but we can give you a little personal attention now and then."

"Doesn't matter how often I see you do that, I'm never tempted to try it for myself."

Lil glanced back to smile at Farley. "You pet horses."

"A horse may kick the hell out of me, but it's not going to rip my throat out."

"She's used to being touched, to being spoken to, to the scents and voices of people. It's not just humans who need physical contact."

"Tell that to Roy. Or Siegfried. Whichever one of them had that real contact with the tiger."

"Mistakes cost." She backed away, ducked under to join Farley. "Even a kitten will scratch and bite when it's annoyed or bored. Nobody who deals with cats gets out without a few scars. Were you looking for Tansy?"

"I wanted to see you, too. I just wanted you to know I'll be sticking close to home, so you don't need to worry."

"This screwed up your plans for last night."

"I was hoping I could work things out for a picnic maybe. That's romantic, right?"

"Meets the top ten requirements."

"But spring's a busy time around the farm and around here."

"Go raid the pantry in my cabin. Use the picnic area over there."

"Here?" He gawked at her. "Now?"

"I'd bet my budget for the next five years you've got the ring in your pocket here and now."

"I can't take that bet. I need to save my money." He looked back around, his face full of excitement and concern. "You think I could ask her here?"

"It's a pretty afternoon, Farley. She loves this place as much as I do, so yeah, I think you could ask her here. I'll make sure everyone gives you some room."

"You can't tell them why."

"Have some faith."

He had plenty of faith in Lil, and the more he thought about it, the more it seemed like the right thing. After all, he and Tansy had gotten to know each other right here at the refuge. He'd fallen in love with her here. And she with him, something he thought she was just about ready to admit.

Lil didn't have much in the way of picnic food, but he found enough to put a couple of sandwiches together. He took apples, a bag of chips, and two Diet Cokes—since that was all she had.

Then he nagged Tansy over to a picnic table.

"I can't take much of a break."

"Neither can I, but I want to spend what I've got with you."

She went soft, he could see it. "Farley, you just kill me."

"I missed you last night." He tipped her face up for a kiss before he gestured her to the bench he'd already brushed off.

She sighed. "I missed you, too. I really did. But I'm glad you went back. It was the right thing. Everyone's trying not to be jumpy, and that makes me more jumpy. I spend a lot of my time in what most people consider a danger zone. And there is risk, of course. But it's calculated and it's respected and understood. I just can't understand any of this. Humans are, to my thinking, the most unpredictable of animals."

"You got that scar right here." He reached out to trace the mark on her forearm with his finger.

"From a cheetah who saw me as a threat. And my fault more than hers. None of this is Lil's fault. None of it."

"We're not going to let anything happen to her. Or you."

"He's not interested in me." Tansy laid a hand over his. "And I'm spoiling this quick picnic. What've we got?" She picked up a sandwich, laughed. "Peanut butter and jelly?"

"Lil didn't have a lot of choices on the menu."

"She always has pb&j." Tansy bit in. "How are things at the farm?"

"Busy. Time for spring plowing soon. And we'll be turning some calves into steers shortly."

"Into . . . oh." She lifted a hand, made a scissor motion with her finger. "Snip, snip?"

"Yeah. It always pains me a little."

"Not as much as the calf."

He smiled. "One of those got-to-be-done things. Living on a farm, well, it's a lot like here. You get to see things as they are. You get to work outside, feel a part of things. You'd like living on a farm."

"Maybe. When I came out here to help Lil, I really thought it would be temporary. I'd help get her up and running, train some staff, and then go to work for one of the big outfits. Make a big name for myself. But this place got its hooks into me."

"You're home now."

"Looks like."

He drew the ring out of his pocket. "Make home with me, Tansy."

"Farley. Oh." She held up a hand, thumped the other on her heart. "I can't breathe. I can't breathe."

He dealt with the problem by spinning her around then shoving her head between her knees. "Take it easy."

"This is crazy." Her breath hitched and pitched.

"Just in and out a few times."

"Farley, what have you done? What have you done?"

"Bought a ring for the woman I'm going to marry. Couple more times in and out."

"Marriage is huge! Huge. We've barely dated."

"We've known each other a long time now, and we've been sleeping together regular the last little while. I'm in love with you." In firm strokes he rubbed her back to help her settle. "And if you weren't in love with me, you wouldn't have your head between your knees."

"That's your gauge of love? That I'm dizzy and short of breath?"

"It's a good sign. Now, are you ready to sit back up so you can get a look at this ring? Lil helped me pick it out."

"Lil?" She popped straight up. "She knows about this? Who else?"

"Well, I had to tell Joe and Jenna. They're my parents in every way that matters. And Ella at the jeweler's. It's hard to buy a ring without her knowing about it. That's all. I wanted to surprise you with it."

"You did. A lot. But—"

"You like it?"

Maybe some women could have resisted taking a good look, but Tansy wasn't one of them. "It's beautiful. It's, oh, it's gorgeous. Really. But—"

"Like you. I couldn't ask you to wear a ring that wasn't. It's rose gold. So that makes it a little different. You're not like anybody else, so I wanted to give you something special."

"Farley, I can honestly say you're not like anyone else either."

"That's why we suit. You just listen a minute before you say anything. I know how to work, make a decent living. So do you. We're both doing what we're good at, and what we like. I think that's important. This is our place, yours and mine. That's important, too. But most important is I love you."

He took her hand and kept his eyes, so clear and serious now, on hers. "No one's ever going to love you the way I do. Joe and Jenna, they made me a man. Every time I look at you, I know why. What I want most in this world, Tansy, is to build a good life with you, to make you happy every day of it. Or most every day, because you'll get mad at me sometimes. I want to make a home and a family with you. I think I'd be good at that. I can wait if you're not ready to wear this. As long as you know."

"I have all these arguments in my head. Rational, sensible arguments. And when I look at you, when you look at me, they all seem weak. Like excuses. You're not supposed to be the one, Farley. I don't know why you are. But you are."

"Do you love me, Tansy?"

"Farley. I really do."

"Are you going to marry me?"

"I really am." She let out a quick, surprised laugh. "Yes, I am."

She held out her hand. He slipped it on. "It fits." Her quiet murmur was thick and shaky.

Dazzled, he stared at the ring, then at her. "We're engaged."

"Yes." Now she laughed, full out, and threw her arms around him. "Yes, we are."

Lil kept the staff working on the other side of the compound as much as possible. She had to shift her own position to keep the picnic table in view when interns led a group around the habitats.

She told herself it wasn't like spying. She was just . . . keeping an eye on things. And when she saw Tansy go into Farley's arms she didn't quite muffle the cheer.

"Sorry, what?" Eric asked.

"Nothing, nothing. Ah, can you make sure everything's set up for the school group tomorrow morning? In the education center. Take a couple of the other interns along."

"Sure. Matt's going to do his exam of the new female tiger this afternoon. I was hoping I could observe. Maybe even assist."

"If Matt clears it."

"The word is you're going to take the barricade down between the enclosures."

"Yes. When Matt finishes the exam. She's still caged, Eric. It's a bigger cage, and it's clean, it's safe. Once we take the barrier down, she'll be free to interact with her own kind, and she'll be able, when she's ready, to roam her habitat, walk in the grass, run. Play, I hope."

"I wanted to make sure it wasn't just rumor. I hate what they did to her. Cleo was different. She was so sleek and arrogant. But this one, she just seemed sad and tired. I guess I feel for her."

"That's why you've been getting better at your work. Because you feel for them."

His eyes brightened. "Thanks."

Was she ever that young? Lil wondered. So that a compliment from an instructor or trainer put that look in her eyes, that spring in her step? She supposed she had been.

But she'd been so focused, so absolutely determined to carve out her route. Not only to reach the goal but to make up for what she'd lost. To make up for Coop.

She drew a breath as she studied the compound. All in all, it had worked out for her. Now it would be her decision, her choice if she wanted to open back up, take back what she'd lost.

She heard the steps on the gravel, slow steps, and whirled to defend. Matt wheeled back so quickly he slid and nearly went down.

"Jesus, Lil!"

"Sorry, sorry." Had she been braced like that all day? she wondered. "You startled me."

"Well, you scared five years off my life, so we're more than even. I want to set up to examine the female tiger."

"Right. Eric wants to assist."

"That's fine." Matt gave her just the lightest pat on the shoulder. For Matt, Lil knew, it equaled a hug from anyone else.

"There's a lot of inside work. You could be doing that."

"He should see me. If he's watching, if he's out there, he should see me. See that I'm doing what I always do. It's about power." She remembered what Coop had said. "The more I hide, the more power I give him. And hell, Matt," she added when she saw Farley and Tansy exchange a kiss by his truck. "It's a really good day."

"Is it?"

"Wait and see."

She stuck her hands in her back pockets and strolled toward Tansy as Farley drove away.

Tansy turned, and her shoulders went up and down with a bracing breath as she walked toward Lil.

"You knew."

"Let me see how it looks on you." She grabbed Tansy's hand. "Fabulous. Perfect. I am *good*. Though he actually picked it himself, unless my mental shove actually worked."

"It's why you were babbling this morning. You thought I was talking about Farley asking me to marry him. Not the e-mail."

"There was momentary confusion," Lil allowed, "but no babbling."

"He told me, just now, how he'd planned to ask me last night. He had a bottle of champagne and candles. He was going to set the stage in my apartment."

"And instead he went to take care of family."

"Yes, he did." Tansy's eyes went damp. "That's who he is, and that's one of the reasons this ring's on my finger. I figured it out. So he's younger and paler than I am. He's a good, good man. He's my man. Lil? I'm going to marry Farley."

With a laughing hoot Lil grabbed Tansy to dance in a circle.

"What the hell is this?" Matt demanded.

"I told you it was a really good day."

"So the two of you are yelling and jumping?"

"Yes." Tansy ran to him, leaped, and nearly knocked him over with a hug. "I'm engaged. Look, look, look at my ring!"

"Very nice." He eased her back, out of his personal space, and smiled. "Congratulations."

"Oh! I've got to go show Mary. And Lucius. Well, mostly Mary."

When she ran off, Lil just grinned. "See? A really good day."

FAMILY CAME FIRST, Lil reminded herself and tried not to worry as she sat at her parents' dining room table. Her mother wanted—insisted on—a celebrational family dinner, so she was where she should be. With them, and Farley and Tansy, with Lucy and Sam, who'd stood as Farley's unofficial grandparents. And, of course, with Coop.

But her mind kept turning back to the refuge. Security system up and running, she reminded herself. Matt and Lucius and two of the interns on-site.

Everything was fine. They were fine, her animals were fine. But if something happened when she wasn't there . . .

As conversation buzzed around them, Coop leaned over and whispered in her ear. "Stop worrying."

"I'm trying."

"Try harder."

She lifted her wineglass and made sure she had a smile on her face.

Late summer wedding. She tuned in. And here it was already April, so much to be done. Debates ran on the venue. The farm, the refuge. On the time. Afternoon or evening.

Did he know she wasn't there? Lil wondered. Would he try to hurt someone just to prove he could?

Under the table, Coop took her hand and squeezed. Not supportive and lover-like, but *cut it out*.

She kicked him, but pulled herself back. "If I get a vote, it's for here at the farm, afternoon. That way we can party right through the evening. We'll close the refuge for the day. There's more room here, and if we have any sort of bad luck with the weather—"

"Bite your tongue," Jenna ordered.

"Well, the house is more accommodating than the cabins."

"Close for the day?" Tansy pushed that single point. "Really?"

"Come on, Tans. It's not every day my best friend gets married."

"Oh, boy, we have to shop!" Jenna winked at Lucy. "Dresses, flowers, food, cake."

"We were thinking to keep it kind of simple," Farley put in.

To which Joe muttered, "Good luck, son."

"Simple's no problem. But simple still has to be pretty and perfect." Jenna emphasized the point by jabbing a finger in Joe's arm. "I hope your mother can come out soon, Tansy, so we can put our heads to-gether."

"There's no stopping her. She's called three times since I told her, and already has a stack of bride magazines."

"We'll have a girl trip when she comes. Oh, this will be fun! Lucy, we have to have a shopping safari."

"I'm already there. Jenna, remember the flowers at Wendy Rearder's daughter's wedding? We can outdo that."

"Simple." Sam rolled his eyes at Farley.

"Before you women get too far along and start talking about releasing a hundred doves and six white horses—"

"Horses." Jenna interrupted her husband by clapping her hands together in delight. "Oh, we could do a horse and carriage. We could—"

"Just hold on, Jenna. Farley's looking pale."

"All he has to do is show up. You leave the rest to us," Jenna told Farley.

"Meanwhile," Joe said, pointing a hushing finger at his wife. "Jenna and I talked about some practicalities. Now, the two of you might have something else in mind, or maybe you haven't thought about it as yet. But Jenna and I want to give you three acres. Room enough for you to build a house, have a place of your own. Close enough to make it easy for both of you to get to work. That is, if you're planning on staying on here at the farm, Farley, and Tansy's staying on with Lil."

Farley stared. "But . . . the land should go to Lil, by rights."

"Don't be an ass, Farley," Lil said.

"I . . . I don't know what to say or how to say it."

"It's something you'll want to talk to your bride about," Joe told him. "The land's yours if you decide you want it. And no hard feelings if you decide you don't."

"The bride has something to say." Tansy rose, went first to Joe, then Jenna, to kiss them both. "Thank you. You've treated me like family since Lil and I were roommates in college. Now I am family. I can't think of anything I'd like more than to have a home here near you, near Lil." She beamed over at Farley. "I'm the luckiest woman in the world."

"I'd say that's settled." Joe reached up to close his hand over the one Tansy had on his shoulder. "First chance we get, we'll go scout out that acreage."

Too overcome to speak, Farley only nodded. He cleared his throat. "I'm just gonna . . ." He rose, slipped into the kitchen.

"Now we've got something interesting to talk about." Sam rubbed his hands together. "We've got a house to build."

Jenna exchanged a look with Tansy as she got up and followed Farley.

He'd gone straight through and stood on the porch, his hands braced on the rail. The rain Lil had scented that morning pattered the ground, soaked the fields waiting for plowing. He straightened when Jenna laid a hand on his back, then turned and hugged her hard. Hard.

"Ma."

She made a little sound, weepy pleasure, as she pressed him close. He rarely called her that, and usually with a kind of joking tone when he did. But now that single word said everything. "My sweet boy."

"I don't know what to do with all this happy. You used to say 'Find your happy, Farley, and hold on to it.' Now I've got so much I can't hold it all. I don't know how to thank you."

"You just did. Best thanks going."

"When I was a boy they said I'd never have anything, never amount to anything, never be anything. It was easy to believe them. It was harder to believe what you and Joe told me. Kept telling me. I could be whatever I wanted. I could have whatever I could earn. But you made me believe it."

"Tansy said she's the luckiest woman in the world, and she's pretty damn lucky. But I'm running neck-and-neck. I have both my kids close by. I can watch them make their lives. And I get to plan a wedding." She drew back, patted his cheeks. "I'm going to be such a pain in the ass."

His grin came back. "I'm looking forward to it."

"You say that now. Wait until I'm nagging you brainless. Are you ready to go back? If you're out here too long Sam and Joe will have designed your house before you get a chance to say whoa."

"Right now?" He swung an arm around her shoulders. "I'm ready for anything."

26

Wicked, windy thunderstorms pounded through the night, hammered into the morning. Then it got nasty.

The first rattle of hail spat out like pea gravel, bouncing on the paths, chattering on the rooftops. Well-versed in spring weather, Lil ordered all vehicles that could fit under cover. She maneuvered her own truck through the mud as the golf balls began to ping.

The animals had enough sense to take shelter, but she watched some of the interns racing around, laughing, scooping up handfuls of hail to toss. As if it were a party, she thought, and the slashes of lightning cracking the black sky were just an elaborate light show.

She shook her head as she caught sight of Eric juggling three balls of hail, like a street performer while the cannon fire of thunder boomed.

Someone, she thought, was going to get beaned.

She cursed as a clump the size of a healthy peach slammed into the hood of her truck. Even as she squeezed the truck under the overhang on the storage shed she snarled at the new dent.

Not laughing now, she noted, as interns scrambled for the nearest

shelter. There would be more dents and dings, she knew. Shredded plantings and an unholy mess of ice to scrape and shovel. But for now, she
was warm and dry and opted to wait it out in the truck.

Until she saw a softball of ice wing into the back of one of the running
interns, and pitch her forward into the mud.

"Crap."

Lil was out and sprinting even as a couple of her other kids rushed to
pick up the fallen.

"Get her inside. Inside!" It was like being pelted by an angry baseball team.

She grabbed the girl, half dragged, half carried her to the porch of her
own cabin. They arrived wet and filthy, with the girl pale as the ice that
battered the compound.

"Are you hurt?"

The girl shook her head, and wheezing, braced her hands on her
knees. "Knocked the wind out of me."

"I bet." Lil flipped through the jumbled data in her brain to find
names for the two of the new crop of interns while thunder roared over
the hills like stalking lions. "Just relax. Reed, go in and get Lena some
water. Wipe your feet," she added. For all the good it would do.

"It happened so fast." Lena shivered, and her eyes stared out of a face
smeared with mud. "It was just like little ice chips, then ping-pong balls.
And then . . ."

"Welcome to South Dakota. We'll have Matt take a look at you. Are
you sure you're not hurt?"

"Um. No. Just sort of . . . wowed. Thanks, Reed." She took the water
bottle, drank deep. "Scared me. And still." She looked past Lil to where
the ice balls hammered the ground, and a vicious pitchfork of lightning
hurled out of the clouds. "Weirdly cool."

"Remember that when we're cleaning up. The hail won't last long."
Already slowing, Lil judged. "Storm's tracking west now."

"Really?" Lena blinked at her. "You can tell?"

"The wind's carrying it. You can use my shower. I'll lend you some clothes. When it's over, the rest of you report to the cabin. There'll be plenty to do. Come on, Lena."

She took the girl upstairs, gestured toward the bathroom. "You can toss out your clothes. I'll throw them in the wash."

"I'm sorry to be so much trouble. Taking a header in a hailstorm wasn't the way I wanted you to notice me."

"Sorry?" Lil turned from where she dug fresh jeans and a sweatshirt out of her dresser.

"I just mean we've been working mostly with Tansy and Matt since I got here. There hasn't been a lot of opportunity to work with you directly with everything that's going on."

"There will be."

"It's just that you're the reason I'm here. The reason I'm studying wildlife biology and conservation."

"Really?"

"God, that sounds geeky." Lena sat on the john to drag off her boots. "I saw that documentary on your work here. It was that three-part deal. I was home sick from school and really bored. Channel surfing, you know? And I hit the part about you and the refuge. I missed the other two parts, because—you know—back to school. But I got the DVD, the same one we sell at the gift shop. I got really into what you were doing, and what you said and what you were building here. I thought, That's what I want to be when I grow up. My mother thought it was great, and that I'd change my mind a dozen times before college. But I didn't."

Intrigued, Lil set the jeans, the sweatshirt, and a pair of warm socks on the bathroom counter. "That's a lot from one documentary."

"You were so passionate," Lena continued, rising to unzip her muddied hoodie. "And so articulate and *involved*. I'd never been interested in science before. But you made it sound, I don't know, sexy and smart and important. And now it sounds like I'm sucking up."

"How old were you?"

"Sixteen. Up till then I thought I'd be a rock star." She smiled and wiggled out of her wet jeans. "Not being able to sing or play a musical instrument didn't seem to be a problem. Then I saw you on TV, and I thought, now *that's* a rock star. And here I am, stripping in your bathroom."

"Your instructors gave you a very high rating when you applied for internship here."

Obviously unconcerned with modesty, Lena stood in her underwear and watched Lil with wide, hopeful eyes. "You read my file?"

"It's my place. I've noticed you work hard, and you listen well. You're here on time every morning and you stay late when you're needed. You don't complain about the dirty work, and your written reports are thorough—if still a little fanciful. I've noticed you take time to talk to the animals. You ask questions. There may be a lot going on, and that's cut into the one-on-one time I like to put into the intern program. But I noticed you before you took the header in the mud."

"Do you think I have what it takes?"

"I'll let you know at the end of the program."

"Scary, but fair."

"Go on and clean up." She started to leave, hesitated. "Lena, what's everyone saying about what's going on? How are you guys dealing with it? You talk," she said. "I was an intern once. I remember."

"Everyone's a little freaked. But at the same time, it doesn't feel really real."

"It'd be good if you all stuck together. As much as you can. Head over next door when you're done."

Lil went down to toss the clothes in the wash, ordered herself to re-member to put them in the dryer when they were clean. While thunder, distant now, echoed, she thought about the girl up in her shower, and realized Lena reminded her of Carolyn.

The idea gave her a quick shiver before she went out to start cleaning up from the storm.

AT THE FARM, Coop and Sam let the horses out to pasture. Sam limped a bit, and maybe always would, but he seemed sturdy and steady enough. Enough that Coop didn't feel the need to watch his grandfather's every step.

Together they watched the young foals play while the adults grazed.

"At least we hadn't gotten any of the spring crop in. Could've been worse." Bending, Sam picked up a baseball-sized hunk. "How's that arm of yours?"

"I've still got it."

"Let's see."

Amused, Coop took the ice, set, then winged it high and long. "How's yours?"

"Might be better suited for the infield these days, but I put it where I throw it." Sam plucked up another ball, pointed to a pine, then smashed the ice dead center of the trunk. "I still got my eyes."

"Runner on second's taking a long lead. Batter fakes a bunt, takes the strike. Runner goes." Coop scooped up the next ball of ice, bulleted it to his imaginary third baseman. "And he's out."

Even as Sam chuckled and reached for more ice, Lucy's voice carried to them. "Are you two fools going to stand around throwing ice, or get some work done around here?" She leaned on the hoe she'd been using to clean the ice from her kitchen garden.

"Busted," Coop said.

"She's mad 'cause the hail tore into her kale. Fine by me. I can't stand the stuff. Be right there, Lucy!" Sam brushed his hands on his pants as they started back. "I've been thinking about what you said about getting more help around here. I'm going to look into it."

"That's good."

"It's not that I can't handle the work."

"No, sir."

"I just figure you should put more of your time into the business. If we get somebody to pitch in with what needs doing around here, that gives you that time for the rentals and guiding. That's what makes practical sense."

"I agree."

"And I figure you won't be using the bunkhouse all that much longer. Not if you've got any sense or spine. If you've got that sense and spine, you'll be adding on to that cabin of Lil's. You'll want more room when you settle down and start a family."

"You kicking me out?"

"Bird's got to leave the nest." Sam grinned over at him. "We'll give you a little time first. See you don't waste it."

"Things are complicated right now, Grandpa."

"Boy, things are always complicated. The two of you might as well untangle some of the knots together."

"I think we're doing that, or starting to. Right now, I'm focused on keeping her safe."

"You think that's going to change?" Sam stopped a moment, shook his head at Coop. "It won't be what it is now, God willing, but you'll be working to keep her safe the rest of your life. And if you're blessed, you'll be keeping the children you make between you safe. Got no problem sleeping with her, have you?"

Coop barely resisted the urge to hang his head. "None."

"Well, then." As if that was that, Sam continued on.

"To get back to the business," Coop said. "I've been wanting to talk to you and Grandma about it. I'm looking to invest."

"Invest what?"

"Money, Granddad, which I've got."

Sam stopped again. "The business is doing well enough. It doesn't need a . . . what's it? Infusion."

"It would if we expanded. Built on to the stables, added pony rides, a small retail space."

"Retail? Souvenirs?"

"Not exactly. I'm thinking trail gear and supplies. We get a lot of customers who buy them somewhere else. Why shouldn't they buy their trail mix, water bottles, trail guides, and disposable camera when they realize their battery's dead from us? If we upgraded the computer, the printer, we could do photographs, make them into postcards. A mother's going to want a postcard of her little cowgirl sitting on a pony. She's going to want a dozen of them."

"That's a lot of add-on."

"Think of it as an organic expansion."

"Organic expansion." Sam snorted. "You beat all, Coop. I expect we could think on it. Postcards," he muttered and shook his head.

Frowning, he shaded his eyes against the beam of the sun that broke through after the storm. "That's Willy coming."

Lucy had seen him, too, and stopped to pull off her gardening gloves, push at the hair the wind blew around her face.

"Miss Lucy." Willy tapped the brim of his hat. "The hail sure did a job on your garden."

"Could've been worse. Doesn't seem to've hurt the roof, so that's a blessing."

"Yeah. Sam. Coop."

"Willy. Did you get caught out in that hail?" Sam asked him.

"I missed the worst of it. Weatherman never said a thing about hail today. I don't know why I listen half the time."

"That's about the amount he gets it right. Half."

"If that. Seems to've blown in some warm though. Maybe that'll stay awhile. Coop, I wonder if I could have a word with you."

"William Johannsen, if you've got something to say about that murdering so-and-so, you say it right out." Lucy fisted her hands on her hips. "We've a right to know."

"I guess that's the truth. I'm going by to talk to Lil, so it's not something you won't hear." With a nudge of his knuckle, he tipped up the rim of his hat. "We found Tyler's wallet. Or what we believe is Tyler's wallet. Had his driver's license and some other ID in it. No cash, no photographs like his wife said he had. But all the credit cards she listed."

"Where?" Coop demanded.

"See, now, that's the interesting thing. Well west of here, only about five miles from the Wyoming border. It looked like he was heading toward Carson Draw. The rain washed some of his trail, but once the men picked it up, they followed it well enough."

"That's a ways from here," Lucy said. "A good long ways."

Out of his current territory, Coop thought. Out of the hunting ground. "He took the pictures but left the ID."

"That's a fact. One theory is he figured he was far enough away from the search area to toss the wallet. Another is he just dropped it by mistake."

"If he wanted to toss it, he could've used the river, or buried it."

Willy nodded at Coop. "That's a fact, too."

"But this is good news, isn't it? If he's that far west and still moving, he's leaving." Lucy reached out for Coop's arm. "I know he needs to be caught, to be stopped, but I won't be sorry if that happens miles from here. So this is good news."

"Might be."

"It's sure not bad news," she shot back at Willy.

"Now, Miss Lucy, in circumstances like this, I've got to be cautious."

"You be cautious. I'll be sleeping easier tonight. Come on in and sit down a minute or two. I've got some sun tea cold and coffee hot."

"I'd like that, I would, but I've got to get on. I want you to sleep easier tonight, but I want you to keep your doors locked just the same. Don't you work too hard now. Miss Lucy, Sam."

"I'll be right back." Coop walked off with Willy. "How long to verify it's Tyler's wallet, and match his prints?"

"I'm hoping tomorrow. But I'm willing to put money down it's Tyler's, and that Howe's prints will be on it."

"Are you putting the same money down that he tossed it, or dropped it?"

"That's not a gamble I'm willing to take."

"I'd put mine on him planting it."

Willy pressed his lips together as he nodded. "I'd say we're on the same page of this book. It just strikes too easy. We barely find a sign of this bastard for days. Then he leaves a trail, even after it rains, that my nearsighted grandmother could follow. I may be small-time law, but I'm not as stupid as he thinks."

"He wants a little time, a little space, to prepare for whatever he has in mind. You make sure Lil understands that. I'll be doing the same when I see her, but I want her to hear it from you first."

"I'll do that." He opened the door of his cruiser. "Coop, the feds are putting their focus on Wyoming. Could be they're right."

"They're not."

"The evidence points there, so they're following the evidence. All I've got is a gut telling me he's hornswoggling us. That's what I'll be telling Lil."

He got in the car, tipped Coop a salute, and drove back down the farm road.

BY THE TIME Coop got to the compound, the dusk-to-dawn lights had glowed on. He knew by the sounds the animals made they were feeding. A group of interns, finished for the day, piled into a van. Immediately, Weezer rocked out.

A glance at the office cabin told him that was locked up for the night. Still, he made the rounds, over gravel, concrete, mud to offices, sheds, stables, ed center, commissary to assure himself all was empty and secure.

Lights shone in the windows of Lil's cabin. As he circled, he saw her—her hair pulled back from her face in a tail, the strong blue of her cotton sweater, even the glint of the silver dangles that swung at her ears. He watched her through the glass, the way she moved as she poured wine, sipped it while she checked something on the stove.

He saw the steam rise, and through it the strong lines of her profile.

Love rolled through him, over him, in one strong, almost violent, wave.

Should be used to it, he thought. Used to her after so much time, even counting the time without. But he never got used to it. Never got through it or over it.

Maybe his grandfather was right. Time was wasting.

He stepped up on the porch, pushed open the door.

She spun from the stove, drawing a long, serrated knife from the block as she whirled. He saw, in that moment, both the fear and the courage.

He held up both hands. "We come in peace."

Her hand shook, very slightly, when she shoved the knife back in the block. "I didn't hear you drive up, and didn't expect you to come in the back."

"Then you should make sure the door's locked."

"You're right."

Time might be wasting, Coop thought, but he had no right pushing now.

"Willy's been by?" Coop asked and got down a second glass.

"Yes."

He glanced at the stove, the bottle of good white wine. "Lil, if you're thinking of a kind of celebration dinner—"

"When did I suddenly go stupid?" She bit off the words. Snapping more out as she took the lid off the skillet and made him lift his brows when she poured the good wine over the chicken she had sautéing. "He's no more in Wyoming than I am. He made sure he left enough signs for them to follow, and might as well have put up a 'Here's a Clue' sign pointing to that wallet."

"Okay."

"It's *not* okay. He's trying to make fools out of us."

"Which is worse than trying to kill us?"

"It adds insult. I'm insulted." She grabbed up her wine and drank.

"So you're cooking chicken using twenty-five-dollar-a-bottle wine?"

"If you knew anything about cooking you'd know if it's not good enough to drink, it's not good enough for cooking either. And I felt like cooking. I told you I could cook. Nobody said you had to eat it."

After she'd slapped the lid back on the skillet he crossed to her. He said nothing, just grabbed her, tightening his hold when she tried to pull away. Drawing her in, holding her to him, saying nothing at all.

"He's up there somewhere, laughing. It makes it worse. I don't care how petty it is, it makes it worse. So I'm going to be pissed off."

"That's fine, be pissed off. Or look at it this way: He thinks we're stupid, that you're stupid. He thinks we bought his little game, and we didn't. He underestimated you, and that's a mistake. It took a lot of time and effort for him to make that trail, plant that wallet. He wasted it on you."

She relaxed a little. "When you put it that way."

He lifted her face to his, kissed her. "Hi."

"Hi."

He ran his hand down the length of her braid, wishing he could ask, demand, even beg. And let her go. "Any hail damage?"

"Nothing major. How about at your grandparents'?"

"To my grandfather's secret pleasure, they lost most of the kale."

"I like kale."

"Why?"

She laughed. "No good reason. There's a ball game on tonight. Toronto at Houston. Wanna watch?"

"Absolutely."

"Good. You can set the table."

He got out plates, laid them with the scent of cooking, of her, filling the air. He decided it wasn't pushing just to ask. "Is that sexy underwear still in your dresser?"

"It is."

"Okay." He glanced at her while he opened a drawer for flatware. "You need to pick a date this summer. I'll give you the Yankee schedule, and you can pick whichever game works for you. I can get Brad to send the plane. We could take a couple of days, stay at the Palace or the Waldorf."

She checked the potatoes she had roasting with rosemary in the oven. "Private planes, fancy hotels."

"I've still got my box-seat season tickets."

"Box seats, too. Just how rich are you, Cooper?"

"Really."

"Maybe I should hit you up for another donation."

"I'll give you five thousand to throw away the red number in the drawer upstairs."

"Bribery. I'll consider it."

"New York and the Yankees were the first bribe. You missed it."

She'd missed this, too, she realized. Just poking at each other. "How much to toss them all?"

"Name your price."

"Hmm. Could be steep. I want to build a dorm for the interns."

He turned back, head angled. "That's a good idea. Keep them on the property. They have more time here, probably more interaction with one another and the staff. And you'd have a number of people on-site at all times."

"The last part wasn't a consideration until recently. Which I just don't want to talk about right now. Housing and transportation aren't huge problems, but they always take some work. I want to build a six-room dorm, with kitchen facilities and a community room. We'd have room for a dozen interns. Fork over enough and I'll name it after you."

"Bribery. I'll consider it."

She grinned at him. "How does it feel? To be loaded?"

"Better than it did to be broke. I grew up with money, so I never thought about it. Part of my mistake when I hit college. I never had to worry where a meal was coming from or how I'd pay for shoes, that kind of thing. I blew through my savings and then some."

"You were just a boy."

"You were just a girl and you made a budget, and lived by it. I remember."

"I didn't grow up rich. You spent plenty on me, too, back then. I let you."

"In any case it was a come-to-Jesus when I got in a hole, which I compounded by going against my father and dropping out of college, wanting to be a cop. Still, I figured I could do it."

He shrugged and sipped as if it didn't matter. But she knew it did.

"I'd have the first chunk from the trust coming along so I could live thin for a while. I didn't know what thin was. But I found out."

"You must've been scared."

"Sometimes. I felt defeated and pissed off. But I was doing what I needed to do, and I was pretty good at it. Getting good at it. When he blocked the trust payment and froze my accounts, what there was of them, it turned desperate. I had the job, so it wasn't like I'd be on the street, but thin got thinner. I needed a lawyer, a good one, and a good one wants a good retainer. I had to borrow the money for that. Brad lent it to me."

"I knew I liked him."

"It took months, close to a year, before I could pay him back. It wasn't just the money, Lil, breaking my father's hold on the trust payment. It was, finally, breaking his hold on me."

"His loss. And I don't mean the control. He lost you."

"And I lost you."

She shook her head, turned back to the stove.

"I had to prove myself before I could be with you, and proving myself meant I couldn't be."

"Yet here we are."

"And now I have to prove myself to you."

"That's not it." Fresh annoyance shimmered in her voice. "That's not right."

"Sure it is. It's fair. A pisser, but fair. There's a lot of thinking time when you're working with horses. I've spent a good chunk of that thinking about this. You've got me on probation, and that's a pisser. You want to make sure I'm not going to leave again, and you want to make sure you want me to stay. But in the meantime, I get to have you in bed, and now and then I get a hot meal I didn't have to make myself. And I can watch you through the kitchen window. That's fair."

"Sex and food and occasional voyeurism?"

"And I can look in your eyes and see that you love me. I know you can't hold out forever."

"I'm not holding out. I'm—"

"Making sure," he finished. "Same thing." He moved, fast and smooth, and had her wrapped in a kiss, layered in the warmth, in the need. He let her go slowly, and with a soft, lingering bite.

"The chicken smells good."

She eased him back a little farther. "Sit down. It should be done."

They ate, and by tacit agreement turned the conversation to simple things. The weather, the horses, the health of her new tiger. They did the dishes together. After he'd checked the locks—the only outward sign of trouble—they settled in to watch the ball game. They made love while the waxing moon poured its light through the windows.

And still, in the night, she dreamed of running. A panic race through the moonstruck forest with terror galloping in her chest and her breath a harsh echo. She felt the sweat of effort and fear slick her skin. Brush tore at that skin as she fought through it, and she scented her own blood.

So would he.

She was hunted.

The high grass slashed at her legs when she reached the flats. She heard the pursuit, steady, always closer no matter how fast she ran, which direction she took. The moon was a spotlight, mercilessly bright, leaving her no place to hide. Flight, only flight could save her.

But his shadow fell over her, nearly bore her to the ground with its weight. Even as she turned, to face, to fight, the cougar sprang out of the high grass, its fangs bared for her throat.

27

A day passed, then another. There were reports of sightings of Ethan in Wyoming as far south as Medicine Bow, as far north as Shoshoni. But none panned out.

The search team in Spearfish thinned, and talk in town and the outlying farms turned to other matters. Spring plowing and planting, lambings, the cougar who'd perched in an apple tree in a yard not a quarter-mile from downtown Deadwood.

People agreed over pie at the diner, across the counter of the post office, between sips of beer at the bar that the man who'd killed that poor guy from St. Paul had run off.

The trail had gone cold.

But Lil remembered the dream, and knew they were wrong.

While those around her lowered their guard, she only strengthened hers. She began to slip a knife in her boot every morning. Its weight gave her peace of mind even as she resented the need for it.

Good weather brought the tourists, and the tourists meant increased donations. Mary reported their seven percent increase for the first quarter held steady for the first weeks of the second. Good news, Lil knew, but she couldn't work up enthusiasm.

The more settled and ordinary the days became, the more her nerves frayed. What was he waiting for?

She asked herself that question as she carried hampers of food, or hosed down enclosures, as she uncarted supplies. Every time she made her rounds of the habitats her muscles braced for attack.

She all but willed it to come. She'd rather see Ethan leap out of the woods armed to the teeth than wait and wait for some unseen trap to spring.

She could watch Boris and Delilah curled together, or see him lead, and her tentatively follow into the grass, and feel pleasure, a sense of accomplishment. But under it brewed worry and stress.

She should be helping Mary and Lucius plan the summer open house, or put real effort into helping Tansy plan her wedding. But all she could think was: When? When would he come? When would it be finished?

"The waiting's driving me crazy." Following another new habit, Lil circled the habitats with Coop after the staff had gone for the day.

"Waiting's what you have to do."

"I don't have to like it."

She wore one of their new Chance Wildlife Refuge hoodies under her oldest jacket, and couldn't seem to stop playing with the strings.

"It's not like sitting in a jeep half the night waiting for a pride of lions to come to the watering hole, or even sitting at a computer tracking a collared cougar for a report. That's *doing* something."

"Maybe we were wrong. Maybe he did head west."

"You know he didn't."

Coop shrugged. "Willy's doing the best he can, but he's got limited resources. There's a lot of ground up there, and a lot of hikers, trail riders, and campers making tracks."

"Willy's not going to find him. I think we both know that."

"Luck plays, Lil, and you have a better chance at getting lucky with persistence. Willy's damn persistent."

"And you have a better chance of getting lucky if you *take* a chance. I feel like I'm locked in here, Coop, and worse, just running in place. I need to move, need to act. I need to go up there."

"No."

"I'm not asking for your permission. If I decide to do this, you can't stop me."

"Yes, I can." He glanced at her. "And I will."

"I'm not looking to argue, not looking to fight. You've gone up. I know you've guided tours on the trail the last couple days. And we both know he'd be happy to hurt you if only to get to me."

"Calculated risk. Hold it," he ordered before she could debate. "If he tried to take me out, he'd bring back the full force of the search. He took the time and effort to point the arrow west and the FBI's followed it. Why bring them back? Second, if he was stupid or impulsive enough to try, I carry a radio, which I show every member of the tour how to use, in case of accident. So he'd have to take me out, and the entire group I'm guiding. Calculated risk," he repeated.

"And you get to sit your ass on a horse, ride. Breathe."

He skimmed a hand over her hair, a subtle show of sympathy. "That's true enough."

"I know you're going up hoping to find some signs, pick up a trail. You won't. You've got some skills, but they're rusty. And you were never as good as I was."

"Circles back to luck and persistence."

"I could go up with you, take a group up with you."

"Then, if he happened to catch sight of us, or you, he might take me out. Then he could force you off at gunpoint, so by the time anyone still alive radioed for help, you'd be gone. Well gone if he used the horses. Waiting means he moves first. He exposes himself first."

She stalked down the path and back. In his enclosure, Baby mirrored her move. The reflected motion had Coop's lips curving. "That cougar's a slave to his love for you."

She glanced over, nearly smiled herself. "No ball tonight, Baby. We'll play in the morning."

He let out a call that Coop would have called a whine if cougars were capable of it.

Lil ducked under the barricade, relenting enough to rub him through the cage, let him butt her head, lick her hand.

"Is he going to be pissed if I come over there?"

"No. He's seen you with me enough. He's smelled you on me, and me on you. A cougar's sense of smell isn't his strongest asset, but Baby knows my scent. Come over."

When he'd joined her, Lil put her hand over his, and laid it on Baby's fur. "He'll associate you with me. He knows I'm not afraid of you, or threatened. And he really likes to be rubbed. Bump foreheads with me. Just lean down, touch your forehead to mine."

"He smells your hair," Coop murmured as he rested his brow against hers. "The way I do. It smells like the hills. Clean, and just a little wild."

"Now rest your forehead on the bars. It's an offer of affection. Trust."

"Trust." Coop tried not to imagine what those sharp teeth could do. "Are you sure he's not the jealous type?"

"He won't hurt what I care about."

Coop laid his forehead on the fencing. Baby studied him for a moment. Then he rose to his hind legs, bumped his head against Coop's.

"Did we just shake hands or exchange a sloppy kiss?" Coop wondered.

"Somewhere in between. Three times I tried to release him to the wild. The first, when I took him and his littermates up into the hills, he tracked me back—to my parents. I'd ridden there to visit. You can imagine the surprise we got when we heard him, then opened the back door and saw him sitting on the porch."

"He followed your scent."

"For miles, and he shouldn't have been able to, he shouldn't have wanted to."

"Love adds to ability, I'd say, and desire."

"Unscientific, but . . . The second time, he tracked me back to the refuge, and the last, I had Tansy and an intern take him. That was guilt on my part. I didn't want to let him go, but felt I had to try. He beat them back. He came home. His choice. Good night, Baby."

She moved back to the path. "The other night I dreamed I was being hunted. Running and running, but he kept getting closer. And when I knew I was done, when I had to turn and fight, a cougar leaped out of the grass and went for my throat."

She leaned into him when he put his arm around her shoulders. "I've never dreamed of being attacked by a cat. Never. Not even after I'd been bit, or come out of some dicey situation. But this has done that. I can't keep being afraid. I can't keep being locked in here."

"There are other ways to get out."

"What? Going into the city to shop?"

"It's out."

"Now you sound like my mother. It'll do me good, take my mind off things. That's when I'm not hearing how Tansy wants her best friend and maid of honor with her when she picks out her wedding dress."

"So you're going."

"Of course I'm going." But she sighed. "Tansy's mother flew in today, and tomorrow we're off on our safari. And I feel guilty about being irritated about it."

"You could buy new sexy underwear."

She slanted him a look. "You've got a one-track mind."

"Stay on track, you eventually reach the finish line."

"I need the hills, Coop." Her fingers went back, tugging and twisting the strings of the hoodie. "How long can I let him take them from me?"

This time he leaned down, pressed his lips to her hair. "We'll take the horses down to Custer. We'll ride the hills all day."

She wanted to say those weren't *her* hills, but it would have been petty and pouty.

She looked toward their silhouette, blank and black under the night sky. Soon, she thought. It had to be soon.

Lil reminded herself, again, she liked to shop. Geography and circumstances meant she did a lot of that online, so when she had the chance to really dig into the colors, shapes, textures, smells of shopping in three dimensions, she did so with enthusiasm.

And she enjoyed the company of women, particularly these women. Sueanne Spurge had charm and a sense of fun, and got along like a house afire with Jenna and Lucy.

She liked the city, too. Usually. She enjoyed the change of pace, the sights, the stores, the crowds. Since childhood a trip into Rapid City had been a special treat, a day of fun and busy doings.

But now the noise annoyed, the people just got in the way, and she wanted nothing more than to be back at the refuge—which only the night before had begun to feel like a prison.

She sat in the pretty dressing room of the bridal boutique, sipping sparkling water garnished with a thin slice of lemon, and thought about what trails she would take if *she* had the opportunity to hunt Ethan.

She'd start on the flat, where he'd disabled the camera. The search had covered that area, but that didn't matter. They might have missed something. He'd killed there, at least twice. A human and her cougar. It was part of his hunting ground.

From there, she'd cover the ground to the Crow Peak trail, where he most likely had intercepted James Tyler. From there to the river, where the body had been found. From that point—

"Lil!"

Lil jolted back so fast she nearly tipped the water into her lap. "What?"

"The dress." Tansy spread her arms to model the off-the-shoulder ivory confection of silk and lace.

"You look gorgeous."

"All brides look gorgeous." A hint of impatience edged into Tansy's tone. "We're taking opinions on the dress."

"Um . . ."

"I just love it!" Sueanne clasped her hands together at her heart as her eyes filled. "Baby, you look like a princess."

"The color's lovely on you, Tansy," Jenna put in. "That warm white."

"And the lines." Lucy rubbed her hand up and down Sueanne's back. "It's very romantic."

"It's a spectacular dress," Lil managed finally.

"And it's an outdoor country wedding. Doesn't anyone else think this is, yes, spectacular, but too much for a simple, country wedding?"

"You're still the showpiece," Sueanne insisted.

"Mama, I know you've got Princess Tansy in mind, and I love you for it. I love the dress, too. But it's not what I have in my mind for my wedding."

"Oh. Well." Obviously deflated, Sueanne managed a wobbly smile. "It has to be *your* dress."

"Why don't we go hunt some more?" Lucy suggested. "Lil can help her out of that one, and into one of the others we've got in here. But maybe we missed the perfect one."

"That's a great idea. Come on, Sueanne." Jenna took the mother of the bride by the arm to steer her out.

"I love it, I really do." Tansy did a turn in front of the three-way mirror. "What's not to love? If we were doing something more formal, I'd snatch this in a heartbeat, but . . . Lil!"

"Hmm. Damn it. I'm sorry. I'm sorry." Setting the water glass aside, she rose to unhook the back of the dress. "I'm a terrible friend. I'm the worst maid of honor in the history of maids of honor. I deserve to wear puce organdy with two dozen flounces and puffy sleeves. Please don't make me wear puce organdy."

"I'm holding it in reserve," Tansy said darkly, "so watch your step. I know you didn't want to come today."

"It's not that. I just haven't been able to get my head here. But now it is. I'm keeping it here. Solemn swear."

"Then help me get into the one I hid behind the one with the enormous skirt. I know Mama wants me in a big white dress, and would like it better yet if it had a twenty-foot train and six million sequins. But I saw that one out there and it hit. I think it's the one."

It was the color of warm, rich honey, its sweetheart neckline outlined with tiny, delicate pearls. It dipped in at the waist then flowed out in a subtle flair. Ribbons crisscrossed the back down to the elaborate bow that flirted from the waist.

"Oh, Tansy, you look . . . edible. If it weren't for Farley I'd marry you myself."

"I glow." Tansy turned in front of the mirror, her face radiant. "That's what I want. I want to glow on the outside the same way I am on the inside."

"You really do. It's not spectacular. It's stunning and it's so absolutely you."

"It's my wedding dress. You have to help me convince my mother. I don't want to disappoint her, but this is my dress."

"I think—"

Lil stopped short as Sueanne bustled back in, leading the parade. Sueanne stared at Tansy, then pressed her hands to her mouth. Tears spilled out of her eyes. "Oh, baby. Oh, my baby girl."

"I don't think she needs convincing," Lil concluded.

Shopping did take her mind off things when she let it. And there was nothing quite like the fun of an all-girl day in the shops. Pretty dresses and pretty shoes and pretty bags, all guiltlessly purchased thanks to Tansy's wedding.

Intermission was a fancy lunch, which included, at Sueanne's insistence, a bottle of champagne. With the mood as bubbly as the wine, they went back to the task at hand, scouring florists and bakeries for ideas and inspiration.

Triumphant, they squeezed back into Jenna's SUV with their mountain range of shopping bags. By the time they dropped off Tansy and her mother in Deadwood, the streetlights burned.

"I bet we walked twenty miles." With a little groan, Lucy stretched out her legs. "I'm going to top off the day with a nice long soak in the tub."

"I'm starving. Shopping makes me hungry. And my feet hurt," Jenna admitted. "I wonder what I can eat in the tub."

"That's because you walked out of the store wearing new shoes."

"I couldn't resist." Jenna curled and uncurled her aching toes. "I can't believe I bought three pairs of shoes at one time. You're a bad influence."

"They were on sale."

"One pair was on sale."

"You saved money on the one, so it's not like buying them."

"It's not?"

"No," Lucy said in reasonable tones. "It's like saving on them. So look at it that way: you only bought two pairs. And one of them's for the wedding. Those you were obligated to buy. Really, you only bought one pair."

"Your logic is wise. And confusing."

In the backseat Lil listened to the old friends enjoy each other's company, and smiled.

She hadn't taken enough time for this, she admitted. Time to just sit and listen to her mother talk, to be with her, with Lucy. She had let that bastard steal that from her too, those little moments of pleasure.

That would stop.

"Let's have a spa day."

Jenna flicked a glance in the rearview. "A what?"

"A spa day. I haven't had a facial or a manicure since before I left for South America. Let's figure out when we can all take a day off and book a bunch of decadent treatments at the day spa."

"Lucy, there's someone in the backseat pretending to be Lil."

Lil leaned up, poked her mother's shoulder. "I'm going to have Mary call and book us as soon as I check my schedule and Tansy's, so you'd better let her know if you've got any day next week that doesn't work. Otherwise, too bad for you."

"Somehow I believe I can clear my schedule. How about you, Lucy."

"I may have to shuffle a few things, but I think I can clear the decks. Won't that be fun." She shifted to smile back at Lil.

"Yes. It'll be fun." And long overdue.

Lil got out when they reached Lucy's to stretch her legs and switch to the front seat. "Let me help you in with those."

"I bought them, I can carry them," Lucy replied.

At the back of the SUV, the three of them pawed through bags.

"That's mine," Lucy said. "That one's your mother's. This one, yes, that's mine. That one there. And, oh, my, I did go a little overboard."

With a laugh, Lucy kissed Jenna on the cheek. "I don't know the last time I had so much fun. 'Night, sweetheart," she said with a kiss for Lil. "I'm going to listen to Sam ask me why I needed *another* pair of shoes when I've only got two feet, then I'm putting these old bones in the tub."

"I'll talk to you tomorrow," Jenna called out, and waited until Lucy was in the house before heading down the farm road.

"What about you? Are you looking to soak or eat?"

"I'm thinking shoes off, feet up, and a big fat sandwich."

"You had a good day, and you're going to be a beautiful maid of honor."

"It's a great dress." Sighing, Lil let her head tip back. "I haven't done a shopping marathon like that in years. Literally years."

"I know it wasn't easy for you to take a full day away like this. And now you're planning a spa day. You're a good friend."

"She'd do the same for me. Plus, great dress, fabulous shoes, and assorted other items I really had no need for."

"It's more fun when you don't need them."

"Too true." Lil toyed with the new earrings she'd bought, and—like her mother and the shoes—had worn out of the store. "Why is that?"

"Buying what you need's the result of hard work. Buying what you don't need's the reward for hard work. You work hard, honey. I'm glad you took the time away. It was nice, wasn't it, seeing how happy and excited Sueanne is? She can't say enough about Farley."

"It makes you proud."

"It really does. It's so satisfying when other people tell you what a good person your child is. I feel so good about it, about knowing how welcome he's going to be in that family. You'll be happy, too, having her living so close."

"You want to bet Dad and Farley ditched the chess game and spent all evening playing with plans for the house?"

"No question. They'll probably be sorry to see me home."

When they got to the gate, Jenna stopped so Lil could swipe her card, and key in her code.

"I can't tell you how much better I feel knowing you've got this security in. Almost as good as I feel knowing you're not going home to an empty house."

"It's an odd situation, having Coop here. I want him here, but at the same time I'm trying not to get used to having him here."

"You're gun-shy."

"I really am. Part of me feels that I might be punishing him for something he did, or didn't do, said or didn't say, when I was twenty. I don't want to do that. Another part of me wonders if we're together here because of the situation, because I'm in trouble and he needs to help."

"Do you doubt he loves you?"

"No. No, I don't."

"But?"

"But if I don't hold something back, and he leaves again, I don't know if I'd get through it."

"I can't tell you what to do. Well, I could, but I won't. I'll just say nothing in this world comes with a guarantee. With people, with love, a promise has to be enough. When it's enough for you, you'll let go."

"It's hard to think straight or feel straight with this cloud over my head. I don't want to make a decision or take a step like that when everything around me is in such upheaval."

"That's very sensible."

She narrowed her eyes at her mother as Jenna set the brake in front of the cabin. "And wrong?"

"I didn't say that."

"Yes you did. Just not out loud."

"Lil, you're my daughter. My shining star." Reaching out, she lifted a lock of Lil's hair, let it slide through her fingers. "I want you safe and happy. I'm not content until I know you're both, as much of both as is possible. I love Cooper, so I'd be thrilled if you decide he's a part of making you safe and happy. But the safe and happy's what I want most for you, however you decide. For now? I like seeing his truck there, and the lights on in your cabin. And . . . I like seeing him stepping out on the porch to welcome you home."

Jenna slid out of the car. "Hi, Coop."

"Ladies." He walked down. "How'd it go?"

"You can judge that by the amount of bags still in the back. We considered renting a U-Haul for the loot, but we managed to stuff it and everyone in for the ride back. Barely."

She opened the back, began to pass him bags.

"Did you leave anything for the rest of the state?"

"Not if we could help it. There. The rest is mine, all mine." She turned, gave Lil a hug. "We don't do this often enough."

"I'd have to give myself a raise to do it more often."

"You call me tomorrow."

"I will."

"Take care of my girl, Cooper."

"Top of the list."

Lil waved her off, watched the tailgate fade. "Is everything all right here?"

"Fine."

"I should check, see if anyone left me any messages."

"Matt and Lucius were still here when I got home. They said to tell you things ran okay without you. Even though you wouldn't like to hear it."

"Of course I like to hear it."

"Then why are you frowning? I'm taking all this stuff inside."

"I'm just not used to being away all day." And now that she was back she wondered what had possessed her to suggest another day away.

"You were in Peru for six months."

"That's different. I don't care if it's illogical, it is different. I should do a circuit around the habitats."

"I already did." He dumped the bags at the base of the stairs. "Baby made do with me."

"Oh. That's good, too. I guess there's no word on Ethan, or anything in that area."

"I'd tell you if there were." He leaned down, kissed her. "Why don't you relax? Isn't stripping stores of all their stock supposed to relax the female?"

"That's very sexist, and mostly true. I'm starving."

"I ate the leftovers."

"I want a sandwich. A really big sandwich."

"Then it's a good thing I went shopping, too," he said as he walked with her to the kitchen. "Because you were out of bread and anything—other than peanut butter—to put between it."

"Oh. Well, thanks." She opened the fridge, and stood staring with her eyes wide. "Wow. This is a lot of food."

"Not if two people actually eat a couple of meals a day."

With a shrug, she pulled out packs of deli meat. "We did fancy for lunch, which means you end up ordering salad. Fancy salads. I nearly ordered a Reuben, but somehow it felt wrong. Especially since we had champagne. I just don't think you can have a Reuben and champagne at the same time."

He sat on the bench, watched her. "You had a good time. It shows."

"I did. It took me a while to change gears, get in the groove, whatever. But thankfully I did and will not be forced to wear puce and flounces at Tansy's wedding."

He cocked his head. "What is puce, anyway?"

"Every bridal attendant's worst nightmare. Tansy got the most fabulous dress. A killer of a dress, which mine will complement perfectly. Then there were the shoes. Watching Lucy and my mother in the shoe department is an education and a thrill. I'm a rank amateur in comparison. Then there were handbags."

She chattered about purses, then the flower shops, reliving little pieces of the day in the telling while she poured a glass of milk.

"We grazed through shops like a herd of starving deer. I think my credit card gasped weakly at the end of the day." She brought the sandwich to the table, plopped down. "God, my feet!"

Even as she bit in, she toed off her shoes.

"It's work, you know. The shopping safari. As physical as mucking out stalls."

"Uh-huh." He lifted her feet onto his lap, and began to rub, running his knuckles up her instep.

Lil felt her eyes roll back in her head. "Oh. This is probably what heaven's like. A huge sandwich, a glass of cold milk, and a foot rub."

"You're a cheap date, Lil."

She smiled and took another bite. "How much of my shopping adventures did you actually listen to?"

"I tuned out in the shoe department."

"Just as I suspected. Lucky for you, you give a good foot rub."

Later, when she hung her new dress in the closet, she thought it had been an exceptional day. Stress-free, once she'd put stress aside, and touched with moments of real joy and wonderful foolishness.

And her mother had been right, she realized as she heard Coop tune in for the baseball scores. It was nice to have someone who'd walk out on the porch to welcome her home.

28

Lil felt him touch her, just the lightest touch, a brush on her shoulder, down her arm. As if he reassured himself she was there before he got out of bed in the predawn dark.

She lay, wakeful now, in the warmth of the bed, the warmth he'd left for her, and listened to the sound of the shower. The hiss of water against tile and tub.

She considered getting up herself, putting on the coffee, getting a jump on the day. But there was something so comforting, so sweetly simple about staying just where she was and listening to the water run.

The pipes clanged once, and she smiled when she caught his muffled oath through the bathroom door. He tended to take long showers, long enough for the small hot water heater to protest.

He'd shave now—or not, depending on his mood. Brush his teeth with the towel slung around his hips and his hair still dripping. He'd rub the towel over it briefly, impatiently, maybe scoop his fingers through it a few times.

Oh, to have hair that didn't require fuss or time. But in any case, vanity wasn't part of his makeup. He'd already be thinking about what needed to be done that day, which chore to deal with first on the daily list of chores.

He'd taken on a lot, she mused. The farm, the business, and because of who and what he was, the responsibility of finding ways to keep his grandparents involved in the day-to-day while making sure they didn't overdo.

Then he'd added her, she thought. Not trying just to win her back but also to help her deal with the very real threat to her and hers. That piled extra hours, extra worry, extra work into his day.

And he brought her flowers.

He came back into the bedroom, moving quietly. That, she knew was both an innate skill of his and basic consideration. He took some care not to wake her, dressing in the half-dark, leaving his boots off.

She could smell the soap and water on him, and found it another kind of comfort. Heard him ease a drawer open, ease it shut again.

Later, she thought, she'd go downstairs to the scent of coffee, the scent of companionship. Someone cared enough to think of her. He'd probably light a fire, to take the chill off the house, even though he'd be leaving it.

If she needed him at any time of the day, she could call. He'd find a way to help.

He came to the bed, leaned down, and pressed a kiss to her cheek. She started to speak, but felt words would spoil the moment, would distract from what was happening inside her. She stayed silent as he slipped out of the room.

The night before he'd come out on the porch to greet her. He'd eaten the leftovers, and gone to the market. He'd walked with her on her evening check of the habitat.

He waited for her, she admitted. But what was *she* waiting for?

Promises, guarantees, certainties? He'd broken her heart and left her unspeakably lonely. It didn't matter that he'd been motivated by good intentions, the hurt still happened. Still existed. She feared it nearly as much as she feared Ethan.

In fact, Coop was the only man who'd ever had the power to break her heart or make her afraid. Did she want to live without that risk? Because she would never get there, not with Coop. Just as she would never, never feel so utterly safe, happy, and excited about anyone else.

As dawn streamed in the windows she heard him leave. The door closing behind him, and moments later, the sound of his truck.

She rose, crossed to her dresser to open the bottom drawer. She dug under layers of sweats to draw out the cougar he'd carved for her when they'd been children.

Sitting cross-legged on the floor, she ran her fingers over the lines as she had countless times over the years. She'd put it away, true. But she took it with her when she traveled, kept it in that drawer at home. Her good-luck piece. And a tangible piece of him she'd never been able to toss away.

Through that roughly carved symbol, Coop had gone with her to Peru, to Alaska, to Africa and Florida and India. He'd been her companion on every field study.

Twenty years, she thought, nearly twenty years since he'd taken a block of wood and carved the image of what he knew—even then—she valued.

How could she live without that? Why would she choose to?

Standing, she set the cougar on her dresser, then opened another drawer.

She felt a tug for Jean-Paul. She hoped he was well, and he was happy. She wished him the love he deserved. Then she emptied the drawer.

She carried the lingerie downstairs. A fire crackled in the hearth, and the scent of coffee tantalized the air. In the kitchen she put the nightwear in a bag, and with a smile ghosting around her mouth put it in the laundry room.

It would wait until he got home, she thought, because this was home now. For both of them. Home was where you loved, if you were lucky. Where someone would light the fire and be there when you came back.

It was where you kept the precious. A baseball bat, a carved cougar.

She poured a mug of coffee and, carrying it with her, went upstairs to dress for the day. It was a good day, she thought, when you opened yourself to both the joys and the risks of love.

COOP WORKED UP the first sweat of the morning mucking out the stalls. They had three group rentals booked for the day, two of them guided, so he'd need to load up a couple more horses and get in to set up. He needed to schedule a visit from the vet and the farrier, both at the stables and at the farm. He had to get in, check the website for future bookings.

And he wanted an hour, a good hour without interruptions to study the files, his notes, the map and try to find a new angle for tracking down Ethan Howe.

It was there, he knew it was there. But somehow he was missing it. A handful of men couldn't cover the hundreds of acres of hills, forests, caves, and flats. The dogs couldn't hold the scent when there was essentially nothing to hold.

A lure was needed. Something to lure Ethan out, just far enough to trap him. But since the only bait that seemed potent enough to accomplish that was Lil, he had to find another way.

Another angle.

He tossed another load of soiled hay into the wheelbarrow, then leaned on the pitchfork as his grandfather came in. Barely a limp now, Coop noted, though it generally increased if Sam stayed on his feet for several hours.

The angle *there,* Coop knew, was to get the man to take periodic breaks without making them seem like breaks.

"Just the man I wanted to see." Coop shifted to stand between Sam and the barrow before his grandfather got it in his head to haul the manure out to the pile. "Do me a favor, will you? We need vet and farrier appointments here and at the stables. If you could set those up it would save me some time today."

"Sure. I told you I'd see to the mucking out."

"Right. I guess I forgot. Well, it's nearly done."

"Boy, you don't forget a damn thing. Now hand over that pitchfork."

"Yes, sir."

"In case you're working your brains trying to find other ways to keep me out of trouble and in the rocking chair, I'll ease your mind." With the grace of long experience, Sam went to work on the last stall. "Joe and Farley are going to give me some time today helping check fences. I'm going to hire the young Hossenger boy to do some chores around here, before and after school. If he works out, I'll keep him on through the summer. He's got it in his head he wants to work with horses. We'll give him a try."

"Okay."

"He's got a strong back and he's not an idiot. I was talking to Bob Brown yesterday. He tells me his granddaughter's looking for a job. Girl can ride, and she's thinking about asking you if you need another guide."

"I could use one, especially with the season coming up. Does she know the trails?"

"Bob says she does, and she's got a head on her shoulders. You can talk to her yourself, and decide."

"I'll do that."

Sam puffed out his cheeks. "Jessie Climp teaches over at the elementary, and she's looking for summer work. You might want to talk to her. She's been around horses all her life, and she's good with kids. Might be she'd do fine for those pony rides we're adding in."

Coop smiled. So they'd discussed the changes and additions he wanted to make. "I'll talk to her."

"New computers and what-all, I'm leaving to you and Lucy. I don't want any more to do with them than I have to."

"We'll look into that, first chance."

"As for adding on, could be I'll talk to Quint about drawing something up for that. I had a conversation with Mary Blunt about this retail business, and she tells me Lil's place does a good turn on things like post-cards and such."

"You've been busy."

"I saw the doctor yesterday. He says I'm fit and I'm sound. The leg's healed up." To prove it, Sam gave his thigh a smack. "At my age I'm going to have to pamper it some, but I can walk and stand and I can sit a horse and ride a plow. So I'll be taking on some of the guideds again. You're not here to work yourself to the bone—that's not what your grandmother and me want."

"I'm a long way from the bone."

As Coop had, Sam leaned on the pitchfork. "I've been dug in about hiring on. Don't like change. But things change whether you like it or not, and the fact is we've got a good business going with the rentals. Better than we ever expected. We need to hire on more help there. We need more help around the farm so you can do what you came out here to do, and if that's adding some things, changing them some, that's the way it is."

"More help's not going to hurt my feelings, but I'm doing what I came out here to do, whether we add on or change a thing."

"You came out to help your crippled grandfather." Sam did a bounce and kick that had Coop laughing. "Do I look crippled?"

"No, but you don't look like Fred Astaire either."

Sam wagged the pitchfork. "You came back to start digging in the roots you planted when you were just a boy. To run the horse business and help with the farm."

"Like I said, I'm doing what I came out to do."

"Not all." This time Sam pointed a finger. "Are you married to that girl? Did you just forget to invite me to the wedding?"

"I didn't come out here to marry Lil. I thought she was going to marry someone else."

"Had that been the case, you'd've been working out ways to win her away from that French guy ten minutes after setting eyes on her again."

"Maybe."

Pleased, Sam nodded. "You would've done it, too. Anyway, we're hiring on, and we're adding on. Your grandma and me decided on it."

"Okay. I'll make it work for you, Grandpa."

"You make it work for you, I expect it'll work for me. And you'll have time to do everything you came out here to do. I'll finish up here. You go in and sweet-talk your grandmother out of some breakfast before you go on. She's got the start of her spring cleaning in mind today, so God help me. I got the names and phone numbers of those I told you about in the kitchen."

"I'll haul this load out first."

"Do you think I haven't got the muscle for that?"

"Grandpa, I figure you can haul your share of shit and everyone else's, but it's on my way."

Coop wheeled out the barrow while Sam guffawed. He headed to the manure pile with a grin.

IN THE CHANCE kitchen, breakfast was on. Farley plowed into flapjacks, dazzled by his luck. Along with them were sausage and hash browns. A kingly breakfast, in his mind, for the middle of the week.

"Our stomachs are getting full because Jenna emptied my wallet yesterday."

Jenna bumped Joe's shoulder with her elbow, then topped off his coffee. It did ease the guilt of the sting she put on their credit card. "That's *our* wallet, mister."

"It's still empty."

She laughed and sat to look over her grocery list, the list for the feed store, and other errands. "It's market day, so I'm going to be putting another dent in that tin can with the spare cash you've got buried outside."

"I used to think you really had one of those," Farley said between bites.

"What makes you think I don't? Take my advice, Farley, get yourself a tin can and bury it deep. A married man needs some backup."

Jenna's eyes twinkled with humor even as she narrowed them. "I know where everything's buried around here. And just where to bury *you* where no one will ever find the body if you're not careful."

"A woman who can threaten your life before you've finished breakfast is the only kind of woman worth having," Joe told Farley.

"I've got one of those. I'm a lucky man."

"The two of you lucky men better finish up and get out of here if you expect to get your work done, then help Sam."

"We'll be the best part of the day. We'll have the radio if you need anything."

"I've got my own full day. Lucy's packing you two lunch so you won't starve, or have need to come back in before you're done. I'll be heading into town later on, then swinging by Lucy's. She's started her spring cleaning, so I'm picking up what she needs at the market."

"Can you go by the hardware? I need a couple things."

"Put it on the list."

Joe wrote down what he needed while he finished his coffee. "We can call the dogs in if you want them around today."

"I'll be leaving in a couple hours anyway. Let them have a good run with you. Are you home for supper, Farley?"

"Well, Tansy's mom's going back today, so I was thinking . . ."

"I know what you're thinking. I'll see you in the morning, then." She added to her list while Farley cleared the table.

"I'll load up the tools," he said. "Thanks for breakfast, Jenna."

When they were alone, Joe winked at his wife. "We'll have the house to ourselves tonight, so I was thinking . . ."

She laughed. "I know what you're thinking, too." She leaned over for the kiss. "Get going so you can get back. And don't work so hard you've got nothing left for what you're thinking."

"I've always got something left for that."

She smiled as she finished her lists in the quiet kitchen, because that was the pure truth.

LIL HELPED CLEAN and hose down the enclosures before going into the offices. It was dental hygiene day at the refuge, so Matt and several of the interns would be busy drugging animals and cleaning teeth. And a shipment of chicken was due to arrive that morning. More interns busy unloading and storing. The winch on the door of the lion's habitat had made unfortunate noises that morning as she'd lowered it to keep Sheba out of the enclosure while they'd cleaned and disinfected it. Maintenance on the list, she thought, and some prayers that it didn't need replacement.

Maybe one day she'd be able to afford hydraulics, but that was not today.

"Don't you look bright and happy this morning," Mary commented.

"Do I?"

"Yes, you do." Mary tipped down her cheaters. "Good news?"

"No news, so I suppose that's good. It's going to hit seventy today, a veritable heat wave. Forecasters claim it'll hang around through tomorrow before we drop about twenty degrees. We do need more feed for the petting zoo."

"I ordered it yesterday."

"I've got news." Lucius waved the whip of red licorice in his hand. "I just checked the website. We're up to five thousand dollars in donations attached to Delilah. People are all excited about her, and her and Boris. It's the love story that's done it, I think."

"If it is, we're going to generate a romance for every animal in here."

"They've gotten more hits than any of the others on the webcam this week, and more comments. I was thinking we could update the bios on all the animals, juice them up a little. And replace some of the photos, maybe do a couple of short videos."

"That's good. And you know what, Lucius, maybe you could get some videos of Matt and his interns working on the dental. It's not sexy, but it shows what kind of care we give them, how much work's involved. It's educational, plus it may stir up donations from people who don't realize what goes into tending them."

"Sure, but it would work better if you wrote up a little piece on it. Something fun that talks about how people hate to go to the dentist and stuff like that."

"I'll play with something."

She went into her office to work on a piece she hoped to pitch for pay on Delilah's rescue. She'd beef it up with the romance angle with Boris, she decided. Good nutrition, proper care, and housing all mattered, she mused, but the connection to another living thing made life rich.

Nodding, she sat down to work on it, and thought romance was certainly in the air.

He was ready, fully prepared. It had taken hours of work, but he felt everything he needed and wanted was now in place. Timing would be an unknown, a risk factor, but it would be worth it. In fact, it would be more exciting, more *important* with that unknown.

He was ready to kill, here and now, and take that risk as well. But as he watched, hidden, he lowered the crossbow. He might not have to kill to retrieve the bait. It would be better if he could make this clean. Take less of his time, his energy.

And make the real hunt-and-kill that much more satisfying.

Look at them, he thought, look at them going about their business, their useless business, without a clue he was close. No idea they were being watched.

He could kill them so easily. As easy—easier—than shooting a buck at his watering hole.

But wouldn't she try harder, run faster, fight more viciously if he let them keep their worthless lives? Too much blood and she might lose heart.

He couldn't have that. He'd waited too long, worked too hard.

So he watched them load the fencing. Fucking farmers, making their rooms out of the land. His land. Trapping their mindless cattle, animals not even worth the hunt.

Go on, *go,* he urged them, setting his teeth as their voices and laughter carried to him. Go. Everything will have changed when you get back. Yes, it was better to let them live, let them suffer when they realized what he'd done right under their noses.

Their tears would be sweeter than their blood.

He smiled as the dogs raced and ran and leaped in anticipation. He'd been resigned to killing the dogs, but he'd have been sorry for it. Now, it seemed, even that blood could be spared.

They rode off, the dogs in joyful pursuit. And the little farm in the valley of the hills went quiet. Still he waited. He wanted them well away, out of sight, out of hearing before he broke cover.

He'd watched the women many times in the past, studied the routine of the farm as he would any herd he stalked. She was strong, and he knew they had weapons inside the house. When he took her, he'd take her quickly.

He circled behind the barn, moving fast and silent. In his mind he wore buckskin and moccasins. His face bore the symbols of the warrior.

Birds sang, and some of the cattle lowed. He heard the chickens humming, and as he neared the house, the sound of the woman's voice singing.

His mother hadn't sung. She'd kept her head down, kept her mouth shut. She'd done what she was told to do or she got the boot. In the end his father had had no choice but to kill her. As he'd explained, she'd stolen from him. Held back her tips. Hoarded money. Lied.

A worthless white bitch, his father had explained when they'd buried her deep. A mistake. Women were no damn good, and white women the worst of the bad.

It had been an important lesson to learn.

He eased up to the side window, letting the lay of the kitchen come into his head from the times he'd scouted it. He could hear clanking and clattering. Doing the dishes, he thought, and when he risked a look, he saw—pleased—that she had her back to him as she loaded the dishwasher. Pans stood stacked on the counter, and her hips moved as she sang.

He wondered what it would be like to rape her, then dismissed the idea. Rape was beneath him. Just as she was beneath him. He wouldn't soil himself with her.

She was bait. Nothing more.

Water ran in the sink, pots clattered. Under the cover of the kitchen noise, he stepped lightly to the back door, tried the knob.

He shook his head, vaguely disappointed it wasn't locked. He'd visualized kicking it in, and the shock on her face when he did. Instead, he merely pushed it open, stepped inside.

She spun around, a skillet in her hand. As she raised it to strike or throw he simply lifted the crossbow. "I wouldn't, but you go ahead if you want this bolt in your belly."

She'd gone white, so her eyes shone black against her skin. He remembered then she had some of his blood. But she'd let it go pale. She'd ignored her heritage. Slowly, she set the pan down.

"Hello, Jenna," he said.

He watched her throat work before she spoke, enjoyed the fear. "Hello, Ethan."

"Outside." He plucked her cell phone out of its charger on the counter, stuck it in his back pocket. "I can put one of these in your foot and drag you," he said when she didn't move, "or you can walk. That's up to you."

Giving him as wide a berth as possible, she went to the door, and out to the porch. He closed the door behind them.

"Keep moving. You're going to do exactly as I say and exactly when I say it. If you try to run, you'll find out how much faster a bolt is than you are."

"Where are we going?"

"You'll find out when we get there." He shoved her forward when he decided she wasn't moving fast enough.

"Ethan, they're looking for you. Sooner or later they'll find you."

"They're idiots. Nobody finds me unless I want to be found." He forced her across the farmyard toward the trees.

"Why are you doing this?"

He watched her head move, left to right, and knew she was looking for a place to run, gauging her chances. He almost wished she'd risk it. As Carolyn had. *That* had been interesting.

"It's what I am. What I do."

"Kill?"

"Hunt. Killing's the end of the game. Against the tree, face-first." He pushed her. She threw her hands out to catch herself, scraping her palms on the bark. "Move, and I'll hurt you."

"What have we done?" She tried to think, to find a way out, but couldn't push past the fear. It crawled inside her, crawled over her skin until there was nothing else. "What have we done to you?"

"This is sacred ground." He looped a rope around her waist, pulled it tight enough to stop her breath. "It's mine. And you, you're worse than the rest. You have Sioux blood."

"I love the land." *Think, think, think!* "I—my family has always honored and respected it."

"Liar." He pushed her face against the bark, drawing blood. When she cried out, he yanked her back by the hair. "Put this on, zip it up." He thrust a dark blue windbreaker into her hands. "And pull up the hood. We're going for a hike, Jenna. Listen close. If we run into anyone, you keep your mouth shut, your head down, and just do what I say. If you make a move, try to get help, I'll kill whoever you speak to. Then they're on your head. Understand?"

"Yes. Why don't you just kill me now?"

He smiled widely. "We have places to go and people to see."

"You're going to try to use me to get to Lil, and I won't let you."

He grabbed her hair again, yanked until she saw stars dancing. "I can use you dead as easy as alive. Alive's more fun, but dead works." He patted the knife sheathed on his belt. "Do you think she'd recognize your hand if I cut it off and sent it to her? We can try that. What do you think?"

"No." Tears born of helplessness and pain tracked down her cheeks. "Please."

"Then do what I tell you. Put this on." He handed her a battered backpack. "We're just a couple of hikers." He gave the rope a yank. "And one of us is on a short leash. Now, walk. Keep up or you'll pay for it."

He avoided the trail as much as possible, kept a hard pace over rough ground. If she stumbled, he yanked or dragged. And since he seemed to enjoy it, Jenna stopped any attempt to slow him down.

She knew they skirted the edges of her daughter's land, and her heart thundered. "Why do you want to hurt Lil? Look at what she's done. She's preserving the land, giving shelter and care to animals. You're Sioux. You respect animals."

"She puts them in cages so people can stare at them. For money."

"No, she's dedicated her life to saving them, to educating people."

"Feeding them like pets." He gave Jenna another shove when she paused. "Taking what should be free and caging it. That's what they want to do with me. Cage me for doing what I was born to do."

"Everything she's done has been to preserve the wildlife and the land."

"It's not her land! They're not her animals! When I'm done with her, I'll free them all, and they'll hunt as I hunt. I'll burn her place to the ground. Then yours, then all the rest."

His face shone with madness and purpose. "Purify."

"Then why did you kill the others? James Tyler? Why?"

"The hunt. When I hunt to eat, it's with respect. The rest? It's sport. But with Lil, it's both. She has my respect. We're connected. By blood, by fate. She found my first kill. I knew someday we'd compete."

"Ethan, you were only a boy. We can—"

"I was a man. I thought, at first, it was an accident. I liked her. I wanted to talk to her, to touch her. But she pushed me away. She cursed at me. Struck me. She had no right."

He yanked the rope so she stumbled against him. "No right."

"No." Her heart skidding, Jenna nodded. "No right."

"Then her blood was on my hands, and I was afraid. I admit it. I had fear. But I was a man and knew what should be done. I left her as a token to the wild, and it was the cougar who came for her. My spirit guide. And it was beautiful. I gave back to the land what had been taken. That's when I became free."

"Ethan, I need to rest. You have to let me rest."

"You'll rest when I say."

"I'm not as strong as you are. God, I'm old enough to be your mother; I can't keep up."

He paused, and she saw a flicker of hesitation on his face. She swallowed on her dry throat. "What happened to your mother, Ethan?"

"She got what she deserved."

"Do you miss her? Do you—"

"Shut up! Just shut up about her. I didn't need her. I'm a man."

"Even a man starts as a boy and he—"

She broke off when he closed his hand over her mouth. His eyes scanned the trees. "Someone's coming. Keep your head down. Your mouth shut."

29

She felt Ethan's arm go around her waist, to keep her still, she imagined, and to cover the rope snaking from under the jacket. She prayed for the life of whoever crossed their path, and at the same time prayed they would sense trouble. She didn't dare give them a sign, but surely they would sense her fear, sense the madness in the man holding her hard against his side.

It was in his eyes. How could anyone not see the murder and madness in his eyes?

They could get help. There was a chance for help. And then Ethan would never get to Lil.

"Morning!"

She heard the cheerful greeting and risked lifting her eyes a few inches. Her pulse picked up speed when she saw the boots, the uniform pants. Not another hiker, she thought, but a ranger.

And he'd be armed.

"Morning," Ethan called back. "It sure is a pretty one!"

"Nice day for hiking. You're a little off the trail."

"Oh. We're exploring some. We saw some deer, and figured we'd follow them for a while."

"You don't want to wander off too far. It's easy to get lost if you go off the posted trails. Just out for the day, are you?"

"Yes, sir."

Can't you hear the madness? Can't you hear it in his overbright cheer? It's licking at every word.

"Well, you've made some real progress from the trailhead. If you're going to stick to this loop it gets pretty steep, but the views are worth it."

"That's what we're here for."

"If you backtrack to the posted trail, you'll have a better time of it."

"We'll do that, then. Thanks."

"Enjoy the day, and this fine weather. Just head over . . ." The ranger hesitated. "Jenna? Jenna Chance?"

She held her breath, shook her head.

"What in the world are you doing out . . ."

She felt it, that moment of awareness. On instinct she raised her head and pushed her body hard against Ethan's. But even as she moved, he swung the bow from behind his back.

She screamed, tried to lurch forward. But he was right. The bolt moved faster, much faster, than she could. She watched it strike home, and the force of it knocked the ranger back and off his feet.

"No. No. No."

"Your fault." The backhand sent Jenna sprawling to the ground. "Look what you did, stupid bitch! Look at the mess I've got to clean up. Didn't I tell you to keep your mouth shut?"

He kicked her, his boot slamming into the small of her back so she rolled and curled up in defense. "I didn't say anything. I didn't say anything. God, God, he has a wife, he has children."

"Then he should've minded his own *business.* Assholes. They're all assholes." When he stomped over to wrench the barbed bolt from the ranger's chest, Jenna began to retch.

"Look here. Got something out of it." He pulled the sidearm out of the holster, brandished it. "Spoils of war." Shoving the body over, he dug out the wallet. He slapped the gun back in the holster, unclipped it, and fixed it to his own belt before pushing the wallet in his backpack.

"Get up, help me drag him."

"No."

He walked over, pulled the gun again, and pressed the barrel to her temple. "Get up or join him. You can both be wolf bait. Live or die, Jenna. Decide."

Live, she thought. She wanted to live. Fighting sickness, breathless from the pain radiating from her back, her face, she got to her feet. Maybe he wasn't dead. Maybe someone would find him, help him. His name was Derrick Morganston. His wife was Cathy. He had two kids. Brent and Lorna.

She said his name, his family's names as she followed orders, took the feet and dragged the body farther off the trail.

She said nothing when he used the rope to tie her to a tree so he could retrieve Derrick's radio, go through his pockets for anything else he found useful.

She kept silent when they began to walk again. Nothing more to say, she thought. She'd tried and failed to find some place in him to appeal to. There was no place inside him. Nowhere to reach.

He wasn't covering the tracks, and she wondered what that meant. She wondered if she would live through the day, such a pretty spring day. See her husband again, her home. Hold her children. Would she speak with her friends, wear her new shoes?

She'd been washing the skillet, she thought, when her life had changed. Would she fry bacon again?

Her throat burned, her legs ached. Her palms throbbed where she'd scraped them against the bark. But those discomforts meant she was alive. Still alive.

If she had the chance to kill him and escape, would she? Yes. Yes, she would kill him to live. She would bathe in his blood if it meant protecting Lil.

If she could get his knife or the gun, a rock. If she could find a way to use her bare hands.

She concentrated on that, on the direction, the angle of the sun, the landmarks. There, she thought, look at the brave pasqueflowers, blooming. Delicate and hopeful. And alive.

She'd be the pasqueflower. Look delicate, be brave.

She walked, one foot in front of the other, with her head down. But she kept her eyes, her body alert for any chance of escape.

"We're home," he announced.

Confused, she blinked sweat out of her eyes. She barely saw the mouth of the cave. It was so low, so narrow—like a slitted eye. It looked like death.

She spun around, launched herself at him to fight. She felt the pain, and the satisfaction when her fist connected with his face. Screaming, she used her nails, her teeth to claw and bite like an animal. And when she tasted his blood, it thrilled.

But when his fist plowed into her belly, he took her breath. When it rammed into her face, the sun went dim in a wash of dark red.

"Bitch! Bitch whore!"

Dimly, she heard the harsh wheeze of his breath. She'd hurt him. That was something. She'd given him pain.

He used the rope to drag her over the rough ground and into the dark.

She fought as he bound her hands and feet, screamed, spat, and cursed until he gagged her. He lit a small lantern, and with his free hand dragged her farther into the cave.

"I could kill you now. Carve you up and send the pieces to her. What do you think about that?"

She'd marked him, was all she could think. Blood welled and dripped from the grooves she'd scored in his cheeks, on his hands.

Then he smiled at her, wide and wild, and she remembered to be afraid.

"The hills are honeycombed with caves. I've got a few nice ones I use regular. This one's yours."

He set the lantern down, then drew out his knife before he crouched. He turned the blade so the soft light stuck the edge. "Need a couple of things from you."

Joe, she thought. Joe. Lil. My baby.

And closed her eyes.

IT TOOK LONGER than he'd hoped, but he was still well within the time frame. The rush, the incidental kill, the unexpected fight left in the mother bitch all added a fresh anticipation. The best part was walking right into the refuge like any other paying customer. It was the biggest risk and the biggest thrill.

But he had no doubt Lil would give him more of both.

He smiled at the pretty intern through the beard he'd grown over the winter. It hid most of the scratches the mother bitch had given him. He wore old riding gloves to cover the ones on his hands.

"Is something wrong with the lion?"

"No, not a thing. She's getting her teeth cleaned. Cats especially need regular dental checks, as they tend to lose teeth."

"Because they're caged up."

"Actually, they'll keep their teeth longer in the refuge than in the wild. We provide them with bones once a week, an important element of dental hygiene. Cats' mouths tend to be full of bacteria, but with regular cleanings, good nutrition, and the weekly bones, we can help them maintain that smile." She added one of her own. "Our vet and his assistant are making sure Sheba's teeth are healthy."

It made him sick, made him furious. Brushing the teeth of the wild animal, as if it were a kid who ate too much candy. He wanted to drag the smiling girl off, plunge the knife into her belly.

"Are you all right?" she asked.

"Fine and dandy. I thought this was a nature preserve. How come you don't let it be natural?"

"Part of our responsibility to the animals here is to give them good, regular medical care, and that includes their teeth. Nearly all of the animals here at Chance were rescued from abusive situations, or taken in when they were sick or injured."

"They're caged. Like criminals."

"It's true they're enclosed. But every effort has been made to provide them with a habitat natural to their needs and culture. It's unlikely any of the animals here would survive in the wild."

He saw the concern, even suspicion in her eyes, and knew he'd gone too far. This wasn't why he was here. "Sure. You know more about it."

"I'd be happy to answer any questions you might have about the sanctuary, or any of our animals. You can also visit our education center. There's a video on the history of the refuge, and on the work Dr. Chance has done."

"Maybe I'll do that." He moved along before he said something to make her worried enough to call for assistance. Or before he gave in to the urge to batter her bloody.

He understood the need. He'd washed carefully, but he could still smell the ranger's blood. And the mother bitch's. That was sweeter, and the sweet wanted to stir him up.

He needed to do what he'd come to do, and get out before he made a mistake.

He wandered, pausing at each enclosure even while the resentment burned in his gut. When he reached the cougars he expected to find his center again, to look into the eyes of his spirit guide and see approval. A blessing.

Instead the cat snarled, showing fangs as it paced.

"You've been caged too long, brother. I'll come back for you one day. You have my promise."

At his words, the cougar called a warning and hurled itself against the fence. In the compound, guests and staff came to attention. Ethan moved on quickly, and the cat screamed behind him.

She'd corrupted it, he thought as rage shook through him. Turned it into a pet. No better than a guard dog. The cougar was *his,* but it had come at him like an enemy.

Just one more sin she would pay for, and soon.

ERIC HURRIED ACROSS the compound to check on Baby. The usually playful cougar continued to pace. He leaped into his tree, over to the roof of his den, leaped down again to rise on his hind legs at the gate at the rear of the enclosure.

"Hey, Baby, hey, take it easy. What's got you all stirred up? I can't let you out for a run. You need your teeth checked first."

"It's that guy." Lena jogged back to Eric. "I swear it's that guy."

"What guy?"

"That one. He's heading toward the ed center. See him? Ball cap, long hair, beard. His face is all scratched up, too. You can't see it from here, but he's got some nasty scratches under that ugly beard. I was talking to him a few minutes ago and, I don't know, something creepy. Something in his eyes."

"I'll go check him out."

"Maybe we should tell Lil."

"Tell her what? Some creepy-eyed guy's taking the tour? I'll just keep an eye on him."

"Be careful."

"My middle name." He walked backward. "There are a couple of groups in the center, and a few of us in there, too. I don't think creepy-eye's going to cause any trouble."

Ethan didn't go to the center, but cut over and circled back to leave the present he'd brought with him on the table on Lil's back porch.

By the time Eric crossed the compound he'd melted into the trees. He moved fast from there. The next phase of the game was about to start.

Once he'd reached the watching post, he settled down, took out his field glasses. He washed trail mix down with water and played with Jenna's cell phone.

He'd never owned one, never wanted one. But he'd practiced on others he'd stolen or taken from the kill. He punched and scrolled until he found the contact list, and smiled when he reached the entry listed as *Lil's Cell.*

Before much longer, he thought, she'd get a phone call she'd never forget.

IN HER OFFICE Lil answered the last e-mail on her list. She wanted to get over to the commissary and make sure the meat had been properly stored before she checked on Matt's progress. She looked at the time, surprised to find it was nearly three.

She'd asked Matt to hold off on Baby and the other cougars until she could help out. Baby hated dental hygiene day. So she'd check Matt first, she decided.

As she rose, Lena tapped on her doorjamb.

"I'm sorry to bother you, Lil. It's just . . . Baby's acting up."

"He probably knows he's about to get put under and have his teeth cleaned."

"Maybe, but . . . There was this guy, and he was weird, and that's when Baby started up. Eric went over to check him out at the center. But I just got this bad feeling and wanted to tell you."

"What kind of weird?" Lil asked and was already on her way out of the office.

"Creepy weird—to me. He was saying stuff like we caged the animals like prisoners."

"We get that sometimes. What did he look like?"

"Long hair, beard. Baseball cap, denim jacket. He had fresh scratches on his face. He kept smiling, but, well, it just made my skin crawl."

"It's okay. I'll head over to the center, just in case. Do me a favor? Tell

Matt I'm handling this, and I'll be over to help with Baby and the others as soon as I'm done."

"Sure. It was probably nothing. It's just he hit the red zone on my Creep-O-Meter."

They parted ways, with Lil veering toward the center. Her phone rang, and absently, she pulled it out of her pocket. Seeing her mother's number, she clicked on. "Hey, Mom, can I call you back? I need to—"

"She can't talk right now either."

A chill arrowed down her spine. When her fingers trembled, she gripped the phone tighter. "Hello, Ethan."

"Funny, that's what she said. Like mother, like daughter."

A terrible fear had her shivering, as if she'd plunged into an icy river. But she fought to keep her tone calm and even. Steady, she thought, stay steady with him as you would with anything feral. "I want to talk to her."

"You want to stop where you are. You take another step back toward the office, I'll cut off one of her fingers."

She stopped dead.

"Good girl. Remember, I can see you. You're wearing a red shirt, and you're looking east. A wrong move, she loses a finger. Understood?"

"Yes."

"Start walking toward your own cabin, around the back. If anyone comes up to you, calls to you, wave them off. You're busy."

"All right. But how do I know you didn't just steal my mother's phone? You have to give me more than that, Ethan. Let me talk to her."

"I *said* she can't talk right now. But you keep walking. I left you something on your back porch. Right up on the table. Yeah, that's right. Run."

She bolted, rounded the cabin, sprinted up the short steps. Everything inside her stopped, heart, lungs, brain, for one terrible instant. Then she made herself pick up the small plastic bag.

Inside was a hank of her mother's hair, and her wedding ring. Blood smeared the gold band.

"I figure you recognize those, so you know I'm not bullshitting you."

She gave in to her shaking legs and lowered to the porch. "Let me talk to her. You let me talk to her, goddamn you."

"No."

"How do I know she's still alive?"

"You don't, but I can guarantee she won't be in two hours if you don't find her. Head due west. I left you a trail. If you follow it, you'll find her. If not . . . If you tell anyone, try to get help, she dies. Toss the phone into the yard. Start now."

He could see her, she thought, but she had the porch rails and pickets for partial cover. She curled into a ball, angling her body toward the house. "Please don't hurt her. Don't hurt my mother. Please, please, I'll do whatever you say, whatever you ask. Just don't—"

She pushed end, cut off the call. "Please God," she whispered, and punched Coop's number. She rocked, made her shoulders shake, let the tears come. "Answer, answer, answer." She squeezed her eyes shut when it switched to voice mail. "He has my mother. I'm heading west from the back of my cabin. He can see me, and I only have seconds. He gave me two hours to find her. I'll leave you a trail. Come after me. God. Come after me."

She clicked off, pushed to her feet. She turned to face west, hoped Ethan could see the tears, the fear. And she threw the phone away. Then ran.

She picked up the trail right away. Trampled brush, broken twigs, prints in soft ground. He didn't want her to go astray, she thought. He might be leading her miles from wherever he had her mother, but there was no choice.

Her wedding ring smeared with blood. The hacked-off hank of her beautiful hair.

She forced herself to slow, to breathe. If she rushed she might miss a sign or follow a false one. He might be watching her still, so she'd have to take care in the markings she left for Coop.

He'd given her two hours. Had he taken her mother from home? It seemed the most logical. Wait until she was alone, then take her. On foot or by horseback?

On foot most likely. A hostage would be easier to control on foot. Unless he'd forced her into the car and . . . No, no, don't think that way, she ordered herself as panic bubbled into her throat. Think simple. Under it, he's simple.

Two hours from her cabin—and he'd want to push her, want it to be close. She put a map in her mind. Somewhere accessible and solitary from the cabin and from the farm. If she was alive— She was alive, she had to be alive. He'd have to hide her. A cave would be best. If he . . .

She stopped, studied the tracks, the carelessly trampled wildflowers. He'd backtracked. She drew a breath, then another, steadying her nerve, and did the same until she found where he'd laid the false trail.

She scuffed out his prints, used her penknife to mark the bark of a tree so Coop wouldn't make the same mistake. She picked up the trail again, then picked up her pace. She had an idea where he was leading her and knew she'd need nearly all the time he'd allotted.

JENNA WORMED AND rolled. She'd lost all sense of direction, could only pray she was inching her way to the mouth of the cave. He'd blindfolded her before he'd left so her dark was complete. Whenever she had to rest she lay still and tried to judge if the air was any fresher. But all she smelled was dirt, her own sweat, her own blood.

She heard him coming, screamed against the gag, struggled against the rope.

"Just look at you, Jenna. You're a real mess. And with company coming."

When he yanked off her blindfold the lantern light burned her eyes. "She'll be along soon, don't you worry. I'm going to clean up a bit." He sat cross-legged on the cave floor, and with a travel razor, a broken piece of mirror, began to shave.

AT THE REFUGE Lena waved to Eric. "Hey! What did you think of Creepy Guy?"

"I never saw him. He must've gone right through the center, or changed his mind."

"Oh. Well, what did Lil say?"

"About what?"

"About the guy. When she came over."

"I didn't see her either."

"But . . . She was going over. I don't see how you could've missed her."

"Maybe she got hung up." Eric shrugged it off. "She wanted to help Matt when he got to the cougars. Listen I've got to get back to—"

Lena simply grabbed him by the sleeve of his T-shirt. "I've just come from Matt. She's not there, and he's waiting for her."

"She's around somewhere. So okay, we'll look around. I'll check the commissary, you check her place."

"She knows Matt's waiting," Lena insisted, but she hurried over to the cabin. She knocked, then pushed open the door to call out. "Lil? Lil?" Baffled, she walked straight through, and out the back. Maybe the office, she thought.

When she jogged down the steps, she heard the jingle of the phone. Relieved, she glanced back, expecting to see Lil striding along with the phone to her ear. But there was no one. She turned back, following the ring.

She snatched the phone off the ground, flipped it open.

"Hey, Lil, I just saw my mother off, so—"

"Tansy, Tansy, this is Lena. I think something's really wrong." She began to run toward the office cabin. "I think we need the police."

———

On a stretch of road between the farm and the stables, Coop tightened the lug nuts on the spare tire of a minivan. The two kids inside watched him like owls while they sucked on sippy cups.

"I really appreciate this. I could've changed it, but—"

"Looks like you've got your hands full." He nodded toward the windows. "It's no trouble."

"You saved me a lot of cursing." The young mother beamed a smile. "And took care of it in probably half the time it would've taken me, not including breaking up the fights inside. We've been running errands all day, so they missed their nap." Her eyes sparkled with a laugh. "Boy, so did I."

After sending the kids a wink, he rolled the flat around the back of the van to stow it. He shook his head when she offered him a ten-dollar bill. "No, but thanks."

She leaned in, rooted around in the grocery bags. "How about a banana?"

He laughed. "I'll take it." He replaced the tools, gave the kids a quick salute with the banana and made them both giggle, then closed the door. "You're good to go."

"Thanks again."

He walked back to his truck, waited for her to pull out. He did a U-turn to head back the way he'd been coming when he'd seen the van on the side of the road. In about half a mile, his phone signaled a voice mail.

"I got your Hefty bags, Grandma," he muttered. "And the big-ass bottle of Lysol." Still, he punched the key to play the message.

He has my mother.

Coop slammed on the brakes, swerved to the shoulder.

After the first flash of heat, everything in him went to ice. He punched the gas, pushed speed dial for the sheriff.

"Put me through to him. Now."

"Sheriff Johannsen's not in the office."

"You patch me through to wherever the hell he is. This is Cooper Sullivan."

"Hey, Coop, it's Cy. I can't really do that. I'm not authorized to—"

"Listen to me. Ethan Howe has Jenna Chance."

"What? What?"

"He may have Lil by now, too. You get Willy, and you get him over to the refuge. Now. Fucking now."

"I'll get him, Coop, Jesus God, I'll get him. What should I—"

"I'm heading to the refuge now. I want Willy there, and as many men as he can get. No air search," he said quickly, fighting to stay focused. "He'll just kill them if he sees copters. Tell him she said she'd leave me a trail. I'll be following it. Do it."

He shut it off and burned up the miles to Lil's.

Lil saw him sitting cross-legged at the mouth of the cave, the crossbow in his lap. His face was raw, cross-marked with vicious scratches under the streaks of war paint he'd applied. She thought of the bearded man who'd set off Lena's radar.

He wore a braided leather strap around his head, with a feather from a hawk woven through it. On his feet were soft leather knee boots, around his neck a necklace of bear teeth.

It would've been funny, she thought, this half-assed play at being Indian. If she didn't know how murderously serious he was.

He lifted his hand in greeting, then slid back into the cave. Lil climbed the rest of the way, held her breath, then followed him in.

It opened after the first few feet, but was still low enough she had to crouch. Deep though, she noted, as she watched the pale light of the lantern.

He sat in that light with a knife to her mother's throat.

"I'm here, Ethan, you don't have to hurt her. If you do hurt her, you'll get nothing from me."

"Have a seat, Lil. I'll explain how things are going to be."

She sat and wanted to tremble. Cuts and bruises marred her mother's face, her hands. Blood stained the rope around her wrists, her ankles.

"I need you to take that knife away from my mother's throat. I did what you asked me to do, and I'll keep doing that. But not if you hurt her more than you already have."

"She did most of this to herself. Didn't you, Jenna?"

Jenna's eyes said everything. *Run. Run. I love you.*

"I'm asking you to take the knife off my mother. You don't need it. I'm here. I'm alone. That's what you wanted."

"It's just the start." But he lowered the knife an inch. "Everything else was just the start. This is the finish. You and me."

"You and me," she agreed. "So let her go."

"Don't be stupid. I'm not wasting time on stupid. I'm going to give you ten minutes. That's a good head start for somebody who knows the hills. Then I hunt you."

"Ten minutes. Do I get a weapon?"

"You're prey."

"A cougar, a wolf, have fangs and claws."

He smiled. "You've got teeth, if you get close enough to use them."

She gestured toward the bow. "You weigh the game heavily in your favor."

"My game, my rules."

She tried another angle. "Is this how a Sioux warrior shows his honor, his courage? Hunting women?"

"You're more than a woman. This one?" He yanked Jenna's head back by the hair and had Lil braced to leap. "Half-breed squaw? She's mine by rights now. I took her as captive, just like our ancestors took captives from the white. Made them slaves. I might keep her for a while. Or . . ."

He knew so little, she realized, about those he claimed as his own. "The Sioux were hunters of buffalo and deer, of bear. They hunted for food, for clothing. How does it honor your blood to kill a woman who's bound and helpless?"

"You want her to live? We hunt."

"If I win?"

"You won't." He leaned forward. "You've disgraced your blood, your spirit. You deserve to die. But I'm giving you the honor of the hunt. You'll die on sacred ground. If you play the game well, maybe I'll let your mother live."

Lil shook her head. "I won't play at all unless you let her go. You've killed before, you'll kill again. It's what you are. I don't believe you'll let her live, however I play your game. So you'll have to let her go first."

He lifted the knife to Jenna's throat. "I'll just kill her now."

"Then you'll have to kill me, too, where we sit. I won't play your game, use your rules unless she's out of it. And you'll have wasted all this time, all this effort."

She ached to look at her mother, reach out to her, but kept her gaze on Ethan's face. "And you'll be nothing but a butcher then. Not a warrior. The spirit of Crazy Horse will turn from you."

"Women are nothing. Less than dogs."

"A true warrior honors the mother, for all life comes from her. Let mine go. You won't finish this, Ethan. It'll never be finished unless we compete. Isn't that right? You don't need her. But I need her to be worthy of the game. I'll give you the hunt of your life. I swear it."

His eyes glowed at her promise. "She's useless anyway."

"Then let her go, and it's just you and me. Just the way you want it. It's a bargain worthy of a warrior, worthy of the blood of a great chief."

He cut the ropes on Jenna's wrists. She moaned as she tried to lift her aching arms to pull off the gag. "Lil. No, Lil. I won't leave you."

"Touching," he said, and spat as he cut the ropes at her ankles. "Bitch probably can't even walk."

"She'll walk."

"I won't. I won't leave you to him. Baby—"

"It's all right." Lil drew Jenna close, gently. "It's all right now. Step back from her," she told Ethan. "She's afraid of you. Step back so I can give her comfort, and say goodbye. We're only women. Unarmed. You can't fear us."

"Thirty seconds." Ethan stepped back three paces.

"Lil, no. I can't leave you."

"Help's coming," she whispered in Jenna's ear. "I need you to go, I need to know you're safe or I won't be able to think to win this. I know what to do. You have to go or he'll kill us both. Give her some water," Lil demanded in disgust. "What kind of honor is it to beat a woman, to deny her water?"

"She can drink her own spit."

"Water for my mother and you can take five minutes off my lead time."

He kicked a bottle over. "I don't need your five minutes to beat you."

Lil uncapped it, held it to her mother's lips. "Slow now, a little at a time. Can you find home?"

"I—Lil."

"Can you?"

"Yes. Yes, I think."

"Won't help you. By the time she gets there—if she does—and they start looking for you, you'll be dead. And I'll be smoke."

"Take the water and go now."

"Lil."

"If you don't he'll kill us both. The only chance I have to live is for you to go. You have to believe in me. You have to give me that chance. I'm going to help her out of the cave, Ethan. You can hold the bow on me. I won't run."

She helped her mother to her feet, cursing when Jenna wept from pain, from grief. Crouched over in the shallow space, she helped Jenna hobble to the mouth. "Help's coming," she whispered again. "I can keep him off me until they come. Get home as fast as you can. Promise me."

"Lil. Oh, God, Lil." As the sun lowered toward the hills, Jenna held her tight.

"I'm going to lead him to the grassland above the river." Lil pressed her face to her mother's hair as if in grief, and murmured against her ear. "Where I saw the cougar. Remember that. Send help there."

"Shut up! You shut up and she goes now, or she dies now, and you after her."

"Go on, Mom." Lil pried Jenna's scraped and bruised arms away. "Go on or he'll kill me."

"Baby. I love you, Lil."

"I love you." She watched her mother limp and stumble, saw the agony of emotion in her battered face when she looked back. For that alone, Lil thought, he'd pay. Whatever it took.

"Start running," Ethan ordered.

"No. The hunt doesn't start until I know she's away. Until I know you won't go after her first. What's your hurry, Ethan?" Deliberately she sat on a rock. "You've waited a long time for this. You can wait a little longer."

30

The compound was chaos. A dozen people raced from various directions when Coop jumped out of his truck, and all of them talked at once.

"Stop! You." He jabbed a finger at Matt. "Sum it up, and fast."

"We can't find Lil. Lena found her phone in the yard behind the cabin. And when I went back, I found this." He held out the plastic bag with Jenna's hair and wedding ring. There was somebody here, paying customer. Lena got a bad feeling about him. Baby didn't like him either. Nobody can find him. We're afraid he took Lil. Mary's inside, calling the police."

"I already called them."

"I think it's Jenna's ring." Tears spilled down Tansy's cheeks.

"Yeah, it's Jenna's. He's got her, and Lil's gone in to find her. Shut up and listen," he ordered when everyone began to talk at once. "I need anyone who can handle a gun without shooting themselves. Lil's got a good hour's head start, but she's leaving a trail. We're going to follow it."

"I can." Lena stepped forward. "I can handle a shotgun. Trap shooting champion, three years running."

"In Lil's cabin. Shotgun in the front closet, ammo on the top shelf. Go."

"I've never shot a gun in my life, but—"

"Stay here." Coop cut Matt off. "Wait for the police, then lock the place down. Tansy, go to the Chance farm. If Joe hasn't heard, he needs to. Listen to me. Tell him it's most likely Jenna was taken from there. He and Farley, and whoever else he can round up, should start from there. He taught Lil to track. He'll pick up the trail. We need radios."

Mary came out of the cabin as two interns sprinted for radios. "The police are on their way. Fifteen minutes."

"Send them in after us. We're not waiting for them. You upstairs, bedroom, top left dresser drawer. Three ammo clips. Get them. Wait." Struck, he held up a hand, looked over to the enclosures. "I need something of Lil's, something she was wearing."

"Sweater in the office," Mary said. "Hold on."

"That cat loves her. Will he track her?"

"Yes! God, yes." Tansy pressed a hand to her mouth. "He followed her back every time she tried to release him."

"We're going to let him out."

"He hasn't been out of the habitat since he was six months old." Matt shook his head. "Even if he leaves the compound, there's no telling what he'll do."

"He loves her." Coop took the sweater Mary brought him.

"We'll have to separate the others." Tansy hurried to the enclosure with him.

"Do what you have to do. Make it fast."

He held the sweater to the bars. Baby prowled over, then grumbled in his throat. Rubbed his face against the sweater. Purred.

"Yeah, that's right. You know her. You're going to find her."

Interns chicken-baited the range area while Eric pulled up the door. Baby lifted his head, looked around while his companions rushed through the feed. Then turned back, pushed his face against the sweater.

"This is crazy," Matt said, but he stood by with the drug gun. "Get back, well back. Tansy."

She unlocked the cage. "Find Lil, Baby. You find Lil." Using it as a barrier, she opened it.

He slunk out slowly toward the unknown, drawn by Lil's scent. Coop held up a hand toward Matt as the cougar approached him. "He knows me. He knows I'm Lil's."

Once more, the cougar rubbed against the sweater. Then he began to track. "She's everywhere, that's the problem. She's everywhere."

Baby leaped onto Lil's cabin's porch, called, called. Then leaped off again to circle around.

"I packed you a kit." Mary pushed it into his hands. "Bare essentials. Put that sweater in this plastic bag. It'll confuse him otherwise. Get her back, Cooper."

"I will." He watched the cat stalk over the yard, then gather himself to run for the trees. "Let's move."

LIL GAUGED HER time, mentally planned out routes while she sat on the rock in the dying day with the man who wanted to kill her.

Her nerves smoothed out with every minute that passed. Every minute took her mother farther away and brought Coop closer. The longer she could keep him here, the better her chances.

"Did your father teach you to kill?" She spoke conversationally, her gaze aimed west, toward the setting sun.

"To hunt."

"Call it what you like, Ethan. You gutted Melinda Barrett and left her for the animals."

"A cougar came. A sign. Mine."

"Cougars don't hunt for sport."

He shrugged. "I'm a man."

"Where did you leave Carolyn?"

He smiled. "A feast for the grizzlies. She gave me a good game first. I think you'll do better. You may last most of the night."

"Then where will you go?"

"I'll follow the wind. Then I'll come back. I'll kill your parents and burn their farm to the ground. I'll do the same with that zoo of yours. I'll hunt these hills and live free, the way my people should have lived free."

"I wonder how much of your view on the Sioux comes from actual truth or your father's bastardization of the truth."

Color flooded his face, warning her not to test him too far. "My father wasn't a bastard."

"That's not what I meant. Do you think the Lakota would approve of what you do? The way you hunt down and slaughter innocent people?"

"They aren't innocent."

"What did James Tyler do to deserve to die?"

"He came here. His people killed my people. Stole from them."

"He was a real estate agent from St. Paul. It's just you and me here, Ethan, so there's no reason to pretend this is anything but what it is. You like to kill. You like to terrorize, to stalk. You like the feel of warm blood on your hands. It's why you use a knife. Otherwise, saying you murdered Tyler because of broken treaties, lies, dishonor, greed perpetrated by people who've been dead more than a hundred years would just be crazy. You're not crazy, are you, Ethan?"

Something—a slyness—came and went in his eyes. Then he bared his teeth. "They came. They killed. They slaughtered. Now their blood feeds the ground like ours did. On your feet."

Fear blew through her again, one icy blast. Ten minutes, she reminded herself, if he kept to his own rules. She could cover a lot of ground in ten minutes. She got to her feet.

"Run."

Her legs quivered to. "So you can watch where I go? Is that how you track? I thought you were good at this."

He smiled. "Ten minutes," he said and backed into the cave.

She didn't waste time. Her first priorities were speed and distance.

Cunning had to wait. The farm was closer, but she needed to draw him away from her mother. Cooper would come from the east. She scrambled down the slope, warning herself not to sacrifice safety for speed and risk a broken ankle. Fear urged her to take the shortest, straightest route toward the compound, but she thought of the bow. He'd track her too easily that way, and he could disable her from a distance with the bow.

And any trail she left for Coop, Ethan could follow.

She veered north, and raced ahead of the dark.

AT THE CHANCE FARM, Joe stuffed extra ammo in his pockets. "We're losing the light. We'll use flashlights until moonrise."

"I want to go with you, Joe." Sam gripped Joe's shoulder. "But I'd just slow you down."

"We'll stay by the radio." Lucy handed him a light pack. "We'll wait for word. Bring them home."

He nodded, moved out of the door ahead of Farley.

"Be careful." Tansy wrapped her arms around Farley, held hard and brief. "Be safe."

"Don't you worry."

Outside, Farley took point with Joe ahead of the three armed men who would join them on the search. Dogs, already on the scent, bayed.

"If he's hurt her," Joe said quietly to Farley. "If he's hurt either of them, I'll kill him."

"We will."

MILES AWAY, Coop studied the signs Lil had left for him. He hadn't seen the cougar since it had run into the forest. He had two college kids with him, and twilight falling fast.

He should've come alone, he thought now. Shouldn't have wasted even the few minutes it had taken to outfit the backup, release the cat.

The others were ten minutes or more behind him, with some steering south, others north. He knew Joe, by the information relayed by radio, led another group headed in from the west.

And still, there were untold acres to cover.

"You two wait here for the rest to catch up."

"You're worried we'll screw up, or get hurt. We won't." Lena looked at her companion. "Right, Chuck?"

Chuck's eyes were huge, but he nodded. "Right."

"If you fall behind, go back. Radio back our new direction," he ordered Chuck, then headed southwest.

She'd left clear markings, he thought as he forced himself not to run, not to run and miss one of those markings. She was counting on him. If he hadn't stopped to play Good Samaritan, he'd have gotten her call, he'd have convinced her to wait until he could go with her. He'd have . . .

No point, no point. He'd find her.

He thought of Dory. Good cop, good friend. And the long, syrupy seconds it had taken to draw his weapon.

He wouldn't be too late, not this time. Not with Lil.

SHE LAID A trail to a stream, backtracked. With sundown the air chilled. Despite the sweat of exertion and fear, she was cold. She imagined the warm sweater she'd shed in her office that afternoon as she took the time to remove her boots, her socks.

Brushing out tracks as she went, she returned to the stream, gritted her teeth as she waded through the icy water. The false trail might fool him, might not. But it was worth a try. She waded downstream ten yards, then ten more before she began to search the banks. Her feet were numb by the time she spotted the tumble of rocks. They'd do.

She climbed out, put her socks and shoes on again, then picked her way over the rocks until they gave way to soft ground. She ran, cutting away from the water, circling the brush until she was forced to shove through it. Her boots thudded as she propelled herself up a slope.

She sought the shelter of trees again to rest, to listen.

The moon rose like a spotlight over the hills. It would help her avoid tripping over roots or rocks in the dark.

Her mother should be halfway back to the farm by now, she calculated. Help would be coming from that direction, too. She had to believe her mother would make it, and would direct the help toward the high ground she'd chosen for her stand.

She had to cut east again. She rubbed her chilled arms, ignoring the sting from nicks and scrapes she'd incurred on the run. If her maneuver at the stream bought her any time, she had the distance to make it. She just needed the stamina.

Gritting her teeth, she pushed to her feet, then cocked her head as she heard a quiet splash.

Some time, she thought as she turned east. But not as much as she'd hoped.

He was coming. And he was closing in.

COOP STOPPED AGAIN. He saw the slash, fresh, on the pine bark. Lil's sign. But he studied the prints—cougar tracks. The first pointed west, and the second north.

Nothing to prove it was *her* cougar, he thought. And clearly, she'd gone west. Following Ethan's trail, to find her mother. But after, he'd want the hunt. Want the thrill.

Coop's head said go west, but his heart . . .

"Head west. Be slow, go quiet. Follow the slash marks. Radio back, tell them I'm heading north from here."

"But why?" Lena demanded. "Where are you going?"

"I'm following the cat."

Wouldn't she have led Ethan away from her mother? Coop asked himself. His heart thudded every time he thought he'd lost the trail. What made him think he could track a cougar? Mr. Fucking New York. She wouldn't leave signs now. No handy slash marks or rock piles. She couldn't leave signs because by now he was hunting her.

Come after me, she asked him. He could only pray he was.

Twice he lost the trail, so desperation and terror made his skin clammy. And his belly would clutch each time he found it again.

Then he saw the bootprints. Lil's. Even as he crouched, touched a finger to the impression she'd left on the ground, his body shuddered. Alive. Still alive and moving. He saw where others—Ethan's—crossed hers. He was following, but she was still ahead. And the cat followed both.

He moved ahead. When he heard the murmur of water on rock, he picked up his pace again. She'd headed toward water, to lose him in the water.

When he reached the stream, he stood, baffled. Her tracks led into the water, while Ethan's moved forward, back, circled around again. He closed his eyes, tried to clear his mind and think.

What would she do?

False trails, backtracking. He had no skill for that. If she'd gone into the water, she might've come out again anywhere. The cat had gone in, that was clear enough. Maybe just to cross, or maybe to follow her. Which way?

His hands fisted at his sides as he struggled to see, to look at the land as she would. Upstream and across, she could cut around to his grand-parents' farm, or other houses. A long clip, but she could do it. Down and across, her parents' farm. Closer.

She had to know help would come from that direction.

He started to wade in, to follow that instinct. Then stopped.

Downstream, and east. The grassland. Her camera. Her place.

He cut back, circled, and ran. He didn't follow tracks now, but the thoughts and patterns of a woman he'd known and loved since childhood.

JOE STARED DOWN at the blood staining the ground. It was black in the moonlight. His head went light, his knees weak, so he knelt down, laying his hand over the blood. He thought, could only think: Jenna.

"Over here!" one of the deputies called out. "It's Derrick Morganston. Goddamn it, it's Derrick. He's dead."

Not Jenna. Not his Jenna. Later, sometime later, he might feel sorrow that he didn't think of the man, his family, and only of his own. But now fresh fury and fear pushed him to his feet.

He started forward again, searching for tracks.

Like a miracle, she came through the shadows and the moonlight. She staggered, fell, even as he raced toward her.

He dropped to his knees again, pulled her up, rocked, wept. He stroked her bruised face with his fingers. "Jenna."

"The grasslands." She croaked it out.

"Here's water. Ma, here's water." Tears gathered in the corners of his eyes as Farley held water to her lips.

She drank to ease her raging thirst as Farley petted her hair, as Joe rocked. "The grasslands," she repeated.

"What?" Joe took the bottle from Farley. "Drink a little more. You're hurt. He hurt you."

"No. Lil. The grasslands. She's leading him there. Her place. Find her. Joe. Find our baby."

HE HAD TO know where she was going now, but it couldn't be helped. She only had to get within range of the camera, trust someone would see. Then hide. All that tall grass, she could hide.

She had the knife in her boot. He didn't know about that. She wasn't defenseless. She hefted a rock, clutched it tight in her fist. Damn right she wasn't defenseless.

God, she needed to rest. To catch her breath. She'd have sold her soul for a single sip of water. She wished the moon behind clouds, just for a few minutes. She could find her way now in the dark, and the dark would hide her.

The muscles in her legs wept as she fought her way up the next slope. The fingers that clutched the rock were numb with cold. Her breath whisked out, little ghosts, as she panted, as she pushed herself to the edge of endurance.

She nearly stumbled, hated herself for the weakness, and braced her hand on a tree until she found her balance.

The bolt slammed into the trunk inches from her fingers. She dropped, rolled behind the tree.

"I could've pinned you like a moth!"

His voice carried through the clear air. How close? How close? Impossible to tell. She lunged up, keeping low in the sprint from tree to tree. As the ground leveled out, she pushed harder. She imagined the shock and pain of one of those vicious bolts in the back. Cursed the thought. She'd come so far, nearly there. Her lungs burned, pushing air out as whistles as she tore her way through the brush, waking her freezing skin with fresh cuts.

He'd scent her blood now.

She burst out, praying someone would see as she flew across camera range. Then she dived, into the grass. Clamping her teeth, she slid the knife from her boot. Her heart pounded against the ground as she held her breath. Waited.

Such quiet, such stillness. The air barely stirred the grass. As the blood beating in her head slowed, she heard the night sounds, little rustles, the lazy call of an owl. Then him, coming through the brush.

Closer, she thought. Come closer.

The bolt cut through the grass a foot to the left. She bit back the scream tearing at her throat, stayed still.

"You're good. I knew you would be. Best I've had. I'm sorry for it to end. I'm thinking I might give you another chance. Want another chance, Lil? Got any left? Go on and run."

The next bolt dug into the ground to her right.

"You've got until I reload. Say thirty seconds."

Not close enough, not for the knife.

"What do you say? Starting now. Thirty, twenty-nine—"

She sprang up, wheeled back, and pitched the rock with the heart of a girl who'd believed she could play in the majors. It struck his temple with a crack of stone on bone.

When he staggered, when the bow fell from his hands, she charged forward, screaming.

He pulled the gun he'd taken off the ranger, plowed a bullet into the ground at her feet.

"On your knees, you bitch." Though he swayed, and blood dribbled down from the wound, the gun held steady.

"If you're going to shoot me, just shoot me. Goddamn you."

"I might. In the arm, in the leg. Not a kill shot." He slid the knife out of his sheath. "You know how it's going to be. But you did well. Even drew first blood."

He swiped at it with the back of his knife hand, glanced down at the smear. "I'll sing a song in your honor. You brought us here, where it's right to end. Destiny. Yours and mine. Full circle, Lil. You understood all along. You deserve to die clean."

He started toward her.

"Stop where you are. Put the gun down. Step away from him, Lil," Coop ordered as he stood on the edge of the grass.

Shock had Ethan's gun hand jerking. But the barrel stayed beaded on Lil. "She moves, I shoot her. You shoot me, I still shoot her. You're the one, the other one." He paused, nodded. "It's only right you're here, too."

"Put the fucking gun down or I'll kill you where you stand."

"It's aimed at her belly. I can get one off, maybe two. You want to watch her bleed? You back off. You fucking back off. We'll call this a standoff. There'll be another time. If you don't lower that gun, I'll put a hole in her. Lower it and I'll ease back. She'll live."

"He's lying." She'd seen it. That slyness again, sliding into his eyes and out. "Just shoot the bastard. I'd rather die than see him walk away."

"Can you live with that?" Ethan demanded. "Live with watching her die?"

"Lil," Coop said, trusting her to read his eyes, to understand. His finger twitched as he lowered his gun an inch.

The cat leaped out of the brush, a streak of gold, of flashing fang and claw in the streaming moonlight. Its scream sliced through the night like silver swords. Ethan stared, eyes dazed, mouth slack.

Then it was his scream as the cougar sank its teeth into his throat and took him down.

Lil stumbled back. "Don't run, don't run!" she shouted at Coop. "It might go for you. Stop!"

But he kept coming. Coming after her, she thought dully as her vision hazed. Kept coming to catch her when her knees finally gave way.

"We found you." He pressed his lips to hers, to her cheeks, her throat. "We found you."

"Have to move. Too near the kill."

"It's Baby."

"What. No." She saw the eyes gleam at her as the cat sat in the grass. Saw the blood staining his muzzle. Then it walked to her, bumped its head against her arm. And purred.

"He killed." For me, she thought. For me. "But he didn't feed. It's not—he shouldn't—"

"You can write a paper on it later." Coop pulled out his radio. "I've got her." Then he brought her hand to his lips. "I've got you."

"My mother. She's—"

"Safe. You're both safe. We're going to get you home. I need you to sit here while I check on Ethan."

"He went for his throat." She buried her face against her knees. "Instinct. He followed instinct."

"Lil. He followed you."

LATER, WHEN THE worst was over, she sat on the sofa with the fire roaring. She'd taken a hot bath, sipped brandy. And still, she couldn't quite get warm.

"I should go see my mother. I should."

"Lil, she's sleeping. She knows you're safe. She heard your voice on the radio. She's dehydrated, exhausted, and bruised up. Let her sleep. You'll see her tomorrow."

"I had to go, Coop. I couldn't wait. I had to go after her."

"I know you did. You don't have to keep saying it."

"I knew you'd come after me." She pressed his hand to her cheek, closing her eyes, absorbing the warmth. "But Matt and Tansy had to be crazy to release Baby that way."

"We were all crazy. It worked, didn't it? Now he's eating his feast of chicken and has hero status."

"He shouldn't have been able to track me, not like that. He shouldn't have been able to find me."

"He found you because he loves you. The same goes for me."

"I know." She cupped his face in her hands. "I know." She smiled when he leaned in to brush his lips to hers.

"I'm not going anywhere. It's time you believed that, too."

She let her head rest on his shoulder, studied the fire. "If he'd won, he'd have come back for my parents eventually. Killed them, or tried. He'd have come here, and killed. He liked to kill. Hunting people excited him. It made him feel important, made him feel superior. The rest, the sacred land, the revenge, the bloodline, that was smoke. I think he'd come to believe it, or parts of it, but it was smoke."

"He didn't win." He thought of how many dead might never be found. How many he'd hunted and killed they'd never know. But those, Coop decided, were thoughts for another day.

He had Lil, had her safe in his arms.

"You were going to shoot him."

"Yes."

"Lower your gun enough to make him believe you meant it—so he'd swing his toward you. Then you'd have killed him. You figured I had brains enough to get out of the way."

"Yes."

"You were right. I was about to dive when Baby came out of nowhere.

We trusted each other—life-and-death trust. That's pretty damn important. Anyway." She let out a long breath. "I'm tired. God."

"Can't think why."

"One of those days. Do me a favor, will you? I left the trash in the laundry room this morning. Would you take it out for me?"

"Now?"

"I'd appreciate it. Small change compared with saving my life, but I'd appreciate it."

"Fine."

She folded her lips on the smile when he strode out, so obviously annoyed. She took another sip of brandy, and waited.

When he came back, he stood in front of her, looking down. "You put that trash in there this morning?"

"That's right."

"Before I saved your life—or had some part in it?"

"Right again."

"Why?"

After shaking back her hair, she stared straight into his eyes. "Because I decided you're not going anywhere, and since I've loved you most of my life, I want you not to go anywhere with me. You're the best friend I've ever had, and the only man I've ever loved. Why should I live without you just because you were a moron at twenty?"

"That's debatable. The moron part." He skimmed a hand over her hair. "You're mine, Lil."

"Yes, I am." She got to her feet, wincing only a little. "And you're mine right back." She went into his arms. "This is what I want," she told him. "So much of this. Will you walk with me? I know it's silly, but I want to walk in the moonlight, safe and loved and happy. With you."

"Get your jacket," he said. "It's cool out."

The moon beamed down, pure and white, as they walked. Safe and loved and happy.

In the stillness, in that chill of early spring, the cougar's call echoed over the valley. And it carried into the hills looming black in the night.